The Girl
Garden

An emotional and uplifting novel set in the momentous times of the 1930s and the Second World War

(The India Tea Series: Book 3)

Janet MacLeod Trotter

This is a work of fiction. Names, characters, organizations, places, events, and incidents are either products of the author's imagination or are used fictitiously. Any resemblance to actual persons, living or dead, or actual events is purely coincidental.

Published by MacLeod Trotter Books Ltd

www.janetmacleodtrotter.com

Cover design by Michael Star

ISBN-978-1-908359-65-0

The India Tea Series

In the fertile valleys of India, the passionate and resourceful women of the Belhaven and Robson tea planter families have always dreamt big, even in the momentous early years of the twentieth century. From the majestic mountains of Assam to the industrial streets of northern Britain, they must learn to cope with hidden secrets, forbidden love, betrayal and adversity as they strive to make life better for themselves and their loved ones. But as they embark on epic adventures across a fast-changing world, will the upheavals of war and the dying days of the British Raj stop their dreams from becoming a reality?

Praise for The India Tea Series

'Irresistible'
Sunderland Echo

'A wonderfully moving, deeply emotional tale'
Daily Record

'Trotter uses her experiences and imagination to bring strength and depth to her novels. Another thought-provoking book'
Lancashire Evening Post

'Another action-packed, emotionally charged page-turner'
Newcastle Journal

'A moving saga set against the backdrop of the thriving tea trade in turn-of-the-century Tyneside'
Peterborough Evening Telegraph

'A gripping and heartrending novel... An unforgettable novel of courage, suffering and enduring love'
Bolton Evening News

Titles by Janet MacLeod Trotter

The Raj Hotel Series
The Emerald Affair – Book 1
The Sapphire Child – Book 2
The Diamond Daughter – Book 3

The India Tea Series
The Tea Planter's Daughter – Book 1
The Tea Planter's Bride – Book 2
The Girl from the Tea Garden – Book 3
The Secrets of the Tea Garden – Book 4

HISTORICAL
In the Far Pashmina Mountains

The Jarrow Trilogy
The Jarrow Lass
Child of Jarrow
Return to Jarrow

The Durham Trilogy
The Hungry Hills
The Darkening Skies
Never Stand Alone

The Tyneside Sagas
A Handful of Stars
Chasing the Dream
For Love & Glory

The Rebellious Woman Sagas

The Suffragette
A Crimson Dawn

Scottish Historical Romance

The Flower of Scotland (formerly The Jacobite Lass)
The Beltane Fires
Highlander in Muscovy

MYSTERY/CRIME

The Vanishing of Ruth
The Haunting of Kulah

TEENAGE

Love Games

NON-FICTION

Beatles & Chiefs

DEDICATION

For Manaal – thank you for your friendship and support.

Chapter 1

Shillong, India, 1933

Adela heard a scream; it was coming from the dormitory. She bounded up the dark wooden staircase two steps at a time and burst through the door. A group of girls stood around the far bed, taunting.

'You have to,' ordered Nina Davidge. 'Every new girl must drink it. I drank twice this much last term.'

'Go on, Flowers, drink it!'

'Stinky Flowers!'

'We'll call you Weedy if you don't.'

'Please stop it,' wailed Flowers Dunlop. 'It's not smelling nice.'

'*Not smelling nice*,' Margie Munro said, mimicking her sing-song Indian accent. 'You're so *chee-chee.*'

'It's for your own good,' Nina said, thrusting it right in the girl's face. 'Else you're not one of us. We're going to teach you how to be a good little memsahib and learn our ways. That's why your parents sent you here, isn't it? Pin her down, girls!'

Adela stood rooted to the spot, heart drumming as her classmates grabbed the new girl by her skinny arms and long plait. Nina was lying about having drunk the stuff herself; she had refused any initiation ceremony when she'd joined the school in the summer term. Her delicate bones needed heat, Nina had told them, and that was the only reason why she was in a dump of a school like St Ninian's in Shillong with the daughters of non-commissioned officers and box-wallahs. Otherwise, according to Nina, she would be at a boarding school at home in England with girls of her own social class. Better for Flowers if she just submitted and got it over with; then Nina might leave her alone. But Flowers was fighting back, squirming out of their hold and shrieking in protest.

Margie caught sight of Adela and called, 'Hey, Tea Leaf! Come and help us.'

Adela winced. Until last term, plump, pretty Margie, the sergeant's daughter, had been her best friend. Then tall Nina, a retired colonel's daughter with her blonde hair in a sleek ponytail, had breezed in and picked Margie to do her bidding. For some reason Nina had taken a dislike to Adela, although she had gone out of her way to be friendly. Margie tried to keep friends with them both, but this term she'd started calling her by the irritating nickname Nina had invented, Tea Leaf, just because Adela's parents ran a tea plantation.

Nina turned. 'Yes, Tea Leaf. Get yourself over here and help with giving this silly patient her medicine.'

Adela hesitated. If she joined in, it might make Nina be friends with her.

'No, help *me*!' squealed Flowers, throwing her a pleading look, eyes wide with distress.

Adela ran forward.

'That's it, Tea Leaf.' Nina gave a malicious little laugh. 'You hold her head back.'

'Give me that,' Adela said, grabbing at the tooth mug of frothy urine-smelling liquid. She dreaded to think what all was in it. 'I'll do it.'

Nina was so surprised she let go. The other girls giggled and chanted.

'Throw it, throw it! Water the Flowers! Water the Flowers! Water the Flowers!'

Flowers Dunlop, a station master's daughter, stared back like a terrified deer caught in a trap. Then she screwed her eyes tight shut and braced herself for the ordeal. Adela felt a wave of guilt, like the first time she had shot dead a blackbuck with the rifle her father had bought her for her eleventh birthday. *Don't be sentimental, Adela.* He had wiped away her tears. *All's fair game in the jungle.*

But this wasn't fair; her thirteen-year-old schoolmates were picking on the unhappy new girl like a pack of jackals smelling her weakness, and all because her mother was a native. Turning from Flowers, Adela spun round and flung the disgusting concoction over Nina.

There was a stunned silence. Until that very second, Adela herself had no idea she was going to do it. Nina spluttered in shock. The other girls loosened their hold and Flowers wriggled free. Margie clapped a hand over her mouth to stifle a nervous snort of laughter.

Nina, her look murderous, shrieked and launched herself at Adela.

'I hate you!' She grabbed hold of Adela's long, dark plait and yanked it hard, scratching at her face like a wildcat.

Adela fought back, shoving Nina on to the bed.

'Serves you right,' Adela panted as they tussled. 'You're just a big bully.'

'And you're a wog just like Flowers!' Nina screamed, digging her nails into her breast. 'Nobody likes you. Your mother's a half-caste and your father's a cad!'

Adela gasped in fury. How dare she speak about her parents like that! She seized Nina's long, pale fingers and sank her teeth into them. Nina let out a piercing scream that brought the young house mother tearing into the dormitory.

'What on earth is going on?' Miss Bensham demanded.

The other girls scattered to their beds. Adela stood up just in time to see Flowers slip out of the room unnoticed. Nina burst into tears.

'She attacked me,' Nina sobbed.

Miss Bensham bustled forward. 'Dear girl, your hair's soaking.' She wrinkled her nose at the sour smell.

'She did it!' Nina burrowed into the house mother's plump hold. 'And she b-bit my h-hand.'

'Oh my word, I can see teeth marks! Adela, is this true?'

Adela stood mutely defiant.

'Girls?' Miss Bensham looked around at the others. 'What happened?'

'Miss,' said Margie, 'she just went for Nina.'

'Whatever possessed you?' Their house mother looked deeply shocked.

Adela hesitated. If she told on the others about what they had been doing to Flowers, they would turn on her. At least Flowers had escaped.

'She insulted my parents,' Adela said.

'I never did,' Nina protested, her blue eyes reproachful.

'Yes, you did!'

'Nina, what did you say?' Miss Bensham pushed her to arm's length and scrutinised her.

'Nothing, miss,' she sniffed. 'I don't even know her parents.'

Miss Bensham looked at a loss as to what to do.

'It's not my fault, miss,' Nina whined. 'Adela picks on me because she doesn't like me being friends with Margie.'

'You must all be friends together, girls. Now go and rinse out your hair before teatime, Nina. Everyone else leave the dormitory now; you shouldn't be up here in the afternoon.' The girls scrambled for the door. 'Not you, Adela Robson. You're coming with me.'

As Adela followed the house mother out, Nina stuck out her tongue and made a rude gesture that only Adela saw.

***

When Adela refused to explain her behaviour to Miss Bensham, she was sent to the headmistress, Miss Gertrude Black. Her office smelled of polish and flowers; a mix of beeswax and the marigolds and wild pink cosmos that stood in a blue vase on a bookcase by the door. For a moment it caught Adela's attention, and she forgot why she was there.

It wasn't the first time she'd been hauled in front of the brown-suited, red-headed Miss Black. By no means. Three years ago, in her very first week at the school, Adela had caused panic among girls and staff by smuggling in her pet tiger cub, Molly, in a laundry basket. She had wept for hours when her father had returned and taken Molly home without her. Then there was the time when she had thrown a jug of water from an upstairs window over a visiting missionary. In the dusk she had mistaken the spindly figure for one of the annoying boys from St Mungo's School who were always daring each other to throw pebbles at the girls' dormitory windows.

Miss Black scrutinised her over horn-rimmed spectacles and did not ask her to sit down.

'I must say, Adela, I am dismayed to see you once more in front of my desk. I'm even more aghast to hear that this time it's not merely your usual high spirits causing trouble, but an attack on another girl. It's completely unacceptable. I've seen the teeth marks on Nina's hand, and I've already had her mother on the telephone demanding that you are expelled. Give me one good reason why you shouldn't be.'

Adela felt her cheeks burn. 'Nina Davidge is a bully!'

'Give me an example.'

Adela was on the point of telling her about Flowers being forced to drink Nina's disgusting potion but hesitated. She didn't want to drag Flowers into her spat with the colonel's daughter, or Nina would only take it out on them both. Flowers would be summoned and forced to tell tales against Nina.

'She says unkind things,' Adela replied. 'She was horrible about my mother and called my father a cad.'

Miss Black raised her eyebrows. 'That's certainly not a nice thing to say. But remember the old adage "Sticks and stones may break my bones, but words will never hurt me." You mustn't be oversensitive. I'll have a word with Nina about it. I expect you girls to set an example to the younger ones. You're thirteen years-old and in the senior school now, so you better start acting your age.'

The headmistress pushed her spectacles more firmly on to her nose. 'In the meantime, you will be punished for such unladylike behaviour. You shall not be allowed to take part in the junior inter-house hockey matches, but instead will be given extra sewing duties by Miss Bensham. A period of calm reflection is what is needed. If anything like this happens again,' Miss Black warned, 'I shall not hesitate in summoning your parents and having you removed.'

Adela's stomach lurched at the threat; how disappointed her parents would be if she was sent home in disgrace. Yet a part of her felt defiant; she would like nothing better than to leave the strictures of St Ninian's and return to her beloved home at Belgooree.

***

Frustrating as her punishment was – Adela loathed sewing and yearned to be out in the fresh autumnal air – she submitted without protest, hoping the trouble with Nina would soon blow over. Perhaps the snobbish colonel's daughter had only said those hurtful things about her parents in the heat of the moment. Adela was sure she couldn't have meant them, for they weren't true.

But the trouble didn't stop. Nina was vindictive. Adela had misjudged quite how humiliated Nina had been, both by the drenching and by being publicly hauled in front of Miss Black.

Nina called Adela a little sneak and organised the other girls into not speaking to her.

'We've sent you to Coventry,' Margie told her, 'for being horrid to Nina.'

'But she started it,' Adela protested.

'Can't hear you!' Margie called as she hurried away and left Adela mending sheets in the common room.

Only Flowers Dunlop smiled warily at her when she entered the classroom or dormitory, and once she realised that Adela didn't hold a grudge against her for what had happened, she was happy to chat about life as a member of a railway family. Her father was station master at the busy depot at Sreemangal in the tea district of Sylhet. He was a second-generation Scot in India. Her mother came from the nearby hill station of Jaflong. Adela had seen them dropping off an excited Flowers at the start of term: a jovial red-faced man and a pretty woman in a lime-green sari who had stood out like a sore thumb because no one else's mother was dressed in native costume.

'I've been fishing at Jaflong with my father,' Adela enthused. 'It's beautiful there, and the fishing boats are like gondolas – just like in Venice.'

'Have you been to Venice?' Flowers asked, wide-eyed.

'No, but I've seen pictures. And one day I'm going to go there – I'm going to travel all over the world and become a famous actress.'

'How will you do that? Are your family very rich?'

'No,' Adela admitted. She waved away such an obstacle. 'I'll marry a prince or a viceroy and he will take me around the world. We'll spend the summers in Europe, or maybe America – yes, we'll have a house in Hollywood so I can star in the latest films.'

Flowers chewed on the end of her pigtail. 'I want to be a nurse and make people better.'

Adela looked at her in pity. 'I can't think of anything worse – all that blood and having to empty bedpans and wash men's bottoms.'

Flowers gasped. 'I wouldn't want to do that.'

'You'll have to. Auntie Tilly's brother is a doctor and he says that's what nurses have to do. He calls them angels, but I think it sounds like a job from hell.'

'Adela!'

'Well, I'm just telling the truth. I think you should become a lady doctor instead, then you can be in charge of all the nurses and wear nicer clothes and still make people better.'

'I hadn't thought of that.' Flowers' slim face looked pensive. 'I don't think girls like me become lady doctors.'

'Why ever not? You're obviously brainy. You've only been here a month and you're top of the class in almost everything – no wonder bossyboots Nina doesn't like you. She was first in everything last term – except for the singing prize, which I won.'

Adela abandoned her sewing and paced to the window. Outside, the leaves of a large chinar glowed brilliant scarlet in the mellow autumn sun. How she longed to be home in the hills at Belgooree, out riding through the tea garden on her piebald pony, Patch, shooting duck by the river with her father or, after an explore through the sal forest, pestering their khansama, Mohammed Din, for scraps of chicken for Scout, her hill dog. Anything but be stuck in school doing endless sewing, with everyone except new-girl Flowers giving her the cold shoulder.

How she loathed St Ninian's! She hated lessons and having to sit still and learn algebra and the names of long-dead kings and queens. School was only bearable when she was out of doors running and playing games on the half-bald playing field or larking around in the spinney with Margie and the others. She used to make Margie laugh with impersonations of the teachers. But Margie wasn't speaking to her.

Adela had to admit the bleak truth that things had been changing with Margie long before the fight with Nina. All term their friendship had been lukewarm. Margie hadn't come to stay at Belgooree over the summer like she had in previous holidays; she had gone to Simla in the Himalayan foothills with Nina and her mother. 'We went to a garden party at Viceregal Lodge,' Margie had boasted, 'and Nina got a part in a play at the Gaiety.'

Adela had been consumed with envy to think that Nina had performed on a real stage with a paying audience and – if she was to be believed – in front of the Viceroy himself! Nina couldn't act for toffee. It should have been her, Adela Robson, with a good singing voice and dancing legs, who entertained India's most important people, the 'heaven-born' – those elite British government officials who spent the hot weather in Simla.

But that was never going to happen, not while she was stuck in a boarding school in Shillong. Here, the only chance to act was in the inter-house plays in front of the headmistress and occasionally Miss Black's missionary brother, Dr Norman Black, who had helped found the school and came to judge the competition – if he wasn't away spreading the gospel to heathens.

Adela gave an impatient sigh. If only she hadn't interfered between Nina and Flowers. Since then school life had become completely unbearable.

'All your troubles are my fault. I'm sorry,' Flowers said.

Adela swung round. The girl was studying her with sorrowful brown eyes.

'Don't be,' Adela said.

'I should just have drunk that ghastly stuff and got it over with.'

'No, you shouldn't have. It's not a tradition – just something Nina made up. We usually just make apple-pie beds and lock the new girls in the laundry room and pretend it's haunted.'

'It doesn't matter – any tradition will do,' Flowers said, shaking her head. 'I just want to fit in here.'

***

'There isn't a part for you,' Nina said callously. 'It's all about Queen Elizabeth the first and Mary, Queen of Scots. I'm Queen Bess and Margie's going to be Queen Mary. We've already decided.'

Adela looked up at them, stunned. They were standing over her desk, where she was struggling with equations, her jotter a patchwork of holes where she'd rubbed out her miscalculations. Everyone else had finished their prep and gone to the common room. Margie glanced away; even she looked sheepish.

'That's not fair!' Adela protested. 'You can't just choose the best parts – it has to go to a vote.'

'We've voted. After the hockey match. You weren't there.'

'I didn't know—'

'Well, now you do.'

Adela was suddenly filled with rage at the injustice. She leapt up and grabbed Nina as she tried to walk away.

'Why are you being so mean?' she cried.

Nina went rigid, as if her touch was contagious. 'Get off me, or I'll scream for help.'

Adela let go. 'Just tell me! Why can't we all be friends?'

Nina's face puckered into a look of disgust. 'You're not like us; you never will be. You pretend to be British but you're not.'

'Of course I'm British. Just because I was born in India doesn't make me Indian.'

Nina gave a malicious little smile. 'You don't know, do you, Tea Leaf? I can't believe no one's told you.'

'Told me what?' Adela's stomach knotted. The glint in Nina's pale blue eyes was frightening.

'You're two annas short of a rupee – ask your mother.' She leant forward and hissed, 'And your father is a blackguard who jilted my mother at the altar, so I'll never *ever* be friends with you!'

With a toss of blonde ponytail, Nina turned her back on Adela. 'Come on, Margie, we've got a rehearsal.'

Adela, shaking with shock, watched them march from the room.

***

That night Adela lay awake, tormented by Nina's hurtful words. What did she mean by them? Two annas short of a rupee was an insult thrown at Eurasians – or Anglo-Indians, as mixed-race families, such as Flowers', now called themselves – but she, Adela, had no Indian blood. The Robsons were British through and through, and her mother was the daughter of Jock Belhaven, English soldier turned tea planter. What incensed her even more, though, was the slur on her father's character; he would never jilt anyone at the altar and he had only ever loved her mother. Auntie Tilly in Assam said it was well known among the tea planters how Wesley Robson adored his Clarissa and had even given up his career at the prestigious Oxford Tea Estates to run the remote tea garden in the Khasi Hills just to please the beautiful Clarrie Belhaven.

The next day, tired out and short-tempered from lack of sleep, Adela confronted Margie in the washroom.

'You don't believe all this nonsense about my parents, do you? You've met them, Margie. You've always said how much you like them.'

Her former friend looked uneasy. 'I shouldn't be speaking to you.'

'Margie! Just tell me you don't believe Nina.'

Margie gave her a cool look. 'I do believe Nina.'

'Why?'

''Cause I've heard Mrs Davidge say as much. She tells Nina everything.'

'What did she say?' Adela blocked her way. 'Tell me. I have a right to know.'

'Very well,' Margie said. 'Don't say you didn't ask for it. Mrs Davidge said she was engaged to your father, but he left her in the lurch and went off with a box-wallah's half-caste daughter who'd been married before.'

'Box-wallah's half-caste . . . ?' Adela felt winded.

'Mrs Davidge said it turned out to be a lucky let-off 'cause she ended up with an officer in a prestigious Gurkha regiment and not stuck out in the sticks with a penniless tea planter.'

Margie pushed past and left Adela gaping after her.

***

Adela hardly ever cried, but that day she ran off to the spinney and howled behind the thick trunk of a pine tree. Crouching down, she eventually forced herself to be calm. She refused to believe Margie's poisonous words. Surely a grown woman like Mrs Davidge wouldn't say such malicious things, let alone admit them to her daughter's friend. She had glimpsed Nina's mother at speech day: a thin woman dressed in a fashionably belted frock and a large straw hat with matching ribbon over a neat blonde perm. She had hung on to the arm of a much older man wearing a military-style topee and an array of medals, presumably Nina's father. Henrietta she was called; Adela had heard her being introduced. She had looked so sophisticated that Adela had felt a guilty stab of relief that her own mother had not felt well enough to travel the bumpy two hours by car from Belgooree. She would have worn one of her ancient tea dresses and an old-fashioned hat, the kind that no one had worn since before the Great War.

But Auntie Tilly had travelled all the way from the Oxford Tea Estates with gruff Uncle James, and her adored father had come from Belgooree looking handsome in a white linen suit and brown fedora hat. Adela had felt so proud marching up on stage to receive a small silver cup for singing.

Had her father and Nina's mother spoken to each other that day? Auntie Tilly had demanded to be shown around her schoolhouse, so Adela hadn't been with her father all of the time. It made her feel strange inside to think her father might have had feelings for another woman. She knew that her mother had been married before; she had run a tea room in Newcastle and named it Herbert's after her first husband. Adela's parents had made no secret of that. But these other hurtful accusations were a different matter.

Suddenly she had an overwhelming urge to run away, to escape the cattiness of Nina and her followers and the strictures of boarding school. She longed for home, for her mother's fussing attention and her father's companionship.

'What are you doing out here?'

Adela looked up to see Flowers peering anxiously at her. Adela rubbed her eyes.

'I hate it here,' she admitted. 'The only thing I was looking forward to was being in the inter-house play competition, and now I'm not even in that. Nina has said horrible things about my parents, and now Margie and all the other girls hate me.'

'I don't hate you,' said Flowers, squatting down beside her. 'I think you're the nicest girl in the class – in the whole house. I'll never forget the way you stuck up for me.'

Adela's eyes watered again. 'Thank you.' She slipped an arm around the girl's bony shoulders.

Flowers said, 'I thought St Ninian's would be like the Chalet School in those novels Daddy used to bring me back from the library – all girls together and having adventures. But it's nothing like that, is it?'

'I don't know – I've never read them – but it doesn't sound like St Ninian's. It was all right when Margie was my best friend, I suppose, but I've always preferred playing with boys.

My cousin Jamie was the best fun – till he got sent back home to school.'

'To England?'

'Yes. Durham, in the north of England. Not that I've ever been there.'

Flowers looked at her with dark, solemn eyes. 'I'll be your best friend if you like. I'm not pretty like Margie and I'm not a boy—'

Adela snorted with sudden laughter. 'No, I can see you're not a boy.'

Flowers giggled and sucked her hair. Adela considered the idea. Flowers was not as timid as she looked; she had fought back when the girls had tried to force her to drink Nina's potion. And she had come out here to find her even though she must know that speaking to her, Adela, would make her more unpopular with Nina and the others. Flowers had a quiet strength and an innate kindness. Adela was growing fond of the railway girl.

'Can you sing and dance?' Adela asked.

Flowers smiled. 'Mummy says I'm her little nightingale, and I went to ballet classes in Sreemangal.'

'Good.' Adela stood up. 'We're going to enter our own act in the inter-house competitions. There's nothing to say we can't.'

Flowers gaped at her. 'But what will the others say?'

'Who cares?' Adela said with a grin, pulling the skinny girl to her feet. 'All that matters is that we get on that stage and show them they haven't beaten us.'

Chapter 2

'Hello, sir.' Sam Jackman gripped Dr Black in a firm handshake. Sam's handsome, expressive face grinned with pleasure under a battered green porkpie hat that sat at a jaunty angle far back on his head.

'So kind of you, dear boy, to collect me from the station,' said Norman Black, delighted to see the son of his old friend Jackman, the steamship captain. The lad had grown into a tall, athletic young man, yet his boyish looks made him look younger than his mid-twenties, as did the mischievous hazel eyes, creased in a smile.

'Delighted to do so,' Sam said, seizing the missionary's battered case from the wiry porter who carried it on his head, then tipping the man in thanks. 'And I'm looking forward to showing off my Kodak cine camera. I think it's a great idea to film the work of the school.'

'Well, the footage you sent me of river life was so very good,' enthused Norman, 'that I thought it would be an excellent way to help my sister fundraise for St Ninian's. She needs donations to cover the bursaries of the disadvantaged girls she takes in.'

Sam smiled. 'A worthy cause,' he said, thinking how the kind doctor had helped him with his own school fees.

Sam strode ahead, leading his old mentor to a dusty motor car – an ancient open-topped tourer that he'd won in a drunken card game from a tea planter in Guwahati, but there was no need to tell that to the good doctor.

Sam's pet monkey jumped up and down in the driver's seat, hooting the horn.

'Nelson still going strong, I see?' Norman's deep-set eyes and craggy face looked amused.

'This is Nelson the Third,' Sam introduced the monkey. 'Nelson One died of old age, and Nelson Two ran off with a young female half his age.'

The monkey screeched in excitement, trying to grab the missionary's dark homburg hat from his head. Sam told him off in colourful Hindustani, and the monkey leapt on to his master's shoulder and clutched him by the ears.

With a loud bang from the exhaust, they set off up the winding road to St Ninian's, chatting loudly over the rattle and grinding gears of the labouring car. Sam hadn't seen Dr Black for over seven years – the missionary had been back in Scotland for five of those and in Southern India the past two – but he would always be grateful for the man's kindness. Norman Black had taken an interest in his welfare since the time his mother had deserted him at the age of seven, separating from his father and disappearing back to Britain without him.

It's me and the heat of Assam she can't stand, his father had told him, *not you, lad.* But it had tipped his world upside down like an earthquake.

'I'm sorry to hear that your father died,' Norman shouted over the straining engine. 'Was it very sudden?'

'Yes,' Sam admitted, feeling a familiar pang of loss. 'It was just a normal start to the day. We'd had breakfast on the boat and were watching the sunrise. Father said he was feeling dizzy and went off to sit in the wheelhouse for a minute. Nelson the Third found him. His heart just gave out.'

Norman patted his shoulder in sympathy. 'Then there was nothing you could have done for him, so stop feeling guilty.'

Sam gave him a grateful look. The missionary's knack of reading his mind was uncanny. Two and half years on, Sam was still blaming himself for not checking on his father sooner. He had been too wrapped up in gazing at the dazzling golden sunrise.

'Thank you,' said Sam.

Norman changed the subject, describing his recent travels and making Sam laugh, like old times.

Norman Black, who had often crossed the Brahmaputra River on the Jackmans' ferry *Cullercoats* on trips to remote tea planters' families to administer medicine and a dose of salvation, had always been a favourite of Sam's. The man had never treated him like a nuisance in the way other grown-ups had. Deeply hurt at his mother's rejection of him, Sam had often been difficult and over-boisterous, but Black had been patient with him and made Sam feel special.

It was thanks to the doctor's generosity that Sam, aged ten, had been given a good education. Black paid for him to go to The Lawrence School, near Simla, in the Western Himalayas – a three-day journey from home – where Sam had been happy. He had baulked at the military discipline, but developed a passion for tennis and cricket and revelled in his studies and the chance to learn about agriculture. He had helped out at a local dairy and went to lectures in Simla on crop rotation and forestry. He would dearly have loved to have sat the civil service exams and joined the government department of agriculture, but at sixteen, having gained his School Certificate, his father had called him back to help on the ferry.

'I miss you, lad,' Jackman had said. 'You can do farming when I'm dead and gone.'

Yet when his father had died over two years ago, Sam had continued as before, steering the ship just as his father had done. He would probably be negotiating the sandbars and swirling currents of the mighty Brahmaputra till he was as old and grey as Norman Black.

They pulled up in front of the iron gates of St Ninian's, and Nelson jumped on the horn. The frantic hooting brought the gatekeeper rushing to open up. On the far side a row of uniformed girls were lined up, ready to greet their distinguished visitor.

Norman got out and spoke to each of them in turn – there were half a dozen youngsters – and they bobbed in a little curtsy as he shook their hands.

'Just like royalty,' Sam teased.

'You drive on while I walk up with the pupils to the school hall,' said Black.

'They can jump in the back,' Sam offered. 'Come on, girls, hop on.'

After a moment's hesitation the tallest girl, a slim blonde with a saucy blue-eyed look, slipped into the seat behind Sam, and the others scrambled in after her. The two who couldn't squeeze on the back seat perched on top of the boot at the back.

Sam grinned. 'Hold on tight,' he said. They arrived at the main entrance in a cacophony of hooting and giggles that brought Gertrude Black hurrying out to greet them with scolding words that belied her obvious delight in seeing her older brother.

'Goodness, what a noise! Mr Jackman, so kind of you to bring Dr Black. Just leave the case – one of the staff will bring it in.

Girls, get back to your houses at once and prepare for inspection. Norman, dear, it's so very good to see you.'

Sam reached into the boot for his camera and bag full of film canisters.

Turning to go, the blonde girl gasped. 'Is that for making films?'

'Yes.' Sam said, smiling. 'I'm going to record life at the school.'

'And the drama competition?'

He winked. 'I'll make film stars of you all.'

She returned the smile, and the others squealed in excitement, which set Nelson screeching. Miss Black clapped her hands for order.

'To your houses, girls! That includes you, Nina Davidge.' She gave the tall blonde girl a warning glare.

The girl stood her ground. 'Shall I show Mr Jackman around the school, miss?'

'No, thank you, Nina. I shall be doing that after lunch.'

Nelson took that moment to swing down from the car and scamper towards the girls. Nina shrieked as the monkey grabbed her school tunic. Sam lunged forward and pulled Nelson away. Nina and the other pupils fled with screams and giggles.

'I'm so sorry,' said Gertrude. 'I don't know what's got into them today. My girls are not usually so unruly.'

'No, I apologise for Nelson's ungentlemanly behaviour,' Sam said, putting Nelson on his lead and keeping a tight rein.

'Perhaps, dear sister.' Norman said with a laugh. 'I shouldn't have brought such a handsome young man into their midst. But maybe they will all perform their plays twice as well for the camera.'

***

'And he's got gorgeous hazel-brown eyes,' Nina told her enthralled classmates, 'and a wicked smile. He's some sort of film director. Absolutely divine – apart from his horrid little monkey that smells of the bazaar.'

Adela listened from across the room; even though most of the girls were speaking to her again (including Margie when Nina was out of earshot), she was no longer part of the gang. She and

Flowers kept each other company and had been secretly practising their routines in Miss Bensham's linen room. The house mother must have felt sorry for them because she was allowing them to use her wind-up gramophone and had added their mystery act on to the programme. They were going to perform a slapstick imitation of Charlie Chaplin that turned into them throwing off their hats and blazers and dancing the Charleston, a more old-fashioned dance than they had wanted, but Miss Bensham's record collection was limited.

Nina was still going on about the good-looking film-maker who had brought Dr Black.

'I've never heard of a film director with a monkey,' Adela chimed in. 'Can't be anyone famous.'

'Nobody asked you, Tea Leaf,' Nina snapped. 'Anyway, it doesn't concern you, since you're not in our play.' She turned to the others. 'And I could tell he liked me – he gave me a wink!'

'And directors don't do their own filming,' Adela persisted. 'If he didn't bring a cameraman with him, then he's not a proper director, is he?'

Nina stormed across the room and jabbed Adela hard with a long finger. 'Nobody cares what you have to say. You're just jealous that I'm going to be filmed, aren't you? I'm the one who will be famous one day – not a little Tea Leaf from the back of beyond. So shut up, two annas!'

Adela stared her out, not flinching from the painful jab or answering back. *Just wait and see,* she thought defiantly. She, not the hateful Nina, would be the star by the end of the day.

***

Sam good-humouredly followed in the wake of the formidable Gertrude Black and filmed what she thought potential benefactors of the school would like to see: the gothic chapel, the hockey field, the science laboratory, with its test tubes and wallcharts, and the moderately well-stocked library.

Norman had long got bored and disappeared off to talk to the pupils.

'Don't you think your supporters would like to see pictures of the girls engaged in their everyday life?' Sam suggested. 'Eating in the dining hall or playing chess in the common room – that sort of thing. I can't do sound, but I can edit-in explanatory titles.'

'Our benefactors will want to know of the good work and education – Christian education – that we give the girls at St Ninian's. It's not a holiday camp.'

'No,' Sam murmured, 'I can see that.'

She gave him a sharp look. 'What I mean is we don't want people to think this is some sort of finishing school. Our girls are being equipped to go out into the world to be useful young women – teachers and administrators, or at the very least intelligent wives and mothers for the Empire.'

Sam laughed. 'The Empire's on its way out, surely.'

Her look was scandalised. 'I hope not. You're not one of those radical young Englishmen who support the Home Rule for India lobby?'

Sam shrugged. 'I believe what my old dad used to say: India belongs to the Indians and we've just got it on loan.'

'I can't agree,' Gertrude replied. 'We have so much more to give India, so much good we can do – men like my brother giving unselfish service. We can't just abandon the Indians, give up and go home.'

Sam, seeing her flustered, said more gently, 'We're moving towards more self-governance for Indians, Miss Black. I believe it's a matter of when, not if, we go. But perhaps it won't happen in our lifetime. Things grind mightily slowly on the Brahmaputra, as my old dad also used to say.'

'You seem very fond of quoting your father; do you not hold opinions of your own?' Her stare challenged him. 'And what are you going to give back to India, Mr Jackman, after the benefits you've had of a first-class imperial education?'

He gave a rueful laugh. 'Help you and Dr Black make a film promoting St Ninian's.'

Gertrude's stern face twitched in a smile. 'Enough of filming buildings then. You are right about showing the girls at recreation. The inter-house play competition will demonstrate how they put their knowledge of history, geography and literature into live performance. Let us go to the central hall; I suspect that's where we'll find my talkative brother.'

Sam fell into step behind the headmistress. He could do with a drink. He hoped the competition wouldn't take all afternoon and that he could make a swift departure. Nelson, who was chained up in the games shed, would not stand his confinement much longer either.

***

The hall was abuzz with excited whispers and shuffling in seats as the girls in the audience awaited the series of mini tableaux and dramas to be performed. Some of the most senior girls were commandeering the front rows. Sam had set up his camera on a tripod near the front, but to the side so that he wouldn't block the view of the smaller girls at the back. Looking through the programme of four plays plus a mystery act, he groaned inwardly, hoping he could make his escape before dark.

'We'll have to put on the hall lights I'm afraid,' he told the Blacks. 'There isn't enough natural light in here.'

'Not a problem.' Norman assured. 'Got everything else you need?'

Sam nodded. 'I won't hang around afterwards – can't leave Nelson for too long in the shed.'

The doctor said, 'I quite understand. I'll come and see you in a week or so on my way up to Tezpur. Will you have the cine film developed by then?'

'I'll have to send it off to Calcutta – probably two weeks.'

Norman clasped him on the arms. 'Thank you for doing this, Sam. We're most grateful.'

'Let's see how it turns out first.' Sam gave a wry smile.

Suddenly there was a screech behind them, and the men turned to see Nelson swinging along the backs of the chairs towards them, an impish-faced girl with a thick, dark plait clutching on to his lead, grinning.

'I found Nelson the Third in the games shed,' she panted as the monkey dragged her quickly to Sam. Nelson leapt on to his master's shoulder, licking his cheek in delight at being reunited. 'Someone had tied him up.'

Sam blushed. 'Well, yes, I did . . . Thank you . . . Er . . . should I know you? I mean, how on earth do you know Nelson?'

Adela stared up at Sam Jackman; she should have known he'd be the man with the monkey. All the tea planters knew the steamboat captain with a flair for photography and a pet rhesus monkey. Not everyone knew that Sam had had three such pets, but Adela noticed these things.

'I'm Adela Robson – Wesley and Clarrie's daughter from Belgooree,' she prompted. 'Don't you remember me? I last saw you over a year ago when I went to stay with Auntie Tilly on the Oxford Estates; she's not my real auntie, just married to a Robson cousin.'

'Of course I remember.' Sam said with a quick smile.

Adela felt a kick of disappointment; she could tell that he hadn't.

'Well, Nelson remembered, didn't you, boy?' She tickled the monkey's chin.

Nelson cackled and swung into her arms.

'What are you doing with that creature?' Miss Black came hurrying over. 'He's supposed to be outside.'

'I'll look after him, miss,' Adela said at once. 'He knows me.'

'Aren't you in your house play?'

'No, miss.'

'That surprises me,' frowned Gertrude.

'Well, if you wouldn't mind keeping him under control,' Sam intervened, 'I'd be very grateful . . . er . . . Della?'

'Adela,' she corrected.

'Adela,' Sam said, smiling, 'that would be very kind of you.'

She grinned back. 'Pleasure.' She swung Nelson on to her hip.

Sam watched her skip off to join another girl, who looked Anglo-Indian. The tall blonde pupil, who had spent the last half an hour flirting with him as he set up the camera and chatted to Dr Black, advanced on the two smaller girls. Sam couldn't tell what was being said, but he saw the look of disdain on the blonde girl's face as she flicked her hand at them. She was obviously telling them they couldn't sit with her.

Adela Robson? No, he had no real memory of her, though he knew Wesley as an experienced planter who didn't suffer fools. Clarrie Robson was a bit of a recluse at Belgooree, but he knew Tilly Robson better. He still remembered the first time Tilly had travelled aboard their boat, over ten years ago, garrulous with nerves at meeting her new husband. He had liked her instantly, which is more than he could say for her hard-drinking, ruthless planter husband, James.

Sam waited till Adela had settled in a seat near the back. She glanced at him with pretty dark eyes, laughing as Nelson nuzzled and nibbled her hair. Sam winked and then turned to the job of recording the plays.

***

Adela and Flowers slipped out halfway through the third performance, a re-enactment of Queen Victoria being made Empress of India and a group of girls dressed as milkmaids dancing around an imaginary maypole, which Adela thought quite bizarre.

They had left their costumes in the games shed; that's how she'd come across Nelson the Third. She'd instantly recognised the patch of lighter-coloured fur around his left ear and the intelligent look in his eye, and he appeared to know her even if his owner didn't. It rankled with Adela that the handsome Sam had not recognised who she was, but then he must get hundreds of passengers every month, so why should he remember her from over a year ago?

'Do you think this is a good idea?' Flowers asked anxiously.

'Course it is.'

'I think we should have told the others, so they won't get a nasty shock when they find out it's us.'

'That's the whole point,' said Adela. 'They think it's just some musical appreciation that Miss Bensham has dreamed up. I can't wait to see the look on Nina Davidge's face when we go on stage. We're going to get ourselves on cine film too!'

'I don't think I can do this. There are so many people in the hall – seniors too. And Miss Black might hate it, 'cause it's not history and serious. What if we get into trouble? I don't want to get sent home.'

'Calm down! No one's going to get sent home. Miss Bensham will back us up – she's going to announce us after Nina's play. Now put your costume on.'

Flowers reluctantly pulled on a pair of baggy trousers they'd made out of old sheets over her dancing dress and buttoned up her school blazer on top. Nelson leapt around them, snatching at their hats.

'He's excited for our performance.' Adela laughed. 'Come on, Flowers, put a smile on your face and let's have some fun for a change.'

They scurried back to the hall and went backstage. They were too early; Nina and Margie were just about to go on.

'What on earth are you two doing?' Margie hissed.

'We're the surprise act at the end,' Adela said, delighting in Nina's astonished look.

Nina, dressed in a sumptuous Elizabethan costume her parents had paid to have tailor-made, gaped at them.

'Come on, Nina, we're on.' Margie pulled her arm.

Nina found her voice. 'You look like a couple of tramps. I wouldn't be seen dead dressed like that.' She shot Flowers a pitying look. 'I bet Adela put you up to this. Well, make a fool of yourself if you want to, but you'll never live it down. You'll make our house look second-rate.'

Nelson, who was swinging on the curtain, reached out and yanked Nina's crown.

'Get him off me!' she squealed, flapping at the monkey. 'Give that back!'

Nelson scampered off across the stage as the curtain went up, flinging the crown into the audience. Laughter rippled through the hall.

'We should be on there,' Margie said in agitation.

'I haven't got my crown,' cried Nina.

'Come on!' Margie pushed her forward.

Laughter grew as Nelson leapt across the seats and evaded capture. Adela whistled for him – a loud one through her fingers like she'd seen Sam do – and the monkey scampered backstage again and into her arms.

Nina flung a look of loathing as she hurried on stage. Adela felt a twinge of remorse as she watched Nina's flustered performance from the wings.

'A real actress wouldn't care if a monkey ran off with her crown,' she whispered to Flowers. 'A professional doesn't need props – she just gets on with it.'

But to stop any more antics from Nelson, she put him back on his lead, which she tied to a chair.

The short play was over even quicker because Margie jumped a whole scene leading up to her execution by order of Queen

Bess, cutting out Nina's long, dramatic final speech. Nina stormed off to halfhearted applause.

'I'll never forgive you for this – or you, stinky Flowers.' Nina pushed past them, eyes smarting with furious tears.

Miss Bensham appeared in the opposite wing, where the gramophone was set up, and waved across. 'Ready?' she mouthed.

Adela nodded and gave the thumbs up. Miss Bensham beamed and gave the signal for the curtains to be pulled aside again. She began announcing the final surprise act.

'Two young ladies have been working hard in secret to put on an extra entertainment for you. This is not part of the competition but just for your pleasure. Let me introduce The Two Chaplins!'

Adela's stomach flipped. 'Come on, Flowers, it's us now.' She took the girl's hand.

Flowers pulled away. Her face was pale with terror. She shook her head, unable to speak.

'This is our big moment,' Adela urged. 'Don't get cold feet now.'

'I-I c-can't,' Flowers gasped. 'Sorry . . .' She turned and dashed away.

'Flowers!'

But she was gone.

The curtains were fully opened, and Adela could hear the crackle and hiss as Miss Bensham put the first record on the gramophone, *The William Tell Overture*. She felt a wave of panic surge through her. The act was ruined before it started; she would be a laughing stock if she went on alone.

Adela looked round in desperation. Nelson. She rushed across and untied the monkey's lead. 'Now's your big chance at stardom.'

She waddled onstage Charlie Chaplin style, turning a hockey stick in place of a walking cane and holding Nelson on his lead. Miss Bensham was looking aghast from the other wing. There was laughter from the hall as Nelson tried to grab the stick and imitate Adela. She improvised, speeding up their act in time to the music and allowing Nelson to chase her around the stage. She tripped over his lead, banging her knee hard, but the audience roared with laughter, so she did it again on purpose.

The record finished and the girls applauded and cheered. Nelson clapped them back. Miss Bensham was so bemused she forgot to put on the second record. Adela did an exaggerated waddle across and reminded her.

As ragtime music blared out, Adela began to shed her comic clothing: blazer, hockey boots, baggy trousers. Each time Nelson scampered after her, trying to put them on or hurling them over his head. The youngest girls laughed until they were crying. Adela, now clad in a skimpy flapper's dress (made out of an old petticoat and fringes from a lampshade), tossed off her hat, and her long, unbound wavy hair fell about her shoulders. She danced and kicked her legs for all she was worth, knowing that the monkey would mimic her. She picked him up and waltzed around the stage, unable to keep the grin off her face at the giggling beyond.

Then abruptly it died away as the headmistress marched to the front and ordered the curtains to be closed. Her face was thunderous. She hissed at Miss Bensham to stop the music. Adela came to a standstill, Nelson still cavorting across the stage. The giggling audience, hands clapped over mouths, disappeared from Adela's view as the curtain fell.

Miss Black's commanding voice could be heard addressing the hall just feet away.

'This is no laughing matter. I would not have allowed such a spectacle if I had known the content of the surprise entertainment. Quite inappropriate. I hope our honoured guests will not think this sort of thing usually goes on at St Ninian's. Now, we will have a ten-minute interval while Dr Black and I decide which play we deemed the best in both content and delivery. And I think you will agree what a high standard we have seen here this afternoon – beautiful costumes and stirring patriotic words. Then Dr Black will present the winner with the Inter-House Drama Cup.'

Adela caught Miss Bensham's horrified look. They were both in trouble. A moment later Miss Black was stalking backstage, face puce with fury.

'What an unseemly performance,' she said, glaring. 'Miss Bensham, I can't imagine what you were thinking of allowing this.'

'I thought it was just some dancing—'

'I shall deal with you later.' She turned on Adela. 'Look at you, dressed like some sleazy cabaret act! And cavorting about with that monkey. Are you deliberately trying to provoke me? You've brought this school into disrepute. How ashamed I feel in front of Dr Black. Have you anything to say for yourself?'

Adela stared back in bewilderment; she thought she had given the performance of her life. How could she have misjudged the situation so badly? Flowers had been right to be afraid of their headmistress: the woman was stuck in Victorian times.

'I suppose I should go and give Nelson back,' she mumbled.

'Nelson?' Miss Black snapped.

'The monkey – I should give him back to Mr Jackman.'

'Miss Bensham will do that,' the headmistress ordered. 'You will put some clothes on.' She pointed at the stage door. 'Now, get out of my sight. I shall be informing your parents of this.'

Adela bundled Nelson into Miss Bensham's arms – the house mother looked stricken – and grabbed at her pile of discarded clothes. Then she fled from the stage, stumbling down the outside steps, numb and humiliated.

***

Sam dumped his camera equipment on the seat beside him and drove off into a purplish dusk, leaving behind a frosty-faced Gertrude Black and a waving Norman. He probably hadn't improved the situation by saying he thought the Robson girl was rather a good dancer and wasn't it brave of her to go on stage alone?

Nelson, at least, had had the time of his life and was still leaping around the open-topped car, overexcited from all the attention. As Sam bumped away down the school drive and headed thankfully for home, he hoped Adela wasn't in too much trouble. Knowing Norman, he was sure the kind doctor would persuade his sister to show some Christian mercy, if not forgiveness.

Sam found himself whistling the Charleston as he drove through the scented pines leading away from Shillong. A glorious sunset was blazing in the west beyond the treetops as they rattled over the hill road.

'Settle down, Nelson,' Sam said, trying to calm his companion, but the monkey wouldn't sit still for a second. He screeched and grabbed Sam around the neck.

Eventually Sam stopped the car and turned sternly to his pet. 'I can't drive with you in this state. What on earth is the matter with you?'

The monkey hopped over the back seat and squatted on the boot. He began drumming his hands on the metal and screaming. Sam got out of the car and circled it, wondering if there was a tyre going flat or if something had got stuck under the chassis that was making Nelson agitated. It was too dark to see under the car, so he went and fetched a torch from the front shelf. Still the monkey squealed and banged on the boot.

Sam saw that the boot had not been properly closed. As he opened it wide to give it a good slam shut, Nelson grabbed the torch and swung on to his shoulders. Something caught in the torchlight. Sam blinked in astonishment. He grabbed the torch from the monkey and shone it at the interior. A girl squinted back at him, raising a hand to shield her eyes. She was cowering under a St Ninian's blazer in a fringed petticoat. Nelson leapt down and squatted beside her, patting her bare legs.

'Is that you, Adela?' Sam asked in alarm. 'What are you—?'

'Are we out of Shillong?' She sat up, clutching Nelson and peering out in fear.

'Yes, but—'

'Please don't take me back. I don't want to get you into trouble, but please don't.'

'I can't leave you in the boot of my car!'

Adela scrambled up and swung long legs over the side. Sam grabbed her hand to help her. She struggled to push him away.

'Let me go! I won't go back!'

Sam held her hard. 'Hey, steady on. Tell me what this is all about.'

'I just need a lift. I need to get away.' She glared back at him with defiant eyes.

'You can't run away at this time of night. People will be worried about you.'

'No, they won't. Nobody cares.'

'Of course they do. Miss Black—'

'Miss Black hates me. I'm a disgrace to the school. She's going to tell my parents.'

Suddenly Sam laughed. 'Is this all because of your dancing act?'

'It's not funny,' Adela raged. 'I can't go back. They all hate me and I don't have any friends. Even Flowers Dunlop let me down – she was supposed to do the dance too.'

'It can't be as bad as you think,' Sam soothed. 'Most of the girls loved it. I'm sure Miss Black will forgive you and it'll all blow over.'

'It won't blow over. Don't treat me like a child. I'm not a child!'

Sam let go of his hold. She stood shivering and barelegged.

'Pretend you never saw me. I didn't want you to find me – I was going to sneak out when you next stopped.'

'Sneak out and go where?' Sam snorted. 'It's dark, and dangerous for a girl to be wandering around in . . . in . . . what little you're dressed in. You'll catch your death.'

'I'm not afraid of the dark. I can sleep under a tree, and then when it's light I'll walk home.'

'Walk to Belgooree?' Sam cried. 'That would take ages.'

'I don't care – I can do it. Nothing is going to make me go back *there* – and you can't make me either.'

Sam, hands on hips, scrutinised the stubborn girl. She looked like an urchin with her dark, unruly hair tumbling about her shoulders, standing knock-kneed in a tatty slip with its fringed hem half off, arms folded tight over small, high breasts. Her dark-lashed eyes – he saw now that they were flecked with green – defied him; her mouth was a mulish pout. One day, Sam thought with a catch in his throat, Adela Robson would be beautiful. Sam dropped his gaze and reached beyond her into the boot.

'Here, put this round you.' He held out a blanket. 'And tell me what you want to do.'

'I want to go home,' she said at once. 'Please, Sam, can you take me to Belgooree?'

Suddenly she looked tired and unhappy, the self-assured defiance vanishing.

'Are your parents on the telephone?' he asked.

She nodded, looking confused. 'There's one in Daddy's office.'

'Hop up front then and I'll take you there. But only if you promise that we ring the school and let them know you are safe as soon as you are home.'

Her pretty, slim face broke into a smile of relief that made his heart squeeze.

'Thanks, Sam.'

She vaulted into the passenger seat without opening the door, wrapping the blanket around her and a squealing Nelson. Sam climbed back into the driver's seat, fleetingly tempted to turn around and take her back to school. That would be the sensible thing to do. But he would lose her trust for ever. And Nelson would never forgive him. Sam started up the engine and set off towards the tea plantation, wondering how much trouble he was heading into with his rash rescue.

Chapter 3

Adela awoke as the car bumped up the familiar track, passing the squat factory, gleaming white in the moonlight, and lurched towards the bungalow. The air smelt of woodsmoke and the sweet scent of night-blooming flowers. She sat up, pulling hair out of her eyes.

'I take it that's the burra bungalow?' Sam nodded towards the gateposts smothered in bougainvillea, with a glimpse of red tin roof beyond.

'Yes, we're home.' Adela grinned and hugged Nelson. Then her smile faltered. 'You will stay, won't you? Please stay and help me explain.'

On the journey she had told him everything about her unhappy time at school and the hurtful things that Nina Davidge had said. Sam had been sympathetic, but hadn't understood. He'd tried to mollify her as if she were a child: 'Best to take no notice. Bullies get bored if you don't rise to their baiting. You're a great girl – you'll find other friends.'

She studied him now, his face in profile: the long nose and smooth jaw that looked like he never needed to shave, the firm mouth and the battered hat perched on his short, thick hair. Under the tweed jacket with leather patches at its elbows, his shoulders looked strong and comforting. Sam's hands on the steering wheel were large and dextrous – a sportsman's hands – and she had an overwhelming urge to touch their roughened edges. With a gasp, Adela realised that she was smitten with Sam Jackman.

'What's wrong?' He glanced over. 'It's okay. I'll stay and back you up.'

Adela gulped. 'Thank you.'

Passing the servants' compound, their arrival set dogs barking. The bungalow, ghostly in the bright moonlight and covered in creepers, emerged out of the dark. Lamps glowed from a room beyond the veranda.

'Scout!' Adela cried and was out of the car the moment they stopped.

Her tan-coloured dog, with bushy tail wagging, came bounding down the steps to meet her. She fell on him, cuddling and stroking as he licked and barked in excitement.

'Who's there?' a strong voice bellowed from the veranda above. 'Good God, Adela! My darling, what are you doing here?'

Wesley Robson dashed down the creaking veranda steps. Adela stumbled into her father's arms, burying her head in his warm chest, breathing in the smoky smell of his waistcoat. She burst into tears.

'What's happened?' he demanded. 'You've hardly got a stitch of clothing on.' He swivelled to the man climbing out of the car, a monkey clinging to his shoulder. 'And who are you?' He peered into the shadows. 'Would you like to explain what the devil is going on?'

Sam came forward, hand outstretched and smiled. 'Sam Jackman of the *Cullercoats*,' he said, 'and happy to deliver your daughter safely home. She's not harmed in any way, but we need to ring the school and tell them where she is.'

'Do we indeed?' Wesley stared at him, dumbfounded.

'Who is it, Wesley?' a woman called from above.

Adela was too overcome with relief and tears to answer.

'It's Adela,' Wesley shouted, 'and . . . and Jackman the boatman's boy.'

Sam bristled to be addressed as a boy. 'Mrs Robson, if I could just come in for a moment and explain—'

'You'll certainly do that,' Wesley blustered, steering his daughter towards the house.

Adela looked up to see her mother staring down from the top of the steps, clutching her stomach. 'Darling!'

'Clarissa, you should be resting,' Wesley chided.

Adela expected her mother to hurry down to meet her, but she hung on to the veranda railing as if she'd been winded.

'Mother,' Adela cried, running up the stairs and flinging out her arms.

Clarrie embraced her, but her hold was awkward. Her mother felt fat, she had put on so much weight. Adela blurted out her woes.

'I'm sorry, but I couldn't stand it any longer. They've been horrid to me all term and no one's speaking and Nina Davidge, the colonel's daughter, has said terrible things about – about both of you – and then they stopped me being in the house play so I did a dance and Miss Black said I was a d-disgrace. And I didn't know what to do, so I got into Sam's boot – it wasn't his fault – and he said he'd get me home. I won't go back – not ever!'

Clarrie hugged her and stroked her hair away from her tear-stained face. 'Hush now. Come inside and tell us properly.' She saw Sam hovering below. 'And you, Sam, please come up. You've had a long, tiring drive.'

With growing reluctance, Sam mounted the steps behind Wesley, who was huffing and muttering under his breath.

Half an hour later, with spicy tea brought in by their khansama, Mohammed Din, who did not hide his delight at seeing Adela, Sam had explained as best he could what had happened earlier that day. Adela, after her first outpouring, was curled up under her mother's arm, exhausted and suddenly overwhelmed by what she had done. She felt embarrassed and shy in Sam's company.

'You should have taken her back,' Wesley berated the young riverboat captain. 'They'll have search parties out looking for her. How could you be so irresponsible?'

'It's what Adela wanted,' Sam defended. 'She was very upset.'

'She won't learn to stand up for herself by running away.'

'Wesley,' Clarrie said calmly, 'go at once and telephone the school. Explain that Adela is quite safe and there's no need to worry further. We'll sort things out tomorrow.'

'I'll take her back tomorrow,' Wesley declared.

'No, Daddy,' Adela protested. 'Please don't.'

'I think that might be a mistake,' said Sam. 'A few days at home won't do any harm, surely.'

'Did I ask for your opinion?' Wesley snapped. 'Our daughter's welfare is our business, not yours, Jackman.'

'Of course.' Sam flushed. 'I'm sorry.'

'Don't pick on Sam,' Adela said. 'He was just trying to help me.'

'He's made things worse.' Her father scowled. 'You'll go back tomorrow and face them like a brave Robson.'

Adela sat up in agitation. 'No, I won't! I'm not a Robson in their eyes. I'm a two annas – and you're a four annas, Mother!'

Clarrie gasped and put a hand to her throat.

'How dare you!' Wesley hissed. He hauled her from the sofa and shook her. Adela gritted her teeth and glared back.

Sam leapt from his seat. 'Don't take it out on her – she's only repeating what the Davidge girl said.' He put a restraining hand on Wesley.

'The Davidge girl?'

'Nina's mother said it,' Adela cried, wincing in pain. 'Henrietta Davidge. Said you jilted her at the altar and you married a half-caste. But it's not true, is it? Tell me none of it's true!'

Abruptly Wesley let go. Adela nearly fell backwards. Her mother heaved herself up, the blood draining from her face as she faced her husband. 'Henrietta? The woman you were going to marry? Did you know she was in Shillong?'

Wesley's face was puce with fury. 'That meddling woman. I did see her at speech day, lording it over the other mothers, but we hardly spoke.'

'Why didn't you tell me?'

'There was nothing to tell. She married a colonel and I married you. She's just being malicious – jealous of you no doubt.'

Clarrie covered her face in her hands. 'Oh, this is all my fault. I should have listened to you and sent Adela back to school in England like you wanted.'

'You wanted to send me to England?' Adela asked in shock.

Wesley's eyes shone with a fierce light, his jaw so clenched he could not speak.

'Only because he thought that way we could protect you from the gossipmongers,' Clarrie said, her voice wobbly. She reached for her daughter. 'But I couldn't bear to have you so far away. It was so selfish of me.'

Adela caught a look of desolation pass between her parents. Her stomach cramped in fear. She flinched away from her mother's hold.

'What do you mean? I don't understand.' She glanced at Sam and saw a look of pity in his kind hazel eyes.

'Tell me, Mother!'

Clarrie clutched her stomach as she faced her. 'Your grandfather Jock married your grandmother Jane Cooper from Shillong. She was the daughter of a British father and an Assamese mother. I spent my childhood being talked about in the cantonments and planters' clubs as being four annas short of a rupee for having an Indian grandmother. I ignored their catty comments and I thought things were changing – but obviously they're not. That's why I've tried to shelter you from the cruelty of petty snobbery among some of the British here.'

Adela stared at her in bewilderment. 'How can you have kept such a thing from me? Why didn't you tell me?'

'It was for your own protection—'

'No, it wasn't,' Adela cried. 'You were just too ashamed to tell me, weren't you? I should have been told. You lied to me! I'm not like the others. Nina was right: I'm a two annas.'

Wesley pulled his daughter to him. 'She isn't ashamed,' he insisted. 'There's nothing to be ashamed of.'

Adela struggled out of his hold. 'I hate you both! I can't believe anything now. I bet you jilted Nina's mother. You're a blackguard just like she said!'

Wesley tried to grab her again. Sam leapt in front and seized his arm. 'Don't touch her!'

The two men struggled, knocking over a side table.

'Stop it!' Clarrie wailed. Suddenly she shrieked and doubled over.

Adela watched in horror as her mother crumpled to the floor. In an instant Wesley was at her side, holding her close.

'Darling, are you all right?' He kissed her hair and rubbed her back. 'I'll send MD for the doctor, shall I?'

'The doctor?' Adela gasped. 'What's wrong?' At once she was full of fear that her mother was dying and she would lose her for ever. She couldn't imagine life without either of her parents. 'I'm sorry, Mother. I didn't mean to upset you.' She threw her arms around Clarrie's neck.

'It's not you, my darling,' Clarrie groaned. 'It's the baby.'

Adela drew back.

'What baby?'

'The baby's coming.'

Adela was stunned. Her mother was far too old to be having a baby, surely.

Her father gave her a sheepish look. 'I thought you would have guessed.' He turned to Sam. 'Please help me get Clarissa to bed.'

Sam didn't hesitate; he helped Clarrie to her feet and shouldered her weight.

Adela gulped. 'I'll go for MD,' she said and fled from the veranda, calling for the khansama.

***

Dr Hemmings in Shillong was out on a call; all Mohammed Din could do was to leave a message. So Adela's old nurse, Ayah Mimi, was roused from her quarters in the garden and hobbled in as quickly as she could to help with the birth. She found Clarrie shrieking in pain while Wesley paced and shouted orders, his fear infecting Adela.

'She's not going to die, is she?' Adela cried, hovering by the bedroom door.

'She is going to have a baby,' Ayah said, issuing instructions to Mohammed Din for hot water and clean cloths. Then the door to the bedroom was firmly closed. Adela could hear Ayah giving encouragement while her father, insisting on being present, blasphemed and pleaded and cried endearments.

Sam came back from telephoning the school to find her weeping in a chair, big Mohammed Din trying to calm her with soft words and tea.

'I feel so terrible,' Adela sobbed. 'It's all my fault for saying those things. If M-Mother dies, I won't ever forgive myself.'

Sam put an arm around her shaking shoulders. 'It's not your fault. Women don't go into labour because of something that's said – it's just that it's time for the baby to come.'

She looked into his face, her eyes swollen from crying.

'But my father will blame me. He hates me now. I think he might have slapped me if you hadn't s-stopped him. Daddy has never ever smacked me before.'

'He was upset – you all were. He was just standing up for your mother. Come now, stop crying,' he chided. 'You're lucky to have parents who love each other so much.' Sam pulled out a crumpled handkerchief from his trouser pocket and dabbed at her tears.

Suddenly he seemed so much older and wiser than she, his handsome face frowning in concern. He might look young, but he was a man of the world and, she imagined, with a lurch of the heart, that he was already experienced with women. She wondered how many grown-up women he had pulled into his comforting arms. She took the large cotton handkerchief and, blowing her nose, pulled away from his hold.

'Why don't we go for a walk in the garden?' Sam suggested. 'Let things take their course in there.' He gestured in the direction of the bedroom, where the noises were getting more muted.

Adela nodded and scrambled to her feet, pulling Sam's car blanket around her shoulders. The night air held the chill of autumn; a bright moon hung over the trees like a lamp illuminating the lawns and paths, making the dew glitter like silver drops.

'Tell me about your parents, Sam,' Adela asked. 'Did they not love each other?'

Sam stopped and gazed up at the moonlit sky. 'Do you mind if I smoke?' he asked.

Adela smirked, pleased that he deferred to her like a grown-up, and shook her head. She watched him pull out a battered packet of bidis – small, pungent Indian cigarettes – and light one up. The tip glowed in the dark as he drew in smoke, and then he exhaled with a sigh, the scented smell tickling her nostrils.

'I thought they loved each other,' he said ruefully, 'until the day my mother walked out and deserted us. I was seven years old. I felt like the sky had fallen in. I don't even remember her saying goodbye.'

'How cruel,' Adela gasped. 'Where did she go?'

'Back to England. My father said she couldn't cope with Assam – or having a husband who was away on the river so much. He said it was nothing to do with me but . . .'

'But what?'

'Well, she never gave me the choice to go with her, did she?' Sam could not keep the anger out of his voice.

'Would you have gone with her?' Adela pressed him.

Sam took a long draw on the thin cheroot and then ground it under his shoe. He shrugged.

'The way I see it, she deserted us both. I wanted my father to change the name of our boat from *Cullercoats* to something Indian so we wouldn't be reminded of her all the time, but he wouldn't.'

'Cullercoats? Was that her maiden name or something?'

'It's the fishing village she came from.' He plunged his hands in his pockets. 'I think my father always hoped she'd come back one day, but she never did. And if she did now, I wouldn't want to see her.'

Adela was shocked by his bitter tone; it seemed so unlike him. She felt suddenly selfish at her tears and complaints, when Sam had suffered far worse as a child. Her mother would never desert her in a million years.

She pulled his hand from his pocket and gave it a squeeze. 'Your mother was a fool to run away from you. But I'm glad you had your dad. At least he cared about you, didn't he?'

Sam swallowed and gave a brief smile. 'Yes, he did.' His voice sounded husky.

After a moment they disengaged hands and walked on down the path. Neither spoke. Adela breathed in the night smells of woodsmoke and damp foliage, her spirit soothed by the presence of Sam in her beloved Belgooree. They wandered as far as the factory before turning back.

As they retraced their steps up the garden path, Adela plucked up courage to ask, 'What did Miss Black say when you rang the school? Was she very cross?'

'Relieved more than cross. When I explained what was happening here and why your father couldn't ring in person, she seemed a bit lost for words.'

'I bet she was.' Adela blushed to think of Sam having to talk of her mother in childbirth. 'So she wasn't hard on you for helping me escape?'

Sam gave a rueful look. 'Well, I don't think I'll be invited back to give out the prizes at speech day.'

Adela couldn't help a snort of laughter. 'Oh, Sam, I'm sorry.'

As they regained the bungalow steps, a door was flung open. Wesley came tearing out of the bedroom and across the veranda.

'It's happened!' he bellowed. 'Adela, where are you?'

Scout was barking and jumping around him in agitation.

Her stomach vaulted. 'Daddy! What's happened? Is Mother all right?'

He lurched at her, his face crumpling into tears. He could hardly get out his words.

Adela flung her arms about him. 'Is it Mother?' she cried. 'Tell me!'

He gripped her tight and almost roared, 'Yes, she's all right and you have a baby brother!'

***

By the time Dr Hemmings arrived from Shillong at daybreak, the newborn had already been swaddled and fed. Adela dozed in a long cane chair on the veranda, wrapped in Sam's car blanket, with Scout curled at her feet, while her father and Sam attempted to finish the bottle of whisky they had begun two hours ago in celebration. Her father's animosity towards Sam had evaporated in the euphoria of the birth.

'I have a son!' Wesley greeted the doctor, climbing unsteadily to his feet. 'Have a whisky with me, Hemmings.'

'Don't feel I deserve it,' the balding doctor said. 'Ayah has done all the hard work. I'll just look in on Mrs Robson first.'

The doctor checked on mother and baby, retreating when he found them both sleeping.

Adela was roused by Mohammed Din, fetching tea and puris for their visitor.

'Umm, my favourite,' Adela said, grinning at the servant, reaching for one of the deep-fried puffed-up breads.

'Guests first,' Ayah Mimi said, appearing out of the shadows wagging a finger. She touched Adela gently. The nanny was like a tiny bird, thin and darting in her movements, yet strong and wise. She had once been the ayah to Auntie Tilly's cousin Sophie in this very house, so when the Robsons had returned to Belgooree from England, Ayah Mimi had become Adela's beloved nanny too.

Adela handed round the plate, while Mohammed Din poured tea. 'Proper tea too,' she announced, breathing in the peachy smell of Belgooree tea. 'Not like at sch—'

Abruptly she stopped, not wanting the conversation to revert to her absconding from school. She felt suddenly leaden inside, her appetite vanishing as the memory of her unhappy flight, and last night's wrangling flooded back. She slid Sam a wary look. What trouble she had caused him, pitching him headlong into a family row and making things difficult for him with the Blacks at St Ninian's for forcing him to aid her escape. He looked exhausted, his eyes glazed with lack of sleep and whisky. His hat had fallen off the back of his head and his hair stuck up at untidy angles. Nelson, tired out from all the excitement, napped in his lap. How Sam must wish he had never set eyes on her.

Wanting suddenly to be with her mother, Adela left the men talking and slipped into her parents' bedroom. The smell of cloves could not mask the stench of blood and afterbirth. She recoiled from the odour, struck anew with shock that her mother could have given birth. She was in her late forties, wasn't she? The thought of her parents having sex at their age, let alone producing a baby, made her feel queasy. But there was the proof, her new brother lying peacefully in an ancient swinging cot by the bedside. Adela peered at him. He was tightly swaddled in a white sheet, his face crinkled like a withered plum, and with a shock of dark hair sprouting from his crown. She didn't know what to make of him.

Once Auntie Tilly had said, 'You and my Jamie get on so well together. It's such a shame you don't have a brother or sister to play with at Belgooree. Don't you wish you had one?'

'No,' Adela had said, laughing. 'Why would I want to share Mother and Daddy with anyone else?'

She turned away quickly from the cradle.

'Mother?' Adela whispered. 'Are you awake?'

Clarrie's face on the pillow looked flushed, dark hair stuck to her glistening brow, and there were purple smudges under her closed eyes. How Adela adored that face.

She burned with shame at the hurtful things she had shouted at her parents – repeating Nina's poisonous words – when all she had wanted was for them to deny it all and for things to be the same between them as before. But they had not been able to calm her fears; instead her father had admitted to being engaged to the hateful Mrs Davidge, and then her mother had admitted to having some Assamese grandmother, whom Adela had never heard of. It couldn't be true! How could they have kept such secrets from her?

Adela sat on the bed trying to hold back the tide of panic rising in her chest. She wasn't who she thought she was. She wasn't one of them – the girls at school, who were proud of being British through and through. They knew where they came from; their allegiance was undivided. Home was Britain, even if half of them had never even been there. Until last night, despite the malicious gossip of Nina, Adela had believed she was every inch a British girl too. But not now. Her great-grandmother was Assamese. Had she been a farmer's daughter or a peasant? Perhaps a tea picker. Adela cringed to think what Nina and the others would have to say about that: 'Two annas has the blood of a chai-wallah in her veins.'

It made her all the more determined that she was never going back to St Ninian's. Adela got up and tiptoed back to the cot. She bent down and stroked the cheek of the baby. It was soft as an apricot. He snuffled like a puppy at her touch. She felt the first stirring of emotion, a stab of pity, towards him. 'Poor baby,' she whispered. 'You're a two annas just like me.'

Chapter 4

Christmas, 1933

Adela heard her parents arguing over her again. She was pulling off her riding boots at the bottom of the veranda steps when she became aware of raised voices from within the bungalow.

'Well, I've invited them to stay. Tilly and Sophie want to see Adela as much as baby Harry,' Clarrie insisted. 'They're concerned about her.'

'There's no need to be,' Wesley snapped. 'We're managing perfectly well teaching her at home.'

'Horse riding and tea tasting do not add up to an education.'

'They do if she's going to go into the family business.'

'She's too young to know what she wants,' Clarrie retorted. 'We can't keep her here indefinitely. She needs to be with girls her own age doing interesting things and passing examinations; only then will she be equipped for the modern world. Things were different when Olive and I were young girls here and—'

'I hope you're not accusing me of being overprotective and selfish like your father was,' cried Wesley.

'That's not fair! And you know I don't mean that.'

'Because if I ever start turning into Jock Belhaven, you have my permission to take me out and shoot me.'

'Oh, honestly!' Clarrie exclaimed. 'You can be just as stubborn.'

'I would never stand in the way of my daughter's happiness.'

'And neither would I,' Clarrie said. 'Anyway, the Robsons and Khans have both accepted our invitation—'

'Your invitation.'

Clarrie gave an impatient sigh. 'You should be pleased they want to come and make a fuss over Harry – Tilly's dying to see him.'

'It's not Tilly I object to, it's that pompous husband of hers.'

'James is your cousin,' Clarrie reminded him, 'and you used to get along fine when you were business partners.'

'James and his bullying father always made it perfectly clear that I was very much the junior partner. He'll relish the chance to come here and lord it over us, tell us how well they're doing at the Oxford Estates compared to us.'

'We're not doing so badly, surely.'

'How would you know?' Wesley accused. 'You haven't been near the factory for months.'

'You haven't let me! You've wrapped me in cotton wool since Harry's birth and treated me like an invalid.'

'You know you haven't been well,' Wesley blustered, 'and Dr Hemmings said a woman of your age will take longer to get over—'

'I'm perfectly fine.'

'No, you're not. You're tired all the time, and now you want to overdo things by having all these people to stay.'

'The only thing I'm tired of is being stuck in this bungalow with a baby that feeds like a tiger while you and Adela ride off and enjoy yourselves around the tea garden.'

'But you refused a wet-nurse when I suggested it.'

'I know I did.' Clarrie sounded tearful. 'I just want some adult company for once. Is that too much to ask?'

In alarm Adela heard her mother break into a sob. At once Wesley was contrite.

'Oh, Clarissa, my darling! I'm so sorry. The last thing I want to do is upset you.'

Her mother's voice was muffled, as if her face was buried into Wesley's shoulder.

'Of course your friends must come and stay,' he relented. 'My insufferable cousin probably won't hang around long – he'll be itching to get back to the Boxing Day drinking and horse racing at Tezpur.'

'Thank you.' Clarrie brightened. 'It's ages since we've had anyone to stay.'

'Well, Tilly and Sophie are so busy with their own lives,' Wesley said.

'Yes, I know. It'll be so good to see them again – have a house full for Christmas. And I'm sure they will have good advice on what to do with Adela.'

***

Adela went straight back to the stables and got the syce to saddle up her pony, Patch, again. The mid-afternoon sun lit the steep hillside of emerald tea bushes as she cantered up through the gardens and into the forest. She only stopped when she reached the clearing with the fallen-down temple and the derelict hut where Ayah Mimi had once lived when she had no children to look after.

Adela had been overjoyed to hear that her special aunties, Tilly and Sophie, were coming for Christmas. They were her mother's friends, not proper aunties. Her only real auntie was Aunt Olive, who lived in England and ran a teahouse, but Adela hadn't seen her since she was two years old and had no memory of her. This had never bothered Adela, as her pretend aunties were more than enough; she adored them. Tilly was plump and talkative, a mother hen who loved children and gave wonderful hugs like a huge, soft hot-water bottle. Uncle James, her husband, was not the least bit cuddly; he was square and pugnacious, with a laugh like a bark who teased Tilly for overindulging their offspring.

'Pack the little devils off home to school as soon as they can catch a ball,' he would decree, and then roar with laughter at his wife's cries of protest. He had got his way, however. Tilly had had to part with two out of the three, Jamie and Libby, taking them back to the North of England to be schooled.

While Auntie Tilly was motherly, Auntie Sophie was glamorous and a little bit notorious. She was a divorcee with a deep laugh and Scottish lilt who had married an Indian and converted to Islam. With her shapely figure and wavy fair hair, she could make a mechanic's boiler suit look stylish – which she often did when helping to fix one of the five cars that belonged to the Raja of Gulgat. Her husband, Rafi, worked as an aide-de-camp and chief forester for the Raja in the neighbouring principality to Belgooree. Rafi Khan, with his dark good looks, startlingly green eyes and film-star moustache, was the most handsome man Adela had ever seen. Together, he and Sophie were like a Hollywood couple, with no children to make them seem ordinary. They were fun and athletic and would organise treasure hunts, party games and camping trips. One day, Adela vowed, when she was grown up, she was going to dye her hair blonde and perm it to look like Sophie Khan.

***

On Christmas Eve in Gulgat, Sophie distributed baskets of fruit, flowers and money to the bungalow servants and their neighbours, explaining how they would be in Belgooree for Christmas. *That's if we ever get away,* she thought, sighing, and went to look for Rafi.

As she mounted the steps to the Raja's modern pavilion, built eight years ago to accommodate his second wife, Rita, she heard her husband's placatory voice.

'Don't worry, sir. He can't make you do anything you don't want to do. Stourton is just here to advise.'

'I don't want his advice,' said Kishan in agitation. 'Why are the Britishers always interfering where they're not wanted? My meddling old mother has him wrapped around his pink little finger.'

Sophie heard Rafi give an amused snort. 'I think it's supposed to be her finger that he's wrapped around.'

'His finger, her finger,' the Raja answered with impatience, 'what does it matter? I want them all to keep their fingers to themselves and let me decide who my successor will be.'

Sophie hung back as the two men discussed the latest palace intrigue: the dowager rani's attempt to force her son Kishan to declare his nephew Sanjay his heir rather than his own daughters. She glanced up through the thick subtropical jungle of banana trees, bamboos and sal to the crumbling fortress on the escarpment above. Somewhere in the gloomy depths of its shuttered rooms, the old rani brooded over the loss, eight years ago, of her favourite son, Ravindra, swept away by a river in spate. Together with her widowed daughter-in-law, the timid and grieving Henna, the old woman kept their bitterness inflamed.

'Was it not Kishan's fault for taking Ravindra fishing when the day had been decreed inauspicious?' she would rail. 'Kishan should never have encouraged his younger brother to enjoy swimming in the first place. He is to blame for our unhappiness!'

In the widowed rani's eyes, her eldest son's sins were many. He had preferred to go overseas and study in Scotland rather than live with his own people. He had neglected his first, high-caste wife, and when she had died in childbirth, he should never have married that woman from Bombay, who refused to live in purdah and could not give him sons. But the Raja's biggest crime to date was to send Ravindra's only son, her beloved grandson Sanjay, away to school near Delhi and to refuse to name him as the heir to Gulgat.

Poor Sanjay, Sophie thought. Alternately spoilt and neglected, the boy was incapable of pleasing them all. She had liked him as a small boy – he could still be charming and friendly – but at seventeen, he could be petulant if he didn't get his own way. Recently he had grown overfamiliar with Rita and with her, making suggestive remarks and trying to kiss them when their husbands were not there. Perhaps it was a phase that boys of his age went through, but it made her uncomfortable.

'Why are you lurking outside?' a silvery voice called from the veranda above.

Sophie looked up guiltily to see Rita's attractive dimpled face grinning down at her. The Raja's wife blew a smoke ring over the balcony. 'Come up at once, Mrs Khan, or I'll report you to that stuffy Britisher, Stourton, for spying on us all.'

Sophie bounded up the outside stairs two at a time.

'So you do possess a dress?' Rita teased, stubbing out her cigarette and eyeing her friend with approval. 'Turquoise suits you. Is it too early for a cocktail? Yes, I suppose it is. Coffee then?' She ordered refreshments and made room for Sophie on the swing seat beside her, gathering in her immaculate cream sari.

Sophie gazed out on the valley below – a shimmer of emerald paddy fields wreathed in morning mist – and breathed in the temperate air.

'I love this time of year, don't you?'

'Yes,' Rita agreed, 'but only because Kishan and I will be going to Bombay. A month of theatre and concerts for me, and parties and dancing for the girls.'

'Are Jasmina and Sabeena very excited?' Sophie smiled.

'Ready to burst,' Rita said, and chuckled. 'And I can't wait to get Kishan away from all this.' She waved a slim be-ringed hand in the air. 'Before his mother poisons us all, or the Britisher brings in the army and hoists a flag over the house.'

Sophie laughed. 'Aren't you being a bit overdramatic?'

‘Me?’ Rita arched her eyebrows in mock surprise over large brown eyes. ‘Don’t pretend you’re not worried too. Why else did you have your ear to the door down there?’

‘I must admit,’ said Sophie, ‘that I’m looking forward to getting Rafi away for a few days. He works so hard.’

‘Next time you must come with us to Bombay.’

‘I haven’t been there since I arrived back in India over ten years ago,’ Sophie mused. ‘We’ve become like hermits in the woods.’

‘Well, you can let your hair down with your tea-planter friends, can’t you? They know how to party from what I hear.’

The coffee came and they sipped it as the sun grew stronger and the mist burned off to reveal a shimmering landscape of pools and jungle. Green-and-red parrots flitted between the trees.

‘Will Sanjay go with you to Bombay?’ Sophie asked.

Rita shrugged. ‘That is one of Kishan’s battles with the old witch and Henna. He would like to take the boy, but they complain they don’t see enough of him as it is. Kishan’s mother will refuse to let him go, but it’s me who will get the blame. Sanjay will be moody and resentful, and the whole thing will give Kishan an ulcer. Happy families, eh?’

‘I wouldn’t know.’ Sophie gave a pained smile.

Rita was contrite. ‘Oh, my dearest, here I am complaining about my family when you have had such tragedy in yours. Don’t listen to me. Let’s change the subject.’

They did, but Sophie couldn’t help dwelling on her lack of relations. Orphaned at six years old in India when her parents had died violent deaths, she had been brought up by a beloved aunt in Scotland, who had died when Sophie was twenty-one. Though she had hardly any memory of her parents, it still made Sophie shudder to think that her own father could have shot her mother and then shot himself. What drove a man to do that? In the aftermath of her parents’ tragedy, she had also lost her only brother. He had been given away at birth and never been seen again. It was a source of pain too that she and Rafi appeared unable to have children. Once she had been pregnant to another man . . . Sophie forced herself not to think of the dark circumstances of her miscarriage and her failed marriage to the forester Tam Telfer. Yet she had Rafi, whom she adored; he was her family, along with her dear cousin Tilly, whom she was impatient to see again at Belgooree over Christmas.

When Rafi appeared with Kishan, Sophie leapt up and went to her husband. The warm smile he gave her was enough to banish the bluest of thoughts.

***

Sophie and Rafi were on the point of leaving for Belgooree when Sanjay appeared, clutching a cricket bat.

'Come on, Rafiji.' The handsome youth gave a winning smile. 'You're the best bowler in Gulgat. Stourton said he'd play too. Just for an hour. You don't mind, do you, Mrs Khan?'

'We really need to be on the road,' Sophie said, dismayed.

'You can field,' Sanjay declared. 'You have a great throwing arm – shapely but strong.'

Rafi gave her a helpless look. She knew how he pitied the boy for losing his father so young. Yet the Raja's nephew was on the cusp of manhood; he was no longer a child, even if the adults around him still treated him like one. His mother and grandmother overindulged him, while his uncle and Rita ignored or excused his outbursts of temper as something he would grow out of. Even Rafi seemed blind to the boy's manipulating charm; she could see how flattered he was to be asked to play cricket for the young prince. Maybe she was being unfair, Sophie thought, and Sanjay was being naturally enthusiastic. Strange, though, how he had waited just until their moment of departure to waylay them with his sudden cricket match.

'Very well,' she relented. 'But we go this afternoon.'

***

On Christmas Day, Adela rushed down the drive when she heard the Khans' car hooting on the tea garden track.

'Happy Christmas! Where have you been?' Adela jumped on board and squeezed in between Rafi and Sophie, flinging her arms about both and kissing their cheeks. 'We thought you were coming yesterday. I'm so sick of baby talk. Auntie Tilly's never put Harry down for a minute. I'm so glad you're here. Now we can have some fun.'

Rafi laughed and Sophie hugged her back. 'Happy Christmas too, my darling lassie. Your Uncle Rafi got embroiled in a cricket match that lasted all day – that's why we are late.'

'Your Auntie Sophie caught out Sanjay,' said Rafi, 'otherwise we'd still be playing.'

'Yes, that didn't go down well at all,' Sophie grimaced.

'Who's Sanjay?'

'The Raja's nephew,' said Rafi. 'Remember he once came on a hunting trip here with his uncle.'

'Was he the boy who said he'd skin my tiger cub, Molly, if I let her out of the house?'

'Sounds like Sanjay,' Sophie said, rolling her eyes.

'He'd have been teasing,' Rafi defended.

'He has a cruel streak,' said Sophie.

'Not cruel, just boisterous.'

'He's still behaving like a spoilt brat, yet he's nearly a man. It's high time you learned how to say no to him once in a while.'

Adela felt uncomfortable at their disagreement; it wasn't like them. 'Well, I remember him as rather good-looking and I was probably being a pest. Anyway, it doesn't matter now. You're both here, and that's the best Christmas present I could have.'

Rafi ruffled her hair and Sophie gave her another kiss, and the topic of Sanjay was dropped.

Shrieks of delight greeted the latecomers as Sophie and Tilly hugged, Clarrie rustled up cocktails and the men swapped news. Tilly's youngest son, Mungo, leapt from chair to chair in a pirate outfit and set Scout barking madly. Around a table set out on the veranda, they ate a huge lunch of chestnut soup, snipe, blackcock, quail, roast potatoes, greens and curried cauliflower, followed by plum pudding and brandy butter and gaudy sugary sweetmeats with coffee. Wesley served up his best claret and a bottle of port he'd kept for ten years. Adela knew her father was doing his best to impress his cousin James and show off Belgooree hospitality.

The conversation was loud and unceasing. Tilly talked of her son and daughter at boarding school in England, while James and Wesley discussed falling tea prices and the likelihood of production having to be cut.

'Oh, James, you promised not to talk shop,' Tilly protested.

'And you promised not to bore about babies,' James grunted.

Sophie intervened swiftly. 'Tell the gossip from Assam, Tilly. Who is the burra memsahib at the club these days?'

'Tilly of course,' James joked.

'Chance would be a fine thing,' Tilly cried. 'James never takes me these days.'

'I take you to the film club once a month.'

'Once in a blue moon,' she retorted.

'Well, you hate it there,' James said. 'You always complain about the men drinking too much and gambling away the housekeeping.'

'Oh, talking of which' – Tilly's plump face was animated – 'have you heard about young Sam Jackman, the ferry captain?'

Adela's heart lurched at the sudden mention of Sam's name. She caught a look pass between her parents.

'Heard what?' Clarrie asked.

'He's a captain no longer,' said James.

'Lost his boat in a card game a month ago,' Tilly said.

'Never!' Clarrie exclaimed.

'Silly ass!' Wesley frowned, throwing Adela a glance.

'Gambling went on all weekend apparently,' James said. 'Drank far too much. Let some clerk from a Calcutta shipping company win it from him. The man offered it back when Jackman sobered up.'

'But Sam wouldn't take it,' Tilly added. 'Said the man had won it fair and square.'

'But the *Cullercoats* was his father's boat,' Adela gasped. 'It meant a lot to him.' Tilly eyed her in surprise, which made her go red.

'Obviously not as much as we thought,' said Wesley.

'What is he doing now?' Clarrie asked in concern.

'Gone,' said Tilly, 'with that chattering monkey.'

'Gone where?' Adela asked in deep dismay.

'No one knows. Just up and left,' Tilly sighed. 'It's the strangest thing. He was always such a sensible boy. Don't think he's ever really got over the death of his father – they were very close.'

'Don't know why you had such a soft spot for him,' James said. 'He could be quite critical of us tea planters. Bit of a Gandhi-Congress supporter. Probably gone off to agitate somewhere else.'

'Good luck to him.' Rafi smiled. 'Congress and India need young men of passion from all communities.'

'And women,' Sophie added.

James gave a wry look. 'So speak the couple who enjoy life in an autocratic kingdom. You don't have agitators coming in to stir up your workforce, do you?'

'We feed them to the tigers,' Rafi joked.

'So you agree with Congress and their incitement to strike and damage our businesses?' James pressed him.

'No more than I agree with boycotts by the British, which damage Indian businesses,' Rafi countered.

'I agree with you there,' said Clarrie. 'The boycotts are petty.'

James pressed Rafi further. 'Is that hot-headed brother of yours still causing trouble in Lahore?'

'Ghulam has been out of prison and out of trouble for five years,' Sophie came to Rafi's defence. 'He's doing social work now.'

'That's good,' said Tilly, 'isn't it, dear?' She gave her husband a warning look. 'And I'm glad to hear you are in touch with your family, Rafi.'

'I'm not exactly.' Rafi gave a wistful smile.

'They still can't accept me as Rafi's wife,' Sophie said, sighing. 'Even after all these years. I told Rafi he should go and visit his parents anyway, but he won't go without me.'

Adela saw them exchange tender looks.

Rafi brightened. 'But Ghulam speaks to me,' he said, 'since the Raja paid for the lawyer who helped get him released from prison. And my youngest sister, Fatima, writes and tells me the family news.'

'Dr Fatima,' Sophie corrected. 'She qualified earlier this year.'

'That's wonderful,' cried Clarrie.

'Isn't it?' Sophie smiled. 'She's working at the Lady Reading Hospital in Simla. I'm trying to persuade Rafi to take a holiday and visit her there – he hasn't been back since his school days at Bishop Cotton.'

'It's finding the time.' Rafi gave a rueful smile.

'Oh, you must!' Tilly encouraged. 'I'd love to go. There's so much theatre, and the air is so healthy.'

'One day,' chimed in Adela, 'I'm going to perform there at the Gaiety.'

James said gruffly, 'From what we hear, young lady, performing on stage has got you expelled from school.'

Adela flushed as silence fell around the table.

'Not now, James,' Tilly murmured.

'Well, I thought we'd come here to give advice on Adela's schooling,' he said bluntly.

'We don't need advice,' Wesley said, bristling.

'And I didn't get expelled.' Adela was defiant. 'I ran away.'

Abruptly Rafi burst into laughter. 'Well, Wesley, if your daughter and my sister are a taste of things to come, the world is going to be run by women of spirit.'

'Amen to that,' Clarrie said, smiling. Wesley laughed, and the awkward atmosphere was broken.

Adela excused herself. She could see five-year-old Mungo, who had eaten earlier with his ayah, was growing irritable and bored. She swiftly took him off to the stables to see Patch. Sophie soon followed. She steered Adela aside, while Mungo helped the syce brush the pony's tail.

'You shouldn't mind what Uncle James says,' she said gently. 'He means well, but doesn't know how to be tactful.'

'He's right though,' said Adela. 'You have all come here to sort me out. I heard my parents talking about it – no one knows what to do with me, do they?'

'It doesn't matter what we think,' said Sophie. 'What do *you* want?'

Adela struggled with conflicting thoughts. 'Part of me just wants to stay here for ever and be with Daddy and Mother, riding every day and never having to worry about grown-up things.' She twisted her long plait. 'But part of me is longing to be an adult and go out into the world and find adventure. Most of all I want to be an actress. Do you think that's ridiculous?'

'Not at all,' Sophie said. 'You have a lovely singing voice and you were wonderful in that school play we came to last year.'

Adela's stomach twisted with regret that she had thrown all that away. 'When I'm on stage,' she said, 'it's the most exciting feeling. I feel twice as alive. It doesn't matter if there are five or fifty in the audience – I just want to make them happy.'

Sophie touched her shoulder. 'Then you better go somewhere that's going to give you that feeling. There aren't many theatres in Belgooree the last time I looked.'

'No.' Adela laughed. 'Just the veranda where I make Ayah Mimi and MD watch me tap dancing. Not that Ayah has any time to do that now because of the baby.'

'Dear Ayah Mimi,' Sophie said, her look reflective. 'Brought out of retirement again for wee Harry.'

'She never lets him out of her sight,' said Adela. 'I think she loves him more than Mother does.'

Sophie turned away abruptly. 'Come on then, Mungo,' she called. 'Uncle Rafi is organising party games.'

With a squeal the boy ran over and took her outstretched hand. Adela wondered if she had said something wrong. She was enjoying having a grown-up conversation with her sophisticated aunt, but perhaps it was the mention of babies that she didn't like. Her mother had said it was upsetting for Sophie and Rafi to be childless.

'You're right,' said Adela as they swung Mungo between them up the path, 'I should go somewhere else. And it's not been the same at home since I ran away from St Ninian's. There was a terrible row with my parents. Did they tell you about it?'

'Clarrie said there was bullying at the school and some unkind things said about the family.'

'Which turned out to be true,' Adela said with bitterness.

Sophie stopped. 'Mungo, you run ahead and tell Uncle Rafi to put the music on.' When the boy was out of earshot, Sophie scrutinised Adela. 'Tell me what was said.'

'That Dad left someone standing at the altar – the mother of the girl who was bullying me. And that I was a two annas because my mother was a half-caste. Did you know that about us?'

Sophie's attractive, broad features creased in a frown. 'You shouldn't use language like that – they're the words of a bigot and you perpetuate their prejudice by repeating them, Adela.'

Adela's eyes smarted at the reproof. Sophie's expression softened.

'Yes, I knew your mother was Anglo-Indian – Tilly told me – but there's no shame in that. Clarrie is the most amazing person. Tilly and I wish we could be more like her. You should be proud to have such a mother.'

'That's what Sam said.' Adela gave a bashful look.

'Sam Jackman?'

Adela nodded. 'Yes, I forced him to help me escape school and then landed him in the middle of a family fight. Got him into trouble with St Ninian's too. He was so kind to me, but ever since then his life seems to have gone wrong. Do you think I'm to blame in some way?'

Sophie took her by the shoulders and shook her gently. 'Stop being so dramatic. You are not to blame for Sam Jackman getting drunk and losing his boat. If you ask me, it sounds like he was looking for an excuse to get rid of it – he wouldn't have given it up so easily if he'd wanted to stay a river captain, would he?'

'Do you think so?' Adela brightened.

'Yes, I do.'

'Then where do you think he's gone?'

Sophie gave her a quizzical look. 'Do I detect that there's more than just passing interest in the young captain?'

Adela blushed and grinned. 'Is it that obvious?'

Sophie put an arm about her. 'Well, I'll get Auntie Tilly to find out – she's better than the telegraph system for picking up gossip.'

***

Back at the bungalow, Rafi wound up the old gramophone, and Mungo screamed with excitement throughout musical bumps. They followed this with blind man's buff, hunt the slipper and hide and seek, while Mungo's father snored under a newspaper and his mother fussed over a fretful baby Harry.

'He's teething,' Tilly declared, plonking him into his pram. She and Clarrie bumped him down the path as far as the factory and back, with Ayah Mimi in attendance.

Tea was served, and later there was a supper of eggs, smoked trout and Clarrie's ginger pudding (a Belgooree speciality), and then the friends sat up late sipping port, whisky and more tea as a huge moon lit up the plantation and the trees rustled with night creatures.

The following day there was a fishing trip to Um Shirpi, where the men fished, Sophie and Adela swam in the chilly river pools, and Clarrie and Tilly chatted and read books. A picnic was served in the early afternoon and they returned to the bungalow for a leisurely supper.

All week the friends went on expeditions: riding, shooting blackbuck and woodcock, walking the hill paths or just lazing on the veranda, talking. To everyone's surprise James did not hurry away to join the other tea planters at the club for the seasonal races and polo matches. He seemed just as happy as Tilly to socialise with the Robsons and Khans and drink his way through Wesley's cellar. With Clarrie's encouragement, Wesley curbed his envy of his cousin's success at the Oxford Tea Estates and sought his opinion on the Belgooree gardens. Together they inspected the pruning of tea bushes and the maintenance of the machinery that Wesley had introduced to the factory a decade ago.

'It's a relief to find someone who will talk tea with James,' Tilly said to her female friends. 'I drive him mad because I get so absorbed in doing my stamps that I don't listen to what he's saying half the time. This holiday is doing both of us the world of good. Thank you so much, Clarrie, for inviting us – we get so sick of our own company. But that's the same for all couples, isn't it?'

Sophie gave a wry smile. 'It's the opposite for us. Rafi is so busy running after the Raja and his family that I don't see enough of him. It's wonderful having him around to talk to at last.'

'Well, maybe it's different for you and Rafi.' Tilly sighed. 'But tea planters' wives live in such isolation, don't we, Clarrie?'

'We do,' Clarrie agreed.

'If we didn't have our children,' said Tilly, 'we'd go quite mad. I don't know what I'll do when Mungo has to go back home to school. It was hell leaving Libby at Easter. Oh sorry, Sophie. I don't mean to keep going on about the children—'

'It doesn't bother me,' Sophie assured. 'It would be worse if you felt you couldn't talk about your children in front of me. And anyway I adore all your kids – especially that girl over there.' She turned to Adela and winked.

'Oh, we all want to adopt that one.' Tilly smiled.

Her mother beckoned her over. 'Come here, Adela, and let's talk about your future before the men come back. Your aunties and I have been putting our heads together.'

Adela gave a dramatic sigh as she perched on Clarrie's chair arm. But secretly she was pleased to be the focus of their attention.

Clarrie was firm. 'You're too young to leave school yet, so you're going to have to finish your education somewhere. Auntie Tilly and Auntie Sophie think you should have a choice.'

Adela eyed them with interest.

Tilly spoke first. 'If you wanted to go to school in England – Newcastle, for example – you could live with your aunt Olive. I know you're very friendly with your cousin Jane, aren't you?'

'Yes, we're penfriends,' Adela said, her excitement igniting.

'Then you'd have a ready-made pal,' said Tilly, beaming, 'and you could go to my sister in Dunbar for holidays – meet up with my Jamie and Libby too. It would be lovely to think of you all getting together.'

'Are there theatres in Newcastle?'

'Of course.' Tilly laughed.

Adela looked at Clarrie. 'What do you think, Mother?'

'It would be a very different life for you there,' Clarrie said, her eyes glistening, 'but if you wanted to go, your father and I would try and arrange it. I made a mistake over St Ninian's. So wherever it is, I want you to be happy.'

'And you, Auntie Sophie?' Adela asked.

'I have a different suggestion – well, it's Rafi's really.' Sophie shook back her wavy blonde hair. 'We think you should go and look at St Mary's College in Simla – they are very keen on drama and the arts. It's a daughter school of the main college in Lahore, where Rafi's sister Fatima went. They take girls from all backgrounds.'

'Simla?' Adela gasped. 'I'd love that.'

'Your mother has certain reservations,' said Sophie.

'Is it too expensive?' Adela's face fell. From her mother's startled look, she knew she had guessed correctly.

'Rafi and I would be only too happy to help with fees,' Sophie offered.

Clarrie held up her hands. 'Wesley wouldn't hear of it.' She saw Adela's disappointment. 'But if you set your heart on going there, we would manage somehow. Perhaps you could live in the town more cheaply as a paying guest. I wish we knew people in Simla.'

'You do,' said Sophie. 'Mrs Hogg – that colonel's wife – is retired there.'

'Is she?' Clarrie remarked. 'I thought she was in Dalhousie.'

'She moved to Simla three years ago to be near friends after the Colonel died. We still exchange Christmas cards.'

'Oh, I didn't know she'd been widowed, poor woman.'

'Do you mean Fluffy Hogg, who sailed to India with us in '22?' Tilly exclaimed. 'I was terrified of her.'

Sophie laughed. 'It's true she won't stand for any nonsense, but she's not the least bit stuffy. She was very kind to me when I first came back to India – in fact, she was the only person in Dalhousie who would speak to me when things got difficult between me and Tam.'

Adela noticed glances pass between the women, but no one elaborated; they obviously didn't want to talk about Sophie's past in front of her.

Sophie smiled. 'Anyway, she'd be an excellent chaperone.'

'Yes, she would.' Clarrie brightened. 'And that would stop Wesley fretting about Adela too much.'

'She sounds like a bit of a battleaxe.' Adela was unsure.

'Forthright, yes,' her mother conceded, 'but she's one of those rare army wives who really loves and understands India. I liked her a lot when I met her on the ship over.'

Sophie winked at Adela. 'I'm sure she'd love the company of a bright young lassie like you.' She added, 'Clarrie, I'd be happy to put you in touch with her.'

'Thank you,' Clarrie said, smiling in relief, 'I'll see what Wesley thinks of the idea.'

But Adela was fairly certain that whatever her father thought, her mother had already made up her mind. If they could afford it, she would be going to St Mary's in the famous hill station.

***

With Rafi's endorsement and the women's enthusiasm for the idea, Wesley was easily persuaded that the Simla school was a good place for his daughter. Even James was approving. Letters were sent to the school principal and to Fluffy Hogg. Adela's aunts and uncles left with hugs and words of encouragement. Back came an invitation from the school to Adela to be interviewed and sit an entrance exam. Mrs Hogg wrote return of post that she remembered Adela as an engaging child on the boat to India and would be happy to offer her a room in her small bungalow should she be accepted. The principal, Miss Mackenzie, was a friend of hers.

In late January, Wesley and Adela set out for Simla. The *mohurer*, Daleep, drove them to Guwahati, where they began the long train journey via Calcutta, Patna, Lucknow and Delhi to the station at Kalka, where the mainline ended.

Adela spent hours gazing out of train windows, drinking in the sights of the North Indian plains: villages of mud huts shaded by banyan trees; boys herding cattle; women in bright saris washing clothes by rivers; hayricks as tall as houses; and the smoke from fires adding to the haze of an orange dusk. Arriving at Kalka on the third day, they transferred to the narrow-gauge railway and a small train pulled by a red-and-black steam engine that wound up into the Himalayan foothills. As they rattled through long tunnels and swept round precipitous bends, Adela's excitement mounted.

'There's Simla,' a fellow traveller pointed out as they rounded a curve and saw a spread of houses clinging to the steeply wooded hillside and a vast palace of turrets and towers rising above the treeline.

'What is that?' Adela gasped.

'Viceregal Lodge of course,' the official replied, 'though it's empty until the Viceroy comes up from Delhi at the end of the cold season.'

Then tantalisingly, the town disappeared as the railway line looped around another spur.

Some clerks in the carriage disembarked at Summer Hill station, which was the stop nearest to Viceregal Lodge; a few minutes later the train was pulling into Simla station, and porters were rushing to help passengers with their luggage. Wesley hired a rickshaw that pulled them through the town and along the Mall, lined with an eccentric hotchpotch of buildings, ranging in style from mock Tudor to Swiss cottage and Gothic Victorian.

Adela squealed in delight as they passed the solid stone frontage of the Gaiety Theatre.

'I wonder what's showing? Can we go there later?'

'Let's get settled in first,' Wesley answered.

He had booked them into Clarkes Hotel, beyond the Mall, with a dizzying view into the valley below. Adela was eager to explore the town and stretch cramped legs after sitting in trains for so long. As the short winter afternoon waned, they walked past a series of shops to the imposing Christ Church on The Ridge, at the top of the Mall, and then up Jakko Hill. Adela breathed in the scent of woodsmoke, thrilling at the sight of mellow sunlight glinting off windows and turning them golden. There were still banks of snow and icy patches on the north-facing paths, and out of the sun the cold air stung their faces. Reaching the temple to Hanuman at the top, they were greeted by the screech of monkeys swinging through the trees and leaping across the temple roofs.

In the fading smoky light, they could just make out the dark backdrop of mountains stretching off to the north and east. Lights were already being lit between the trees, betraying where bungalows nestled among the woods of pine and deodar.

'Isn't it beautiful?' Adela gasped. 'Oh, Daddy, I really want to come here!'

He gave her a wistful look and then smiled. 'Well, you better put on a good performance for the principal tomorrow, eh?'

Adela hardly slept. She was up early, washed, dressed and with her hair neatly tied back long before a breakfast of porridge and eggs, which she could hardly swallow.

The college lay on a hill spur to the north of the town, past the Lakkar Bazaar and along a ridge among some of the oldest buildings in Simla, including the original home of the viceroys before the vast baronial palace, Viceregal Lodge, was built at the other end of the town. St Mary's was a rambling two-storey wooden building with covered-over verandas, surrounded by narrow strips of lawn and tennis courts that appeared to cling on to the cliff edge.

An older girl with short brown hair came stepping towards them with the poise of a ballerina and swept them inside, introducing herself as 'Prudence Knight – but call me Prue.'

The principal was a middle-aged woman with a jowly face and a jovial smile. She bundled Adela off with Prue to look around the school while she gave Wesley coffee in her study.

Prue winked at Adela. 'It's so she can interview your father and make sure he understands the ethos of this place.'

'Which is?'

'Each girl is special and must be allowed to develop in her own unique way,' spouted Prue. 'The brainy ones get pushed to university standard, and the artistic ones can spend as much time in the art room or on stage as they like. I love painting and I'm allowed to go along to the Simla Art Club every week too.'

'I love acting. Will I be allowed to join the amateur dramatics in Simla, do you think?'

'Very likely.' Prue was enthusiastic.

Adela clapped her hands with excitement. 'I really hope I get in.'

'Do you sing?' asked Prue. Adela nodded. 'Well, Miss Mackenzie loves Gilbert and Sullivan, so give her something of theirs as your party piece.'

Adela tried to concentrate on the entrance exam, but she couldn't think of anything interesting to write about the topic of 'My Family', and the maths questions completely baffled her. All she could think about was how, if she came here, she could start again where nobody knew about her parentage, reinvent herself as thoroughly British Adela Robson, who was destined to become a film star. The last thing she wanted to do was to write about her family, her quarter-Indian mother or her dark-haired baby brother. It made her guilty to think how often she scrutinised Harry to see if he betrayed their Anglo-Indian blood. In panic, Adela ended up scrawling something about her tiger cub, Molly, and how an Indian prince had threatened to skin it. In place of equations, she wrote out a list of tea pickings and leaf varieties just to fill up the page.

The look of dismay on the face of the teacher overseeing her exam made Adela want to burst into tears. Her chances of being accepted appeared to be dwindling as fast as the dew on the school lawn. When she was summoned into Miss Mackenzie's study, Adela decided to be bold. Better to make an impression than not to be remembered at all was her motto.

Ignoring the chair she was offered next to her father, Adela marched right up to the principal's desk, bowed and burst into a rendition of 'Three Little Maids from School' from *The Mikado*.

Miss Mackenzie gaped in amazement. When Adela finished, she glanced at her father, who obviously thought she had taken leave of her senses. Then behind her, in the doorway, Prue began clapping enthusiastically.

'Well, goodness me,' said the principal, 'I wasn't expecting that. But what a sweet voice you have, Miss Robson. You can sit down now. Prue, I imagine this was your idea of a bit of fun. You may go, thank you.'

Adela glanced round at the retreating girl, who winked at her as she went. Had she been duped into making a fool of herself? Adela was too anxious to sit.

'I know you didn't ask me to sing, miss, but I made such a mess of my exam paper and Prue said you liked Gilbert and Sullivan so I just wanted you to know I can sing and I really, *really* want to come here and it's just the sort of school where I know I'd be happy 'cause Prue says if you like drama you can do as much as you want and I only ran away from St Ninian's because they wouldn't let me act and I got into trouble for standing up for Flowers Dunlop, but I would never run away from here—'

'Adela!' Wesley hissed. 'For heaven's sake, sit down and be quiet for once.'

Adela flopped into the seat next to him. 'Sorry,' she mumbled.

'Don't be.' Miss Mackenzie smiled. 'Your entry was unorthodox, but entertaining. I think Prudence might have raised your expectations of St Mary's somewhat. We do encourage creative subjects, but every girl who comes here must achieve a good level of academic achievement too. I'm sorry you were unhappy at St Ninian's; it is a well-run school and I am a personal friend of Miss Black's.'

Adela's hopes plummeted. For the rest of the interview she tried to answer the principal's questions, but her replies were faltering and short. Her stomach churned and her eyes smarted with tears. They left shortly afterwards, with Miss Mackenzie promising a swift decision. Trudging back past the well-stocked furniture stalls of the Lakkar Bazaar, Adela turned to her father and demanded tearfully, 'Do you think Prue told me to sing to get me into trouble?'

'Why would she do that?' Wesley asked.

'Perhaps she's another school bully, like Nina Davidge.'

'She didn't seem like that to me,' her father said, 'and even if she is, you can't spend your life avoiding people like that. You have to stand up to them.'

Wesley steered her back into town and declared they would treat themselves to afternoon tea at the Cecil Hotel and whatever was showing that evening at the Gaiety Theatre.

Adela revived as they ate cake and drank Darjeeling in the ornate and lofty dining hall while a string quartet played Strauss waltzes and foxtrots for those who wanted to dance.

'Your mother would love this,' Wesley smiled.

'Come on, Daddy. Show me how it's done.'

As Wesley swept her around the dance floor, Adela had never felt so grown-up. She noticed the interested glances from older women at her handsome father and felt proud of him.

Later in the theatre, they sat in the plush green seats of the stalls in front of the viceroy's box and laughed at the antics of the amateur players, who were still doing the pantomime *Cinderella*. Adela determined that, even if she didn't get into St Mary's, she would one day return and perform on the Gaiety stage.

The next day, before leaving for Kalka and the long journey home, they called on Fluffy Hogg at her small bungalow, Briar Rose Cottage, on Jakko Hill. Although almost seventy and of solid build, Fluffy was fit and red-cheeked from constant walking, and her manner was breezy and welcoming. They sat drinking tea on her narrow veranda with a view north to the snow-capped Himalayas. The early-morning sun struck their peaks, turning them rapidly from rose pink to glistening white.

'Don't worry about the exam,' the colonel's widow consoled. 'If Lilian Mackenzie thinks you are right for her school, then she will take you even if you wrote gibberish.'

Before they left, she showed Adela the simple bedroom that would be hers if she was successful. It was painted pale green, with a moss-green bedspread and faded curtains patterned in roses. There was a small writing table, an upholstered chair and a dark chest of drawers with an oval mirror above. Hanging on the wall next to a brightly painted Tibetan scroll was a photograph of a young woman in a long riding habit, sitting side-saddle on a pony.

'Me in Quetta,' said Fluffy.

'You're beautiful,' Adela cried.

Fluffy chuckled. 'All girls are at that age.'

Suddenly there was a loud clatter across the corrugated-iron roof that made Adela jump.

'Simla monkeys,' Fluffy said, unperturbed. 'If you come here, you'll have to get used to those little devils. Keep the windows shut or they'll steal your worldly goods.'

Adela glanced out of the window at the mountains retreating into a blue haze. A road wound its way along the hillside into the distance, already busy with carts, mules and porters.

'Where does that go?' Adela asked.

'That's the road to Narkanda and beyond,' said Fluffy. 'It goes all the way to Tibet.'

Adela's heart leapt with excitement at the mention of the fabled name. When she turned round to face her father and the elderly widow, they could both see the yearning shining in her dark eyes.

***

A week after returning from Simla, Mohammed Din hurried into the sitting room, where the family were struggling to listen to music on the gramophone over Harry's squalling.

'I think our little tiger is hungry again,' Clarrie said, plucking him from the cradle.

'Sahib,' interrupted Mohammed Din breathlessly, holding out a silver tray, 'the *chaprassy* has been. There is a letter from Simla for Adela Missahib.'

Adela sprang out of her seat. 'Thank you, MD.' She grabbed at the letter and tore it open.

The khansama stood waiting as tensely as Adela's parents. Clarrie bounced a fretful Harry in her arms. Adela felt sick as she unfolded the single page with the St Mary's College crest embossed in blue at the top. She stared hard.

Adela looked up. 'I can't believe it,' she said, and then gulped.

'Well?' Wesley demanded. 'Put us out of our misery. Are you in or not?'

A huge grin spread across her face. 'Yes – *yes* – I'm in! I'm to start after half-term in March.'

'Oh, my darling, well done!' Clarrie cried above the noise of the baby.

Wesley jumped out of his seat and hugged her. 'My clever girl! Let me see.' He took the letter and read it. 'By Jove, Clarissa, they say they're looking forward to having her.'

'Of course they are,' Clarrie said, beaming, 'and they'll be lucky to have her. Oh, come and give me a hug!'

Adela went to her mother; it was an awkward hug with Harry in the middle. Within a couple of minutes Mohammed Din had returned with celebratory glasses of nimbu pani – Adela's favourite lemon drink – and ginger biscuits. He smiled and congratulated her too.

'Thank you, MD. I'll miss you all, but I'm so excited about going.'

As the khansama handed round the drinks, Wesley gave a toast.

'Although we don't want you to leave us, Adela, your mother and I would rather have you a three-day train ride away in the Punjab than a three-week sea voyage away in England.' He smiled. 'No running away this time though,' he warned. 'Your mother and I won't have you back a second time – you'll just have to join the circus.'

'Oh, Wesley!' Clarrie chided. 'Congratulations, dearest Adela.' She smiled and raised a glass in one hand while clutching her son with the other. 'You will always have a home here with us.' Clarrie kissed the baby's head. 'Won't she, Harry?'

Adela noticed the adoring look on her mother's face as she spoke to the baby. Clarrie put down the drink. 'Sorry, I'll have to go and feed him.'

'Little monster,' said Wesley, but his expression was one of pride.

With a stab of envy, Adela watched her mother disappear to the bedroom, humming a tune to pacify Harry. She knew her parents would not miss her half as much now that they had Harry. It would never again be just the three of them, always four. Perhaps that was part of the reason why she was looking forward so much to a future in Simla. But what excited her the most was that she was being offered a fresh start in a school far away from her tormentors at St Ninian's, with countless possibilities to act on a real stage. Adela could not wait.

***

St Mary's College, Simla
June, 1935

Dear Cousin Jane

Thank you for the lovely homemade birthday card with fifteen cats on it! Airmail takes just over a week to get here now, so it arrived in plenty of time. You are very artistic, and cats are one of my favourite animals. I know you are always busy in the café, so it's kind of you to paint the picture in your spare time. I'm sorry to hear that Aunt Olive is bad with her nerves again. Just as well you have a good manageress in Lexy. I think Lexy's idea of changing the name from Herbert's Tea Rooms to Herbert's Café is a good one – much more modern. I'm sorry to hear that her friend Jared Belhaven has died though. Wasn't he some sort of cousin of ours?

Is Cousin George still courting the usherette at The Stoll? Uncle Jack must be doing really well if he's taken over from Mr Milner in the running of the Tyneside Tea Company. Well done, Uncle Jack! Is that why you've moved to a bigger house? Send me a photo or do a drawing of it when you can.

My best friend, Prue, has been exhibiting at the Simla Art Show this month and I'm in a production of Saint Joan *next week. We're performing it in Davico's Ballroom because it holds a much bigger audience than the school hall. I was hoping to be Saint Joan, but they gave the part to Deborah Halliday – I'm sure it was because she's got blonde hair. But anyway I'm Brother Martin, a young priest who is kind to Joan at the end. At least I've got a part. Also I'm singing in the end-of-term concert. I'm so excited because Auntie Sophie and Uncle Rafi are coming to hear me. They're visiting Dr Fatima (that's Rafi's sister), who works at the hospital and lives in a flat in Lakkar Bazaar so she can be near her work. She's very beautiful for a doctor.*

Sometimes I go and visit the sick with her and help make the patients cups of tea. Mrs Hogg ('The Fluff', as Prue calls her) thought it would be a good idea if I did some volunteering work, so I do that on Saturdays after classes. Sometimes Prue comes with me, and Dr Fatima says we are very useful, especially on the purdah wards, where the women can't be seen by male doctors or any male staff at all. Dr Fatima also goes into the hills and takes her travelling clinic to very remote places. Maybe next year I might go too.

The town is filling up with visitors. The Delhi government lot have been here since the middle of April, but now there are army and civilian wives escaping the heat of the plains, and young single officers on leave – some of them very handsome! You wouldn't believe the amount of flirting that goes on, and there are dinner dances and entertainment almost every night. I see the partygoers passing below the bungalow in rickshaws dressed up to the nines in satin and sequins (the men in white mess kit or tails) and they often wake me up on their return, laughing their heads off or singing. The lights of the rickshaw lamps bump up and down in the dark like fireflies as the rickshaw-wallahs pull their passengers up the slope. It looks so romantic. It makes me think of Sam Jackman. I still wonder a lot about what happened to him. Perhaps Auntie Sophie will have news of him.

I can't wait till I'm allowed to go to parties – real grown-up ones – where I'll have a dance card filled with the names of young men dying to dance with me! Aunt Fluffy says I have to wait till I'm seventeen. Although she does hold dinner parties that I'm allowed to be at, the guests are usually pretty old and talk a lot of politics, but she often has Indians to dinner, like Dr Fatima, who isn't in purdah, or Indian Army officers that Colonel Hogg used to know. There's a really jolly Sikh officer called Sundar Singh who used to be with Rafi in the Lahore Horse. He's here on some survey. He's had a sad life, as his wife died in childbirth, and he doesn't get to see his son much as he's being brought up by Sundar's sister near Pindi, but he's full of fun and always telling jokes and I think he's a bit smitten with Dr Fatima – though I don't think Sikhs are allowed to marry Moslems, which is a bit of a pity, as he makes her laugh, which is quite hard work because she is a serious sort.

I'm allowed to go to the pictures. Last week Sundar took Aunt Fluffy, Dr Fatima and me to see The Merry Widow. *It was wonderful and I've been pretending I'm a Maxime's dancer and practising steps ever since. Aunt Fluffy complains that I make more noise upstairs than the monkeys on the roof!*

Write to me soon and tell me how you are. Give my love to Aunt Olive and I hope she cheers up soon.

Your loving cousin, Adela

(Alias film star Jeanette MacDonald!)

***

Briar Rose Cottage, Simla
July 1936

Dear Cousin Jane

*Sorry this is such a belated thank you for your lovely birthday card with the sixteen dragonflies – they really are that brightly coloured here – shimmering green and blue and red. I've been so busy with the end-of-term play (*She Stoops to Conquer *– I got the part of Constance, which I think is a more interesting one than leading lady, Kate) as well as helping out at the Gaiety Theatre – Aunt Fluffy complains that since the school holidays started I practically live backstage and that she might as well send round all my meals.*

But guess what? I've got a part in the musical No, No, Nanette *dancing and singing in the chorus!! I'm so thrilled I could burst. I especially love 'Tea for Two', as it reminds me of singing it in the car with Daddy at the top of our voices. Prue is helping behind the scenes painting stage scenery. It's much easier doing that at the Gaiety than at school because they have a clever system of painting the canvas over two floors with a slit between the two, where the backcloth can be wound up and down on a roll, so Prue is often upstairs painting away. You can always tell it's her because she has a very loud whistle and whistles along to all the songs, which sometimes annoys the lead actors, but makes me smile and dance even harder. Prue left school this term and is staying up for the season, then will be joining her parents in Jubbulpore (her father works at the Gun Carriage*

Factory). I'll miss her terribly, but at least we've got till the cold season together.

I won't be going home this summer because I'm involved in the musical, and now the monsoon has come there's been bad flooding on the way up to Shillong, so the family are a bit marooned at Belgooree. But as I wrote in a previous letter, I'm glad I got home for the Easter holidays, and all seemed well.

You asked about my brother because I forgot to tell you last time. Harry had grown so much since Christmas – he's going to be tall like Daddy and he's got the same dark wavy hair that won't lie down even when it's brushed. He's speaking now but he chooses not to say very much – at least not to humans – but he talks to Scout like a best friend and I think he would sleep with the dog on the veranda if he was allowed to! He'll be three in three months' time. Harry hums a lot and he loves building towers with wooden bricks and then knocking them down. Ayah Mimi is forever searching for bricks under the furniture. The best day of the holiday was going riding with Daddy and Mother over to Um Shirpi for a picnic and a swim, while Ayah looked after Harry. It was like old times. Daddy said that next year he might take me hunting in the jungle around Gulgat with Rafi and the Raja. That would be so much fun! Mother didn't like the idea, but Daddy laughed and said that I would be a match for any tiger!

They have leopards in the forests here. I saw one late at night when I was returning with Dr Fatima from the clinic near Kufri. It walked right across the path in the moonlight in front of our ponies. It stopped and stared at us with big yellow eyes and twitched its tail, then bounded off into the trees again. Luckily the ponies and the baggage mule didn't get spooked or bolt for their lives, but I had my heart in my mouth, I can tell you!

I love going into the hills with Dr Fatima – it gives me a chance to ride properly and not just promenade around The Ridge and Jakko Hill like the richer girls at school, who have riding lessons. Sometimes Sundar Singh gives us a lift in his old open-top Chevrolet, but Dr Fatima doesn't like to be beholden to him. She can be very stubborn for someone so shy – well, not shy exactly, but very reserved about her feelings. She says I'm far too open with mine!

I like going to visit the hill people. They are friendly and welcoming and they live very tough lives – the men are employed as coolies in the town, so the women do all the work in the fields and look after the families while they are away. They look old very quickly, though the young women are beautiful (except for those with pockmarks from smallpox), with rings in their noses and colourful clothes. They sing and laugh and tease us for not being married. You should see them dressed up for the native Sipi Fair in May, weighed down with necklaces and earrings of silver and bright jewels and the most enormous hoops in their noses – you could practically skip with them! Aunt Fluffy doesn't approve of the Sipi Fair because she says some of the young girls are sold off as brides like at a cattle market, but she doesn't stop me going because it's a fun day out and I like seeing the hill people letting their hair down, as they lead such hard lives the rest of the year.

At the hill clinics Dr Fatima performs small operations and gives out medicines. There are some terrible accidents – children with burns from falling into fires or women who have cut themselves chopping wood, and their wounds have gone septic before they can be treated. Sometimes Dr Fatima can get them sent to hospital in time, but not always.

One time a young woman came in carrying a baby who had been mauled by a dog. The baby was screaming and the mother was weeping. Dr Fatima treated the wounds and we sat up all night with the baby and you could tell she was in great pain crying in her mother's arms. In the morning she seemed more calm, but later that day she went into a fit and died. The dog must have been rabid. We were there when they cremated her little body and put the ashes into the river. I couldn't stop crying, until Dr Fatima told me not to be so emotional, as it didn't help. But I know that she sometimes cries quietly at night from all the sorrow she sees. She wants to make everyone better; that's her mission in life.

Sometimes Tibetans come to the clinics at Kufri and Theog. They walk all the way from Tibet through the high mountain passes to sell jewellery and homespun cloth in the Indian towns, carrying everything on sturdy yaks, which are like shaggy oxen. They are the gentlest people I've met – they smile a lot and their faces are creased and weathered by the fierce mountain sun. If they can't pay, Dr Fatima accepts a few apples or a bracelet of a couple of beads on a leather strap.

There are some missionaries at Narkanda who grow apples – the orchards were planted in the 1920s – and it gives the hill people something to sell at market. I haven't been up that far yet, but Dr Fatima promises she'll take me soon. The monsoons have come now and the days are very misty and wet, so I prefer to be here in Simla, working at the theatre.

Next summer I'll be leaving school – I refuse to stay on any longer than I have to. It's not that I don't like St Mary's, but I'm not in the least bit academic and I want to get out into the world. What do you think I should do? What's it like now that you are working at Herbert's Café? I'm not sure I am cut out to join the family business. I don't really want to go back to Belgooree and work in tea like my parents. I know Daddy would like me to, but Mother understands that I want more excitement from life. She often talks about her childhood at Belgooree with Aunt Olive. It's strange how your mother has no real memory of it because according to my mother, Aunt Olive was about fifteen when she left, which is just a bit younger than me. I couldn't possibly forget India if I'd had to leave at that age.

I hope the excursion to the seaside is a tonic for both your parents – it sounds like they work very hard. How is Cousin George's romance going with the telephonist?

Please send me a photo of you all at the seaside.

Your loving cousin, Adela.

PS Aunt Fluffy says I can go to the after-show dance at the finish of the musical in August even though I'm not yet seventeen. It's going to be at The Chalet (it's part of the United Services Club) and they are famous for putting on really good parties!

PPS. Have you fallen in love yet, Jane? I still think often of Sam, even though I'll probably never see him again. I can't really explain why he's still on my mind, as I haven't seen him since I was thirteen – but it's more than just about good looks when you fall in love, isn't it? I adore everything about him.

Chapter 5

Simla, June 1937

Adela hurried out of the back of the Gaiety Theatre still caked in stage make-up and ran up the Mall. The military band at the bandstand was packing up; she gave a wave as she dashed past, unable to keep the grin from her face. It was her seventeenth birthday and tonight she was coming out in Simla society. Fluffy Hogg, who had become her surrogate mother these past three years, was hosting a small supper party: Dr Fatima; Sundar Singh; Prue, who was back in Simla with her mother for the summer season; school rival Deborah Halliday, because she was good fun; and Boz, a lanky Scots friend of Sophie and Rafi's from the Forest Service who was posted to Simla and was bringing along his young assistant, Guy Fellows, who was considered one of the best catches in Simla that season.

Guy had fair good looks, had rowed for Cambridge and was full of understated charm. Both Prue and Deborah were amazed and excited that The Fluff had managed to secure such a guest for Adela's birthday meal. Afterwards they were joining a larger party under the wing of one of Fluffy's retired friends, Colonel Baxter, and going dancing to the Full Moon Dance at Davico's Ballroom. Adela had been firm with her friends that she expected to get Guy's name on her dance card before they did.

Fluffy had paid for a local tailor to copy a dress that the actress Vivien Leigh had been wearing in a magazine. Adela and Deborah – they were always competing for the same parts in school plays and town shows – had sighed over it backstage. Adela had torn out the page, taken it back to Briar Rose Cottage and pinned it to her bedroom wall. She had been thrilled when her guardian had suggested having a copy made. The photo was black and white, so they had no idea of the original colour, but Adela chose dusky pink. It was full-skirted and made of crêpe de chine, with a pinched waist and a strappy bodice that showed off Adela's trim, curvy figure. She loved the way it swished from her hips when she moved.

'Auntie, I'm back!' she called as she ran up the veranda steps, throwing off her jacket and kicking off her shoes as she went.

Mrs Hogg was dressed in an old-fashioned floor-length green gown with long sleeves that was already making her perspire in the warm June evening.

'Quick sticks, young lady,' Fluffy ordered. 'Our guests will be here in twenty minutes. And you can't be seen with your face painted like Columbine.'

'You look gorgeous.' Adela kissed her, leaving a smudge of red lipstick on the older woman's warm cheek. 'I'll be ready in ten.'

She scrubbed herself down quickly in the bathroom, removing the make-up, and pulled on the new dress. She squirted on perfume that her parents had sent. Fluffy came in to help her pin up her hair. On a whim Adela plucked a cream-coloured rose from the bowl of flowers by the window and stuck it in her dark hair.

'What do you think, Auntie?'

Fluffy appeared lost for words. When she spoke, her voice was shaky.

'You're a beautiful young woman, and I'm very proud to be showing you off to the world tonight. I wish your parents could be here—'

Adela rushed and hugged her. 'Stop it, you'll make me cry. I'll be seeing them soon enough – just two more weeks of school and then it's all over, unless I can find a job here.'

Fluffy cleared her throat and pulled away. 'Let's just enjoy tonight and not think about that,' she said firmly.

***

Prue and Deborah were the first to arrive as the mali was lighting the lamps that hung in the trees. Adela could hear their excited chatter and giggling even before they appeared in the flickering light around the box hedges of the narrow garden. Just as they did, the telephone rang in the sitting room.

'Go and greet them,' said Fluffy. 'I'll just be a minute.'

Prue, now eighteen, was wearing a sophisticated long dress of midnight blue, her brown hair permed into stylish waves. Deborah's straight blonde hair was swept off her high forehead with a hairband that matched her silk lilac dress. Her father was high up in Burmah Oil and the Hallidays had plenty of money, but Deborah had no airs and graces; St Mary's discouraged boastfulness.

'Adela, you look wonderful!' Prue cried, clattering on to the veranda in her new high heels and hugging her friend.

'Vivien Leigh will die of envy.' Deborah winked, handing over a present. 'Open it later.'

'Have the others arrived yet?' asked Prue.

'She means, is Guy Fellows here?' Deborah gave a roll of her large blue eyes.

'No, you're the first.' Adela smiled. 'Come inside. Auntie says we can drink sherry.'

Prue pulled a face. 'I've been drinking gimlets in Jubbulpore.'

Deborah gave her a playful shove. 'I hope you're not going to be a bore about Jubbulpore all evening.'

'That's the first time I've mentioned it.'

'Third. Bet you can't have a conversation with Guy Fellows without saying the *J* word.'

'Bet I can.'

The two girls spat on their palms and shook hands. Adela pulled them indoors.

'Come on you two: no arguing on my birthday.'

Fluffy appeared and asked Noor, her bearer, to pour four sherries.

'Who was that, Auntie?' Adela asked.

Fluffy raised her glass and made a toast before answering. When they had all taken a sip, she said, 'That was William Boswell.'

'Boz?' Adela queried. 'He is still coming, isn't he?'

'Yes, but I'm afraid that Mr Fellows is not.'

There was a chorus of dismay from the three friends.

'Why not?'

'How disappointing!'

'That's very late in the day to cancel.'

'He's come down with a dose of hill fever,' explained their hostess. 'He's very apologetic – was hoping he would rally in time for tonight.'

Adela tried to put on a brave face; she could see how disappointed her friends were.

'Poor Guy,' she said. 'That's very bad luck.'

'Isn't it?' agreed Fluffy. 'But all is not lost. Boz has managed to find a replacement for the party – someone he knows from up in the hills. The man just happened to be in Simla, and Boz has persuaded him to stay the night.'

'Good for Boz.' Adela brightened.

'Ooh, who is this mystery man?' Prue smiled.

'Some Raja's son I hope.' Deborah gave a wicked grin.

'Deb!' Prue admonished.

'Not exactly.' Fluffy gave Adela an apologetic glance. 'He's a missionary from Narkanda.'

'A *missionary*?' Deborah exclaimed.

'Oh no.' Prue pulled a face.

'Better hide the sherry, Auntie,' Adela said with a rueful look, trying to make light of it.

'Now, girls,' Fluffy said, 'I'm sure he'll be very pleasant.'

'And boring,' muttered Prue.

'Well, he probably won't want to stay beyond dinner, will he?' Adela asked in hope.

'That's true. Missionaries don't usually hang around Davico's,' agreed Prue.

'Except to stop young innocents from entering,' Deborah said in a dramatic voice, 'and save their mortal souls!'

Prue and Adela snorted with laughter. Just then Sundar called out a greeting as he arrived with Dr Fatima.

'The bet about the *J* word still stands,' Deborah hissed to the others.

They came bearing more gifts, Sundar looking magnificent in the evening mess kit of the Lahore Horse with a ruby-red turban, and Fatima in a dark blue sari with gold brocade.

'You really shouldn't,' Adela said, kissing Fatima's cheek. 'All I wanted was a party with my favourite people.'

'Nonsense,' Deborah declared. 'Presents are the best part of birthdays.'

'And it's a good excuse to spoil a very special young lady.' Sundar grinned. 'Tonight, you look like a princess!'

'Thank you.' Adela beamed while her friends giggled. Fluffy welcomed them, and Noor handed fruit juice to the new arrivals. The noise level grew as they chatted and laughed. Prue told them about the gorgeous Guy being replaced by a missionary.

'Some dry old stick that Boz has dragged in at the last minute – probably as old as the hills too.'

'You're going to have to be on your best behaviour, birthday girl,' Deborah teased Adela.

'As will you.' Adela laughed.

'No unsuitable jokes, ladies' – Sundar wagged a finger in mock disapproval – 'or bursting into barrack-room songs.'

'The only ones we know are the ones you taught us,' Adela teased back.

'Not all the missionaries in the hills are ancient,' Fatima said, 'or lacking in humour. Most of the ones I've met are kind and well meaning.'

The girls groaned.

'You never have a bad word to say about anyone, do you?' Adela rolled her eyes.

'Maybe we should practise some hymn singing before he arrives.' Prue smirked.

'What a friend we have in Jesus!' Deborah began at once.

'Honestly, you girls,' Fluffy cried. 'You would think you were seven, not seventeen.'

'Some of us are eighteen,' Prue corrected.

'Because some of us,' Deborah mimicked, 'have had a year in . . .'

'*Jubbulpore!*' Adela chimed in with Deborah.

The friends burst out laughing.

A deep Scottish voice called out of the dark: 'Good evening! Glad to see the party's already started.'

'Boz!' Adela cried, rushing forward to the veranda steps, while her friends stifled their giggles. His tall, wiry frame loomed out of the shadows dressed in kilt and black jacket, his long craggy face scored by years in the sun and his red hair receding, making him look older than Rafi, his contemporary and friend.

'Thank you for coming.' Adela greeted him with a warm handshake, half hoping that he had decided against bringing the missionary with him.

'Wouldna miss it for the world, lassie,' Boz said with a grin. 'And neither would ma friend here when he heard it was Miss Adela Robson's birthday.'

'Oh?' Adela gave a quizzical smile. 'I didn't think I knew any missionaries from Narkanda.'

Boz stood aside as his companion leapt up the steps behind him. Adela's instant impression was that the man was not old at all and that his shoulders were too broad for the suit that Boz had obviously lent him.

'Adela.' He gave a generous smile, and she found herself looking up into familiar laughing hazel brown eyes. He held out a large hand. 'Happy birthday.'

For a moment she just stood there winded, staring at him in disbelief. How was this possible? Fluffy gave a polite cough, which galvanised her out of a state of shock.

'Sam?' Adela gulped, reaching out a hand to meet his. His warm, roughened fingers closed around hers, sparking off an electric storm in her chest.

'You know each other?' Fluffy asked in surprise.

'Yes, from Assam,' Adela said, her voice husky as she held on to Sam's hand a fraction more than was polite.

Sam disengaged and stepped towards his hostess, thrusting a jute bag at her. 'Sam Jackman.' He smiled. 'Some cherries from the orchard. Sorry I don't have anything more exciting. It's very good of you to invite me.'

'Well, it's good of you to come at such short notice,' Fluffy answered graciously.

'I realise I'm the understudy for the lead man, Mr Fellows,' Sam joked. 'So sorry to disappoint, ladies.' He bowed to Prue and Deborah. Adela noticed their looks of amazement. Then Sam caught sight of Fatima. 'Ah, Dr Khan. How delightful.'

'How do you do, Mr Jackman?' she said, smiling in greeting and introducing him to Sundar.

As they made introductions around the room and fell to small talk, Adela felt ridiculously tongue-tied. Fatima had mentioned the mission on a couple of occasions, but Adela had never been curious enough to ask about the missionaries themselves. She tried not to stare at Sam, but failed. It was nearly four years since she had last seen him, and he had lost his boyish looks: his chin was nicked from a recent shave with a blunt razor and there were new lines about his eyes and mouth. He had broadened out – perhaps from manual work – his shirt buttons straining at his chest and the collar digging into his ruddy neck. Sam's hair was still as brush-like and unruly as before, and the teasing familiar smile came just as easily to his firm lips. Her heart hammered from the shock of his sudden arrival, and she felt breathless at his nearness.

For the first year after her flight from St Ninian's, she had thought about him every day, wondering what had become of him, especially after the scandal of him losing his steamboat in a card game. But even Auntie Tilly and her network of gossips in the tea gardens had been unable to find out where he had gone. Some rumours had put him in Calcutta; others that he had joined the Merchant Navy or gone home to England. None had come anywhere close to guessing that the wild Jackman boy had become a missionary. She had never forgotten him, but as time had gone on she had resigned herself to never seeing him again. Yet here he was, conjured up like a magic trick on Fluffy's veranda.

Then Adela's euphoria at seeing him again suddenly deflated. If Sam had found God, perhaps he had also found a missionary wife to help him in his vocation. Wasn't that what most missionaries did?

'Well, Adela dear,' Fluffy said briskly, throwing her a curious glance, 'why don't you lead our guests into dinner?'

Adela took a deep breath. Whatever Sam's situation, nothing was going to stop her enjoying her birthday celebrations. 'Of course.' She smiled, and led the way into the dining room.

***

It was the pudding course before Adela plucked up the courage to ask Sam how he had ended up in the hills beyond Simla. Prue had dominated the conversation early on with chatter about life in the cantonment in Jubbulpore, with trips to the Smoke Cascade, a dramatic waterfall, and dances at the Gun Carriage Factory Club. Deborah had switched the conversation to the forthcoming show at the Gaiety, and Adela had found her voice and joined in with amusing stories about clashes on stage and off. The men had discussed road-widening schemes for the route up to Kufri and unrest in some of the princely states. Sundar had been critical of interference from Congress activists stirring up dissent among the labourers.

'Our contractors are finding it harder to hire men at prices they can afford.'

'The men have families to feed,' replied Sam. 'They shouldn't have to work for nothing.'

'Nobody is asking them to.'

'I'm afraid that's exactly what the old system of *begar* is doing. It's time the hill rajas abolished it – and the British, who have been taking advantage of the free labour on offer.'

'I agree wi' Sam,' Boz said. 'Fair day's pay for a fair day's work.'

'Quite so,' said Fluffy. 'If we expect that for ourselves, we should grant it to the Indians.'

Abruptly Sundar laughed. 'Help me, Dr Khan. Am I the only one at this table prepared to uphold the British administration?'

A smile twitched at Fatima's lips. 'It would seem so.'

As Adela's favourite fruit fool was served, along with Sam's cherries, she asked, 'You still haven't told us how you ended up in Narkanda, Sam. The last we heard was you'd lost your boat!'

Sam gave a short laugh. 'Ah, so you know about that?'

'Auntie Tilly said it was the talk of Tezpur.'

'I'm sure it was.' Sam's look was rueful. 'I went off the rails for a while.'

'How dashing,' said Deborah. Adela could see her friend was quite taken with the handsome, candid missionary.

'Not really,' said Sam, a look of pain flickering across his face. 'It's a sorry tale.'

'Do tell,' urged Prue.

'You don't have to,' murmured Fatima. Adela saw a look flit between them, and she wondered for the first time if they might know each other better than they had let on.

'Maybe it will be a salutary lesson,' Sam said with shrug of self-deprecation. 'I drank and gambled too much – lost everything I had, including the few long-suffering friends who put me up in their bungalows until I drank their godowns dry. Even my monkey ran off.'

'Nelson?' Adela exclaimed.

Sam nodded, his look remorseful. 'Couldn't look after myself, let alone poor Nelson. I was a drunk and a bore and heading for an early grave. And then somehow my old friend and mentor Dr Black found me.' He turned again to Adela. 'You remember Dr Black, the missionary?'

She nodded, blushing to think how the doctor had seen her final humiliation at St Ninian's.

'He rescued me from a dosshouse in Delhi – somewhere in the old city. Anyway, he took me to his home, sobered me up and brought me back to life. I started helping out at the mission, doing odd jobs fixing up shelters and growing food. For the first time in a long time, I felt a purpose in life. When the mission at Narkanda needed help with the orchards, I jumped at the chance to come back to this area.'

'Were you a Bishop Cotton pupil?' Fluffy asked.

'No, a Lawrence boy.' Sam smiled. 'I'd forgotten how much I loved the hills and wanted to work on the land – good for body and spirit.'

Deborah said, 'So you're not really a missionary? I mean, you're more of a farmer than one of the holy brigade.'

'Deborah!' Prue cried.

Sam laughed. 'I'm both I suppose. I grow fruit, but I also believe in feeding the soul. Dr Black saved me from the gutter and gave me a second chance. I made him a promise that I'd dedicate my life to helping others, so that's what I'm trying to do. As a confirmed bachelor I have no wife or family to consider, so I can just serve God. Except' – he gave his boyish smile – 'for the odd trip into Simla to have my cine films developed and attend delightful birthday parties.'

There was an awkward pause; it was bad etiquette to air such personal details and talk about God. Adela thought how his words echoed what Fatima was doing – dedicating her life to serving others. It struck her, looking at the serene doctor and the vigorous Sam, how they suited each other – more so than Fatima and the boisterous, but conventional Sundar did. They must be a similar age too; Fatima could only be a couple of years older than Sam. Adela felt a pang of disappointment at the thought. Even though she was coming of age in society, Sam would probably still think of her as the rebellious child he had known and not a woman to excite his interest.

'Sorry, Mrs Hogg,' Sam said. 'I see I've shocked your young ladies. I know it's bad form to lay your soul bare at the dinner table.'

'Only before the port,' Fluffy replied with a guarded smile.

Adela saw the situation needed rescuing. She shouldn't have put such questions to Sam in front of the others. 'Don't worry. Briar Rose Cottage is infamous for its dinner conversation,' she reassured him. 'Auntie allows just about anything to be talked about at her table, unless it's blasphemous about the Liberal Party or the Indian Army.'

'I'll drink to that.' Sundar grinned and raised his glass of soda water.

Boz stood up, relief on his face. Adela thought the bashful Scotsman was probably keen to veer the conversation away from religion and personal matters.

'Let's raise our glasses to bonny Adela on her seventeenth birthday.'

With enthusiasm, the dinner guests and Fluffy got to their feet.

'To Adela!' they cried in unison.

'Thank you,' she said, beaming. 'And thank you for coming tonight and making my birthday special.'

'And we've still got the dancing to come,' Deborah squealed.

'Better go and freshen up, girls,' said Fluffy. 'The rickshaws are booked for nine o'clock.'

Adela turned to Sam. 'You will come with us to the dance, won't you?'

He hesitated a moment, then smiled. 'If you don't mind a man with two left feet, then I'd be honoured.'

'Good.' She smiled back.

As they applied some of Prue's lipstick in Adela's room, the girls demanded to know how Adela knew Sam. She told them about her escape from St Ninian's in the boot of Sam's car.

'You dark horse!' Prue cried. 'Why did you never tell us this before?'

'Didn't like to be reminded of St Ninian's and that bully, Nina Davidge.'

'Why was she so horrid to you?' Deborah asked.

Adela shrugged. She was never going to tell them the shameful things Nina had said about her parents. 'She was jealous of my friendship with Margie Munro I suppose. Anyway, that's all ancient history, and I don't want to think about it.'

'Well, if she ever shows her face in Simla,' Deborah declared, 'we'll cut her dead.'

Adela felt a guilty wave of relief that that was never likely to happen now. Over a year ago her mother had heard that Colonel Davidge had died, and Nina and her mother had gone back to England.

'Sam's always been a bit of a rebel then,' mused Prue. 'Hiding stowaways and gambling away his boat!'

'Not now,' said Deborah, adjusting the Alice band on her flyaway hair. 'He's living like a monk in the hills, with no interest in girls.'

'Except for Dr Fatima.' Prue smirked.

Adela reddened. 'Whatever do you mean by that?'

'Couldn't keep his eyes off her all supper. You must have noticed.'

'Well, maybe . . .'

'They all love the fabulous Fatima,' said Deborah with a roll of her eyes. 'Sam will have to form an orderly queue behind Sundar and Boz.'

'It's just not fair,' Prue said and sighed. 'She's not the slightest bit interested in men as far as I can see.'

'It's not that she isn't interested,' said Adela, 'it's more that men aren't a priority. She's already made excuses not to come on to the dance with us tonight.'

'Girls, that's the secret,' Deborah said, laughing, 'stay aloof and unobtainable – drives the men wild.'

'If you stay aloof,' said Prue, 'you don't get asked to dance. At least that's what happens in Jubbulpore.'

'Jubbulpore!' Adela and Deborah crowed at once.

'The hundred and tenth mention tonight,' Deborah said. 'Let's make it our code word for action with any boys this evening.'

The three friends spat on their palms, shook hands and hurried downstairs shrieking with laughter.

***

Davico's Ballroom was ablaze with electric lights, perched on its steep slope like a sentinel overlooking the lamplit native bazaar and the shadow-filled valleys. The night air was warm and scented with roses and pines.

Colonel Baxter greeted them and ushered them into the ballroom, introducing Fluffy's party to his own and making a fuss of Adela.

'I first met this beautiful young lady when she was three years old,' he announced, 'and I was ADC to the Raja of Gulgat. We were camping at Um Shirpi at the invitation of her father – tea planter and excellent shot, Wesley Robson.'

Adela laughed. 'I remember a huge dog on a gold chain that I thought was a wolf. And I was so excited to have a prince camping close to the gardens.'

'Ah, so *you* are the girl from the tea garden.' A tall, distinguished-looking man with iron grey hair and pale blue eyes viewed her with interest. 'Boswell has talked about you. Bit of an actress, I hear.'

Boz, red-faced, leapt forward and introduced them. 'Adela, this is Mr Bracknall, the Chief Conservator of Forests in the Punjab.'

Adela noted Boz's discomfort and tried to remember what he'd said about his boss. Some complaint about Mrs Bracknall refusing to let her husband retire because she didn't want to return to England and do without the luxury of servants. Promotion for men like Boz was being denied as long as Bracknall stayed in post.

'How do you do, Mr Bracknall?' Adela shook his hand. He had a crushing grip, and she tried not to wince.

'Very well.' His smile was brief, his eyes assessing. 'Let me put my name on your dance card before all the young bucks fill it up, eh? I insist on the first waltz – leave the more energetic dances to the youths.'

Adela hid her dismay; she had hoped to waltz with Sam. 'Of course,' she agreed, taking her card out of her evening bag and writing his name with the short pencil attached to its gold cord.

Soon all three girls were being booked for dances and whirled around the floor to the beat of the ten-piece dance band. Theatre friends, army subalterns and junior officers of the Indian Civil Service flocked around Colonel Baxter's lively party. There was a smattering of Indians in the room: magistrates and their wives up from Delhi, a maharajah from Bengal and a film producer from Bombay, along with some middle-ranking officials in the Indian branch of the ICS.

Bracknall complained about it as he pulled Adela around the dance floor. 'Would never have been allowed when I was starting out in the service. First World War was when the rot set in. It's not that I object to mixing with Indians – I work with them all day long with absolutely no problem – but it's a class thing, isn't it? You just want to socialise with your own kind, don't you?'

'I would have thought that a maharajah ranks rather higher than any of us, Mr Bracknall,' Adela replied.

'Oh well, yes,' he blustered. 'There's always an exception to the rule. Indian royalty is quite acceptable.'

Adela wondered if it was attitudes like Bracknall's that kept Fatima away from social events like the Full Moon Dance, even though there was no bar to Indians entering Davico's. Sundar had also stayed away, insisting on escorting Fatima safely home to her flat in Lakkar Bazaar. It was only a five-minute walk from the ballroom, and he could have joined them later, but for all that Sundar championed the institutions of the British Raj, Adela suspected he still felt an outsider when it came to socialising with its elite.

'And now that you are out in Simla society,' Bracknall said, winking, 'no doubt you're planning a full season of balls and picnics.'

'Not really,' Adela said, 'apart from performing in the musical next month. In fact I'll have to go home to Assam before the summer ends if I don't find a job here. Mrs Hogg has been so kind to me; I don't want to take advantage of her generosity more than I already have.' She decided to be bold. 'Mr Bracknall, do you need any clerical help in your office? I'm very tidy and organised.'

For a moment he seemed taken aback. 'Well, hiring menial staff is not really my concern.' Then his hold on her tightened, and he smiled. 'But I'm sure we can find something here to keep you occupied.'

'I'd be so grateful,' Adela enthused. 'I really want to be able to stay.' She didn't like to admit how her desire to remain in Simla had now increased tenfold since discovering Sam was living a few hours' ride into the hills.

Bracknall gave her that assessing look again, which made her feel acutely aware of his hot hand on her back and the way he brushed his barrel chest against her breasts as he twirled her around.

'We can always do with some extra help in the Forest Office,' he suggested. 'Though I can't promise you'll get paid much. Can you bash away at a typewriter?'

'Oh yes. I used to help my father with letters,' Adela exaggerated, having only done so a couple of times.

'I'll have a word with Boswell; see what we can do, eh?'

'Thank you, Mr Bracknall, you're so kind.' She smiled. 'That would be wonderful.'

As soon as the waltz was over, she disengaged quickly. 'Just need to powder my nose.' She grabbed her bag and slipped from the hall.

Outside, Adela stood under a deodar tree and gulped in the cooling night air, thrilled that she had so easily found a way of staying on in Simla. Lifting over the dark forested hills, the huge shimmering disc of the full moon lit the earth below, casting shadows like sunlight. She sighed at its beauty.

'Not running away again, are you?' The voice, so close by, startled her. Her hand flew to her chest. Sam stepped round the tree.

She laughed with a mix of relief and excitement. 'No, but it looks like you are.'

'Mrs Hogg saw you bolt from the dance. Wanted me to make sure you were all right.'

'Oh.' Adela felt a pang of disappointment. He hadn't come after her of his own accord. 'Well, I'm fine. Just needed fresh air, so there's no need to worry. You can report back to Auntie.'

Sam leant against the tree and pulled out a squashed packet of bidis from his too-tight jacket. He offered her one. Adela hesitated, then took it. He struck a match and lit hers before his, the flame flaring between them. She held the bidi gingerly between finger and thumb and inhaled. The fiery taste stung her tongue, but she managed not to cough. She and Deborah had experimented with cigarettes – Camels – that Mr Halliday had been given by an American oilman. The Indian cigarette was more pungent and raw in her mouth and yet more calming.

They stood close, smoking in silence, Sam pulling free his tie and unbuttoning his collar. It had left a welt across his neck that was visible in the moonlight. Adela resisted the urge to trace her finger over it.

Abruptly he asked, 'What do you want to do with your life, Adela?'

She was taken by surprise; it wasn't the usual grown-up enquiry such as, what are you going to do after school? Or, what are your plans for the cold season?

'More than anything I want to act – go on the stage, sing and dance. That's when I'm happiest. I want to be as famous as Gracie Fields. My cousins in Newcastle went to hear her sing, and so many people wanted to hear her that she sang on the cinema roof! Imagine giving that much pleasure.' She watched his lean profile, the straight nose and the firm mouth and chin. 'You probably think that's a very frivolous thing to want to do.'

He shook his head. 'If it's what you've always wanted, then you must do it. You're lucky to know at your age what you really want.' He smiled. 'So what are you doing about it? Are you going to apply for drama school?'

Adela laughed. 'My parents couldn't afford it – the tea garden has been struggling for a few years now – but I really want to stay here and keep performing at the Gaiety and maybe do some touring. I've asked Mr Bracknall for a job in the Forest Office. Even if it's not much, I can live simply. All I need is to cover my rent at Auntie's. I don't mind eating in the bazaar if I have to.'

'Then do it,' Sam encouraged. 'If you can stand the pompous Bracknall as your boss. Boz says he's a devil to work for. If he takes a dislike to you, he can make your life hell.'

'Well, I think he quite likes me.'

'That's the other thing,' warned Sam. 'Boz says he has a roving eye.'

Adela scoffed. 'He must be older than my father!'

'Men like that don't see themselves as old – they think they are still attractive to women, however young. You might be better finding somewhere else.'

'Is this my first sermon from Missionary Jackman?' she teased. 'Don't worry, I can look after myself.'

Sam gave a rueful laugh. 'Yes, I'm sure you can. Far better than me. I've no right to lecture.'

She put out a hand and briefly touched his arm. 'I'm so sorry about Nelson.'

Sam grunted. 'I thought you'd be more concerned about my rascal monkey than me,' he teased.

'You brought all that on yourself,' Adela said dryly. 'Poor Nelson didn't have a choice.'

He swivelled round, propping his hip against the tree trunk, and gazed down at her. 'You're quite right. That's what I like about you, Adela: you say exactly what you think.'

She swivelled to face him too. 'And what am I thinking?'

'That you wish it was the young Guy Fellows who was here under the tree in the moonlight with you just now.'

Adela gave a short laugh. 'Wrong. I'm glad it's you.'

They stared at each other. Adela's heart thumped like a bass drum. Maybe it was the dazzling moon or the narcotic effect of the bidi, but she found herself saying, 'I've thought about you a lot over the past years, wondering where you'd gone, whether you ever thought of me. Did you ever think of me, Sam?'

She held her breath. He let out a sigh. 'Yes,' he murmured.

'What did you think?' Adela's heart quickened.

'How brave you were.'

'Brave?'

'Sticking to your guns and not going back to St Ninian's. Standing up to all the adults in your life, making things happen!' His voice took on that passion she had heard when he'd spoken of Dr Black's work. 'After I left Belgooree, I began to realise how empty my life was – my father dead; a mother who had up and left me years ago – how I got no enjoyment any more from working on the river.' He fixed her with an intense look. 'It was all so aimless, pointless, and it was little Adela Robson who made me see it.'

Adela swallowed down disappointment and laughed. 'So I'm still just a plucky little girl in your eyes?'

She dropped the burning bidi and ground it underfoot. He did the same. But as she moved around him, he caught her arm.

'Yes, you were plucky,' he said, 'but I'd have to be blind not to see what a beautiful young woman you've become.'

She shivered at his touch and at the way he stood over her, looking into her eyes. She was sure she saw desire in his. Any moment now he was going to kiss her and her life as a woman would really begin. She had been yearning for this moment since the day she climbed out of his car at Belgooree, impatient to be grown-up, impatient to feel his lips on hers.

He swallowed hard and then dropped his hold, turning away.

'Better get you back into the hall before Mrs Hogg sends out the cavalry to rescue you from the mad missionary.' He ushered her forward.

Adela's eyes stung as she held herself erect and walked purposefully back into the dance hall; she didn't want him to see how much his rejection of her hurt. Her instincts had been wrong; his feelings for her were merely platonic. And if for a moment in the moonlight he had let himself think otherwise, she knew that Sam Jackman the missionary would quell such feelings. She was too young for him, and if ever he began to look for someone to marry, Adela, the would-be actress, would hardly be a suitable wife on an isolated mission. Besides, she wasn't ready for marriage either; she wanted a lot more fun and experience of life before that. The world beyond school dazzled like the bright footlights of the stage, and she was impatient for it.

For the rest of the evening Adela threw herself into the dancing, accepting every invitation, even another waltz with Bracknall. She avoided Sam and wasn't sure at what point he left the party.

'He's decided to travel back the night wi' the moon being so bright,' Boz explained. 'Said tae thank you, but didn't want to drag you away frae the dancing.'

Adela pretended not to care. There he was running away again, she thought in exasperation. Perhaps he just didn't need the company of other people in the way she did. Sam was a puzzle. One minute he was open and friendly, the next impossible to fathom. She gave up trying to work out what it all meant and went back to dance a military two-step with Boz.

Chapter 6

The musical at the Gaiety was a huge success. For a week they played to a full house every night and for two matinees. Adela's solo verse and tap dance in 'Tea for Two' got loud applause and wolf whistles from an overenthusiastic artillery captain, Jimmy Maitland, who spent his leave dating her. She accepted two invitations from him to tea dances at the Cecil Hotel and a picnic at the racetrack in Annandale, which was cut short by a thunderstorm.

Between her job at the Forest Office and theatre performances, she had little time for socialising, but squeezed in what she could. Forewarned by Sam and Boz about the predatory Bracknall, she made sure she was never left alone with him. Employed to help the junior officers sort dak in the post room, she soon took it upon herself to bring order to the chaos in the godowns, piled high with ancient camping equipment and abandoned kit left behind by former forest officers transferred to other areas.

'Throw it out,' Bracknall said without interest. 'Some of it's been here since the twenties – they won't be coming back for it now.'

Adela lost no time in passing on some ancient hats and tennis racquets to the theatre props department; the men's clothes and a couple of mildewed tents she had taken round to Fatima for her hill clinics.

'I'm sorry that I don't have time to help out at the moment,' Adela said, tracking her down at the hospital.

Fatima smiled. 'I quite understand, and these are very useful. Thank you so much, kind girl.'

'Have you seen anything of Sam Jackman?' Adela couldn't resist asking.

'Yes, when I was in Narkanda two weeks ago. He was very busy picking plums.' Fatima's look was enquiring. 'Do you have a message for him? I could take a letter the next time I'm at the clinic.'

'No.' Adela blushed. 'Well, just tell him that it's working out well at the Forest Office, so he has no need to worry.'

When Maitland, the amorous Scottish captain, left Simla, pleading with Adela to write to him often, she was then pursued by a district officer from Patna who was recuperating from a dose of malaria. He managed to string out his sick leave, taking her riding to the forest glades of Mashobra on her Sundays off, until she discovered from Prue that he was married with two sons, and so ended the liaison.

By this time Adela and Deborah were rehearsing for a Noël Coward play. Adela had won a good speaking part of a society flapper while Deborah was playing the housemaid, a role she was determined to ham up for all it was worth to make up for her lack of dialogue. Tommy Villiers, the leading man, a clerk in the Public Works Department and an enthusiastic amateur actor, took a shine to Adela, telling her, 'Whenever you get sick of these chaps on leave, my girl, then Tommy is ready and waiting in the wings.'

She liked Tommy, with his curly brown hair and breezy good-natured banter. Thirteen years older than her, but still single, he was one of those British who, like her, had grown up in India. As an actor he was unflappable, rescuing a scene when others forgot their lines and calming nerves backstage. He never got embroiled in theatre rivalries or spats.

'You can take me to the pictures to see the latest Cary Grant film,' she said, grinning, 'but it doesn't mean we're courting.'

'Strictly professional,' Tommy agreed, 'to brush up on our acting skills.'

He had a good tenor voice and organised a singing trio with Adela and Prue, naming them The Simla Songsters and organising impromptu performances at parties.

Sometimes Tommy joined Adela on outings with Prue and Deborah; they had an ever-shifting circle of friends, depending on who was on leave or out in camp. Deborah had moved into Fluffy's home as a paying guest for the summer rather than go back to stifling Rangoon in Burma, before completing one more year at St Mary's. To the girls' disappointment, the desirable young forester Guy Fellows had spent most of the monsoon season trekking up the Hindustan-Tibet road with Boz, supervising tree felling in remote camps at Kalpa and Purbani. As the Himalayan snows melted, the sawn timbers were launched from precipitous mountainsides into the churning grey water of the thundering Sutlej River and thrust downstream.

Prue had been to two dances with Guy before he joined the forest camp and was deeply in love. They discussed it one afternoon in Fluffy's tiny garden, with its view to the distant mountains wreathed in mist.

'He won't be back till the cold season now,' Prue said and sighed, 'and Mummy and I will be back in Jubbulpore by then.'

Adela gave her a sympathetic pat on the shoulder.

'Talking of which,' said Deborah with a wink, 'has anyone else had any "Jubbulpore" recently? Adela, you've been to see a lot of films with Tommy.'

'That's all we do.' Adela laughed. 'He doesn't even try to hold my hand. I think I'm just an excuse for him to see as many films as he can without going on his own.'

'Well, that's not very romantic,' said Prue.

'I'm really not bothered – I'm just enjoying being unattached, and he's good company.'

'Still holding out for your missionary?' Deborah nudged her.

Adela flushed. 'Course not. I've not even seen him since my birthday. He's not the least bit interested.'

'He was in the audience at the musical,' Prue said.

'Was he?' Adela was astonished.

'Up in the circle. I saw him but not to speak to.'

'Well, he never came to say hello. Was . . . was he with anyone, did you notice?'

Prue shrugged, 'I couldn't say. But it was definitely him.'

'Why didn't you say anything?' Adela cried.

'Sorry, I forgot.'

'Mind too full of the wonderful Guy,' Deborah teased. Prue gave her a shove.

'Anyway, I didn't think you were interested. I mean I know he's good-looking,' said Prue, 'but he is a bit odd.'

'No, he's not!'

Deborah was grinning, obviously bursting to tell. 'Well, do you want to hear my latest Jubbulpore?'

'Of course,' said Adela.

'I got a letter from that American who gave Daddy the Camel cigarettes, Micky Natini. He's coming to Simla on leave next week, and he's going to take me out to dinner.'

'Dinner?' Prue gasped. 'Just the two of you?'

'Well, maybe not dinner,' Deborah backtracked, 'but he said he would look me up.'

'So what did he say exactly?' asked Adela.

Deborah took off her sunglasses and chewed the end before replying. 'He said he was coming to Simla.'

'And what else?' Prue pressed her.

'And could I recommend any good restaurants.'

Adela and Prue burst out laughing.

Prue smirked. 'Not quite Jubbulpore then.'

'Okay, not yet,' admitted Deborah, 'but wait till he sees me in my chambermaid's outfit.' She dissolved into raucous giggles.

Micky Natini turned out to be a good addition to the summer parties. A smallish squat young man with dark Mediterranean good looks and a thick moustache, he was humorous and ready to enjoy himself after eight months in the Burmese jungle supervising pipe laying through the oilfields.

He arrived in Simla on a noisy motorcycle, which he had to leave garaged below the main town, unaware of the prohibition on motorised vehicles along the Mall.

'Only the Viceroy, Governor of the Punjab, or Chief of the Army can drive through the town,' Deborah explained.

'Gee, you Brits just love making up rules.' Micky chuckled.

He organised games of softball at picnics, taught them jive steps on Fluffy's veranda and smuggled in cigarettes and bottles of gin. Deborah basked in his attention – 'He thinks I look swell in my maid's outfit!' she snorted with amusement – and on his final evening took her out to dinner at the Grand Hotel.

'Write to me and be my girl?' Micky pressed her before he left. She knew her parents probably wouldn't approve – her mother was a bit of a snob about colonials and Americans – but she knew he was lonely in his jungle posting, and she had fallen a little bit in love with his enthusiastic charm. He'd kissed her under a cloudy night sky, the air about them moist and chill.

'Who needs stars when your pretty eyes light up the night?' said Micky.

After he left, Deborah pined for him more and more and was still repeating his romantic words to her friends by the time term started.

***

Prue and her mother left for Jubbulpore in early October.

'Tommy and I are going to miss you so much,' said Adela, hugging her friend goodbye. 'The Simla Songsters won't be the same without you.'

As the first snow flurries of November arrived, the foresters came plodding back from camp into Simla on tired ponies and laden mules. By this time Edith Bracknall was chivvying her husband back to temperate Lahore and their winter social calendar of dinner dances, polo matches and tennis tournaments.

'He's Master of the Lodge,' Mrs Bracknall told Adela on the last of her many casual calls to the office to check up on her husband, 'so it's very important for him to be there for the start of the cold season. And everyone's leaving now the weather is turning. Will you be staying here or coming to Lahore HQ, dear?'

The older woman eyed her keenly. She was thin, almost scrawny at the neck and arms, her face deeply lined under greying hair. She must have been pretty once, thought Adela; her blue eyes still were.

'Staying here, Mrs Bracknall.'

She saw the relief on the woman's face. 'Oh well, no doubt we'll see you next season – unless you've gone off in search of stardom.'

'You never know.' Adela smiled.

Suddenly Edith leant forward and dropped her voice. 'Our son Henry works as a radio presenter for the BBC in London.'

'Really?' Adela's eyes widened. 'Mr Bracknall's never mentioned it.'

'No.' Edith looked sad. 'He's not very proud of poor Henry Junior. Wanted him to join the ICS or at least the forces. Doesn't think much to entertainment.'

'Well, I think it's marvellous,' said Adela. 'Lucky Henry, I say.'

For a moment Edith covered her hand with cool bony fingers. 'Thank you, dear.'

The snow came in earnest, and the British residents of the town who remained through the winter – Boz and Guy among them – took to the slopes of Prospect Hill with tin trays for tobogganing and skated on the frozen pond at Annandale. Guy showed interest in Adela, but she kept him at arm's length, knowing how Prue would never forgive her; she valued her friendship far more than any liaison with the handsome forester.

It galvanised her to arrange a trip home to Belgooree for Christmas. She hadn't been home since the previous one; Scout, their beloved hill dog, had died in March, and by staying away she kept him alive in her mind. She knew it was nonsensical and, once she saw her parents' delight at her homecoming, Adela felt guilty for staying away.

Clarrie squeezed her daughter so tightly, Adela squeaked that she couldn't breathe.

Wesley protested, 'You've cut off all your lovely hair!'

'No, I haven't, Dad.' Adela laughed. 'It's still down to my shoulders.'

'I'm Dad now, am I?' Wesley raised an eyebrow.

'Daddy sounds a bit babyish, don't you think?'

'Your hair is lovely,' said Clarrie. 'It suits you that length. You look so grown-up, my darling.'

'Too grown-up,' Wesley chuntered. 'I bet all the boys are chasing you like bees around honey.'

'Do bees chase honey?' Adela teased. 'I thought they made it.'

'You know what I mean, you cheeky girl.'

Adela hugged him, breathing in the dusty tea smell of his jacket, and was glad to be home. Four-year-old-brother, Harry, after some initial shyness, followed like her shadow, even when she retreated to the bathroom for some privacy. He was much more talkative and less solemn than a year ago.

Best of all, her beloved honorary aunties, Sophie and Tilly, were coming with their husbands for Christmas again. But right from their arrival there was tension and bickering between Tilly and James. James did not linger, but took nine-year-old Mungo home after two days to join in a hunt in the Naga Hills around Kohima.

'If Tilly won't take him home to school,' grunted James to Wesley, 'I might as well be teaching the lad to shoot.'

Later, Tilly confided to the women, 'He's insisting this is Mungo's last year in Assam. He's put his foot down. Once the boy's ten, then it's off to school in England to join his brother and sister. But he's not as independent as Jamie and Libby – he's still such a home boy really. He'll hate it.'

Clarrie put a hand on her friend's in sympathy. 'Wouldn't James consider somewhere like Bishop Cotton in Simla? We're hoping Harry might go there in time – Adela's been so happy in Simla.'

'Yes,' Adela agreed, 'and Uncle Rafi went there, didn't he?'

Sophie nodded. 'It's a very good school.'

Tilly looked uncomfortable. 'I wouldn't mind but – well, James is more old-fashioned. Still believes an English education is the best.'

'Or Scottish,' Adela added with a wink at Sophie.

But Sophie bristled. 'You mean as long as Mungo doesn't have to go to school with Indians.'

Tilly's plump face reddened. 'It's not the way I think.' She gave an apologetic shrug.

'Of course it isn't,' Clarrie said, intervening. 'So will you be taking Mungo back this coming summer?'

'Yes.' Tilly sighed. 'We'll book a passage in July probably – have the summer holidays with Mona in Dunbar and then settle him into school.'

'Perhaps I could go with you for a visit home,' Clarrie suggested.

'Really?' Tilly brightened.

'I've been putting off going to see Olive for years, but her letters worry me. She sounds full of anxiety about Jack's business. Things are very tough on Tyneside these days.'

'But Olive has Herbert's Café too, doesn't she?' Tilly asked.

'Yes,' said Clarrie. 'I handed that over to her when we returned to India in '22. With Lexy in charge as manageress, I never worried about Olive coping. But that was before the slump. I should have gone back ages ago to make sure she was managing, but then Harry came along unexpectedly.' Clarrie gave a bashful smile.

'Well, you've had enough on your plate here,' said Sophie. 'It's been hard for the small tea plantations too.'

'All of the gardens,' Tilly said. 'Even the Oxford Estates have had to tighten their belts and cut back production. Doesn't seem to effect James's whisky consumption at the club though.'

Adela feared her aunt was going to start one of her long grumbles about Uncle James, which made everyone else uncomfortable. Sophie in particular was fond of the gruff tea planter, as he had been kind to her when she'd been orphaned and had paid for her education in Edinburgh. Adela and her mother also felt a little sorry for James being the constant butt of Tilly's complaints about life in Assam without her two elder children.

'I wouldn't worry about the café, Mother.' Adela tried to lighten the conversation. 'Cousin Jane seems to be running it with Lexy these days, and her letters are always cheerful.'

'Why don't you come with us too, Adela?' Tilly enthused. 'Wouldn't it be a grand idea, Clarrie?'

'Yes,' agreed Clarrie, smiling at her daughter, 'it would be wonderful – if we can afford the passage for us both, and Harry of course. You have no memories of Newcastle, do you, darling? And you could finally meet your cousin Jane.'

Adela hesitated. Yes, she would love to meet her Newcastle family, but right now she was having so much fun in Simla that she didn't want to go thousands of miles away.

'Well, I'd love to visit England – of course I would – but I wouldn't want to go for too long. It would be right in the middle of the theatre season, and I might lose my job at the Forest Office.'

'You're bound to pick something else up when you get back,' Sophie said. 'Boz will make sure of that. Take the opportunity to travel when it's offered, I say.'

'Speaks the woman who's hardly been out of Gulgat in years.' Tilly chuckled.

'Travel's more fun for the young and fancy-free.' Sophie grinned.

'But it's not really up to Boz,' Adela persisted. 'It's the Chief Conservator who did me a favour in the first place by creating a job in the post room and having me type up the occasional letter for him.'

'Who is chief now?' Sophie queried.

'Mr Bracknall,' said Adela. 'He's back in Lahore now but—'

'*Bracknall?*' Sophie cut in, her smile vanishing. 'He's still in charge?'

'Is he the awful man who made life hell for Rafi?' Tilly asked.

Sophie took a moment to answer, her manner suddenly agitated. 'Yes, he's the reason Rafi left the forest service.' Abruptly she reached out to Adela and seized her hand. 'He's a vindictive bastard!'

'Sophie!' Clarrie remonstrated.

'I'm sorry to use such language, Clarrie, but Adela shouldn't be working for him. He preys on young women.'

'Surely a man in that position wouldn't behave—'

'He poisoned my first marriage to Tam – made up lies about me and Rafi, humiliated Tam—'

Adela winced from her tight grip, alarmed to see her aunt so upset. 'It's fine. He hasn't tried anything improper; he's an old man.'

'He's only in his fifties. I can't believe Boz would allow you anywhere near him.'

Adela didn't like to say that Boz had been far away in the mountains until a month ago, by which time the Bracknalls had gone. And there had been moments when Bracknall's hand had lingered too long on her shoulder as she'd typed or when he had made her blush with comments about her appearance and pressed her for information about the men who courted her. But none of it added up to very much.

'Please don't worry about me, Auntie Sophie. I can look after myself.' Adela made light of the matter. 'Besides, Mrs Bracknall is an eager chaperone – she comes round to the office almost every day.'

'Sophie,' Tilly weighed in, 'aren't you making too much of this? Adela is just doing a few hours of typing and sorting the post – and I bet there are half a dozen other staff around too. What's the harm in that?'

Sophie let go of Adela's hand and sank back in her chair, still shaking.

'I'm sorry. It was just a shock to hear he was still around. I thought he would have retired by now and Edith Bracknall would have set up as the burra memsahib of some Hampshire village.'

'It's she who doesn't want to go apparently,' said Adela. 'Can't bear to be without a house full of servants and the status that comes with her husband's rank.'

Sophie retorted, 'I bet it suits Bracknall to blame his wife for his clinging on to power. It's he who thrives on it all.'

'Well,' Clarrie said, turning to her daughter, 'I don't like the sound of this Bracknall. I think you should definitely consider a trip back to England next year.'

'I agree,' said Sophie. She fumbled for a silver cigarette case. 'Do you mind if I smoke?'

'Go ahead,' Clarrie allowed. 'You've had a shock. Adela, we'll speak to your father and see what he thinks. We'd go for three or four months I suppose.'

'No point going all that way for less,' Tilly declared.

Adela's heart sank at the thought of being away from India that long, yet she could see her mother's interest sparking. After Adela's escape from St Ninian's, her mother had opened up about her past as never before. Adela had been left with the impression that Clarrie had never been that happy in England. Life had been quite a struggle until she'd married the elderly Herbert after being his housekeeper. At least that's what her father had told her. *Your mother ran the most successful teahouse in Newcastle,* Wesley had said proudly. *Built it up from nothing – and in the roughest part of town. A marvellous businesswoman, your mother. I had to marry her to stop her putting the Robsons out of business!* It was her father's perennial joke that always made her mother laugh and throw cushions at him.

But Adela could tell that Clarrie hankered after seeing her sister again. They were both growing older, and it would be up to her mother to make the journey. Olive, according to Cousin Jane, hardly left their neighbourhood and had no desire whatsoever to return to India.

To divert the conversation, Adela decided to tell them the gossip she had been storing up for her aunts. She had kept it quiet from her parents up till now too, not wanting them to question her about it.

'Guess who turned up out of the blue in Simla just before the monsoon.'

'Give us a clue,' Tilly said, her interest piqued.

'He's a missionary in the Narkanda hills and he used to have a pet monkey.'

She watched Tilly's jaw drop and Sophie's eyes widen.

‘Not Sam Jackman?’ Tilly gasped.

Adela nodded.

‘A *missionary*?’

‘Well a sort of missionary-cum-farmer.’ Adela smiled.

‘Good to hear he’s alive and well,’ said Clarrie.

‘Start at the beginning,’ said Tilly, ‘and tell us all you know.’

Adela had a sudden stomach lurch that she had been unwise to spill her secret, but she was keen to steer the conversation away from Bracknall. Besides, talking about Sam at least brought him closer as they conjured him up in their conversation – and that was better than nothing.

***

Restless: that was how Sam felt these days. Climbing up through snow-laden oaks to the crest of Hatu Peak, he stopped to catch his breath. He had come to take a cine film, but the arc of the Himalayas had disappeared behind lowering clouds; the air was stingingly cold, and he was glad of his yak hat with its warm flaps and his Tibetan coat. He was going mad sitting indoors all day. He couldn’t endlessly read like the Reverend Hunt, his fellow missionary. Hunt was a genial but private man, content in his own company and a house full of books.

Sam found the winter months frustrating, with not enough to do in the orchards to keep him occupied. He enjoyed visiting the locals in their homes, especially on festival days, such as Christmas, but he was no good at preaching religion or telling Bible stories like Hunt was; he preferred to help them mend their gardening tools and champion their causes with the local landowner over rents or harvests.

‘Don’t get involved in local politics,’ Hunt had warned. ‘Things are very sensitive these days, and we don’t want the mission closed down.’

Fatima’s clinic would not return until the snows melted, so he didn’t have her welcome company either. She was a handsome woman with beautiful eyes, and he always felt a lifting of the spirits when her grave expression broke into a rare smile. He knew she only smiled or laughed for those who earned her respect – or possibly her affection.

But it wasn't the dedicated doctor who robbed him of his peace of mind; it was the thought of Adela Robson being a day and a half's ride down the road in Simla. How surprised he had been to hear from his friend Boz, the hearty Scotsman who had befriended him two summers ago on his way up to Spiti, that Adela was living so close by. He had assumed she would have been packed off to England to finish her schooling far from the wagging tongues of Assam, so had been amazed to find that she had ended up at St Mary's and was making a name for herself in the local theatre.

He had stepped willingly into Guy Fellows's shoes to make up the numbers at Adela's birthday supper, for he was curious to learn more about the headstrong, impishly pretty girl who had shaken him out of his quiet life four years previously. Ducking under the lamplit trees of Fluffy Hogg's bungalow that June evening, he had caught his breath at the sight of the beautiful woman at the top of the veranda steps. Her dark, lustrous hair was piled up, revealing a slender neck and bare shoulders, her shapely figure and slim legs flattered by a shimmering pink dress. As he'd stepped closer, feeling ridiculously gauche in Boz's old dinner suit, he'd realised that this woman with the large eyes and heart-shaped face was Adela.

She had rushed to greet Boz, while Sam had hung back in the shadows, trying to compose himself, but when Boz had stepped aside to introduce him, Sam had bounded up the steps and stuck out his hand. For a moment Adela had just stared at him as if he had dropped out of the trees; whether it was a look of disbelief or disappointment, he was still not sure. But she had recovered quickly and shaken his hand – neat, warm fingers that had lain in his rough palm and set off a hammering of excitement in his chest – until he had pulled away, quite unnerved at her effect on him.

There had been a lot of small talk and excited giggling among Adela and her friends, while he had talked politics with the amiable Sikh surveyor Sundar and tried to engage Fatima in conversation about the clinic. But Fatima was happy to sit back and let the others talk; observation was what the doctor did best. Yet it was Adela whose curiosity had overridden social niceties; it was she who had questioned him about the crises in his life that had led to his new start in Narkanda. She was different from her friends – more enquiring and mature in thought and yet with the same thirst for life as any seventeen-year-old.

He was unsettled by the intense look she gave him with her brown-green eyes framed by thick dark lashes, her creamy skin flawless in the candlelight. He had felt almost winded by her scrutiny and yet he had spilled out his story, unable to stop himself. Her young friends had squirmed with discomfort, but Adela had made a joke and diffused the strained atmosphere. Why had it seemed so important that he tell her about Dr Black saving him from the gutter? Was it because she had once confided in him so completely about her Anglo-Indian origins and the school bullies?

Sam had not intended to continue with them to the dance – he was a hopeless dancer and he was a fish out of water in such glittering palaces as Davico's Ballroom – but Adela had been keen for him to join them. Or perhaps it had just been politeness, for she had been inundated with requests from other young men to dance and her promise of a waltz (the only dance he half knew) had come to nothing. The odious Bracknall, reeking of hair oil and ogling the young women, had monopolised Adela for the slow dance.

He remembered craving a cigarette, so when Adela had slipped out, he had suggested to Mrs Hogg that he make sure she was all right and gone in pursuit. Adela and he had smoked together, and Sam had felt the tension fall away as they stood side by side under the bright moon. So why had he spoilt the moment by lecturing her on Bracknall as if she were a child without a will of her own? For a dangerous moment he had thought he would kiss her, felt an overpowering urge to pull her into his arms and smother her moist cherry-red lips with hungry kisses, but he had drawn back.

What could he possibly offer her apart from a snatched moonlit embrace? He had no wealth or security and had sworn to dedicate his life to the work of the mission. He was single and unencumbered by emotional ties of any kind; life was a lot simpler and more bearable that way. So he had turned his back on Adela's amorous looks and playful words, and she had taken the hint and ignored him for the rest of the evening.

Then why had he made excuses to go back to Simla a couple of weeks later and slip into the Gaiety Theatre to watch her perform on stage? Late summer and the apple-picking season had come as a blessed relief; weeks of mindless labour, picking, packing, hauling heavy boxes and getting the produce to market. If he had any energy left at the end of a hard day's graft, Sam would organise a game of cricket among the villagers or ride up Hatu to see the sunset burning through the brown oaks.

But however much he exhausted himself physically, Sam could not rid his mind of thoughts of Adela. She came to him on the edge of sleep, a laughing sensual face and a swaying body in a pink dress who robbed his peace of mind and left him sweating and full of frustrated desire long into the night. Tormented, he would take himself in hand and slake his lust on his narrow single bed, falling asleep for a few hours of blessed oblivion, yet waking ashamed at his nocturnal weakness. He prayed hard that he would overcome such desires and accept his celibate life. It was the hardest part of being a missionary. In Assam there had been no shortage of bored British wives looking for seduction and brief liaisons; Sam had been happy to oblige, for these women wanted no emotional involvement beyond a broad shoulder to cry on.

Retreating from Hatu Mountain that day in late December, Sam packed a small haversack of provisions, told Reverend Hunt that he was going hiking for a few days, and set off for Simla. Part walking, part hitching lifts in a milk cart and a timber wagon, Sam arrived in Simla the following day with no clear idea of what he would do.

Boz was out of town for two weeks of leave, Sundar told him when Sam tracked him down to his modest digs in Number Four of the United Services Club barracks. The rows of identical flats were built of deodar and so seasoned by the harsh winters they were almost black, but looking picturesque with overhanging icicles.

'Gone back up to Quetta to visit old friends. He's a Pathan at heart – a tartan Pathan!' Sundar laughed at his own joke. 'Stay here. I can put up a camp bed in my sitting room in a jiffy, as you Britishers say.'

Sam took no persuading and spent three enjoyable days in the Sikh's lively company, strolling the town, whiling away hours at the Simla Coffee House playing draughts and talking politics, skating at Annandale and eating at Sundar's favourite Punjabi café, where they served Lahori dishes of spicy dal and golden puffs of wheat glistening with ghee.

'Hassan serves the best puri outside Lahore,' Sundar declared, belching contentedly. 'I'd have had to return home a long time ago if it hadn't been for him. Isn't that so, Hassan?' He clapped a hairy hand on the café owner's back.

'That is so.' Hassan gave a gap-toothed grin under thick moustaches.

Over many cups of tea – Sam having refused the whisky that Sundar kept for guests – they talked late into the evening. Sam learnt of the loss of Sundar's wife and his pride in his ten-year-old son, Lalit, whose school photograph hung above the small fireplace.

'You would like him,' said Sundar, his eyes glistening. 'He loves cricket – he's a fast bowler. And he can hunt with a hawk.'

'Is that for swooping on the ball at the boundary?' Sam teased. 'You must miss him.'

Sundar nodded and cleared his throat. 'So when are you going to find a wife and sire a healthy son to carry on the name of Jackman?'

Sam laughed with embarrassment. 'No time soon.'

'You must marry,' Sundar encouraged, 'some pretty British rose to keep you company up in the hills. Or you will grow old too quickly.' The Sikh gave him a wicked grin. 'Perhaps someone has already caught your eye.'

'Such as?' Sam drained his tea.

'Miss Adela Robson.'

Sam spluttered into his cup.

'So I guessed correctly,' Sundar said in triumph.

'Not on her part.' Sam laughed wryly.

'That's where you are wrong, my friend. Dr Khan says that Miss Robson asks about you every time she sees her.'

'Does she?' Sam felt his pulse begin to thud. Did Adela have feelings for him after all, or was she just being curious? 'Is she . . . has she . . . is she being courted, do you know?'

Sundar chuckled. 'Half of Simla was in love with her and her pretty friends last summer. But is there not thrill in the chase, young Jackman?'

'Perhaps.' Sam laughed. 'And you, Sundar,' he said, deflecting the attention. 'What about you and the fair Dr Khan?'

He'd never seen Sundar blush before, but he did so to the roots of his magnificently groomed beard.

'Ah, a man can dream,' said Sundar. Abruptly he got up and turned away, staring into the dying fire. 'If I thought she would say yes,' he murmured, 'I would ask her tomorrow and not care what my family thought.'

***

Sam called at Briar Rose Cottage early the next morning under a clear blue sky, his spirits lifting at the sight of the glistening, snow-capped Himalayas in the far distance. Fluffy Hogg was taking her *chota hazri* of tea and toast on the veranda, wrapped up warm in her husband's old army coat and reading a newspaper.

'Mr Jackman, how very nice to see you!'

'Call me Sam, please.' He grinned as they shook hands.

'Will you join me for breakfast? Noor can scramble you some eggs. I didn't know you were in town.'

'I've been staying at Sundar's. And breakfast would be very welcome, thank you.'

They sat and chatted as the sun spread across the sparkling trees, melting the morning frost. Sam kept glancing into the bungalow, wondering when Adela would rise from sleep, impatient to see her.

'It's so good to have young company again.' Fluffy smiled. 'I can't tell you how much I'm missing Adela, so your coming here is a real tonic.'

'Adela isn't here?'

'She went home to Belgooree for Christmas,' said Fluffy. 'Won't be back for another week or so. Oh dear, I can see you are disappointed. No doubt that's why you came.'

Sam hid his dismay. 'Not at all. It's a pleasure to call on the most delightful and interesting person in Simla.'

'Charming, but untrue.' Fluffy laughed.

They talked some more about life beyond the cosseted world of Simla and the troubles in far-off Europe: Hitler's Nazis wiping out all opposition in Germany, Fascist Italy's land grab in East Africa and civil war in Spain.

‘They tell me that even in England young men dress like militia in black uniforms and parade through the towns.’ Fluffy shook her head in disbelief. ‘I’m glad I chose to stay here in retirement. Though India is also changing, of course.’

Sam nodded. ‘We’re impatient for change here too.’

She gave him a considering look. ‘Do you see yourself as Indian, Sam?’

He shrugged. ‘I know I’m British, but India is my country. I have no wish to live anywhere else.’

‘Yes.’ Fluffy smiled. ‘I’m exactly the same.’

Chapter 7

Simla, 1938

Adela returned to Simla in January, the trip with her mother and Auntie Tilly set in motion and their passages booked for July. The end of the holiday had been marred by the fuss over Bracknall. Sophie had been uncharacteristically tearful and upset with Rafi on discovering that her husband had known all along from Boz that his former boss was still in position. Rafi said he had kept it to himself so as not to upset her. Yet Rafi had been aghast to hear that Adela had been working for the hated man. Their virulent dislike of the chief forester baffled Adela, but neither Sophie nor Rafi would explain their strong revulsion, other than to say that Bracknall was a bully who in the past had made their life hell. So Adela had promised that she would look for a job somewhere else if Bracknall should return in the hot season.

'Don't stay away so long again,' Wesley had urged when hugging his daughter goodbye. 'Your mother and I miss you terribly, and Harry will wander round like a lost puppy, I know it. And if you are all going to desert me in July, I must see you before then.'

'You will, I promise.' Adela burrowed in like she used to as a girl and gave him an extra hard squeeze around his waist.

'How about I arrange that hunting trip in Gulgat with Rafi before the monsoons? We've been meaning to do that for ages, haven't we?'

'Yes, let's,' Adela agreed, although her appetite for hunting had waned as her passion for the stage had soared. Still, she wouldn't miss a chance to go on shikar with her father.

'It'll be your birthday treat in June,' promised Wesley.

***

Adela was touched by the enthusiastic welcome she received from Fluffy Hogg.

'How I've missed you! It's been so quiet; don't stay away so long next time. Now what would you like for supper? I thought kedgeree.'

Adela was just as pleased to be back in Simla, catching up with Deborah and other friends. At the theatre, where *Jack and the Beanstalk* was in its final week, Tommy greeted her dramatically.

'Thank goodness you're back – the pantomime is on its knees. Another of the chorus has gone down with laryngitis. You must save the day.'

Adela went on that night, coping with multiple costume changes and dancing as a fairy, a maid and a flower. Helping behind the scenes before Christmas, she had watched them in rehearsal and remembered the routines easily. After the final curtain call, the cast repaired to The Cottage – the Club annex, where women could mix with men – and partied late into the night. As they left, Tommy was already talking about what productions they would put on for the summer season.

'I think we should do another of those exotic tableaux,' he enthused, '*The Arabian Nights* perhaps, and invite any visiting nawabs and rajas to take part. The Viceroy is keen to encourage greater mixing of the races – thinks it'll keep those Congress agitators happy.'

Adela gave a wry smile. 'I think Gandhi and Nehru are looking for a bit more than just Indian princes performing at the Gaiety.'

'Well, we've got to do our bit towards extending the hand of friendship.' Tommy winked.

***

The flurry of holidaymakers over the Christmas season soon scattered and Simla experienced a lull in social activities. The theatre closed for redecoration and would be used by Indian drama groups before the annual migration of government departments and personnel at the start of the hot season.

There was little for her to do in the Forest Office, and the amiable Guy had been sent off on a course in silviculture to the college at Dehra Dun so Adela quickly grew bored. She and Tommy spent a lot of time at the cinema together. Wet, blustery weather set in that brought down trees and smothered the mountains in thick mist for days on end. The air smelt of sodden earth and pines.

'Ah, reminds me of holidays in the Scottish Highlands,' said Fluffy, relishing the stormy weather and insisting on taking Adela out for walks. 'Breathe in that air. Isn't it so invigorating?'

From the top of Jakko Hill, they held on to their hats and leant into the wind as if invisible arms held them up. Looking north-east towards the forested hills of Bashahr province, Fluffy said, 'I quite forgot to tell you. Sam Jackman paid me a visit while you were away.'

Adela's stomach flipped at the unexpected mention. 'Did he?'

'Yes, he was down visiting Sundar; it's nice they've become friends, isn't it? I often think Sundar is still sad about his wife, despite putting on a brave face all the time.'

'So what did Sam have to say?'

'We talked a lot of current affairs. He's very knowledgeable about such things despite being cut off in the hills – such a nice young man. I think he was sorry not to see you.'

'Did he say so?' Adela blushed.

'Well not exactly, but I'm sure he didn't just come to see a wrinkled old widow like me.'

Adela linked arms with Fluffy. 'You're not at all wrinkled. And by the sounds of it he enjoyed his visit.'

'He did stay till after tiffin.' Fluffy smiled. 'We found so much to talk about. I think he must get quite lonely in Narkanda.'

In the last week in January, Boz took Adela and Fluffy to a Burns Night at Clarkes Hotel, where the Scots in the community put on dinner and entertainment in honour of their famous bard. After much whisky and reciting of poems, the tables were shoved back, a Gurkha piper struck up a reel and they danced late into the evening. Emerging into a suddenly starlit night, the women decided to walk home rather than take a rickshaw, Boz insisting on escorting them to their door.

'What's going on down there?' Adela asked, peering into the Lower Bazaar. Most of the lights were out, but she could make out shadowy figures hanging things between the trees and the balconies of tightly packed houses.

Boz gave a grunt. 'They're putting out the Congress flags for Freedom Pledge Day.'

‘Of course,’ said Fluffy. ‘It’s the twenty-sixth tomorrow. I wonder who will be speaking.’

‘They get bolder every year,’ Boz said. ‘No doubt there’ll be some bigwig sent from Delhi to put fire in their bellies and stir up the coolies from the hill states.’

‘The Praja Mandal movement, you mean?’ asked Fluffy. ‘Is it having any success?’

‘Aye, there have been disturbances up in Dharmi and Nerikot. It’s just a matter o’ time before the rulers bow tae pressure.’

‘Pressure to do what?’ Adela asked.

‘They want changes like abolishing the old serfdom,’ explained Boz, ‘where the rajas’ people have tae work for free so many months a year.’

‘Sounds like a good thing, doesn’t it?’

‘Aye.’ Boz dropped his voice to a murmur. ‘But the government doesnae like anything that rocks the boat with the princely states. We like to have good relations wi’ them.’

Adela gave him a knowing look. ‘So you can extract their timber and employ their coolies I suppose.’

‘Exactly,’ Boz agreed.

Adela gazed down at the covert activity; she could just make out the Ganj, the open area in the heart of the bazaar, where a platform was being decorated. ‘Will it be quite a spectacle? We weren’t allowed to go anywhere near it when I was at school.’

‘I’ve never been,’ said Boz. ‘It’s frowned upon for government servants to be seen there – CID keep an eye on who goes to listen. You’d better steer clear, in case Bracknall gets tae hear about it. That’ll be the end of your wee job at the office.’

‘Well, no one can stop me,’ Fluffy declared, ‘from going to listen to the speeches.’

***

Adela hadn’t intended to go – it was a raw day with a biting wind and flurries of sleet – but returning at lunchtime for tiffin, she found Fluffy on the point of leaving for the Ganj.

‘You’re not going on your own.’ Adela was firm.

‘I don’t want to get you into trouble, my dear,’ Fluffy was anxious.

'I sort out camp beds and file post.' Adela laughed. 'No one's going to worry about a minion like me.'

They skirted the Mall, taking the steep steps opposite the theatre down to the Lower Bazaar. They could hear the demonstration before they saw it, a cacophony of drumming, singing, shouting and horns. The streets were crammed with Indians come to take part or watch the procession along the lower road. A phalanx of young men and a few women (dressed in homespun cotton under woollen jackets that marked them out as Gandhi's followers) carried aloft the tricolour flags of the Congress Party, while behind them pressed scores of hills men in their bright caps. Many of the town's porters and a smattering of office workers swelled the crowd too.

'It's a bit of a scrum,' Fluffy faltered.

'Are you sure you want to go on, Auntie?'

'I'm still keen to hear the speeches.'

'Come on then; we'll just stay for a little longer.' Adela linked her arm protectively through her guardian's and they jostled forward towards the Ganj.

They couldn't get near enough to hear what the speakers were saying, apart from a few snatched words of Hindustani about *swaraj*, which Adela knew to mean freedom, and how soon the Britishers must leave India to the Indians. Adela saw a stocky youngish man take to the stage dressed in simple Punjabi *shalwar kameez* and a black beret.

'Looks like a communist,' Fluffy surmised.

He raised his fist in the air and saluted the crowd, his face animated. He shouted above the hubbub and soon they were cheering and repeating his slogans. There was something oddly familiar about him, but Adela couldn't possibly know him.

'Oh dear,' Fluffy said, tugging on her arm. 'Looks like trouble.'

Adela tore her gaze away from the speaker and his mesmerising performance and looked round. Blocking the steps from where they'd come were dozens of police armed with their long baton-like lathis. Her stomach tensed. Abruptly the officer in charge raised a loudhailer and bellowed out commands in Hindustani for the crowds to disperse. He repeated them in Urdu and English.

'Go home! Your demonstration is over. This meeting is breaking the law. Go home now and no one will get hurt!'

The fiery speaker made some repost, standing his ground, but at the sight of ranks of police, the crowd began to break up. The other activists on the stage spoke urgently to the communist, who remonstrated with the police in their attempts to close down the meeting. But soon his supporters were bundling him off the stage.

At this the police officer barked an order, and his men began to push forward, cutting a line through the melee towards the stage. Adela and Fluffy were elbowed and shoved as people tried to get out of the way. Pandemonium broke out.

'They're after that man,' gasped Fluffy.

'We need to get out of here,' Adela cried over the shouting and confusion.

But they were being carried by the tide of people in the opposite direction to the steps, caught in the crush. Adela seized Fluffy's arm and held on for all she was worth. There was nothing to be done but let themselves be carried along. Tugged and jostled, Fluffy cried out, 'My shoe – it's come off!'

'Don't stop, Auntie,' Adela screamed, heart banging with fear. 'Hold on tight.'

Suddenly a man wrapped in a cloak grabbed Fluffy's other arm and pulled.

'Let go of her!' Adela shouted.

'This way, memsa'b,' he urged. 'In here.'

'Noor?' Fluffy gasped as the cloak fell back from her bearer's face. 'How . . . ?'

He didn't answer, but hurried them into an alleyway and then through a low door. All at once they were out of the mayhem, standing in the back kitchen of a food stall, a large vat of steaming dal cooking on an open fire. The skinny boy who was tending it, gaped at them in astonishment. Noor said something to him that Adela didn't understand, except for the word 'chai'; the boy nodded and disappeared behind a curtain. Outside they could hear shouting and police whistles. Fluffy let out a gasp of relief.

'Please sit, memsa'bs.' Noor indicated a couple of low stools. 'We will wait for men to go.'

The boy reappeared with a metal tray of small glasses filled with tea and handed them round. Adela sipped gratefully at the sweet, milky *chai*, the pounding of her heart slowing. Fluffy was grey-faced, her hat askew and a shoe gone; her stockinged foot filthy.

She trembled. 'Noor, how did you come to be there?'

'I followed you, memsa'b.' Noor's lean face smiled. 'In case there was trouble.'

Fluffy's eyes welled with tears. 'Thank you. You are my guardian angel.'

'Do you know who that last speaker was?' Adela asked.

Noor shook his head. 'Someone from the city, not local.'

'What was he saying?'

'Something about the Praja Mandal,' Noor said, glancing round as if fearing he might be overheard, 'and bad things about the hill rajas.'

'The police knew him,' said Fluffy. 'That's what seemed to set them off.'

'Yes,' Adela murmured, thinking of the passionate speaker so full of energy and rage. 'I wonder if he got away.' Silently she hoped he had evaded a beating from the police sticks.

They waited half an hour and then Noor summoned a rickshaw. Rain had set in again. The bazaar was strangely deserted and quiet, the Congress flags torn down and trampled in the mud. The women sat in silence as they were pulled back up the slope to the Ridge and Jakko Hill. Noor ordered hot water for baths and more tea with cake.

'I'm so grateful, Noor,' said Fluffy, 'and feel terrible for putting you and Adela at risk.'

Noor shook his head. Adela felt full of bravado now they were safely home. 'I'm glad I went – it was a great piece of theatre.'

Fluffy gave an impatient tut. 'It's not play-acting for the Indians,' she said. 'For some people the cause of *swaraj* is a matter of life or death.'

***

The next day Adela scanned the newspaper for any mention of the meeting or the scuffles with the police, but there was none. She talked it over with Boz, who was cross that she had gone.

'Lassie, I warned you to stay away. I hope no one saw you.'

'They weren't interested in me,' she retorted. 'Who do you think the man in the beret was?'

'Some hothead by the sounds of it. There's real trouble brewing in the Hill States – Dharmi in particular – and the government is trying to keep a lid on it.'

'But surely it's up to the hill chiefs whether they decide to hand over more power to the – what do you call them? – Praja Mandal.'

Boz sighed. 'Aye, you're right, and many of us are sympathetic to their aims, but we don't want unrest spreading or things falling into the hands of extremists like the communists.'

They talked no more about it, but it preyed on Adela's mind. Up until now she had taken little interest in politics, preferring to read the magazines that Cousin Jane sent her from England rather than the piles of newspapers that Fluffy waded through each day. She knew more about what was happening in Hollywood than New Delhi, let alone the Hill States that bordered Simla.

Yet she liked the tribal women she had met through Fatima's clinics and felt ashamed that she had not been more curious about their lives beyond the daily humdrum. She wondered what Sam's opinion would be of those who came from outside the region agitating for change. Did they make life difficult for him in his mission in the hills, or did he support them? She had a vague memory that he had discussed such things at her birthday supper, but she had taken none of it in, except to steal glances at his handsome animated face.

Oh, Sam! Had he really come seeking her out just a few days before she returned from Assam, or had it just been a social call to Fluffy? Adela could not stop thinking about him. While far away in Belgooree having a busy social time with her family, she had suppressed her feelings. She had even promised herself that this coming season she would look for a romantic friendship among the many young beaux in Simla society who would come up from the hot plains in search of love. She would be eighteen in a few short months and was impatient for romance. Captain Maitland's robust kisses the previous summer had whetted her appetite for physical love, and Adela wanted to go further.

Thoughts of Sam made her discontented, and the incident at the Ganj spurred her on to seek out Fatima. She would volunteer for the clinics again. Better to be helping the hill women than rearranging camping equipment for the umpteenth time. Besides, her parents had given her a small allowance so that she could stay on in Simla until June without relying on a job at the Forest Office.

***

At the hospital they told her that Fatima was ill and hadn't been in for a couple of days. Concerned, Adela went straight round to the doctor's third-storey flat in Lakkar Bazaar, mounting the dark stairway and knocking on the door. No one came. Adela's alarm mounted. Perhaps she was too sick to come to the door. Surely her housekeeper, Sitara, a low-caste Hindu widow who had come with the doctor from Lahore, would answer. She knocked again harder and called out, 'Dr Fatima, it's me, Adela. Are you all right?'

To her relief she heard the soft tread of bare feet and the door being unlocked. It opened a fraction. Fatima peered out.

'Are you okay? They told me at the hospital that you were unwell.'

Fatima hesitated. 'I am fine thank you.'

'Can I come in? I want to talk to you about helping out at the clinics again. I know you'll start going up into the hills soon,' gabbled Adela, 'and I'd like to help. There's too little to do in the office, and I'm driving Boz mad asking for jobs.'

Again Fatima hesitated, glancing over her shoulder and then back at Adela. 'Are you alone?'

'Yes—'

'Come in quickly.' Fatima opened the door just enough to pull Adela through it, close and lock it. Fatima appeared nervous; Adela had never seen her like this before. Adela respectfully took off her shoes, then wondered if she should stay. The doctor forced a smile. 'I'm sorry; I'm being a bad hostess. Take a seat please. I'll see if Sitara can make us tea.'

While Fatima disappeared into the next room, Adela went and sat at the table in the bay window, with its plummeting view over Lakkar Bazaar. The wooden houses and open-fronted shops seemed to defy gravity, pegged to the slope by occasional trees. The day was dank and the buildings drab in the steel-grey light of the late January day.

The room was high-ceilinged and plainly furnished with the bare essentials: a table and two chairs; a large desk and reading lamp; a bookcase jammed with textbooks; an armchair; a locked medical chest; and cushions against the far wall, where Fatima preferred to sit when she didn't have company. The cushions were still rumpled. There was something amiss. A cigarette, hastily stubbed out, was still half burning in a brass ashtray on the floor. Fatima didn't smoke.

Adela stifled an amused gasp. Had the prim doctor been entertaining someone when she'd called unexpectedly? No wonder Fatima had been flustered. If so, the man must be hiding in the back or have slipped out some other way. It can't have been Sundar, for he didn't smoke. Suddenly Adela had a jealous thought that it might be Sam. She couldn't bear it to be Sam. Adela jumped out of her seat and rushed to the far door; she had to see for herself.

They looked around, startled – three figures crammed into the tiny kitchen. Fatima, the dark-skinned Sitara, and a man. Adela stared back. It was the communist speaker she had last seen being chased by police.

The man was the first to speak. He came forward, his look assessing. He didn't extend his hand in greeting but gave a fleeting smile.

'I'm Ghulam, Fatima's brother. You are Miss Robson, the Britisher she told me about who helps on the purdah ward.'

Adela nodded and blurted out, 'You're the man who spoke at the rally. I knew you were familiar. You look like Uncle Rafi.'

Fatima gasped, 'You were at the demonstration?'

'Yes, with Auntie.'

Sister and brother looked at each other and said something rapidly in Punjabi, which Adela didn't understand. He shrugged.

'Let's go into the sitting room,' Fatima said, taking charge again, 'now that the cat is out of the bag.'

Adela couldn't help glancing at Ghulam; this was the notorious younger brother who had been to prison for setting fire to the governor's car in Lahore. Like Rafi, he was an outcast from the rest of the family – apart from Fatima, who appeared to stand by her brothers whatever they did. Ghulam was shorter and stockier than Rafi, and not quite as handsome – he was square-jawed and his nose was imperfect, as if it had been broken – yet he had the same startlingly green eyes as his brother. He moved with a quick restlessness and pent-up energy.

'Why do you call my brother, Uncle?' Ghulam asked, squatting back down on the cushions. Adela joined him, tucking her legs and stockinged feet under her woollen skirt.

'Because he's married to my mother's friend Sophie – she's a pretend auntie.'

'I've never met her,' Ghulam said, 'though my sister tells me she's beautiful.'

'Very. Like a film star.' Adela smiled.

'I admire her for defying her own kind to marry my brother. Especially as your days here are numbered.'

'Ghulam,' Fatima warned.

'What do you mean by that?' Adela bristled. 'India is my country just as much as yours.'

'No, Miss Robson, it is not. Your family may have been here for a couple of generations; mine have been here for centuries. Yours are imperialists who reap the benefits of India's wealth – tea, I believe – while we Indians are supposed to be grateful for menial jobs as coolies and tea pickers.'

Adela wanted to shout out that her great-grandmother was Indian, but feared that he might be just as contemptuous of Anglo-Indians. Besides, it was none of his business.

'My parents do their best to provide for their workers,' Adela defended. 'My mother grew up among them, as did I.'

'Do you know how much they get paid? Or where they all come from?'

'Well, not exactly—'

'No, I didn't think so. It's not your fault, Miss Robson, it's the system. People like your parents are no doubt kind in a patriarchal way, but their efforts are just tinkering at the edges. The whole colonial machine of oppression must be broken up. We have been crushed by it for far too long.'

'Is that what you were saying at the demonstration?'

Ghulam gave a bitter smile. 'They don't need telling about their oppression – they experience it daily. I was giving the workers heart to press ahead with the demands for social and political change in the princely states, where they are kept like medieval serfs. But then you have been there with Fatima and know their conditions.'

'Enough, Brother,' Fatima interrupted. 'You are not on your soapbox now, and you say too much.' She gave Adela an anxious look. 'You mustn't speak of this to anyone.'

'Of course not,' Adela said, affronted that she might think she would betray them.

'Ghulam has done nothing wrong,' Fatima insisted, 'but there are those who would like to see him back behind bars. So far the police have not made the connection between my brother and me, but he cannot stay here long in case they do.'

They paused as Sitara brought in tea and gingerbread. Ghulam lit another cigarette. Adela tried to control her nervousness and act normally, as if she were not sharing afternoon tea with a hunted activist.

'Oh, my favourite. Thank you, Sitara,' said Adela, biting into the moist cake. 'Delicious.' The dark-skinned woman smiled.

'Tea and cake,' Ghulam said, his look mocking. 'So very British.'

'And Indian,' Adela sparked back. 'India's consumption of tea is catching up with Britain's – and as for cake, I bet your tooth is as sweet as mine.'

This made Fatima laugh. 'You are right. Ghulam was always the plump one for eating too many sweets.'

Adela was pleased to see his face darken in a blush. He drew heavily on his cigarette.

'So, Miss Robson, what brings you to my sister's door?'

'You do, Mr Khan, in a sort of roundabout way.' Ghulam's eyes widened. 'Your campaign to improve things for the hill people – it made me guilty that I've neglected the clinic these past few months. I've had a job at the Forest Office, you see, and I'm very involved in the theatre here.' She turned to Fatima. 'But I want to help out more this year – at least before I go to England.'

'England?' Fatima exclaimed.

'Just for a holiday.'

Adela explained all about Tilly's reluctance to take Mungo back to Britain for schooling and how she had seized on the idea of Adela and Clarrie accompanying her too.

'She thinks it will soften the blow if we go with her, and Mother is keen to visit my Aunt Olive – she hasn't seen her for fifteen years. And I suppose I'm quite looking forward to the adventure now it's being planned, as long as we don't stay away too long.'

'Adventure indeed,' Fatima said and smiled. 'I'll be happy to have as much help as you can give in the meantime.'

'Perhaps,' Ghulam mused, 'you will fall in love with your homeland and not come back. Better that you get used to it now because one day you will have to leave here for good.'

'Ghulam!' Fatima remonstrated. 'Don't be unkind.'

'I'm already in love with my homeland,' Adela said with a defiant look, 'and it's India.'

'Then you are in a minority of Britishers,' snapped Ghulam, his eyes suddenly blazing. 'The ones I have met talk of Britain as home – they are happy to take the best jobs here in India but send their children to school in England and retire there on their Indian pensions. They want, and get, the best of both worlds. But we Indians – millions of us – get no say in how we run our own country. Imagine for one minute what it would be like to be the other way around – if an elite few thousand Indians ruled in London over millions of Britishers.'

Adela tried to think what Fluffy might say. 'Things are changing – maybe not as fast as you want, but there are provincial governments now run by Congress, aren't there? And I see a lot of Indian administrators all over Simla these days.'

Ghulam gave a contemptuous laugh. 'You sound just like Rafi – he was always telling me to be more patient.'

'I'm not telling you to do anything,' said Adela, 'but I think you're being unfair to brand all us British as the same. And Indians for that matter. I know Indian rajas who don't in the least want what you want.'

'Indian princes hardly represent the masses of India,' protested Ghulam. 'It's true that we Indians have differing views on how India should be run after the Britishers leave – I want a socialist state without religious interference; my devout brother Amir has his heart set on a homeland for Moslems—'

'I want democracy and women's rights,' Fatima added eagerly.

'But we are *all* agreed on one thing,' said Ghulam. 'You Britishers must hand over power and soon.'

Adela was in awe of the passion that lit his heavy features and made him handsome, his flashing green eyes holding her gaze.

'You'd be surprised,' said Adela, 'how many of us British think the same as you. The argument is just about when we hand over, not if.'

Her empathy seemed to disarm him; he relaxed back.

'And what would you do, Miss Robson, in a free India?'

'Become a film star,' she said at once.

'Adela is a wonderful singer,' said Fatima.

'And has the looks for the silver screen too.' He gave a flash of a smile. 'I promise to watch your films when we have *swaraj*.'

Adela flushed at the compliment. 'And I promise to give you tickets to my premieres,' she sparked back.

She left shortly afterwards; they told her nothing of Ghulam's plans, and neither did she ask. 'You must tell no one of this,' Fatima warned, 'not even Mrs Hogg. And don't ask me about Ghulam when we meet. It's safer for you if you know nothing of his whereabouts.'

Adela wanted to rush home and blurt out her encounter, but promised she wouldn't.

***

Over the next few days, it was a strain to keep her secret to herself and not discuss it with either Fluffy or Boz. The situation was made worse by an impromptu visit from Inspector Pollock. Adela returned to find the tall bald police officer taking tea at Briar Rose Cottage. Fluffy said with a warning look, 'The inspector has kindly come to make sure we are all right.'

'That's kind, but why shouldn't we be?' She shook his hand.

'You were seen at the Freedom Pledge demonstration,' said Pollock, 'and we were worried you might have been caught up in the fracas.'

'I've told him we were perfectly fine,' Fluffy interjected.

'Perfectly.' Adela smiled. 'We just viewed it from afar.'

'So why were you there, Miss Robson?' he persisted. 'Do you take an interest in politics?'

'Not especially.'

'It was my idea to go,' Fluffy said, 'not Adela's at all. As you know, I've always taken an interest in current affairs.'

Adela sat down, trying not to let her alarm show, and changed the subject.

'I hope you're going to come and see our production of *The Arabian Nights*, Inspector Pollock. It's going to start the season with a bang.'

'I'm not really a theatregoer, Miss Robson, but my wife is. I'll make sure she knows about it.'

They talked about trivial matters: the change in manager at the Simla Bank, a new dinner menu at the Cecil and an art exhibition at the town hall. As he stood up to leave, he turned to Adela and asked, 'Does the name Ghulam Khan mean anything to you?'

Her heart stopped. She met his assessing grey eyes with a puzzled frown.

'No, should it do?'

'You went to hear him speak at the demonstration.'

'Well, I had no idea who he was.' Adela gave a dismissive shrug. 'I just went for the drama of the occasion. I didn't understand a word of what he said as I don't speak Punjabi.'

He scrutinised her. 'He was speaking in Urdu and Hindustani. But he's from Lahore, so Punjabi is his first tongue. Strange that you should mention it.'

'Oh goodness, I'm pretty hopeless at languages – they all sound the same, don't they?' She laughed.

'So you've never met Ghulam Khan,' he pressed.

'We never got anywhere near him, did we, Auntie?' Fluffy shook her head. 'I'm not sure I would even recognise him again, Inspector.' Adela gave a dismissive wave. 'And I don't see how I'd ever come across him.'

'Easier than you might think,' said Pollock. 'It turns out his sister is a doctor at the hospital – a friend of yours, Dr Fatima Khan.'

'Dr Fatima?' Fluffy exclaimed.

Adela's stomach clamped with fear. 'Goodness me, is that so? Well, she's never talked about him, has she, Auntie? Probably ashamed – black sheep of the family and all that.'

Fluffy was giving her an odd look; she knew very well that they had all discussed Ghulam around the dinner table, and Fatima had defended her brother as an idealist and not a terrorist.

'So you think it unlikely that Dr Khan would have harboured her brother in Simla.'

'Very unlikely,' Adela said, trying to keep her breathing even. 'She's very law-abiding.'

'Dr Khan is the most hard-working, conscientious doctor you could ever find,' said Fluffy stoutly, 'and we're lucky to have her in Simla. Adela helps out at her clinics and is most admiring of her, aren't you, my dear?'

Adela nodded. 'Have you been to see Dr Khan?' she asked as casually as possible.

'Yes,' said Pollock, 'and she claims not to have seen him in years.'

'Well, there you are then,' said Fluffy with satisfaction.

The inspector jammed on his hat and pulled on his gloves at the door. 'You will tell me if you hear anything of Ghulam Khan, won't you, Miss Robson? Especially if you venture into the hills with Dr Khan. She might know more than she's telling us, so keep your ear to the ground – we suspect that's where he's gone to make trouble.'

Adela felt distaste; he was asking her to spy on Fatima. She managed to nod and smile in agreement as they waved him away.

Fluffy made sure he was gone and out of earshot before she turned to Adela and said, 'What was all that performance about?'

'What do you mean, Auntie?'

'Pretending to be the dizzy little English memsahib with no knowledge of Indian languages. You're hiding something from me, aren't you?'

'Ask no questions, tell no lies,' Adela murmured.

Fluffy put a hand on her arm, suddenly anxious. 'You won't put yourself in danger, will you?'

Adela covered Fluffy's veined hand with her own warm one. 'Me? I'd run a mile from any danger.'

Fluffy snorted, 'I know that's not true.'

'Well, you're not to worry; I'm not mixed up in anything.'

'One day, dear girl,' Fluffy said with an affectionate pat, 'you are going to make a great actress.'

***

Adela was glad of the clinic work to keep her busy, though she often wondered where Ghulam had gone and was frustrated she couldn't talk to Fatima about him, except a hurried exchange to say she'd been questioned by Pollock.

Adela started back at the hospital, helping out on the purdah ward: rolling bandages, fetching and emptying bedpans and occasionally helping to wash and swaddle newborn babies. Labour and childbirth were still a mystery to her – she never witnessed the births – but she was astonished how all new mothers seemed to think that their crinkled, squalling infants were beautiful.

As spring arrived in the hills and lily of the valley began to carpet the wooded slopes, sending up flurries of perfume in the strengthening sun, Adela set off for Kufri with Fatima, a handful of nursing assistants and orderlies and the mobile clinic. Sitara came to cook. The nursing staff crammed into Fatima's newly bought second-hand Ford. Adela took her turn at the wheel, negotiating the narrow bends of the Hindustan-Tibet road, while the equipment followed on horse-drawn carts and strapped to mules.

After three days at Kufri they travelled on to Theog and at the end of the week struck camp again and continued on to Narkanda. Adela had never been so far up the route before. She arrived in the bustling village, her nerves in shreds after hitting patches of ice on the road. They abandoned the car near the river and continued uphill by cart and mules.

'The mission lets us camp in the grounds of their bungalow and use the washing facilities,' explained Fatima.

'Luxury indeed.' Adela gave a wry laugh. As the convoy jolted up the uneven track in the fading light through budding orchards of apple and plum, Adela's heart pounded at the thought of seeing Sam again.

They came out into a clearing; a broad sweep of pasture and a modest bungalow with a green tin roof were lit by the last rays of the sun. She sensed him there before she saw him, a quick-moving, vigorous figure emerging from the shadow. The sun struck his handsome ruddy face and caught fair lights in his wayward hair. His shirtsleeves were rolled up over strong arms as he strode towards them, grinning with delight at Fatima.

'Welcome, Dr Khan. I was beginning to worry you wouldn't arrive before it got dark . . .' He stopped in his tracks at the sight of Adela climbing off a mule in jodhpurs, her hair tangling in the evening breeze. 'Adela? I didn't realise—'

'Hello, Sam,' she said, trying to keep her voice steady. 'I hope you've got gallons of hot water, as we're desperate for baths.'

He quickly recovered his composure. 'Well, this is hardly the Cecil, but we'll see what we can do.' He smiled. 'Come inside. Hunt is away in Nerikot, so you and Fatima can use his room.'

Despite her exhaustion, Adela's heart soared at Sam's obvious delight at their arrival; she hoped it wasn't just for Fatima. She had reached elusive Narkanda at last. They ate in the shuttered veranda with kerosene lamps on the tables as the wind sighed outside and set the old bungalow creaking. They talked of their work and their plans for the next few days.

That night Adela climbed into a sagging spare bed between sheets that were damp with lack of use. Yet she couldn't have been happier, knowing that Sam lay on the other side of the wall – she could hear his bed creaking as he turned over. It was the last sound she remembered before falling asleep.

Chapter 8

The next days were full of hard work. From dawn until after dusk the medical team saw patients at the clinic that they set up on the edge of the village in the tents that Adela had donated from the Forest Office supplies. Sam called in from time to time, bringing in supplies, patching up the torn canvas where the rain leaked in, and keeping the urn topped up with water from the river. Adela was amazed that Sam seemed to know everyone, stopping to chat and joke with patients and distract the grizzling children with a conjuring trick. The locals loved him, and he did all he could to help them.

At night they returned, exhausted, to the mission house to wash away the day's grime and share simple meals of dal, vegetables and chapattis.

'I prefer this any day to the overdone chops and soggy vegetables that Hunt makes us eat,' Sam said, grinning, 'so I've got to make the most of him being away. Mind you, our cook, Nitin, makes the best rice pudding and treacle sponge in the Himalayas, so we'll keep to British puddings.'

Afterwards they would linger on the veranda steps and listen in the dark to night birds calling in the trees and the hum of insects. One evening, while Adela was sitting out with Fatima and Sam, they heard the haunting sound of a flute being played in the distance.

'That's beautiful,' gasped Adela. 'Who's playing?'

'Sounds like a Gaddi shepherd,' said Sam. 'The Gaddies are on their way back now.'

'Back from where?' asked Adela.

'The plains where they've been wintering their sheep. They're nomads. They spend the hot season in the high pastures – sometimes as high up as the dry mountains of Spiti. It's quite a sight to see them driving their flocks back up Hatu.'

'Can we go and see?' Adela enthused.

'If you can drag yourself out of bed before dawn, I'll take you up the mountain,' Sam said, 'before the clinic starts.'

'Yes, of course we will,' Adela agreed. 'Won't we, Fatima?'

'Not me.' Fatima yawned. 'I need my sleep. I'm not that interested in sheep.' She gave a dry smile that reminded Adela suddenly of Ghulam – the way their mouths twisted in lopsided amusement.

'Well, I used to get up before dawn regularly at home to go out riding with my dad,' Adela said, 'so it's no hardship for me.'

Adela slept lightly and heard Sam moving around in the next room as the predawn purple light filtered through the shutters. She pulled on her jodhpurs and a warm jacket, and then went to find him on the veranda. He was smoking a bidi. With just a word of greeting they made for the stable, where the syce was saddling up two ponies. Sam exchanged a joke with the young man, thanked him and mounted his dappled grey mare. Adela swung herself up on to a small brown pony.

They trotted up through the orchards and into the deodar forest that covered the lower slopes of Hatu. It was dark, but the ponies were sure-footed and picked their way over the rough stones of the uneven path. Adela breathed in the fresh, damp mountain air that reminded her fleetingly of Belgooree. How good it was to be in the saddle and out riding before daybreak, the trees alive with the dawn twittering of birds.

The slope became steeper, and clouds of steam rose from the ponies' nostrils and flanks as they laboured up the steep incline. Light was beginning to filter through the trees as the evergreens gave way to brown oaks. A white-faced monkey, startled by their unexpected appearance, swung overhead, screeching in alarm, then disappeared. Suddenly they were emerging into open pasture on the ridge of the mountain. Sam reined in his pony and dismounted, indicating for Adela to do the same.

'We'll watch from here,' he whispered.

In the deeply shadowed hillside, she couldn't see anything of interest, but was content to stand in the clear air while the ponies bent to graze on the dew-soaked grass. Away to the east, where the far peaks of the Himalayas were emerging out of the dark, the first pink rays of dawn seeped into the sky. As the light spread and strengthened, Adela began to pick out figures and a huddle of tents across the slope.

From far off she could hear a low rumble of hooves and high-pitched bleating. The noise grew like approaching thunder. A few minutes later scores of horned and long-haired sheep swept past them, encouraged by a turbaned elder with a long staff and his team of young shepherds. They whistled and chivvied the flock up and over the hill. As they reached the summit, the sunrise lit them in a golden light: a mass of shaggy brown, white and black sheep jostling around boys in homespun jackets, pyjamas and jaunty embroidered caps.

One of them caught sight of the watching riders. Adela waved, and the boy grinned back, waving his stick.

'What a sight!' She turned in excitement to Sam, who was taking rapid photographs with his Kodak camera.

'Smile,' he ordered on the spur of the moment, focusing on her.

Adela laughed and pulled a pose. Then he was pointing the camera back at the Gaddi shepherds, before they disappeared from view.

'Can we get nearer their camp?' she asked.

Sam nodded, stringing the camera round his neck and securing the ponies to a nearby tree. They set off on foot across the high meadow. The wet grass soon soaked Adela's shoes, but she didn't care; she was spellbound by the sparkling dew and the carpet of starlike white and yellow flowers. The whole hillside glittered like a jewel-studded blanket.

At the far side they could see the glow of early fires and smell sweet woodsmoke. Women in gaudy flared skirts belted with woollen rope were already out foraging for kindling and cutting sheaves of grass for the animals. Adela went near enough one group to hear their chatter and see the glint of silver jewellery at their wrists as they worked their knives.

Impulsively, she ran forward to greet them, pressing her palms together.

'Namaste!' she called out.

They stopped and stared. A rapid conversation ended in a peal of laughter, and then a young, pretty girl with braids of black hair stepped towards her and returned the greeting. She ran to an elderly woman who was cooking at an open fire and came back with a flat steaming chapatti – unusually golden in colour – and offered it to Adela. A gaggle of children crowded around her.

Adela turned to Sam and beckoned. 'Come on, let's share it.' She tore the hot bread in two, stuffing a piece into her mouth. It tasted strongly of corn. 'Delicious,' she said, beaming.

The women laughed and pulled their shawls over their hair as Sam came striding towards them, grinning. Munching some chapatti, he struggled with a few words, which made them laugh harder.

'What did you say to them?' asked Adela.

'I was trying to thank them,' Sam murmured, 'but maybe I've just proposed marriage.'

Adela laughed. He reverted to Hindustani and thanked them again. One of the little boys hung on to Sam's hand and pointed at his camera.

'Would you like me to take your photo?' he asked. The boy grinned. Sam asked permission of the women. There was much loud discussion, and then one of the older women decreed that he could.

Quickly he took pictures of the children, and then the young woman who had given the chapatti stepped forward and solemnly posed, regarding the camera with bold dark eyes. The older women upbraided her and chased her inside the tent.

'Time to go,' Sam said, swiftly packing away his camera in the hard brown case, 'before the men find us distracting the breakfast makers.'

Adela, wanting to give them something in return, pulled an embroidered handkerchief out of her pocket and held it out to the older woman who had sent Chapatti Girl indoors and seemed to be in charge.

'Please,' she said, smiling.

The bemused woman took it, running her work-roughened fingers over the flowers that Clarrie had once embroidered in bright silk threads. She gave Adela a gap-toothed smile of thanks. As Adela and Sam retreated, the woman was handing around the handkerchief for the others to admire.

Back at the treeline, they retrieved the horses. The sun was now up.

'Sorry I've made you late for the clinic,' Sam said with a rueful look.

'I'm not sorry at all.' Adela smiled. 'I wouldn't have missed this for anything. You'll show me the photographs someday, won't you?'

'Of course. It'll give me an excuse to come into Simla and see you.' He winked.

Adela's stomach fluttered. 'I'd like that.'

He gave her his hand and helped her up into the saddle, even though they both knew she didn't need it. She held on to his strong grip, looking down at him.

'Auntie said you called at Briar Rose Cottage while I was away at Belgooree. Did you come to see me, Sam?'

She saw the colour creep into his jaw. His hazel eyes held her look.

'Yes, I hoped you would be there.'

She squeezed his hand. 'I'm sorry I wasn't.' A muscle twitched in his lean cheek, as if he struggled with whether to tell her something.

But he dropped his hold and turned away. 'Better get you back to the mission before Fatima sends out a search party.'

Disappointed, Adela coaxed her pony into a trot and set off into the forest, leaving Sam to follow.

***

Later that day Hunt returned from Nerikot in a foul mood.

'Mandalists are causing no end of trouble. People don't feel safe to come out to prayer meetings, in case they get caught up in a demonstration.'

Scandalised to find two unchaperoned young women living under the same roof as his fellow missionary, he turfed Fatima and Adela out of his room and sent Sam off to distant Sarahan to plant more apple trees.

'Take my room,' Sam insisted to the women. 'Sorry about Hunt – he's not usually this territorial. The protests in Nerikot have unnerved him. I'll be back before you leave.'

'We need to speak,' Fatima said, taking him aside. Adela observed them in the garden, heads bent together and talking intensely. Soon afterwards Sam packed and left.

In frustration Adela watched him go. She was sure that he felt something for her, but perhaps not as deeply as she did for him. There was something about Sam Jackman that was always held in check, as if he didn't trust himself to show his true feelings. Or maybe she was wrong and he just didn't share those feelings.

She drove herself at work, filling every minute so that she wouldn't dwell on his absence. Hunt stayed out of their way and ate alone in his room, though he did help Adela collect supplies for the nomads. She persuaded Fatima to make a visit to the Gaddi encampment and take ointment, bandages, children's clothes and blankets, as it was still cold up the mountain. She liked the friendly, independent nomads, who welcomed them to their tented homes and sat around in the evening sun smoking hookahs while their women cooked and sang songs.

Only one man seemed to resent their presence and gave them hostile glances. He appeared to be the guardian of the bold young woman with the braided hair who had befriended Adela previously, for he shouted at the girl for her curiosity. The Gaddi girl – who was called Pema – stroked Adela's wavy hair and creamy skin with smiles of appreciation. Adela gave her two hair clips, which delighted Pema but enraged the older man. He hit the girl with a stick and chased her inside the tent. When Adela and Fatima protested, the man snarled at them to leave. The others seemed afraid of him. How Adela wished that Sam could have been there to stand up to the bullying man; Adela was worried that he obviously mistreated Pema.

Lying at night on a camp bed in Sam's room under one of his blankets, next to his bed where Fatima slept, Adela was consumed with thoughts of him. A week later there was still no sign of him.

Just before they were due to return to Simla, two agitated Gaddi shepherds appeared at the clinic carrying a young woman bundled in cloths and shrieking in pain. While the woman had been sitting by the fire, someone had knocked over a cauldron of boiling water and badly scalded her right side from her hand to her cheek.

Adela gasped in horror. 'It's Pema!'

Fatima got to work immediately, tending and binding her burns.

'From the looks of it they delayed bringing her here,' Fatima said in frustration. 'One of her wounds is infected.'

Adela tried to calm Pema and hide how upset she was to see her new friend in such agony. She kept watch at the clinic overnight. The men wished to take her straight back to the camp, but Fatima was adamant Pema should stay in their care.

'She's feverish and shouldn't be moved; her injuries are serious.'

The young men said that they were due to move on very soon to Spiti, where they had grazing rights.

'We'll take good care of her at the mission,' Adela promised. They seemed nervous about leaving the girl behind, but reluctantly went.

Fatima delayed their return to Simla, deeply worried about her patient. 'Thinking of that bullying man,' she said, 'it makes me wonder if it was really an accident.'

That night Pema's temperature soared and she babbled incoherently. Adela stayed by her side, singing to her softly and wiping her brow, occasionally allowing one of the auxiliaries to take over while she snatched some sleep. After three days Pema's fever went, and she was comfortable enough to move up to the mission bungalow. Even though her face was still half-hidden in a dressing, Pema rewarded Adela with her wide smile. They made a bed on the floor in Sam's room, where the girl was happier than on a framed bed. Nitin, Sam's cook, made her soups and dals that were easy to eat. When he discovered she had a sweet tooth, he made her rice pudding with cinnamon and gur.

Through Nitin – a hills man who understood her language – Pema explained that her parents had died in an avalanche, so she belonged to her uncle. He was a strong, loyal man, but had a terrible temper, especially after drinking *sur*, their homemade liquor.

A few days later the belligerent uncle returned with half a dozen henchmen to claim Pema, insisting that they had delayed long enough. Pema was upset at their abrupt arrival, but when Fatima tried to stall them, the uncle shouted at her and raised his stick. Fatima prepared a bag of fresh dressings and impressed upon the younger men that they were for Pema and that her dressings had to be changed regularly. The young Gaddi woman wept in distress as she said hurried goodbyes. Adela gently hugged her and told her they would meet again. She pushed a handkerchief into Pema's pocket that was wrapped around a cheap chain Adela sometimes wore that Pema had admired. She hoped Pema's uncle wouldn't take these from her.

There was nothing now to keep them in Narkanda. The next day Fatima and her helpers packed up the clinic and returned to Simla.

***

Sam returned two days later.

'I can't say I was sorry to see them go,' Hunt said, emerging from the sanctuary of his room. 'Those women took over the whole house, as well as the garden. What a noise they made, laughing and chattering till all hours. And we had a dozen ruffians at the door demanding the return of some shepherd girl. I know we're here to serve the natives, Jackman, but in future they can stick to their clinic in the village, can't they?'

Sam was deeply disappointed to have missed them. He could just imagine the house ringing with Adela's fits of laughter. How quiet it would be without her.

'What shepherd girl?'

'One of those Gaddies. Badly burnt. Terrible business, but that man who came for her looked like he would gladly cut all our throats. Anyway, they've all gone,' Hunt said and sighed with relief. 'Now we can have a quiet supper. It's lamb chops. Bet you're glad to be back.'

It was Nitin who explained the drama of Pema's injuries, of her being rushed down to Narkanda and then recuperating at the bungalow.

'Dr Khan saved her life, and Miss Adela looked after Pema like her own sister. Now they are gone.' Nitin gave a mournful shrug. He seemed as sad as Sam that the bungalow was empty of guests. Sam sat on his bed, pressing his face to a blanket that still held a scent of Adela.

He would have come back sooner if it hadn't been for Fatima's request that he seek out Ghulam. On his way up the Sutlej Valley, Sam had come across the activist openly distributing leaflets in Nerikot, just as Fatima had suspected. Sam had found Ghulam a highly persuasive man, and had given him sanctuary at the remote bungalow at Sarahan, knowing that Boz and his foresters would not be using it until midsummer.

Ghulam had rekindled in Sam his fierce anger at the injustice suffered by the poorest in India at the hands of the rich and powerful. Ever since his boyhood, when he'd watched impotently as destitute and starving tea pickers had thrown themselves into the Brahmaputra River and tried in vain to reach his father's steamer, Sam had raged that such things were allowed to happen. It was why he had joined the mission. It was why he must remain single and dedicate his life to bringing about a better world. Ghulam was the same, though he believed in revolution by force if necessary, whereas Sam was against violence. Yet meeting Fatima's brother had reminded Sam that only by being single-minded and without emotional ties could you hope to achieve such goals.

Sam steeled himself to put away the blanket and bury his desire for Adela. He knew that she cared for him – it shone from her beautiful green-brown eyes – but she deserved better. The warm-hearted Robson girl would find no difficulty in attracting others to her – of that he was sure.

Chapter 9

Adela, in camisole and knickers, was rifling through the wardrobe in the green room looking for the yellow sari she was to wear for the tableaux. Deborah was already dressed in green pyjama-trousers, a tunic and a gold-edged shawl, and was applying her make-up.

There was a knock at the door.

'Come in, Tommy!' Adela called. 'Any idea where my sari is? Tommy, if you've hidden it, I'll string you up by you know what—'

Deborah's squeal cut her off. Adela emerged from the wardrobe to see a handsome young Indian in a glittering gold coat, tight white trousers, curling slippers and a magnificent blue turban studded with jewels.

Adela gaped.

'I'm terribly sorry, ladies,' he said in a cut-glass English accent. 'I'm looking for Mr Villiers; I'm to be in his play.' By the amused look on his slim moustachioed face, he didn't look at all sorry. Adela dived behind the wardrobe door, pulled on a silk dressing gown, and re-emerged with a smile.

'I thought you were Tommy Villiers; he'll be here somewhere. Do you want me to find him for you?'

'Well, that's most kind' – he eyed her – 'but shouldn't you put something on first?'

'Oh, Tommy's seen it all before,' Adela said, and then laughed, 'hasn't he, Deb?'

But her friend was too shocked at the appearance of an Indian in their dressing room to speak.

'I must say,' Adela said, padding barefoot to the door, 'you look terrific in that outfit. Wardrobe have really pushed the boat out for this production, haven't they? Are you with the Indian Army?'

'No, I'm not.' He gave her a bemused look.

'You're not with the forestry lot, are you? It's just that you look familiar.'

He looked amused. 'No, not the forestry either. But I think I know who you are. Miss Robson from Belgooree, isn't it?'

'Yes.' Adela smiled. 'So you're something to do with tea?'

He shook his head. 'Sophie Khan told me to look out for you.'

'You know Auntie Sophie? How lovely!'

She led the way into the corridor and stopped in astonishment. Two liveried guards, standing either side of the door, saluted. For a dazed moment Adela thought they must also be part of the production of *The Arabian Nights.* Then realisation dawned; they were wearing the yellow-and-turquoise livery of the Raja of Gulgat.

She turned and stared at the Indian actor, blood rushing to her cheeks.

'Oh Lord.' She gasped. 'You're – are you a *real* prince?'

He gave a charming smile. 'Sanjay Singh of Gulgat, the Raja's nephew.'

Adela dropped in a curtsy, clutching her dressing gown and feeling ridiculous. 'I'm so sorry, Your Highness. I thought you were an Indian officer or someone on leave – just dressed up for the play.'

He chuckled and swept her with a look. 'No need for ceremony, Miss Robson, especially given the circumstances.' He held out a hand. 'My friends call me Jay.'

'Call me Adela, please.' She shook his hand. 'What a fool I feel.'

'Your openness is refreshing,' he assured her. 'I prefer it any day to the fawning of courtiers or the stuffiness of British officials. And yes, I am dressed up for the part. You're much more likely to see me in cricket whites than all this.' He swept a mocking hand over his appearance.

'We must find Tommy,' she said hastily, pointing up the corridor. He insisted she went ahead. 'It's very good of you to volunteer for the play,' she said over her shoulder as she led the way. 'Have you acted before?'

'No, but Colonel Baxter approached me at the club – he's an old friend of my uncle's – and I didn't think it would take a great deal of effort to play an Eastern prince. I gather I just stand around looking decorative and don't speak.'

Adela laughed, liking his droll humour. 'Colonel Baxter is a dear. How are Auntie Sophie and Uncle Rafi?'

'A couple of junglis,' said Sanjay. 'I don't know how they stand being in Gulgat all year round. Even the Raja's wife, Rita, insists on getting away to Bombay or France once in a while.

I've spent the last three years in Europe, so Gulgat is a bit of a shock I can tell you.'

'I was hoping they might come to Simla this summer to see me in a play.' Adela stopped outside Tommy's door.

'If I'd known there was a Belgooree rose blooming in Simla,' he said, smiling, 'I would have come a lot sooner too.'

They stood for a moment assessing each other. He was stunningly handsome in his princely garments, but she remembered how his demanding behaviour had caused Sophie and Rafi to argue one Christmas. According to Sophie, Sanjay had been sent off to university – was it Oxford? – to keep him out of palace intrigues and give him an elite education. He was a man used to getting his own way – a spoilt brat, Sophie had called him – but that was years ago, and no doubt he had matured.

'We've met before,' Adela said, wanting to wrong-foot him for catching her half-dressed and causing consternation.

'We have?' He raised an eyebrow.

'On a hunting trip when I was six and you must have been about ten. You threatened to skin my pet tiger and made me cry.'

His dark eyes widened an instant. 'What a little brute I must have been.' He laughed. 'I hope you won't hold it against me for ever.'

'I forgive you as from now.' Adela smirked.

'Good,' said Sanjay, 'and I will endeavour to make amends. You must come out to the villa at Mashobra – with your guardian of course – and I can tell you all about the intrigues of the Gulgat court. That is what women like to hear, isn't it? The latest gossip? And I'm sure Sophie Khan will have given you quite the wrong impression of me. Promise me you will come, Adela.'

She couldn't help but be flattered. 'Promise.' She smiled and then knocked on Tommy's door and walked in before he answered.

***

It soon became backstage gossip that Adela was being pursued by the young Prince Sanjay, who spent his days riding or playing polo at Annandale and his evenings in the clubs and card rooms of Simla, with the occasional appearance at the Gaiety for rehearsals, causing a flutter among the young actresses.

'You should watch your step with that one,' Deborah warned. 'Prince Sanjay's got a reputation for trying to get his way with European girls. I know someone who knew someone who was with him at Oxford. Word has it he was sent down for having a woman in his rooms.'

'Stop listening to tittle-tattle,' Adela said breezily. 'Jay's a perfect gentleman. Aunt Fluffy is always there chaperoning me anyway, and she thinks he's a real charmer. They share a love of Tagore's poetry.'

She dismissed Deborah's disapproval as a dose of envy at Jay singling her out rather than her friend; blonde Deborah was used to basking in men's attention during the Simla season. Why Jay had done so, Adela wasn't at all sure, except that she was young, unattached and popular among the theatre crowd, and he was in Simla to have some fun.

Sometimes he would send a rickshaw to bring her out to the forested spur of Mashobra – with its exclusive mansions, including the Viceroy's country retreat – and she would join a large hunting party of his club friends and one or two rajas from the surrounding hill states. Jay was particularly friendly with the Raja of Nerikot, who shared his love of shikar and good living. Any trip would entail a stop for a sumptuous picnic of caviar, salmon, curry puffs, puddings and champagne, served at tables and eaten off exquisite china, all of which was brought on the backs of dozens of mules and hill porters. Adela felt uncomfortable at the lavishness of these al fresco dinners, knowing how little the Raja's coolies had to eat and how the hill families struggled for their daily existence.

She thought how much Sam would disapprove and then pushed him from her mind. Weeks had gone by since the trip to Narkanda, and Sam had made no attempt to get in touch. And there would be no chance to go back to the mission any time soon, as Fatima was too busy at the hospital and Adela was committed to the theatre season.

Adela much preferred the times when Jay appeared without ceremony to go riding, rather than the grand hunting expeditions. They would trot up Jakko Hill to see the sunrise, with just a retainer on horseback keeping a discreet distance behind.

'Best part of the day,' Adela said on one such ride, breathing in the sweet air of early morning while monkeys swung and screeched between the trees by the temple.

'I normally hate early mornings,' said Sanjay. 'I only do it to keep Robson Memsahib happy.'

'I'm honoured, Your Highness.' She returned his mocking smile.

'You should be. There is no one else I would do this for – except perhaps the Viceroy or my Uncle Kishan.'

'You're very fond of your uncle, aren't you?'

'Yes, very.'

'Uncle Rafi is too,' she said. 'He'd do absolutely anything for the Raja.'

'I wish he was as loyal to me,' Sanjay said, his tone suddenly petulant. 'He still insists on backing the claim of Rita's brat, Jasmina, although it's quite obvious that I, as a man, would make a much better ruler.'

'I don't think it's anything to do with Rafi,' Adela defended. 'Surely it's up to the Raja.'

'Oh, Rafi Khan has a great deal of influence over my uncle, believe me. If he said the word, I would be Uncle Kishan's successor. Stourton, the British Agent in Gulgat, thinks it should be me, but Rafi won't listen to him. But then Sophie and Rita stick together – they're as thick as thieves. If Rita says jump, then Sophie and Rafi jump.' Sanjay turned to look at her intently with his dark, almond-shaped eyes. 'You could speak to Rafi on my behalf.'

Adela hesitated, not wanting to get embroiled in Gulgat politics.

'If you persuaded Sophie, then she would persuade her adoring husband.' There was still an edge to his voice.

'Well, if you think it would do any good.'

Abruptly he smiled. 'Of course it would. Two beautiful goddesses could bewitch Rafi and change his mind, I know it.'

Adela laughed. How quickly he could switch from belligerence to utter charm. She studied his profile as he turned to look at the sunrise. His skin was as light as hers and his sculpted features – the straight nose and high cheekbones – were perfect. With his long, dark lashes, Sanjay was almost beautiful; she could look at him for hours. She wasn't in love with him, but he stirred her physically.

Above the canopy of deodars, the light was turning the distant mountain peaks marigold orange. Soon they would be hidden in haze. That way lay Narkanda and Sam. Adela felt a sharp pang for the elusive man. Why did she have to fall in love with such a hopeless case? Sam could be passionate and impulsive yet funny and down to earth; appearances and possessions meant nothing to him, only the welfare of others did. He would be happy to stay in the hills for ever and probably hadn't given her a second thought since she'd left. Out of sight and out of mind; she was sure that Sam only lived in the moment.

On the other hand, Adela was quite sure that every thought and gesture of Sanjay's was calculated. He took great pride in his appearance; for all his protesting that he preferred to lounge in cricket whites, he was always immaculately dressed and manicured. He planned things down to the last detail, but made them look effortless, such as this morning ride. She knew from the looks he gave her and the attention he lavished on her that he desired her. It would be so very easy to give into his seductive charm.

'I know what you're thinking.' Sanjay turned to her suddenly.

'Oh?' Adela blushed.

'That you would like to dine with me after the show finishes on Saturday night.'

Adela laughed with relief. 'Well, there'll be the after-show party at The Chalet . . .'

'I thought Wildflower Hall would be nice.'

'Wildflower Hall?' Adela gasped. 'I've only ever been when Rafi and Sophie visited and they treated me to Sunday lunch there.'

'This will be better,' declared Sanjay. 'And perhaps afterwards you would like to spend a few days at Eagle's Nest relaxing after the show is over. We can go to the Sipi Fair. It's always good for amusement – all that wife-swapping that the coolies do.'

Adela's stomach tightened in excitement. She and Fluffy had been entertained to dinner at the Raja of Gulgat's villa beyond Mashobra, but never stayed over.

'And Auntie can come too?'

He hesitated for just a heartbeat, then said, 'Naturally Mrs Hogg is invited.'

'That would be lovely, thank you, Your Highness.'

'Please' – Sanjay stretched out a hand and clasped her arm – 'you really must start calling me Jay. I think we know each other well enough by now.'

'Jay,' Adela said and smiled. 'Let's go and tell Auntie now. She'll be expecting you for *chota hazri*.'

Jay rolled his eyes. 'Porridge and devilled kidneys. The things I do for my sweet English rose,' he teased.

***

Fluffy was captivated by the idea of a few days at Eagle's Nest. Fatima was more critical.

'We hardly ever see you at the hospital these days.' Fatima eyed her. 'You spend so much time with Prince Sanjay.'

It was the first time Adela had been back to the doctor's flat since she had found Ghulam hiding there. She had just called in to make sure Fatima was going to come to the show.

'The play has been taking up most of my time,' Adela replied, avoiding her look and glancing out of the window as if something had caught her interest. A woman was spreading out washing on a roof to dry. 'I'm sorry. I'll have more time once it's over.'

'Not if you are going to spend it at Eagle's Nest.'

'That's just for a day or two.'

'I'm surprised at you wanting to spend time with a man like that.' Fatima was blunt.

'Like what?' Adela bristled.

'One that spends his time in gambling and indulgence and keeping company with autocrats like the Raja of Nerikot, who cares nothing for ordinary people.' Fatima was disdainful. 'My brother Ghulam would be rotting in his palace prison if it hadn't been for Sam Jackman.'

'Sam?' Adela's stomach jolted at his sudden mention.

'Yes, he rescued Ghulam from Nerikot and hid him in a forest bungalow. If the authorities found out – or the Raja – Sam would be in big trouble.' Fatima gave her an anxious look. 'You won't say anything, will you? I shouldn't have said—'

'Of course I won't,' Adela cried. 'How could you think I would?'

'Sorry,' Fatima said, touching Adela's head in affection. 'I didn't mean to get on my high horse. I just worry about you with that man. He's from a different class to us, Adela, and thinks he can have whatever he wants. You will be careful, won't you? There can't be any future in it.'

'Who cares about the future?' Adela was impatient. 'I'm just enjoying this season. I won't pretend I'm not flattered by Jay's attention – who wouldn't be? – but I know he's not going to propose to a girl like me. We're friends, that's all. So stop worrying.'

Sitara brought in tea and ginger cake. Fatima talked about the hospital and no more about Sanjay. Before she went, Adela asked, 'Is your brother safe?'

Fatima shrugged. 'I don't know where he is and it's probably best not to.'

'Does Sam know?'

'I haven't heard from him for a month or so – he sent word that Ghulam was safely away from Nerikot, that's all.'

'So Sam hasn't been to Simla?' Adela could feel her cheeks redden despite her attempt to sound nonchalant.

Again Fatima shrugged. 'I think Sundar would have told me if he had; they are good friends now.'

Adela grinned and nudged her friend. 'So even the busy Dr Khan finds time to see her admirer Sundar Singh.'

To her delight, Fatima also blushed. 'Very occasionally,' she admitted, 'I beat him at backgammon.'

'Well, I hope you will drag him along to the play too,' Adela said with a departing hug.

***

Rushing to the theatre on the eve of the first night of the play, Adela ran into her former boss, Bracknall, by the bandstand, where a military band had just finished playing.

'Hello, sir,' Adela said. 'When did you arrive in Simla?'

He took her hand and held on to it. 'Mrs Bracknall arrived last week to set up house; I came two days ago.' He swept her with a look. 'I've been hearing things about you, Miss Robson. Running about with some Indian prince, my wife tells me.'

Adela laughed, trying to withdraw her hand. 'Prince Sanjay is a family friend, that's all.'

'I thought your family were tea-wallahs?'

Adela winced at his derogatory tone. Pulling her hand away, she said proudly, 'My Aunt Sophie and her husband, Rafi Khan, are good friends of the Rajah of Gulgat. Prince Sanjay is the Raja's nephew.'

Bracknall stared at her as if she had grown a second head. Adela said, 'Well, I must get to the theatre . . .'

He grabbed her arm to stop her. 'Rafi Khan from Lahore?'

'Yes.' Adela regretted at once mentioning them. Too late she remembered Sophie's antipathy to Bracknall and that he had once been Rafi's boss. She didn't like the twisted smile on Bracknall's craggy face.

'Well, well. So Sophie Telfer is your aunt – or Mrs Khan, as she no doubt prefers to be called.'

'That is her name,' said Adela.

Still gripping her, he said, 'Perhaps I'm old-fashioned, but I'm not one of those who believe in these mixed racial marriages. Can't quite see how a Christian marrying a Mohammedan can be lawful, but then Sophie Telfer would do anything to escape the shame of her first failed marriage I imagine.'

Adela was shocked at his words. She threw off his hold. 'Auntie Sophie married Rafi for love. They're devoted to each other.'

Bracknall gave an indulgent laugh. 'Oh, the innocence of youth is quite charming. I could tell you a few stories about your aunt and uncle that would have your eyes on stalks.'

'I must go.'

'I'll see you at the office next week, my girl, and we can talk more about the Khans.'

'I don't work at the Forest Office any more, Mr Bracknall.'

'What do you mean?'

'I haven't been there since January.' Adela noticed his annoyance with triumph. 'Did Boz not tell you?'

'No, he did not.' Bracknall quickly recovered. 'But then your role was very minor, wasn't it? And I suppose if you have caught the eye of a rich native you don't need an office job to keep you in stockings and lipstick.'

Adela felt revulsion at his lascivious look and turned away with a curt goodbye. No wonder Sophie disliked the overbearing man; he made her skin crawl too. But his words troubled her; they had been full of menace for Sophie. Sam had warned her about Bracknall – Boz too – but she had dismissed their concerns. It struck her for the first time that anyone who crossed the bullying Bracknall would be made to pay for it.

Chapter 10

Whistling with hands in pockets, Sam walked away from the photographers' shop on the East Mall with a pack of newly developed photographs in his inner jacket pocket. He had some duplicates too. Although tempted to splash out his meagre pay on tea at Clarkes Hotel, he bought Sundar's favourite sticky jalebis from a street stall in the Lower Bazaar instead. His friend was treating him and Fatima to the theatre that night for the final performance of *The Arabian Nights*, Simla style.

'It will be awful, my friend,' Sundar had promised. 'All the stoutest matrons of Simla dressed up like dancing girls and all the portly retired colonels pretending to be Errol Flynn. But our dear Adela will save the show with her sweet singing and a flash of shapely leg. At least that's what they're saying at the club.'

Sam could not deny his feeling of anticipation. It was thoughts of Adela that had plagued him and driven him to town. The photographs were his excuse, but he knew that he would find no relief until he saw her again. He had tried and failed to banish her from his mind. But every morning as the sun came up he remembered riding with her at dawn, and every night when the sun set behind Hatu Mountain he thought of her excitement at meeting the Gaddi nomads. The Tibetan women who sold trinkets in Narkanda; the children who played by the river; a passing chestnut pony with a bright blanket for a saddle; Nitin's rice pudding served on the veranda – all these reminded Sam constantly of Adela's lively presence and how much he missed her.

After the play – when she was able to relax and take time off – he would call round with some photos for her and invite her to tea at Clarkes. If things went well, he would stay for the Sipi Fair – they could ride out there together – and he would tell her exactly how he felt about her. Lying alone in his narrow bed at the mission, listening to Hunt snoring in the next room, Sam had questioned his resolve to remain single. Would his work not be better served with a wife and partner who could be his companion and equal, two of them striving for a better world rather than one? He had seen how good Adela was in helping at the clinic; she didn't flinch from any task, however distasteful.

Even the beggar with leprosy outside the hill shrine had not repulsed her; she had greeted the woman and touched the stump of her hand as she put coins in her bowl.

Yet Adela was still so young, despite her mature handling of people. She might hate the thought of being stuck in the hills far from the bright lights of Simla, its theatre and glittering social life. Since that time she had stowed away in his car as a rebellious thirteen-year-old, he knew she had burned with the ambition to be an actress. Now she was doing what she wanted. Why would she give that up to live with him in a leaky mission bungalow in the back of beyond? Well, unless he asked her he would never know. And Sam was never afraid to ask awkward or challenging questions. He gave a self-deprecating laugh as he sauntered back up the hill to Sundar's quarters, where he was staying. Whatever happened, he was looking forward to sitting in the comfort of the Gaiety Theatre, sucking on jalebi with Sundar and Fatima and watching the prettiest girl in Simla dancing across the stage.

***

'There's someone at the stage door wants to see you,' Deborah said as she came rushing into the dressing room. Adela was still removing her make-up, the clapping and wolf whistles from the army contingent in the stalls still ringing in her ears. Despite Deborah fluffing her lines in the final scene, Tommy forgetting to come on just before the interval and the stage hands bringing on the magic carpet a scene too early, they had received a standing ovation. Perhaps it was because it was the last night, but the atmosphere had seemed almost feverish and the audience raucous.

Sanjay had got a clap all to himself when he appeared dressed in his magnificent clothes and turban glinting with jewels. At the curtain call he had kissed the hands of the leading ladies and caused gasps to ripple through the auditorium. When the curtain finally fell, the cast dissolved into hysterical giggles and laughter.

'A male admirer I hope.' Adela smiled, pausing at the mirror.

''Fraid not. She seems rather formidable. Says she was at school with you.'

Adela gave her a puzzled look. 'Then you should know who she is.'

'Not St Mary's,' said Deborah, sitting down and pulling off her stage shoes. 'She said you were at school in Shillong together. St Ninian's or somewhere.'

Adela felt her stomach clench. 'What did she look like?'

'Bit horsey looking. Blonde hair.'

Adela felt sweat break out on her brow. If it was Flowers Dunlop or even Margie Munro, she wouldn't mind. But it sounded like the one girl from St Ninian's she hoped never to set eyes on again. Yet how was that possible? Her mother had told her that Henrietta Davidge and Nina had gone back to England after Nina's father had died over two years ago.

'Did . . . did she say her name?'

Deborah was pulling off her tunic and wafting perfume under her arms. 'Oh, just go and say hello. She says you'll remember her. Nora or Nina I think it was.'

Adela felt sick. A wave of panic rose up inside and stuck in her throat. At once she was back at school, Nina taunting her and pulling her hair, spitting out cruel words about her parents. *You're just a two annas; nobody likes you. Margie never wanted to be your friend. Go and play with stinky Flowers*. Her heart hammered and she struggled to breathe. This was ridiculous. Nina could do nothing to hurt her; they were grown women. Even if it was her, she had just come to congratulate her, not to cause trouble, surely.

She swallowed hard. 'Please, Debs, can you just say I've already gone? I really don't want to see her.'

Deborah laughed as if she were joking. 'Don't go all Greta Garbo on me, as if you have so many admirers. I'd *pay* someone to hang around backstage and ask for my autograph.'

'If it's who I think it is, that's the last thing she wants. She couldn't stand me at school.'

Realisation dawned on her friend. 'Is she the girl who was so ghastly to you? The one you told me and Prue about?'

Adela nodded. 'Sounds like her. Please, Deb, just do this one thing for me and tell her I left out the front entrance. Anyway, Jay is waiting for me.'

Deborah scrutinised her. 'Are you really going to Wildflower Hall instead of the party?'

'Yes, I am.' Adela held her look.

'What does Mrs Hogg say?'

'She's coming too. It's all above board.'

Deb arched her eyebrows. 'That's not what they'll be saying in the Simla drawing rooms.'

'They can say what they like,' Adela retorted.

Abruptly her friend laughed. 'Quite right. I wish I had your brass neck. Tommy will be heartbroken at you missing the party though.'

'Tommy's heart may break one day,' said Adela, 'but it won't be for me. I'm like his kid sister.'

Deborah pulled on her dress. 'Zip me up then, and I'll go and get rid of Horse Face out there.'

Adela went and helped her. 'Thanks, Deb.' Adela enveloped her in a hug. 'I'll do you any favour in return.'

'Just find me a rich, handsome prince like your one.' Deb winked as she sped out of the door.

Twenty minutes later, dressed in a red satin evening gown bought by Jay, Adela stepped into the yellow-and-blue Gulgat rickshaw sent for her and Fluffy and was pulled away into the dark. At the end of the Mall, they transferred into the Gulgat Bentley and were driven to the exclusive hotel Wildflower Hall, on the wooded hilltop outside the town.

The driveway through the trees was lit with lanterns, and light spilled out of the tall wooden mansion – which had once belonged to Lord Kitchener – on to the lawned gardens. Jay, who had gone straight there to bathe and change, appeared and greeted them. He was wearing an expensive cream dinner suit cut with a mandarin collar over a peacock blue silk shirt, which matched his turban. He was making a statement among the throng of British diners in their formal tails and bow ties, that for all his Westernised ways he was still an Indian prince in his own country and proud of it.

They mingled with others over cocktails. Colonel and Mrs Baxter were entertaining three protégées up from Delhi and Lucknow for the hot season, along with polo-playing officer friends of Jay's. They greeted Adela warmly.

'You stole the show,' said a young captain.

'Wish I could sing like you, Miss Robson,' gushed one of the girls.

'Thank you.' Adela blushed.

'Don't let her get too big-headed,' Fluffy warned.

'It's no more praise than she deserves,' Jay said, smiling and giving a light possessive touch to her elbow.

Adela drank her cocktail too quickly, aware of the looks of speculation passing among the others as they wondered at her relationship with Jay. Only Fluffy's no-nonsense presence gave it respectability, but she doubted that would stop tongues wagging.

'Oh, my dear,' Colonel Baxter said, turning to her, 'there's an old friend of yours just arrived in Simla; I served with her father in Mesopotamia. You might remember him, Fluffy: Colonel Davidge. Sadly died a couple of years ago. Married late – pretty wife and one daughter.'

Adela felt the blood drain from her face. So it was true: Nina was back.

'Davidge?' Fluffy frowned and shook her head.

'Yes, you must remember,' Mrs Baxter prompted. 'Wife's family were in jute – plenty of money. His widow and daughter are renting Sweet Pea Cottage for the season. Henrietta Davidge couldn't settle back home – spent the winter in Bengal, now Simla. Nina recognised Adela in the play.' Mrs Baxter leant towards Adela and squeezed her arm. 'Think she was a bit envious – rather sees herself as a bit of an actress. Henrietta, her mother, has promised to pay her through RADA.'

'The Royal Academy in London?' Fluffy raised an eyebrow. 'She'll need to be jolly good to get in first.'

Adela gulped. 'I remember her enjoying acting at school. Lucky Nina.'

'Yes, isn't she?' said Colonel Baxter. 'We must get you two together soon, mustn't we? It'll be nice for the poor girl to have a friend here, show her some fun. She's been stuck away in some dreary Bengali jute mill town with an uncle.'

Adela forced a smile, downing her second cocktail. Fluffy put a warning hand on her bare arm and gave her a look that asked, *Are you all right?* She nodded and let the waiter refill her glass. Perhaps Fluffy had guessed that this was the dreaded Nina she had run away from, though Adela had never told her the full story, because her guardian steered her away from the Baxters until drinks were over.

By the time they went into dinner, Adela's head was spinning. In the vast teak-panelled dining room, hung with portraits of past viceroys and hunting scenes, she was glad to sit down. To her dismay Colonel Baxter insisted that the prince and his ladies should join their party, so Adela found herself sitting between the Colonel and one of the officers. In her befuddled state, she wondered if the Baxters were deliberately keeping her and Jay apart.

She felt exhausted trying to keep up with the conversation while all the time worrying about the appearance of Nina back in her life. How long before snide rumours about her parentage would surface around the Simla tea tables? And she wanted to avoid the awful Bracknall too. Jay's offer of a few days at Eagle's Nest was suddenly even more appealing. By the end of dinner all she could think of was getting away from Simla and out of the spotlight for a short while.

She observed Jay. He was enjoying himself with his sporty friends and revelling in the attention from the other young women. She saw how important it was for him to be liked; he started issuing invitations to visit Eagle's Nest for shooting and dinner.

'We should all go to the Sipi Fair together,' he declared. 'I'll lay on a banquet afterwards.'

Jay ended up paying the bill for them all.

As he dropped her and Fluffy off at the bungalow, promising to send a car for them in the morning, Adela wondered if she was doing the right thing. Tired as she was, she had half a mind to see if the after-show party at The Chalet was still going on. She felt a pang of regret that she had given in so easily to Jay's insistence on dinner instead of celebrating with her theatre friends. Still, she couldn't wait to get away into the hills for a few days. And Jay was so very generous and kind; tonight he had given her a beautiful cashmere shawl as they had left the hotel.

'What's wrong?' Fluffy came into her bedroom to say goodnight. 'You didn't seem yourself tonight. Is it this Nina Davidge that worries you?'

Adela nodded. 'I know it's ridiculous, but I'm still afraid of her.'

'Well, the worst thing you could do would be to let it show,' said Fluffy robustly. 'You're quite capable of standing up for yourself, my dear. And anyway, what possible harm could she do you?'

Adela slept badly, clock-watching through the night, impatient for the dawn. She was up and dressed with a suitcase packed long before breakfast was served.

***

Sam spent the morning patching up the roof of St Thomas' Church in the Lower Bazaar. 'The native church' as the British in Simla dubbed it. He was friendly with the welcoming priest, who did his best for his flock with a fraction of the resources of the prestigious and well-heeled Christ Church, which looked down on St Thomas' from the Ridge.

Sam was glad of the physical labour, hammering at the corrugated iron sheeting with vigour, sleeves rolled up and shirt sticking to his back from exertion in the hot May sun. With each blow he tried to erase the memory of the previous evening. Adela had looked captivating on stage, playing a variety of parts, dancing and singing in the chorus and then coming on for the final tableaux in a brilliant yellow sari, like some exotic butterfly next to the handsome prince. From the loud whispers around him, he soon discovered that it was Prince Sanjay of Gulgat and that his name and Adela's were being linked by the town's gossips.

He'd slipped away from Sundar and Fatima at the end of the performance and gone for a cigarette by the bandstand, hoping to catch Adela as she came out of the theatre. But there'd been a rather imperious young woman in a fashionable summer coat and pillbox hat demanding to see her. Sam had recognised Adela's friend Deborah, who was trying to put her off. He'd held back in the shadows, but had been near enough to overhear the exchange.

'I'm afraid she's already left – a rickshaw picked her up on the Mall.'

'I don't believe you – she couldn't have left that quickly. She's ducking me, isn't she?' the tall girl had demanded.

'What if she is, Nina? The way you treated her at St Ninian's, I'm not surprised.'

Nina had looked affronted. 'I don't know what you mean.'

'Oh, I think you do. You bullied her. Even hearing your name still upsets her. So I'd rather you just left her alone.'

'I came to congratulate her, but I see I'm wasting my time. It's not my fault if she holds a silly grudge. I'm the one who was wronged by her – she ruined my performance of Queen Bess at the house plays. You wouldn't be so eager to be her friend if you knew what I knew.'

'Well, just stay away from her, why don't you?'

It dawned on Sam that this was the same Nina that had made eyes at him when he visited St Ninian's and had bullied Adela all those years ago. Why was she seeking her out now if not to make trouble for her? Sam had stepped forward, smiling.

'Good evening, Deborah! You were wonderful in the play. Congratulations.'

The young women had spun around. 'Hello, Sam, thank you. I didn't know you'd come to see it.'

'Wouldn't have missed it for anything.'

'Adela will be sorry to have missed you.'

'She's off to the after-show party no doubt.'

Deborah had hesitated, then thrown a defiant look at Nina. 'No, actually, she's gone to dine at Wildflower Hall. With Prince Sanjay.'

Nina had given a disapproving tut. 'Well, that's the difference between us and the likes of Adela Robson, isn't it?'

'Frankly,' Deborah had replied, 'I'd jump at the chance of dinner with an Indian prince.'

Sam had hidden his frustration. 'Well, enjoy your evening, ladies.'

Abruptly Nina had said, 'I thought I knew your face. You're Jackman the film-maker, aren't you?'

Sam had given a wry laugh. 'Not any more. I'm a missionary now.'

'Oh, really.' Nina had looked disappointed. 'Well, that sounds very worthy.'

Sam had left swiftly and rejoined his friends for tea and chat at Fatima's flat. He had listened to them discuss Sanjay's keen interest in Adela.

'He appears quite single-minded,' Fatima had said. 'I worry for her. She assures me there's nothing in it, but it's obvious how flattered she is by all the attention.'

Sundar had laughed. 'Listen to us, turning into Simla gossips. I'm sure Mrs Hogg won't allow anything remiss to happen to her protégée.'

Sam had had to see for himself. Walking back to Sundar's billet, he'd made an excuse to go further. 'Just need to stretch the legs a bit more – not used to all this sitting around.'

In the moonlight he'd stridden out of town the five miles to Wildflower Hall. By the time he got there, dinner guests were spilling out of the electric-lit mansion and climbing into rickshaws. He'd recognised Colonel Baxter and his wife. Suddenly his heart had leapt to see Adela emerge in a figure-hugging red dress, her dark hair loose around her shoulders like a film star, Fluffy beside her. Then Sanjay had followed, beckoning a servant, who came forward with a soft shawl, which the prince draped around Adela's bare shoulders. She had looked up at him with a huge smile of surprise and thanked him. Sam's guts had twisted with jealousy.

He'd watched as a large gleaming black Bentley pulled up and a footman sprang forward to open the passenger door and help Fluffy inside. The prince had taken Adela's hand and helped her into the back, then climbed in after her. The car had slipped away down the drive; his last image of Adela was of her face upturned towards Sanjay, still smiling.

Now Sam tried to shake off the leaden feeling he was carrying. Finishing his job at St Thomas', he declined the priest's offer to stay for tiffin.

'I've another visit to make.' Sam thanked him and left. He thought about returning to Sundar's to wash and change out of his damp shirt, but couldn't put off the moment when he would confront Adela any longer. Pulling on his jacket, he went to buy a box of coconut fudge for Fluffy and then made his way quickly out of the bazaar.

All was quiet at Briar Rose Cottage, the veranda empty. He waved to the mali, who was watering the dahlias and roses. Noor appeared on the terrace. Sam greeted the bearer.

'Hogg Memsa'b and Robson Memsa'b are not here.' He gave a regretful sweep of his hands.

'When will they be back?'

He gave a noncommittal shake of the head. 'Three days, perhaps four.'

'Four days?' Sam cried. That would be after the Sipi Fair, and he would have to be back in Narkanda by then. 'Where have they gone, Noor?'

'Eagle's Nest, sahib.'

Sam's hopes plummeted. 'The Raja of Gulgat's place?'

Noor nodded. Seeing his disappointment, the bearer beckoned Sam on to the veranda. 'Stay, sahib, and I'll arrange tiffin.'

'No, thank you, I can't stay—'

'Yes, yes, yes.' Noor was insistent. 'Hogg Memsa'b would want it.'

Sam gave in quickly. 'Thank you, that's kind. But only if I can take it on the terrace with you. Tea and a chillum.'

Noor smiled in agreement; he liked the young missionary with the open face and cheerful manner, despite his shabby clothes and battered green hat. People from the hills spoke highly of his hard work and lack of airs and graces.

In the shade Sam and Noor sat cross-legged drinking tea, eating boiled eggs and sharing a water pipe. Sam broke open the sweets he'd bought for Fluffy and shared those too. Soon he had the older man talking of his home in Kashmir – Srinagar, by Dal Lake – and his four sons and two daughters, three of whom had children of their own. He liked living in Simla because the hills reminded him of home, but he missed the lakeside; nowhere was as beautiful as Dal Lake on a spring morning with the cherry blossom in full bloom. Two sons worked on houseboats. He would return one day, when Hogg Memsa'b had no more need of him, and live out his days being looked after by his daughters-in-law, inshallah.

'Don't you mind having to live far from your family?' Sam asked.

Noor shook his head, pouring out more hot, sweet chai. 'It's the path I've been given. It's the same for you, sahib. You live far from home and your family too?'

Sam felt an overwhelming loneliness. 'I don't know where home is, Noor my friend. And I don't have any family.'

The older man looked shocked. 'No one?'

Sam felt his jaw clamp as it always did when he thought of his mother. He muttered, 'Perhaps my mother is still alive, but who knows.'

'You do not know where she is, sahib?'

Sam shook his head. 'In England if she's anywhere.'

Noor placed a comforting hand on his shoulder. 'If it's God's will, you will find each other again.'

Sam gave a bitter smile. 'I don't think she's looking.'

Noor patted his shoulder. 'You have many friends here, and God will take care of you.'

Sam's eyes stung at the simple kindness of the man. He envied Noor's children; their father loved them with a fierce pride. It made him grieve anew for his own father and wonder what it must be like to be part of a large and loving family. Suddenly he knew how much he had wanted to see Adela again – spurred on by not just his physical longing to see and touch her, but by his yearning for someone to love and share his life with. Noor and Adela, with their close loving families, had no idea what it was like to feel so alone or hollow inside.

Sam pulled out the small cardboard folder of duplicate photographs he had brought. 'Please will you give these to Miss Robson?'

Noor took them and assured him that he would. Sam thanked the bearer and left. For the rest of the day he wandered aimlessly, hands plunged in pockets, wrestling with dark thoughts. Up Jakko Hill, down Lakkar Bazaar, along the Elysium spur to stare out in the direction of Mashobra. Should he go there and put up a fight for Adela?

He set off along the Mashobra road and then lost courage. What a ridiculous idea! He would only make a fool of himself. He walked for miles: Sanjouli, Chota Simla, through the tunnel and back across the ravine. Why was he here? He had work he should be doing. What was the purpose of it all? He should stop feeling so sorry for himself! Adela was being courted by an Indian nobleman; she was far out of his league. She wasn't the girl he thought she was. She wanted a life of glamour and satin dresses and luxury cars and sumptuous hotels. They had nothing in common after all. Perhaps she'd never really loved him. She was just friendly and approachable to everyone. Standing among the tall deodars, Sam let out a roar of anger and frustration. A monkey scampered past, screeching in alarm.

Sam returned to the Lower Bazaar. He bought a bottle of whisky – rough country liquor made in the hills – and took it back to Sundar's. He stared at it for an hour, then for the first time in three years he drank from the bottle. When Sundar returned from work, Sam was passed out on the floor, the empty bottle clutched to his chest.

Chapter 11

The Eagle's Nest was a little piece of paradise. Its spacious wooden villa was surrounded by verandas that gave spectacular views over the treetops in all directions – across sun-scorched south-facing slopes towards hazy Simla, and north to the forest-clad jungle of the foothills, stretching away to the jagged Himalayas.

The interiors were dark and cool, the rooms panelled in teak and the walls hung with colourful paintings – French impressionists and Persian hunting scenes – as well as photographs from tiger shoots and the Raja's visits to the French Riviera. There were statues of Hindu gods and goddesses, rich-patterned carpets, antique furniture and a library jammed from floor to ceiling with books. The verandas were furnished with cane chairs, comfortable hand-embroidered cushions and ivory-inlaid tables. All around was a profusion of potted ferns and flowers lining the verandas and steps down to sloping lawns and walkways through the trees hung with lanterns. There were the usual dahlias, stocks and wallflowers of the British gardens, but intermingled with local species of mimosa, rhododendrons and azaleas, and all tended by an army of malis.

For two days Adela relaxed, ate and slept deeply, playing the occasional game of tennis with Jay on a lawned court and taking short walks through the forest with Fluffy. The day before the Sipi Fair, the Raja of Nerikot arrived to stay with his entourage. They had a long dinner, with the conversation turning to local unrest.

'Glad to get out of Nerikot to tell you the truth,' he said to Sanjay. 'Wretched Mandalists are stirring things up again.'

'Surely you will have to give up on the practice of bonded labour, won't you?' Fluffy challenged. 'It's happening in other hill states already.'

'Perhaps.' The Raja shrugged, seemingly at a loss.

'Can't have anarchy though,' Sanjay said. 'You have to keep a tight rein on your people – let them know who's in charge.'

'Yes,' agreed the Raja, feeling encouraged. 'I won't be dictated to by rabble-rousers. But how do you control things when these agitators from outside stir up the crowds? Sometimes I don't feel my family are safe at the palace.'

'Surely it's not that bad,' said Adela. 'They don't mean you any harm – they just want a bit of democracy.'

'What do you know about such things?' Jay gave her a curious look.

'Just from what I've read,' Adela said quickly.

'Well, it doesn't concern the British.' He gave a tight smile. 'The princely states will do things our own way and in our own time.' He turned to his friend. 'If your family are threatened, then you have every right to defend them. If I can be of any help, just say the word.'

Adela felt uneasy; was Jay inciting his friend to retaliate with violence? The subject was left unresolved as they turned to talk of the Sipi Fair.

'It's always a jolly affair,' the Raja said, grinning, 'all that wife-swapping.'

'I find it rather distasteful,' said Fluffy, 'to think young women can be sold off like that.'

Sanjay gave an indulgent laugh. 'Is it so very different from the British upper class, who sell off their daughters for titles and big houses?'

'Quite different,' Fluffy declared. 'Upper-class girls have a say in who they marry; these native girls are bartered like sheep.'

'It just speeds up the transaction of marriage,' Sanjay said. 'The coolies living away in the towns have no time to go home and find themselves wives.'

'But the girls have no say in it,' said Adela. 'When I marry, it will be for love.'

'What a romantic you are.' Jay smiled. 'That's what comes of watching too many Hollywood films at The Rivoli.'

'No, it's from seeing how happy my parents are. My father says he's as in love with Mother as the day they first met. And then there's Auntie Sophie and Rafi – they're so happy together.'

Jay pulled a face. 'I wonder. Rafi Khan's family will have nothing to do with him. It puts a strain on a marriage if the families are not in agreement.'

'His sister Fatima and brother Ghulam haven't turned their backs on him.'

'Ghulam Khan the radical?' the Raja interjected.

'Well, yes—'

'You know him?'

Adela flushed. 'I know of him.'

Fluffy said, 'I'm afraid that was my fault. I went to hear him speak at the Pledge Day rally and Adela came along to keep an eye on me. Unfortunately it ended in scuffles.'

'Of course it would,' snorted the Raja. 'They are hooligans who shouldn't be allowed on our streets.'

'You should take more care, ladies.' Jay frowned in concern. 'Don't involve yourselves in communist propaganda. These are bad men intent on removing the British by force as well as overthrowing the princely states.'

Adela thought of Ghulam. He wasn't a bad man, but he was an impatient one. She recalled the way he had challenged her to look beyond her cosy world in Simla, how he was working eagerly for a free India without barriers of class or religious interference. Could he be a danger to them all if he was thwarted in his goal? If so, should she warn the Raja and Jay about him? But to do so would be a betrayal of Fatima and be bound to get her friend into trouble. She just hoped that the latest unrest in the hills died down and that Ghulam took his campaigning elsewhere.

She wished she could talk it over with Sam; he would have a sensible view on it all. Thinking of him made her wonder if he would travel down from Narkanda to the fair. She felt a gnawing longing for Sam. How awful it would be if she never saw him before she sailed for Britain in July.

Fluffy retired to bed. The moon was full, and Jay suggested an evening stroll in the garden. The Raja declined. Together, Jay and Adela walked down the path as a night mist stole up from the valley, looking like a silver sea in the moonlight. Ghostly light filtered through the trees, making bright patterns on the path. The air was heavy with the scent of golden champa. Reaching a garden seat set under an arch of overhanging flowering creepers, Jay indicated they should sit.

'You were quiet at dinner. What is on your mind?' he asked.

'Nothing really.'

'You mustn't worry about all this local politics.'

'Is the Raja's family really in danger?'

'He can take care of them. And I can take care of you and your guardian. You are safe from any harm here; I'll make sure of that.'

'I don't worry for myself.'

'What a remarkable girl you are.'

He lifted her hand to his lips and brushed her fingers with a kiss. Adela felt a delicious frisson all over. She looked into his handsome face, chiselled in the moonlight, and saw the desire in his dark eyes. Her heart began a slow thudding. He leant closer and ran a finger from her brow down her cheek, pushing stray hair behind her ear. He hardly touched her, but it set off tiny shocks like electricity in her chest and the pit of her stomach. He traced the pad of his finger across her throat and collarbone, brushing the back of his hand against her breast.

She couldn't help a sigh escape her parted lips. Jay tilted her chin and kissed her, a soft exploratory kiss that tickled her lips. She knew she shouldn't encourage it, but there was something hypnotic about their secret scented bower, the ethereal light and the pulsing sound of night insects that seemed to suspend them in the moment. It was like a romantic scene from a film. So when he pulled her closer and kissed her with more force, she responded, their mouths opening, tasting, exploring each other.

'You are quite beautiful, my English rose,' he murmured, kissing his way across her face, nibbling her ear. 'Can I come to your room tonight?'

Adela pulled back. This was going too fast.

'I'm sorry,' he said. 'I didn't mean offence. I just thought . . .'

Adela gulped. 'I'm not offended, but I'm not ready . . .'

'I understand.' He smiled. 'You are too irresistible on such a night. But for you, Adela, I will be patient.'

She felt overwhelmed with mixed emotions: desire, trepidation, disloyalty to Sam, whom she loved, yet excitement at being wanted by this powerful, handsome prince, who ought to be far beyond her reach.

'What do I mean to you, Jay?' she asked. 'I need to know.'

'You are as desirable as the stars in the sky,' he said. 'I fell in love with you the moment I saw you in the dressing room in your underclothes. It's an image I can't get out of my head.' He gave a sensual smile.

Adela gave a laugh of embarrassment. He was teasing her, and it helped break the spell.

'I'm a virgin,' she said, 'which must be obvious to a man of the world like you. But the man I give myself to will be the man I marry. It can't be any other way.'

His eyes widened at her boldness. For a moment he was at a loss for words.

'Marry me then, Adela Robson,' he said impulsively. 'Come and live with me at Gulgat, or we can go to the South of France or London or wherever you want.'

'Marry you? Now you are teasing me!'

'I mean it.'

'Surely you have a wife chosen for you already,' she challenged.

'I can do what I want,' he retorted. 'My uncle Kishan married that woman from Bombay. We're in a changing world.'

'I'd never be acceptable to your family, Jay.' She laughed in disbelief.

'Why not?' He seized her hand. 'I can make you the Rani of Gulgat. With you at my side, even Rafi Khan couldn't object to my becoming the next Raja, could he?'

'And your mother and grandmother?'

'They will do anything to make me happy,' Jay declared.

Adela pulled away. 'I can't deny I'm attracted to you – flattered by your words – but what you say is impossible.'

But the more she set up obstacles, the keener he seemed to be on the whole fantastical idea.

'At least think about it,' pleaded Jay. 'I want you, Adela. I've never wanted anyone as much.'

That night Adela hardly slept, tossing in her feather bed, disturbed by memories of Jay's thrilling touches and kisses, wondering if anything he said could be taken as true. Deborah had warned her about Jay's reputation for falling in and out of love with women. Fatima had been filled with worry about her getting involved with someone of Jay's status. So why did she allow herself to be tempted by his sweet words? Was it because being chosen by Jay would bury for ever her feelings of inferiority to the Ninas and Margies of this world? As wife of an Indian nobleman, her parentage would never matter again. And women married across the racial barrier – Sophie had shown how it could work.

How shallow and pathetic she was! She didn't love him. She would only be using him to win herself status, security and a ticket to the world. Falling asleep finally as the dawn crept in at the cracks between the curtains, Adela woke exhausted but with sudden clarity. She would resist Jay's advances, return to Simla after the fair and throw her energies once more into helping Fatima at the hospital.

***

Sam's temples pounded like tom-toms. He had gone on a drinking binge – he wasn't sure for how many days – until Fatima and Sundar had found him wandering confused around Sanjauli. He had a vague memory of trying to find the old dairy where he had helped out in his school days, when he had still had hopes of working for the Agriculture Department. He had been swamped in a tidal wave of remorse for causing them worry and for falling so easily off the temperance wagon.

If Hunt or – God forbid – his mentor, Dr Black, ever got to hear of it, he would probably be dismissed from the mission. How often had he heard his fellow missionary fulminate against excessive drinking and opium smoking among some of the natives? Hunt had been offended by Sam's suggestion that often the porters and coolies took opium to deaden their hunger and help them through long days of gruelling marching and carrying.

But he, Sam, had no such excuse. He had allowed anger and despair to overwhelm him simply at seeing Adela enjoying the sumptuous surroundings of Wildflower Hall and the attentions of Prince Sanjay. When he had sobered up, he had been profuse in his apologies to his long-suffering friends. He would head straight back to Narkanda. Sundar had clapped him on the back like an indulgent uncle.

'Let's enjoy a day out at the Sipi Fair, Jackman; then you can run for the hills,' he had said and laughed.

Sam had agreed. They set off along the road to Mashobra, joining the crowds of holidaymakers heading for the forest glade at Sipi and jumping aside for cars full of British residents going to watch the spectacle too. The sun was bright and the sky cloudless; Sam was glad he wore dark glasses. As they drew near, his head began to pound in time to the noise of the drums and horns of local bands.

A temporary camp of tents and awnings had been erected under the trees; the air was filled with woodsmoke and the smell of pots bubbling with spicy stews. Pans sizzled as cooks dropped balls of dough into hot smoking oil, transformed in seconds into puffs of puri like magic balloons.

Fire-eaters and jugglers entertained the crowds, and children ran squealing from Tibetan dancers dressed up in hideous masks. The hill women sat apart on a grassy slope, dressed up in their finest clothes, bedecked in glinting silver necklaces, bangles and earrings, heavy with jewels, their delicate noses pierced with huge hooped rings. When the sun struck, they dazzled the eye, their chatter excited as they surveyed the scene and passed ribald comments on the British come to gawp at them.

Sam chain-smoked, trying to throw off his edgy mood; usually he enjoyed the fair, but this year he detected an excited tension about the place. Perhaps it was nothing and it was just his own nerves that were jangling.

'Come, Jackman,' Sundar said jovially, 'let's go and inspect the ponies. Then you can help me choose a shawl for Fatima. She never spends anything on herself.'

Sam followed obediently and they jostled through the crowds. The British were picnicking on a slope adjacent to the hill women with a good view over the proceedings. They were being attended to by dozens of servants, cooking and serving food and drink. The smells made him nauseous. It was then that he spotted Ghulam. He was dressed in a white tunic and a Congress cap, with no attempt to blend in among the hill people. He was moving towards the women's section. Sam couldn't believe Ghulam would risk being seen so publicly at a country fair. This was no political rally. Unless he was going to turn it into one, Sam thought grimly. He was startled by Sundar's sudden cry.

'Look, there's Adela and Mrs Hogg.'

Adela was sitting on a camping chair, slim legs crossed, wearing a summer frock of bold orange flowers and a topee, chatting animatedly with Fluffy. Sundar called out. Adela turned, waved and jumped out of her chair. Sam was torn between excitement at seeing her and trying to keep an eye on Ghulam.

Adela beckoned them over.

'Come on,' Sundar encouraged. 'Now is your chance to impress Miss Robson.'

Sam hesitated, but Sundar pushed him forward. Adela met them halfway and greeted them warmly.

'Hello, Sam.' She smiled up at him quizzically. 'I hoped you might be here today. Will you be staying for a few days? Auntie and I are returning to Simla after this.'

Sam shook his head. 'I'm on my way back to the mission – I've been in Simla for a week.' He glanced back to see if Ghulam was still in sight.

'Oh, I see.' Adela did not hide her disappointment. 'We've been having a few days' holiday—'

'Yes, I know. You've been at Eagle's Nest.'

'Word does get round Simla quickly, doesn't it?' she said with a nervous laugh.

'You look very well, Adela.' Sam smiled. 'And you stole the show at the Gaiety.'

'You came to see it?' she gasped.

'Of course he did.' Sundar grinned. 'All your fans were there.'

'So why didn't you let me know?'

'Because someone else seems to be monopolising you these days,' Sam teased.

'Oh, Prince Jay.' Adela blushed. 'Well, he's been very generous.'

As if on cue, Jay strolled over. Adela hurriedly introduced them.

Jay gave an urbane smile. 'Gentlemen, would you like to join us for tiffin? The Raja of Nerikot is with us too.'

Sam's gut clenched. Was this why Ghulam had come out of hiding? Was he preparing to confront the Raja? He looked over his shoulder, scanning the crowd, but he'd lost sight of the young activist. His feeling of dread grew. What if Ghulam was planning a violent protest, one that would whip up the already excited crowd of revellers? Prince Sanjay's party could be the target and Adela's life might be in danger. Sam had to find out where Fatima's brother had gone.

'That's kind,' said Sundar. 'We'd like—'

'We can't stay I'm afraid,' Sam cut in rudely. 'We have to be elsewhere.'

He grabbed Sundar by the arm and pulled him away.

'Sam,' Adela chided, 'please stay.'

Jay put a possessive hand to her elbow. 'Mr Jackman seems in rather a hurry. Best just to let him go. Another time perhaps.' He gave Sam a cursory nod and turned, steering Adela back to the picnic awning.

***

Adela sat down in frustration as Jay went off to speak to the Raja. Fluffy was fanning herself; she looked glassy-eyed in the heat.

'Was that Sam and Sundar?' she asked breathlessly. 'Are they not coming to join us?'

'No,' Adela said. 'Sam made up some excuse not to.'

'Perhaps he has duties to attend to.'

'Sundar wanted to stay, but Sam wouldn't let him. You could tell he couldn't get away fast enough – kept glancing round as if he wanted to be anywhere but here with us.'

'I think you're imagining that.'

'No, I'm not. He probably disapproves of all this,' said Adela with a sweep of her hands around the prince's picnic spot.

'Yes, probably.' Fluffy sighed.

'Are you all right?' Adela was suddenly concerned. 'Would you like to go into the tent?'

'No,' Fluffy said, flapping her fan. 'It'll be even hotter in there. We could do with a good downpour to clear the air, don't you think?'

'Not while the fair is on I hope.' Adela smiled. 'We don't want the day spoilt for everyone. Would you like some nimbu pani to cool you down, Auntie?'

'Yes please, dear.'

While Fluffy sipped and closed her eyes, Adela scanned the crowd, trying to pick out Sam. He had come after all to see her in the show; if only she had known he was there, she would have sought him out. So why hadn't he told her? Perhaps she had never crossed his mind until that evening, and he had only gone because his friend Sundar had taken him along. To think he had been in Simla all this time and she had not known. If she had, she would never have gone to Eagle's Nest. Or would she? An inner voice mocked her. She had jumped at the chance of staying in the luxurious mansion and being lavished with attention by the handsome Jay. If she had to choose again, would she not still pick Jay? Only last night she had been contemplating the prince's wild promise of marriage. Was she really so fickle?

But just catching sight of Sam today, Adela's heart had jumped in her chest and set off a pounding excitement. No one else had ever had that effect on her. He was looking a little dishevelled, his chin stubbled with a few days' growth and his hair messy. It was hard to tell what he was thinking behind his dark glasses, but the fleeting smile he had given her had raised her hopes, only for her to have them dashed so quickly by his brusque refusal to join their party. She strained in vain to spot Sam, but he had melted back into the teeming crowds.

As the afternoon wore on, the revelries grew more boisterous and the noise increased. It seemed rowdier than the year before. Fluffy was dozing in her chair, and Jay was growing bored with it all.

'We can leave anytime you want,' he said. 'Nerikot is going shortly too.'

Adela was about to agree when a commotion broke out further round on the slope. Some men were arguing over a woman. Adela stood up and peered over, shielding her eyes. No doubt this was one of the transactions that Fluffy so disapproved of, but which the British found titillating to watch: men getting rid of women they didn't want and handing them on to men who did.

There was something familiar about the beautiful young woman bedecked in silver jewellery. Adela started to walk towards them.

'Adela, stay away from the coolies,' Jay called out.

'It's Pema!' She picked up speed. She recognised the belligerent uncle. He was pushing Pema at another man. Pema was trying to hide her right cheek, the side that was scarred from her accident, with her shawl, but the other man was ripping it away to expose her.

'Leave her alone!' Adela cried, rushing towards them.

Pema looked up, her eyes beseeching as she spotted Adela hurtling across the slope. A crowd of onlookers jostled around, whether in support of Pema, her uncle or the other man she wasn't sure. Just at that moment Adela caught sight of another face she knew: Ghulam Khan. She stopped short, confused by his sudden appearance. He was pushing towards the fracas from the opposite direction. The men in dispute over Pema were shouting at each other, shoving the girl between them, the younger man demanding money back.

As Ghulam reached them, he raised his arms as if to speak. At that moment Sam appeared out of nowhere and barged Ghulam out of the way, knocking him sideways. Sam elbowed his way between the arguing men. Pema cringed under her shawl and stared at Adela with terrified eyes. Adela held her breath, expecting violence to erupt around Sam for daring to interfere. But Sam cajoled and placated them with words and back slaps, letting each of them have their say. The mood was volatile. Sam glanced once at Adela with a tiny nod that told her to leave.

'Give him his money back,' Sam ordered the uncle.

The uncle protested he would not, so Sam there and then emptied his pockets of all the money he had.

'It's all yours,' he said to the younger man. 'Now she's mine.' Then he reached a protective arm about Pema and pulled her away from them both. The younger man scrambled for the money at his feet. The uncle stared in suspicion at Sam, but did not try to stop him taking Pema. The crowd parted for the tall missionary. Adela watched stupefied as Sam led the Gaddi girl away. Sam had just bought himself a woman right in front of her very eyes! Adela stood for a long time, staring after him, but he didn't look back once. In the heat and press of bodies, she felt faint, yet was rooted to the spot. She could not believe what she had just witnessed.

Jay sent a bearer to fetch her safely back. By the time she had walked unsteadily to the picnic spot, trying to hide how upset she was, the news was spreading among the British onlookers like a forest fire. The maverick missionary Sam Jackman had bought a wife – haggled enthusiastically for her like one of the local peasants.

Jay, concerned by Adela's shaken appearance, ordered transport back to Eagle's Nest for his guests and left his servants to pack up the camp. It was only as they travelled back in the car, leaving the chaotic fair behind, that Adela remembered seeing Ghulam. What was he doing there? Or had she mistaken him for someone else? Her concern had been all for Pema, so she had only seen him for a few brief moments. But deep down she was sure she was right. Ghulam had not left the area at all; he was still around and no doubt active. It didn't bode well for peace in the hills.

But Ghulam left only a nagging unease, whereas Sam's dramatic intervention at the bridal bidding had shocked her to the core. The gossips were already exaggerating the story as they left.

'Fancy a man of God behaving like that.'

'He must have been drunk. I hear he's been drinking his way around Simla for days.'

'Damn disgrace if you ask me. Church should kick him out.'

'Got to admit the man's got balls.'

'Arthur!'

'Reflects badly on us all.'

'That's what happens when a man goes native.'

Adela had not been able to resist rounding on them for their cattiness. 'He was just standing up for the poor girl. I know her – she's a Gaddi shepherdess – and her uncle was selling her off like she didn't matter.'

But they had just looked at her askance and clicked their tongues when she'd walked on.

By the time they got back to Eagle's Nest, Adela was beset by doubts. What had really possessed Sam to intervene? He could have called in the police if he'd thought Pema was in danger. Why had he acted so impulsively and paid over money? Unless he'd wanted Pema for himself. Perhaps he was so lonely in Narkanda that he saw his opportunity and took it. She recoiled with distaste at the very idea. Whatever the reason, Sam's reputation was in tatters. If he was half the man she believed he was, he would have to stand by Pema now. There was no undoing what he had done. And there was no hope now, Adela thought with sickening realisation, of Sam ever marrying her.

Chapter 12

Fluffy retired to bed as soon as they reached Eagle's Nest.

'I think she's picked up a summer fever in the heat,' Adela explained to Jay. He was full of concern.

'She must recuperate here in the cool and quiet,' he insisted. 'I'll send for a doctor. My cooks will prepare anything she wants.'

'I'm sure she'll be fine to travel tomorrow,' said Adela. 'Noor and I can manage at home. I'll get Dr Fatima to check her over.'

'No.' Jay was firm. 'I won't hear of dear Mrs Hogg being turfed out. You shan't go home till she's better.'

With the Raja of Nerikot having returned home, Jay and Adela dined alone. Afterwards they sat drinking vintage tawny port on the veranda. Adela felt light-headed and utterly drained by the day.

'It was a mistake to go to the fair,' said Jay. 'I hate to see you upset.'

'I'm not.'

He caught her hand. 'I can tell when a woman is upset, Adela. Is it just because of the Gaddi girl?'

Adela shrugged but did not pull away.

'Then you should be happy for her,' Jay said. 'The handsome young Englishman stepped in and saved her from the native coolie and her rascal of an uncle.'

Adela didn't like his teasing tone; to him the whole episode was just a passing amusement. She stood up.

'I'm very tired. Thank you for a pleasant evening and for being so kind to Auntie and me.'

Jay stood too. 'I'm not being kind, Adela,' he said quietly. 'I do it because I'm in love with you.'

She jolted at his words.

'Look at your beautiful eyes – as big as dinner plates – but you shouldn't be so shocked. You must know how much you mean to me.'

'Jay, I—'

'Walk with me in the garden please, Adela. It is such a lovely night. What a waste it would be to retire this early and miss its magic.'

She gave in to his persuasive words. The sky was littered with stars, and far off they could still hear the faint throb of drums as the fair-goers celebrated into the night. He led her down a path she had not walked before; it was steep, with steps cut into the bank that Fluffy had thought too hazardous. It levelled out along a small ridge, the whole way lit by flickering lanterns like fireflies in the trees. At the end was a small pavilion perched on the very edge, looking out over the dark valley plunging below.

'This is how the place got its name,' Jay said, leading the way into the summerhouse. 'It's on the site of an eagles' eyrie. Some long-ago officer of the East India Company built a house here. Uncle Kishan's grandfather bought it at the turn of the century and built a new house, but kept the old name.'

Someone had already lit lamps in the room; the warm light pushed back the shadows enough for Adela to see a large divan covered in plump cushions facing out over the view. The windows had been thrown open, and the room was filled with a spicy scent from burning incense sticks to keep insects at bay.

'Sit beside me,' Jay coaxed, 'and tell me how I can chase your sadness away.'

Adela perched on the edge of the vast sofa. Moonlight lit the dramatic mountainsides all around; night birds sang. From somewhere below she thought she heard the call of a leopard.

'This is one of the most beautiful places I've ever seen,' she said, her voice hushed, as if to raise it might break the spell. 'I don't want to be sad in such a place. I want to forget all about today.'

She turned to look at him. He ran his fingers through her hair, sending shivers down her back.

'Let me make love to you, Adela,' said Jay, 'here in this special place.'

Desire flooded through her at his seductive words. She had drunk too much wine and port at dinner to think clearly about what she was doing, yet she didn't want to think. She was enjoying the here and now, the magical setting and the loving that Jay was offering. She yearned for romance and to bury once and for all her feelings of disappointment over Sam. Only Jay could chase away her anger and misery. She had longed for Sam for the past five years, hoping that one day he might return her love. Today that dream had disintegrated before her very eyes.

Now the most handsome man she had ever met was being explicit in his desire for her; Prince Jay was offering her exciting, forbidden pleasure.

Adela's throat was dry with nervous anticipation. Her voice was a husky whisper. 'Yes, Jay, I want you to love me.'

For an instant she saw surprise register in his dark eyes; then his sensual mouth curved into a satisfied smile. He leant towards her and kissed her slowly, softly on the lips. He eased her back into the cushions. Adela closed her eyes and gave herself up to him.

***

Once was not enough. Every evening, while Fluffy kept to her room, dosed up with infusions to fight off the cold that had followed two days of fever, Adela and Jay slipped off to the pavilion. She couldn't wait to be alone with him; she hungered for his kisses and the feel of his soft skin and toned, muscled body against hers. She shed her initial inhibitions at him seeing her naked and delighted in the way he admired her in the lamplight, kissing his way down the length of her, making her cry out with ecstasy.

One night, when the spell of hot May weather was broken by a storm – a precursor of the July monsoon – Jay had declared the path too dangerous for a night excursion. Adela had crept to his apartment in the dead of night, unable to bear the thought of a night without his lovemaking. Jay had been startled but amused, though he had hushed her enthusiasm with a finger to her lips, and they had made love in suppressed silence for fear of alerting Fluffy. Adela didn't care. She felt reckless and alive and in love. Jay had become her heady addiction.

By the end of another week, Fluffy was up and about and impatient to be home. She was suspicious at Adela's reluctance to leave.

'I hope you haven't been foolish while I've been confined to bed, young lady.'

'I'm in love,' Adela blurted out. 'And Jay loves me back. He's even talked about marriage.'

Fluffy snorted. 'Don't be ridiculous. It would never be allowed.'

Adela was hurt. 'If two people love each other, anything is possible.'

Her guardian gave her a sharp look. 'I thought it was young Sam Jackman you were sweet on.'

Adela blushed to be reminded of her infatuation. 'That was a girlish crush. This is the real thing. Anyway, Sam has chosen to marry a native woman.'

'Native woman?' Fluffy echoed, raising an eyebrow. 'I hope you're not turning into a snob.'

'Auntie, please can we stay longer?' Adela implored. 'Or let me stay on if you want to go home.'

'Certainly not,' Fluffy replied. 'We'll return together. If Prince Jay thinks the same way as you, he'll follow you back to Simla.'

Adela determined to ask him to do so the minute he returned from his hunting trip with Nerikot. He had gone before dawn, setting off for his friend's estate, leaving her to creep from his bed before the servants were about, promising to be back by nightfall. She had been frustrated by his refusal to take her with him.

'Nerikot is a backward state – more traditional. They wouldn't approve of you hunting with us like a man.' He had smiled and kissed her nose. 'I'll be back tonight – tomorrow at the latest.'

He didn't return that day or the day after. Adela, filled with worry, determined she would ride to Nerikot and make sure he was all right. Fluffy would hear none of it and sent a message instead. Back came a chaprassy with word that the prince had been unavoidably detained on business and advising them to return to Simla in the meantime.

'What on earth does that mean?' Adela fretted. 'Do you think he's in danger, Auntie? There might be trouble up in Nerikot.'

'Nonsense,' said Fluffy.

'I saw Ghulam Khan the communist at the Sipi Fair,' Adela confessed.

Fluffy looked taken aback by this. But her words were bullish.

'The prince is quite capable of taking care of himself. And we must do as he says and return home before we outstay our welcome.'

***

Back at Briar Rose Cottage, they soon picked up stories that unrest had broken out in Nerikot.

'There was a big demonstration,' Noor said. 'In the bazaar they are saying that things got out of hand. Shots were fired.'

Adela was aghast. 'I told you Jay wasn't safe!'

'How terrible,' Fluffy said in agitation. 'I hope the Raja and his family weren't hurt.'

Noor gave them a strange look. 'No, memsa'b, quite the opposite. It was palace guards that fired on the demonstrators. They say dozens have been killed.'

The women looked at each other, appalled and speechless. The bearer hesitated and then held out a small buff folder to Adela.

'Jackman Sahib left these for you.'

'For me?' Adela tensed as she took it. 'When was he here?'

'Just before the Sipi Fair, Adela Mem'.'

Alone in her room, Adela opened the folder. Her heart lurched to see photos from Narkanda. She flicked through them quickly, pausing over one of her and Sam leaning on the veranda, smiling; Fatima must have taken it. But most of them were of the Gaddi shepherds, including a close-up of a grinning, pretty Pema. In annoyance, Adela threw them into a drawer.

Daily, Adela waited for some word from Jay to say he was safely returned from Nerikot, but none came. Simla was rife with rumours. The police were investigating the shootings. Fluffy and Adela called to see Inspector Pollock for news.

'The rumours of multiple deaths were grossly exaggerated,' he assured them. 'As far as we can tell, two men were shot dead and three more were injured.'

'That's still terrible,' gasped Adela.

'What will happen to the Raja?' asked Fluffy. 'We met him at Eagle's Nest.'

'What did you make of him?' asked Pollock.

'He's a nice man,' said Adela.

'Nice, yes,' agreed Fluffy, 'but a weak one. Prince Sanjay was trying to stiffen his resolve to deal with the Mandalist protestors.'

Adela jumped to Jay's defence. 'But he said nothing about using violence.'

Pollock scrutinised her. 'But you can confirm that Prince Sanjay was staying at Nerikot at the time of the shootings?'

Adela felt cold sweat prickle her brow. 'He could have been out on shikar up in the hills.'

'Well, it's a mess. Someone fired on unarmed men. We have to be seen to be doing something if we're to keep a lid on all this unrest. The Raja will have to explain himself to the British authorities.'

'So might the Raja be prosecuted?' asked Fluffy.

'It's possible,' said Pollock, giving Adela a hard look, 'and anyone else who was involved.'

Soon afterwards Sanjay's name began to be bandied about by the gossipmongers in the Mall shops and club rooms.

'They say it was Prince Sanjay who gave the order to fire – thought the Raja was being too weak.'

'I heard he was the one who fired the first shot, as if the natives were fair game.'

Adela was furious at their attempt to sully Jay's name and chided Fluffy for putting the idea into the inspector's head.

'We shouldn't have gone to see him – and you shouldn't have dragged Jay's name into it, Auntie.'

'And perhaps you are being a bit blinkered about the prince,' Fluffy snapped. 'If he's got nothing to hide, why isn't he back here in Simla paying you some attention?'

Unable to talk about it with Fluffy, Adela went to seek out Fatima and talk about the trouble in Nerikot. They were both relieved to hear that Ghulam's name was not among those of the casualties. But there was rumour of further lawlessness as a result of the shootings, and the police in Simla were on alert for trouble spreading. The atmosphere was tense. Sundar, attempting to raise their spirits, treated Adela and Fatima to tea at Davico's, but Adela was sure people were whispering about her behind her back. A tipsy Bracknall confronted her.

'Ah, Miss Robson, you'll be able to shed some light on the Nerikot affair. Did your native beau, Prince Sanjay, give the order to shoot or not?'

'Mr Bracknall, I find your words offensive,' she sparked back.

'Well, he is your beau, isn't he?' Bracknall leered. 'You've been holed up in his love nest for weeks. Everybody's talking about it.'

Sundar rose. 'Please, sir, leave Miss Robson alone.'

Adela shook with indignation. 'Prince Sanjay would never fire on unarmed civilians, *never.*'

'Oh, I think he's quite capable of it,' slurred Bracknall. 'They don't have the same scruples about fair play that we do.' He threw Sundar a contemptuous look and moved on.

When he'd gone, Adela asked, 'Have people really been talking about me and Jay like this – in such an unkind way?'

Fatima and Sundar exchanged uncomfortable looks. 'What did you expect?' Fatima said bluntly. 'Unmarried memsahibs and Indians, even princes, are not supposed to fraternise, beyond the occasional cocktail party.'

Adela blushed deeply to think how much further she had gone.

'Still,' said Sundar with bleak humour, 'it's nothing to the gossip that Sam's caused with buying the girl.'

'Oh, the silly man,' Fatima said with impatient affection. 'What on earth possessed him?'

Adela's heart twisted at the memory. She glanced around and dropped her voice. 'I think it might have had something to do with your brother.'

Fatima gave her a sharp look. 'Meaning?'

'He was there too. I think he was going to make a song and dance about the confrontation. Sam pushed him out of the way and intervened instead.'

Only as Adela spoke her thoughts aloud for the first time did she believe that might be the reason for Sam's actions. She had been so angry, believing that what he had done that day was a deliberate rejection of her. But perhaps it was something else entirely. Had Sam just acted on the spur of the moment to protect not only Pema but Ghulam too? The idea threw her emotions into turmoil. Whatever the reason – even if it had just been gut instinct – Sam was saddled with his rash actions. And she was too. Adela felt a wave of panic. She had thrown herself at Jay and revelled in their romantic affair. But where was he now?

***

A week later, with no sign of Jay in Simla, Fluffy ordered a listless Adela out of the house.

'Go and see your friends at the theatre,' she ordered. 'They'll be casting for *Charley's Aunt*. It's your last chance to perform before your trip to England.'

Adela steeled herself to go that afternoon. The town was pearly grey under heavy clouds, the air sultry. Another storm was brewing.

In the auditorium Tommy was handing out scripts and trying to herd a chattering crowd of players out of the wings and into seats. He was taken aback to see her. An awkward silence fell as Adela mounted the steps.

Deborah came forward and greeted her. 'Look who the cat's brought in.' She brushed Adela's cheek with a kiss. 'You're brave,' she whispered.

Adela's insides tightened.

'Take a seat in the stalls, girl,' Tommy said, smiling briefly, but avoiding her look. 'You can listen in if you want.'

'Listen in?' Adela laughed. 'I've come to audition.'

To her left someone moved out of the shadows, and a familiar voice said, 'What a shame you've missed the auditions. All the parts are taken, aren't they, Tommy?'

'Nina?' Adela gasped.

'Hello.' Nina smiled. She missed Adela's cheek with a loud kiss. 'We meet again at last. I've been telling everyone all about our school days together and what a little terror you were.' She gave a brittle laugh.

Adela's heart began to thud in dread. Even before anything was said, she knew that Nina had been spreading her poison. All she could do was to try and counter it with courtesy.

'I was sorry to hear about your father's death. It must have been such a shock for you and your mother.'

For a moment Nina seemed thrown; then just for an instant her top lipped curled in that familiar gesture of contempt Adela remembered so well, before it changed to a smile of regret. 'No need to be sorry. You never really knew him. We received so many letters of condolence; that was a great comfort. It's a shame you and your parents never thought to write, even though your father had been a close friend of my mother's. I can't deny that was a little hurtful.'

Adela stuttered, 'I'm s-sorry, but I'm sure—'

'I accept that,' Nina said with a sad expression. 'It's not your fault you don't know what it's like to lose a dear father. Shall we just get on with the rehearsal? I'd rather not talk about upsetting things.'

'Of course,' Tommy said hastily. 'Where were we?'

Adela's frustration swelled. Her mother had insisted on writing a note of condolence despite the smears by Mrs Davidge against the family. She threw a look of appeal at Deborah to stick up for her, but her friend was looking intently at her script.

Adela retreated and sat in the stalls. At first the read-through was stiff and the atmosphere awkward – was that because she was there? – but soon Tommy was putting them at their ease and they began laughing at the comedy and making suggestions. Adela stayed on, stubbornly determined not to be hounded out of the group by Nina's spitefulness, sugar-coated though it was. All the old feelings of inferiority and nervousness that the bullying girl had instilled in her five years ago came flooding back. But she had stood up to her then, and she wasn't going to back down now. They were grown women; it was ridiculous to harbour resentments from when they were thirteen. Yet Nina had power over her; in her head Adela could hear the taunt 'two annas' as if it were yesterday.

At the end of rehearsal she waited for Deborah, but her friend was hanging back with a group of girls clustered around Nina. Was her friend deliberately avoiding her? Adela steeled herself to walk forward and join them.

'Are you going to Davico's?' she asked brightly.

Nina half turned and spoke over her shoulder. 'No, I'm having the girls back to our bungalow for tennis and afternoon tea.'

'Adela can come too, can't she?' Deborah asked. 'She's great at tennis.'

'So sorry,' Nina said. 'I don't mind a bit, but Mother might be awkward – all that past history with Adela's father.'

Adela rose to the bait. 'I don't know what you've been saying, but my father did not jilt your mother. That's just nonsense.'

'Well, how would you possibly know?' Nina asked with that sad smile that Adela was growing to hate. 'Your father would never admit it, would he? But it's a devastating thing for a woman to experience. Surely you can see that.'

'Only if it were true!'

'Mother would never lie.' Nina put her hand to her mouth as if to stifle a sob.

'Adela!' Deborah remonstrated. 'Don't be so unkind.'

'Okay, ladies,' Tommy intervened, 'time to clear off and let me lock up. See you at rehearsal tomorrow.'

They scattered off with calls of goodbye and disappeared, leaving Adela and Tommy alone.

'It's been just three weeks since the last show, yet somehow I've gone from everyone's best friend to the girl no one wants around.' Adela fixed Tommy with troubled eyes. 'What's happened in three weeks?'

Tommy met her look. 'For starters, you and Prince Sanjay are what's happened. They were jealous – I was jealous – you chose to go with him rather than with us to the after-show party. Should never turn your back on the pack, my girl.'

'I regret that now . . .'

'But they would have got over that,' Tommy went on. 'You were providing some juicy gossip going off to his country retreat – we love all that stuff, don't we?'

'It's Nina, isn't it?' Adela guessed. 'She's changed people towards me.'

Tommy sighed. 'Yes, she's been busy with her wagging tongue. Nothing too bitchy, just little titbits dropped now and again with that sorrowful look in her blue eyes that she's so good at. She's a pro that one.'

Adela gulped. 'So you know . . . you know things . . . about my family.'

Tommy nodded. 'She's made sure they all know about you being Eurasian – says your granny was a tea picker or some such.'

Adela felt bile in her throat. She swallowed it down and said with emotion, 'My great-grandmother was an Assamese silk worker – a skilled woman – and my grandmother was a teacher. My mother is a successful businesswoman who has run her own tea rooms in England and tea gardens in India. Why should the likes of Nina Davidge look down her long nose at me? Tell me that, Tommy!'

Tommy gave her a look of pity. 'You know why, Adela.'

She gave a bitter smile. ''Cause my family have let the side down? 'Cause I'm not a pure-blooded English girl?'

'It's cruel, but that's the way a lot of British still think. They like to feel superior – it's been fed to them with their mother's milk.'

'Is that the way you feel, Tommy?' Adela challenged. 'Is that why you don't want me in your play either?'

'I would have let you audition if you'd bothered to turn up.'

'Would you really?'

Tommy dropped his gaze. 'Sit down a minute, will you?' Adela stood where she was, defiant. 'Please.' He tugged her gently into a seat and sat beside her.

For a moment or two he said nothing. He looked around, making sure there was no one else there listening in.

'Villiers isn't my real surname,' he said, his voice so low she had to lean in to hear him. 'I don't know what it is.'

'What do you mean?'

'I was adopted as a baby. My parents – my adoptive parents – had lost three babies, and my mother couldn't bear the thought of another pregnancy, so they went to an orphanage and chose me.' Tommy gave a mirthless laugh. 'I must have been the palest skinned and the fairest haired they could find among the half-castes, 'cause that was what the orphanage was for: the babies the Brits disowned or the Indians were too ashamed to keep.'

Adela struggled to take in his startling revelation. All this time they had been friends yet never known that they shared the same secret. She covered his hand with her own. 'Sorry, Tommy. I had no idea.'

'Of course you didn't. We all keep it locked up inside like something shameful, scared witless in case people find out.'

'That's the worst thing,' Adela agreed, 'the shame you're made to feel. Why should it matter so much?'

Tommy shrugged and let out a long sigh. Adela squeezed his hand.

'But you don't know that you're Anglo-Indian, do you? Your parents might have been British and died or something.'

'Highly unlikely,' Tommy grunted.

'But possible. Have you ever gone back and tried to find out?'

'Why on earth would I do that? I'm a proud Villiers through and through,' he mocked himself.

'Do you know where the orphanage was?'

Tommy laced his fingers through hers. 'Your neck of the woods I think. My father was posted to Shillong with the Public Works Department for a couple of years.'

'When was that?'

'They think I was born in 1907. There was a bit of the jitters going on around then – fifty years since the Indian Mutiny – and all the British were worried about attacks. Plenty of Eurasian babies being abandoned; my parents had the pick of the crop.'

Adela gasped. 'How strange.'

'What is?' Tommy asked.

'It's something I discovered a couple of years ago when I was home. My family told me of a tragedy that happened at our house – before we were living there. My Auntie Sophie and her parents were staying at Belgooree in 1907. Something terrible happened. Her father was ill – sick in the head – he must've been 'cause he shot his wife and then himself, leaving poor Sophie orphaned at six years old. But there was also Sophie's baby brother. Their ayah – who later became my nanny too – said he was taken to an orphanage in Shillong.' She looked at Tommy critically. He had brown eyes and light brown hair. Was there a passing resemblance to Sophie? He was staring at her aghast.

'My God,' said Tommy, 'what an awful story.'

'Isn't it? Mother says Sophie still longs for the brother she never knew.'

Tommy gave her a look of disbelief. 'Don't tell me we could be related.'

Adela smiled. 'Don't worry, Sophie is no blood relation. But what if you were that baby—?'

'Doesn't do to dwell on what ifs,' Tommy cautioned.

'I suppose not,' Adela sighed. 'So can we carry on being friends?'

'Of course.'

'But won't you get sent to Coventry for fraternising with the enemy?'

'I like living dangerously.' Tommy grinned and kissed her fingers.

She kissed his cheek. 'Things would've be a lot simpler if we could just have fallen in love with each other, wouldn't they?'

Tommy looked rueful. 'A lot simpler.'

***

Despite Tommy's promises to remain friends, Adela soon found that her presence at the theatre was unwelcome. Nina was outwardly friendly, but the other girls were cool towards her. She waylaid Deborah outside St Mary's.

'You know half the things Nina says about me are untrue.'

'So half are true,' Deborah mocked.

'What difference does it make?' Adela was impatient. 'We've been friends for years. I'm still the same person I was a month ago, so why are you treating me like a leper?'

'Because you're not the same, are you? You should have been honest with me – with all of us – letting me think you were, well, like the rest of us.'

Adela's look was scathing. 'I thought our friendship was stronger than that.'

Deborah appeared uncomfortable. 'If it was just up to me—'

'It is just up to you, Deb. No one is forcing you to break our friendship – not even Nina can do that. The choice is yours.'

'Don't make me choose,' Deborah said in annoyance. 'Nina has been really nice to me, and her mother has offered to let me stay there after school finishes. My parents are pleased with the idea. Why don't you just make a bit more effort to be kind to Nina?'

'Kind to Nina?' Adela was incredulous. 'The girl who made my life hell at school.'

'So you say,' Deborah retorted. 'Nina tells it differently. She still has a scar on her finger where you bit her. Sounds like you were the one out of control.'

Adela felt sick at the way Nina had twisted things round to make her seem like the bully. Now she was doing her best to turn her Simla friends against her too. She gave Deborah a helpless look.

'Listen,' said Deborah, 'just keep a low profile until all this hoo-ha with the prince and the shootings dies down. I'm sure in time we can all go back to being friends again.'

Adela nodded, although she knew Deborah was just placating her to avoid a further scene. Deborah smiled in relief.

'So what was it like?'

'What?'

'Being with Jay? Bet he's an expert lover like they say.'

Adela was winded by the unexpected remark. She answered without thinking. 'You make it sound sordid, but it's not. We love each other.'

She turned and walked away quickly before Deborah could show her disbelief.

***

In early June a letter came from Sophie.

My dearest lassie,

We have been thinking of you such a lot, Uncle Rafi and I. We have read the newspaper reports about the riots in Nerikot with great alarm and are greatly concerned about Jay's involvement. I know you have a soft spot for him, my darling, so I thought you would want to know that he is back in Gulgat at the palace. I fear he has taken advantage of your affections, but he will tell us little, if anything, of his time in Simla. It is Fluffy Hogg who wrote and told us you had stayed at Eagle's Nest.

I hope you will be home for your eighteenth birthday and that we can all spoil you on your special day – especially if you will be away in England for a while afterwards. Tilly is growing ridiculously excited at the thought of your trip home together – she misses Jamie and Libby so much and can't wait to see them again. It makes me rather wish Rafi and I were coming with you too. I should love to see Scotland again, though I have no relations left there since my Great Uncle Daniel in Perth died.

Come home soon – it's been far too long since we hugged and chatted! Give our greetings to Mrs Hogg. I imagine Boz is away on tour in the hills, but send love to Fatima.

Your adoring Auntie Sophie xxx

Adela sat down on her bed and wept. She had been waiting an age for word that Jay was safe, for him to return to Simla to be with her, but now he was hundreds of miles away in Gulgat. How long had he been there? He had not even sent word himself, but left her to hear of his return second-hand! Did he think so little of her? Or perhaps he was still in danger and was lying low? Maybe Sophie shouldn't have told her and was putting him at risk by writing it down in a letter; the authorities could have intercepted and read it.

Adela read the letter again, so full of tenderness, and felt ashamed at resenting Sophie for breaking the news. Jay had fled from the hills without a thought for her; otherwise he would have sent a message himself or tried to see her one more time before parting. Adela curled up on her bed and wept until she felt hollowed out.

That evening she sat on the veranda with Fluffy watching an electric storm. It crackled and rent the sky into jagged pieces. She told her guardian about Jay being in Gulgat.

Fluffy didn't seem surprised. 'I rather suspected he had left the area.'

Adela felt her eyes sting again with unwanted tears. 'Perhaps it was too unsafe for him to be seen in Simla,' she said, searching for an excuse.

'Perhaps,' agreed Fluffy. 'What do you want to do now, my dear?'

Adela thought bleakly how her life in Simla had collapsed around her so swiftly: she was outcast from the theatre group, gossiped about along the Mall and deserted by Jay. She had given up her job and neglected her duties at the hospital in favour of a social life of dances, dinners and riding expeditions, revelling in the limelight and encouraging Prince Jay. And worst of all, Sam lived close by in the hills and yet forever beyond her reach.

'I think I should go home to Belgooree,' Adela said quietly. 'What do you think?'

'I agree, and I think it will make your parents very happy.'

Adela felt a stab of guilt at how little thought she had given her parents and brother these past months. She had been having too much fun and had hardly spared the time to reply to their long, affectionate letters. A scribbled note shoved into an envelope with Fluffy's longer epistles was all she had given them.

'You've been so good to me, Auntie. The person I'll miss most in Simla is you.'

Fluffy smiled. 'I'll miss you too, my dear. You've been such a good companion. Noor and I will find the house very empty without you.'

'Quiet, you mean.' Adela gave a sad smile.

'You know you can come back any time you want.' Fluffy gave one of her direct looks. 'But I think you are ready to move on. Go and pursue your ambition to be an actress. Don't let the petty-minded of Simla put you off.'

Adela felt her heart squeeze. 'Auntie.' She swallowed, forcing herself to ask, 'When did you find out about my . . . about Mother's parentage? Was it just since Nina came? That's not why you want me to go, is it?'

Fluffy looked at her, shocked. 'Goodness me, how could you think such a thing? I've always known about it – ever since I met your dear mama on the boat coming out in '22 and you were a wee thing rushing about on deck like an eager kitten. Some of the women were unkind to her, but she put them in their place with her polite but firm manner. It didn't bother her that they knew she was Anglo-Indian – at least she didn't show it – and it shouldn't bother you.'

Adela gave a teary smile at Fluffy's brusque, wise words; they eased a fraction of the emptiness she felt. She leant across the wicker sofa and hugged her stout benefactor, breathing in her smell of camphor and lavender. 'Thank you, Auntie. Thank you for everything and more.'

Chapter 13

Adela had forgotten how beautiful Belgooree was. She saw it with fresh eyes as her father drove her back up from Shillong into the Khasi hills. The orchids bloomed and the air smelt of honey; the car stirred up showers of butterflies as they drove by. The jungle parted like stage curtains from time to time to reveal cultivated terraces of potatoes. Cattle meandered out of the trees to cross the road, tended by boys in mountain caps who sang as they prodded the beasts out of the way.

When the engine strained at the steeper gradient and they bumped along the plantation tracks between the emerald tea bushes, Adela felt emotion catch her throat. She waved at the women returning to the weighing machine with baskets of leaves strapped to their heads.

'Second flush from Eastern Section?' she asked.

Wesley grinned and nodded. 'Glad to see you haven't forgotten everything about tea.'

'I haven't been away that long.' She smiled.

'Well, it seems like an eternity to me and your mother.' He ruffled her hair like he used to when she was little. She leant in and hugged him.

'Give it a week and you'll be wishing me back to Aunt Fluffy's.'

'Very likely,' he said and winked, accelerating past the factory and in through the compound, tooting the horn repeatedly.

The noise brought Clarrie and Harry clattering down the bungalow steps.

Harry threw himself at his big sister as soon as she climbed from the car. 'Delly's home!'

She picked him up and swung him round in her arms, dropping him back swiftly. 'Goodness, you're like a sack of potatoes! I can hardly pick you up.'

He reached up to be swung around again, but Adela was rushing to her mother for a much-needed hug. They clung on together.

'I've missed you, Mother,' she mumbled into Clarrie's hair, noticing threads of grey for the first time.

'Me too, my darling.' Clarrie squeezed her tight and kissed her head. They broke apart and Clarrie scrutinised her. 'You're looking a little thin and pasty. Mohammed Din will have to feed you up. None of these faddy diets from Simla in this household.'

'Glad to hear it,' Adela said and smiled, 'but I'm fine really.' There was something about the way her mother eyed her that made her self-conscious. Was it possible for a mother to tell just by looking that her daughter had lost her innocence? Adela turned away. 'Where's Ayah Mimi?'

'You can go and see her,' said Clarrie. 'She keeps to her hut most of the time these days – sleeping and praying.'

'She's well though?'

'She's fine,' said Wesley. 'Still refusing to come and live in the house. She eats less than a mynah bird, but she'll outlive us all.'

***

Adela's first days back were spent early-morning riding and accompanying her father around the tea garden. The temperature was climbing and there had been a couple of half-hearted storms, but the main monsoon was yet to arrive. They listened on the temperamental radio to reports of its progress up the Subcontinent. The rains had started in Ceylon.

Clarrie was once again busy in the factory, overseeing with an eagle eye the processes of withering, rolling, fermenting, drying and sorting, as well as taking part in the tea tasting. Their mohurer, Daleep, had a flair for tea and had been trained up as a taster; Clarrie enjoyed debating with him about the character of their teas and whether they were bright and brisk or a touch flat and dull.

'Never try and argue with Clarissa Belhaven when it comes to the merits of Belgooree tea,' Wesley had joked with the eager young Daleep when he had first been promoted. 'Just listen and learn.' Daleep was now as expert as Wesley and gaining on Clarrie.

Adela greeted the women in the sorting room as they sat on the floor over sieves, sifting the processed tea leaves into grades, their shawls pulled over their noses to keep out the dust. She breathed in the heady aromatic smell of tea that permeated the sheds, a safe, secure smell that conjured up her early childhood.

Each day she called on her old nurse, Ayah Mimi, bringing her bowls of dal and making her tea. No one knew her age, but Sophie had guessed she was in her seventies, though she looked older. The woman had had a hard life after being Sophie's nanny, eking out a living and ending up as a holy woman sheltering in the forest hut at the hilltop temple clearing, where Sophie had found her again. She was the last of the household to have seen Sophie's baby brother after the fateful day Sophie's father had shot his wife and turned the gun on himself. Ayah Mimi had fled with the baby, but been forced to hand him over to a police officer, who had dumped the newborn in an orphanage. For years Ayah Mimi had searched for him in vain, as had Sophie after her return to India as an adult.

Adela waited a week before she brought the subject up, knowing it was painful for the old nurse. But the nagging thought that Tommy might be the missing boy would not go away. She sat on a rush mat on the bare floor of the ayah's hut and talked about Sophie coming for her birthday.

'One of the reasons Auntie Sophie likes to come here is to see you, Ayah Mimi. She's always asking after you in her letters to Mother.'

Ayah smiled and nodded.

'I wonder how much she remembers being here when she was little. Can't be much, can it? And her feelings about the place must be mixed.'

Again the old woman nodded, the expression in her eyes reflective.

'Ayah, you don't have to talk about this if it upsets you, but do you mind if I ask you something about Sophie's baby brother?'

Ayah didn't flinch but fixed Adela with a steady gaze. After a long moment she nodded her assent.

'A male friend of mine in Simla came from an orphanage in Shillong – he was adopted by a British couple – and he'd be the right sort of age for Sophie's brother. I know it's a long shot, but can you remember the name of the orphanage where you . . . where the Logan baby was taken? Was it the Catholics or the Welsh Baptists?'

Ayah began to twist her hands in her lap. Her eyes focused on something distant. Her voice when she spoke was thin and high-pitched, like wind through reeds.

'I don't know which orphanage.'

'But I thought you went to work in one in the hope of finding him.'

'I did,' she whispered, 'but only because I thought that's where the police officer would have taken him.'

'Oh, I see.' Adela felt a stab of disappointment.

'That night – before the terrible thing happened – I took baby sahib in a basket to the village like Logan Memsahib said,' Ayah recalled painfully. 'She thought the baby was in danger from Logan Sahib – he was shouting so much at the baby. Ama, a wise local woman, sheltered us. But afterwards Burke Sahib, the policeman, found me and took him away – said I was stealing a white baby and I was never to try and find him or Sophie again or I would go to prison—'

A dry sob broke from her throat. Adela immediately threw her arms around the tiny woman.

'Even though he made bad threats,' croaked Ayah, 'I did everything to try and find Sophie because I knew from Burke Sahib that she was still alive. Logan Memsahib had kept her daughter safe by getting her to play hide and seek. But it was many years before I knew this – not until Sophie came back to me . . .'

'Oh, Ayah, I shouldn't have made you remember!' They rocked back and forth.

'I never forget,' said Ayah, 'not one day of my life. The little sahib is always in my heart.' She looked at Adela with a spark of hope in her rheumy eyes. 'Perhaps this Simla sahib is him.'

'That's what I keep wondering,' Adela said. 'Do you think I should mention it to Auntie Sophie?'

'What is his name? Is he a nice man?'

'Tommy Villiers – and yes, he's nice. He's fun and a bit of a show-off, but that's an act he puts on – underneath he's kind and really quite caring.'

'Tommy Villiers,' Ayah repeated. 'What does he look like?'

Adela pulled from her pocket the recent programme from *The Arabian Nights*.

'It's not very clear and he's dressed up in a turban, but that's Tommy sitting in the front. Do you think he looks anything like either of Sophie's parents?'

'The eyes,' said Ayah, 'they are kind, like Logan Memsahib's.'

It didn't seem much to go on. 'Would it be cruel to get Auntie Sophie's hopes up?' Adela said, sounding worried.

'It is much more cruel never to know. If there is a chance, then tell her,' Ayah urged.

'But how can we ever prove it?'

Ayah sighed at the impossibility. 'If the gods have been good, then he will still possess the elephant bracelet.'

'What bracelet?'

'Logan Sahib had two that she wore. One she gave to Sophie, and one to me to sell if needs be to feed the baby. I tucked it into his shawl when that man took him away.'

'I've seen Sophie's bracelet – it's made of ivory elephants' heads. I used to count them as a child. Twelve heads.'

Ayah Mimi nodded in agreement.

'I'll write to Tommy and ask him.'

The old woman smiled and cradled her face with slim bony fingers. For the first time in ages Adela heard her old nanny break into a song of joy.

***

On the thirteenth of June, Adela's aunties arrived for her birthday, Tilly with ten-year-old Mungo and Sophie with Rafi. Harry shrieked with excitement to see the older boy, who at once started showing him his homemade catapult. They ran off into the garden to try it out.

'Uncle James sends apologies and happy returns,' said Tilly, kissing Adela, 'but it's too frantically busy at the Oxford Estates for him to get away. Doing as much as he can before the monsoons make the roads impassable.'

'I quite understand,' Adela said. 'I'm just sorry he'll miss the picnic.'

She hadn't wanted a big fuss made of her turning eighteen; somehow she felt so much older. It embarrassed her to hear her parents make teasing comments about their little girl being so grown up now and ready for the world.

They went down to the river and swam in her favourite rock pool, where the waterfall gushed out of the steep cliff and tiny fish flashed beneath water lilies. Harry and Mungo splashed so much that Adela gave up and lounged on the rocks in her bathing suit next to Tilly, who was eating a slice of the massive ginger cake with buttercream icing that Mohammed Din had made for the picnic, and sweating under a large topee.

'Don't you look gorgeous and trim?' Tilly said between mouthfuls. 'You are made for the silver screen with a body like that, Adela.'

Adela self-consciously pulled her knees to her chin and swiftly changed the subject.

Late in the afternoon they returned to the compound and played tennis on the uneven court of dry grass at the side of the house: she and Rafi against Sophie and Wesley, with the boys rushing about fetching balls from the bushes and under the house. Adela and Rafi won. Rafi was still athletic and fast, and she knew her father had paired her up with Sophie's husband so that she would win on her birthday.

'He didn't always used to beat me, you know.' Sophie smiled. 'Rafi, do you remember the first time we ever played?' Sophie reminisced. 'With Boz and Auntie Amy in Edinburgh?'

Rafi's mouth twitched in amusement. 'I will never forget it. You beat me three sets to one and totally ignored me. I was smitten from that very moment.'

'No, you weren't.' She laughed. 'You thought I was a snobby little memsahib and I wasn't very nice to you.'

'You've made up for it since,' he said and grinned, catching her hand and pulling her to him for a quick kiss on the lips.

Adela thought with a pang of Jay's sensual kisses. He'd been wrong about Rafi and Sophie; anyone could see how in love they still were after years of marriage. They didn't seem to need anyone else to make them happy, and it threw her once again into a dilemma about whether to mention Tommy Villiers.

At dinner that night Wesley announced their present to her.

'A shikar trip to Gulgat, just like I promised.' He beamed. 'The Raja will accompany us too. Isn't that an honour?'

Adela's heart thudded at the mention of Gulgat. 'Yes, it is. How wonderful!' She glanced at Sophie who was watching her with an anxious frown. 'Will . . . will anyone else be going with us?'

'Rafi of course,' said her father, 'and probably Stourton, the British Resident. He never misses a chance to bag a tiger.'

'Tiger?' Adela said in excitement.

'There's a pair of tigers the Raja wants shooting,' Rafi explained. 'They've been carrying off cattle from a riverside village.'

'It's worse than that,' Sophie said. 'A villager has gone missing, a grass cutter. They think the tigress might be lame and has attacked the man as easy prey.'

'A man-eater?' Clarrie gasped. 'I don't like the sound of that.'

Tilly exclaimed, 'Don't tell Mungo, or he'll want to go. I can't think of anything worse. Stuff of nightmares. James can't understand it. He thinks hunting is the best thing about being in India.'

'We won't take any risks,' Rafi assured Clarrie. 'Adela will be kept out of harm's way.'

'But man-eaters are cunning,' Clarrie fretted.

'You must trust me to look after our daughter,' said Wesley. 'You would have jumped at such a chance at her age, Clarissa.'

Clarrie smiled. 'You're right of course. I used to go with my father on shikar. I'll stop fussing.'

'Oh, I can't wait,' Adela cried. 'My first tiger shoot. We better get some rifle practice in before we go, Dad.'

'We'll go out at dawn,' he promised with a wink.

Two days later Tilly and Mungo departed. 'Next time we meet will be in Guwahati' – she beamed and gave Adela a clammy hug – 'on our way home! Isn't that exciting?'

Adela tried to sound enthusiastic, but she hadn't really given the trip much thought. She had agreed to it to please her mother, yet somehow it didn't seem real. England, Aunt Olive and the Brewis family were a place and people she had no memory of; if it wasn't for Cousin Jane's chatty letters, she wouldn't know them at all. Her thoughts were consumed with the pending hunting trip and the possibility of seeing Jay again.

Before the Khans left Belgooree, she was determined to get Sophie alone. Adela had handed over a letter from Fatima with news of Ghulam that the doctor had been too nervous to post, but she'd had no chance to confide in her favourite aunt about the events in Simla that summer. Adela took Sophie into the garden, sat her down and told her about Tommy. Sophie's brown eyes widened in astonishment and then abruptly flooded with tears. She grabbed Adela in a fierce hug.

'Do you think it's possible? When can I meet him? Should I write to him first?'

Adela was taken aback by Sophie's ecstatic reaction, latching on to the idea of Tommy being her brother as if it was already proven. She had a surge of misgiving; she wasn't sure that Tommy even wanted a sister. He had treated the whole idea as a bit of a joke. He was happy being a Villiers – to the world, that's who he was – and he might resent being unmasked as someone else entirely.

'Perhaps I should write to him first,' Adela said hastily. 'Explain that you would like to be put in touch – if he's willing.'

'Would you?' Sophie smiled tearfully. 'I'd be so very grateful. You might find this hard to understand, but I still feel there's a little part of me missing, knowing that I have a brother, but not knowing who or where he is. Or even if he lived beyond babyhood. No grave, no explanation, nothing.' Her eyes shone. 'I make up stories about him – I know it's silly – but my favourite one is that he was given to a kind maharajah with a large loving family, and he's grown into a strong handsome man who helps run his father's estates wisely when he's not playing polo or writing sitar music.'

'Well,' Adela said and gave a dry smile, 'doesn't sound much like Tommy – except he could probably bash out a tune on the guitar. He's great on the piano.'

Sophie laughed. 'If he's been a good friend to you, I'd be happy to have a brother like Tommy.'

Adela turned the conversation to Jay, unburdening herself to Sophie. 'I'm in love with him and I thought he was with me, but I've heard nothing since all that Nerikot business. Has he said anything to you about me?'

Sophie shook her head. 'He's been up at the old palace since he came back, so I've hardly seen him. Stourton has told him to keep his head down. Jay and Rita argue whenever he's at the new palace; Rafi tries not to interfere. From what Rafi can gather from Stourton, the Simla authorities are backing the Raja of Nerikot – a case of self-defence against armed communists. If that's the case, Jay will be able to go where he wants again, and I imagine it won't be hanging around Gulgat.'

'What a relief that would be if the Raja and Jay are cleared.'

'Rafi is more worried about Ghulam. Fatima told him everything in the letter you brought from her. But Ghulam cares nothing for his own safety.'

Adela told her aunt about the incident at the Sipi Fair and how she'd seen Sam push Ghulam out of harm's way.

'I think Sam Jackman saved him from being caught by the police, but landed himself in a terrible mess. Goodness knows what Sam's doing now.'

Sophie stroked Adela's hair. 'You were fond of Sam, weren't you?'

'Very,' Adela admitted. She didn't want to think of Sam; it made her sad and angry and aching inside. 'But it's Jay I love now. I just want to see him again to find out . . . Can you get Rafi to invite him on shikar?'

'Adela, you worry me.'

'Please!'

'You know it can't come to anything even if Jay loves you back.'

'Why not?'

'He's already betrothed to another – has been since he was twelve. They're not married yet – she's in East Bengal – but it's just a matter of time. Surely you knew?'

Adela felt punched in the stomach. *Betrothed?* Why had he never told her? He'd asked her to marry him! She'd believed it could be possible.

'No, he said we could be together.'

'Oh, that wretched boy,' Sophie said angrily. 'He was leading you on.'

Adela thought she was going to be sick. She got up from the garden bench, gasping for breath and retching.

'Adela, darling,' Sophie said, rising, 'are you all right?'

Adela croaked, 'No, I must—' She ran across the lawn and down the drive and didn't stop until she was hidden in tea bushes. She crumpled to her knees and sobbed out her pain.

***

She spent the next day in bed with stomach cramps. She didn't know what her parents and the Khans were saying, but she could hear hushed conversation beyond her room and knew they were talking about her. Perhaps Sophie was telling of her humiliation at being led on by Jay. At least she had stopped herself from telling Sophie that she had lost her virginity to the prince; she would keep that secret to the grave. How stupid she felt. He was deceitful! She was furious with him. But she couldn't banish his handsome face; it was there whenever she closed her eyes, and her sleep was disturbed with dreams of him.

The Khans left. To Adela's relief, no one mentioned Jay, so perhaps Sophie hadn't told her parents about her foolish infatuation. She emerged to sit listlessly on the veranda. Harry annoyed her with his boisterousness, clambering over her and twanging her with a rubber band he said was his catapult.

'Perhaps we should call off the shikar,' Wesley suggested. 'If you're not feeling up to it.'

He looked so disappointed that Adela roused herself. 'You mustn't do that. I'll be okay. Just a tummy bug.'

'Are you sure?'

'Of course I am.' She forced a smile. 'I'm really looking forward to it.'

Wesley brightened and kissed the top of her head. 'So am I, my darling.'

Three days later Wesley and Adela were waved away by Clarrie and Harry – the latter tearful at being left behind – and drove to Gulgat. The temperature soared as they descended from the misty pine-covered Khasi Hills to the undulating jungle and river valleys of Gulgat. They stuck to the leather seats in the humid air; the sky pulsed with heat and reduced the vivid green of bamboo and banana trees to shimmering grey.

Adela revelled in having her father to herself – it seemed an age since they had done anything together without her mother or Harry – and he was in high spirits too, singing 'Tea for Two' at the top of his voice.

On the journey they talked of many things: childhood anecdotes of Wesley teaching her to shoot partridge; raising orphaned tiger cub Molly; going to see a troupe of gypsies perform in Shillong on her third birthday.

'It's one of my very first memories,' said Adela. 'I wanted to be a tightrope walker and dance in the sky – it seemed like magic to me.'

'You were terrified of the fire-eaters.' Wesley chuckled. 'Hid inside my jacket till they stopped.'

'I thought they were hurting themselves – I still don't understand how they do that.' She smiled in bemusement.

'There wasn't much that made you afraid.'

'I never felt any real fear because you were always there to protect me. And you've always stuck up for me, even when I made things difficult – like running away from school. I know I wasn't a very obedient child. You must have despaired at times.'

'Never! You have my single-mindedness and your mother's big heart – it's a powerful combination. Your mother and I wouldn't want you to be any other way. It doesn't matter what you do: you're the joy of our lives.'

Adela felt a wave of gratitude and leant across to kiss his craggy cheek. 'Thanks, Dad. I wouldn't want any other parents but you two.'

He gave her a tender smile. After a few moments he asked, 'Did we do the right thing in sending you to Simla? You have been happy there, haven't you?'

'Most of the time very happy,' she assured. 'Aunt Fluffy was the most amazing guardian – firm with me, but always interested in what I was doing and introducing me to some of the best people in Simla. I don't mean the heaven-born, who think they are the best because they hold the top jobs in government; I mean people like Dr Fatima, Sundar Singh and Boz, who became real friends. And I loved St Mary's and acting at the theatre and going into the hills with Fatima's clinic.'

Wesley glanced over. 'And seeing young Sam Jackman? For a while your letters were full of him.'

Adela felt her heart squeeze at his name. 'Yes, and Sam.' She found herself telling him all about her time at the mission and riding out with Sam to see the Gaddi nomads and the awful confrontation at the Sipi Fair.

Wesley put a hand on her knee and gave a comforting squeeze. 'I'm sorry if he's messed things up for himself again. I like

Jackman, but he seems a troubled soul. And I'm sorry if you were holding out hope for him and you. I wouldn't have objected.'

Adela's eyes prickled with sudden tears.

'So he was the man who broke your heart?' asked Wesley. 'The reason why you came home sooner than planned? Sophie said that someone let you down.'

Her heart jolted. She shook her head. 'No, that was someone else.'

'Are you going to tell me who?'

'I'd rather not.'

'Well, damn him,' Wesley said fiercely. 'We'll not talk about it. You and I are going to have the best few days' shikar ever, and to blazes with wretched young men who break my daughter's heart! What do you say, darling girl?'

Adela flicked a tear from her cheek. 'I say that's the best tonic a girl could have,' she said, laughing, 'to go on shikar with her dad.'

At that moment she made up her mind to put the affair with Jay behind her. She had been just as foolish and selfish in her desires as he had. But she was determined to get over him. And for the next few days she was going to enjoy life with her father and Uncle Rafi.

***

To Adela's relief they were not going to the palace but meeting the Raja and his party at the camping ground on a clearing by the river. They drove past work gangs of men and women lifting rocks from the riverbed – the Raja's wealth was partly based on stone sold for building and milling – then afterwards the road deteriorated into a rutted track. Wesley parked up, thankful they had avoided a puncture. Rafi greeted them, linking his arm through Adela's and giving it a squeeze.

'Bearing up okay?' he murmured with an anxious smile.

'Fine, thanks,' said Adela, embarrassed but grateful for his concern.

She gasped at the magnificent tents furnished with carpets, tables and chairs for dining and proper beds for her and Wesley, with a dressing table and mirror and a tin bath behind a curtain for private bathing. To her amusement the Raja and Rafi preferred canvas camp beds and washing in the river.

'Part of the enjoyment of being on shikar,' Kishan said smiling, 'is to get away from all the pomp of the palace.'

Adela remembered the Raja from early childhood and liked him enormously. He was kind and patient and good-looking, though she thought how he had aged since last seeing him: his brow was scored with worry lines.

'The shikaris have been out looking for tracks,' he told them as they ate a dinner of curried vegetables, roast fowl and saffron rice. 'Two days ago they spotted pugmarks in the sand further upriver. They're certain the pair have retreated into the ravine – a boar was found half-eaten up there.'

Rafi said, 'We can go so far by elephant, but not if they're in a narrow side ravine – we'll just have to tempt them out with bait.'

'Not with humans,' joked the Raja, 'so don't look so worried, Miss Robson.'

They got up before dawn and had *chota hazri* of tea and toast. Just as they were about to set off on the elephants, the noise of a car engine disturbed the quiet, and lights came flooding over the hill.

'Ah, this will be Stourton,' said Kishan, 'in the nick of time.'

In the light of the kerosene lamps, two men climbed from the Resident's car: Stourton and another more familiar figure. Adela tensed as the second man strolled towards them.

'Sanjay!' the Raja cried.

'Uncle,' Jay greeted him respectfully. 'It's a good job Stourton told me about the hunt. Wouldn't have wanted to miss it for anything.'

'I assumed Rafi had,' said Kishan, turning to his ADC.

Rafi apologised. 'Your Highness, I thought Prince Sanjay was keeping to the palace for the time being.'

'No need for that, Khan,' said the Resident gruffly. 'Who is going to cause a fuss in such a remote part of Gulgat?'

Jay smiled. 'Quite so.'

Wesley, sensing a slight tension, came forward and greeted Stourton and then the prince. 'Sir, I believe you know my daughter, Adela. She tells me you've acted on stage together.'

Jay bowed. 'Indeed we have. Not only acted but ridden together. Miss Robson is an accomplished horsewoman. How is dear Mrs Hogg?'

Adela's heart hammered. It was too dark to read the expression on his face.

'Very well, thank you.' Her voice sounded squeaky and nervous in her ears.

'Your Highness,' Rafi intervened, 'the elephants are ready, and we should get started if we are to pick up the fresh tracks.'

Adela was thankful for the diversion of the trip getting underway. With her rifle, she clambered on to an elephant called Rose, and Wesley climbed into the howdah beside her. One of the Raja's most experienced mahouts straddled Rose's neck, and they set off behind the Raja and Rafi, with the others following on behind.

'Darling, you're shaking,' Wesley said in concern. 'Are you feeling all right?'

'Yes.' Adela breathed in hard. 'Just a little nervous now it's happening.'

'Don't be,' he said, smiling and patting her shoulder.

They followed the sandy left bank of the largely dried-up river, where the shikaris had found the tiger footprints, and then moved on into the jungle. As dawn broke over the trees, flocks of green parakeets rose noisily, and monkeys screeched and swung overhead as the elephants advanced. Adela was soon enjoying the rhythmic swaying of the huge animal, amazed at how silent and footsure it was for its size. The dewy freshness of the forest and the apricot light filtering through the leaves and creepers were magical; she would be happy just exploring the jungle all day.

They emerged into open grassland and some cultivated terraces of peppers and orange trees. Bamboo huts with thatched roofs were dotted about the slope, tall spikes of ginger plants growing around them. A small girl was tending half a dozen goats by the stream. They disembarked for something to eat, making for the awnings that were being erected in the shade of some sal trees.

'This is the village the grass cutter disappeared from,' Rafi told them.

'Have they found him yet?' Adela asked.

Rafi shook his head. 'He's unlikely to be found alive now, not if the tigress got him.'

'Poor man.' She shuddered.

Jay held court around the table with anecdotes about various hunts he had been on in the hill states around Simla. He spoke to Adela with an easy grace, as if they were friends who shared similar interests, but as if their intimacy had never been. It was astonishing to remember that her last sight of him had been from the warmth of his bed and that since then he had run for his life, leaving her not knowing what had happened to him. She answered him with polite indifference; she would not give him the satisfaction of knowing how much he had hurt her.

They moved on beyond the village into a high-sided valley of dense jungle, the elephants having to trample down the undergrowth to make a path. In the heat and with the swaying motion of Rose, Adela was lulled almost to sleep when a cry went up from the front of the procession. She started awake. There was a commotion among the trackers. Wesley reached for his double-barrelled shotgun.

'Is it a tiger?' she gasped.

Rose padded forward after the other elephants. She swung her trunk at a low branch and pulled something away. The mahout leant forward and took it, holding it up for inspection. It was a shred of red-and-white cotton. He shouted something to the men ahead. There was a quick-fire exchange. The procession halted.

'What's happening?' Wesley asked.

The mahout answered, 'They have found the drag.'

'Of the boar?'

'No, the villager.'

Adela's stomach churned. She knew what he meant by 'drag': the remains of the kill that the tiger had dragged away to hide and feast on when hungry again.

'Oh dear God!' Wesley exclaimed. 'Adela, you mustn't look.'

She stared again at the cloth in the mahout's hand; it was a bloodied piece of clothing. Suddenly the joy drained out of the day. This was someone's father or brother or son, carried off and eaten by a savage predator; she could only imagine the terror of the hapless victim as he'd fought in vain for his life.

They carried on, the Raja ordering one of his men to alert the villagers to come and claim the remains of their neighbour.

Adela averted her eyes as they passed, but not in time to avoid catching an unwanted glimpse of a legless torso with its clothes ripped away. She thought she might be sick.

'We must kill the tiger before this happens again,' she said with vehemence.

'We will,' her father promised.

Soon afterwards, they emerged on to a dried-up riverbed. It was strewn with boulders and small islands covered in scraggy trees between isolated pools of water. The head of the river disappeared into a steep ravine; the line of elephants plodded towards it. At the point where a narrower defile cut into the right-hand slope, they halted. Word came back that this was where the boar had been killed. Now a young buffalo stood there, tied up as bait for the tigers.

At the mouth of the smaller ravine, the shikaris had been busy erecting machans – hideouts – in the overhanging trees, from which the hunters could survey the hunted. Behind, the slope rose steeply to a ridge just above the height of the trees. Rose knelt down and helped the passengers to the ground with her trunk. Adela hardly had time to stretch before her father was chivvying her up the rope ladder into one of the makeshift bamboo cradles. It was hardly bigger than a child's cot, but Wesley squeezed in with her. They covered themselves with leaves and waited. Stourton took the next machan, Jay the one beyond, while Rafi and the Raja went to the other side of the ravine and disappeared into the trees.

The heat was oppressive. Nothing stirred, not even the docile buffalo tethered to its tree. They sat completely still. After a while Adela's legs grew numb from pins and needles and she longed to move.

'Is it him?' her father whispered. Adela met his look. Sweat trickled down his face. 'Is Prince Sanjay the man who trifled with your affections?'

She could barely breathe. She closed her eyes. Not now; she didn't want this conversation now.

'I know I'm right,' he hissed. 'I can tell by the little comments he makes – the innuendoes. I could punch his arrogant face.'

'Don't, Dad,' Adela pleaded. 'Don't let him spoil our trip.'

Just then there was a cry from a deer further up the ravine, and birds flew up from the tightly packed bushes. Something was on the move. They went deadly still. The grass stirred, yet there was no breeze. The tiger was so well camouflaged in the pattern of light and shade between the trees that Adela didn't see it till it was almost right below them, a huge male about nine feet long. The magnificent beast crept forward, tail twitching, sniffing at the elephant tracks. The buffalo began to bellow and twist in its ropes. The tiger gazed around, swiftly crouched, ready to spring. A shot went off like a deafening firecracker. The tiger dropped to the ground, a bullet lodged in its neck.

'Got it!' shouted the Resident. 'Bloody well got the beast.'

'Good shot, Stourton,' Jay called.

The shikaris appeared from among the elephants to survey the tiger, making a din with whistles and firing off into the air to make sure that any other tiger or wild animal was chased away before the hunters descended from the machans. The Resident was cock-a-hoop with his kill.

'Rafi, take a photograph of Stourton with his tiger,' the Raja ordered.

Stourton posed, rifle in hand and foot on the head of the beast, while Rafi took shots with his box camera. It made Adela think of Sam and his passion for taking pictures. She had thrown away all but one of the photos he had left for her at Fluffy Hogg's; she couldn't bear to be reminded of those happy, innocent times in Narkanda. Yet she hadn't been able to bring herself to part with the one of her and Sam leaning against the veranda balustrade, arms touching as they smiled down at Fatima.

She stared in awe at the huge muscled tiger, with its jaws locked in a snarl at the point of death. It had white patches above its eyes that looked like another pair of eyes staring blindly up at them. Its teeth were like daggers and its claws curved like deadly miniature kukris. Her heart banged in relief to be so near a tiger that could no longer harm them, yet she felt a stab of pity for the animal. Her pet Molly, long ago released into the jungle, would now be a fully-grown tiger trying to outwit hunters like them.

There was much animated discussion about how best to transport the hefty animal back to camp without damaging its magnificent pelt.

'It'll make a wonderful rug for Mama's hearth at home,' said Stourton. 'I'll keep the head for my bungalow – get it sent to Van Ingen's to have it stuffed.'

With the help of half a dozen shikaris, the dead beast was loaded on the back of an elephant and transported back to camp. The hunting party retreated to the nearby village for a late tiffin.

'We could shoot some partridge or blackbuck on our way back to camp,' suggested Kishan.

'We can't go back yet,' Jay protested. 'There's still the tigress out there – and she's the dangerous one.'

His uncle gave a weary laugh. 'We'll return to the ravine tomorrow and hunt her down.'

'She might have gone by then,' said Jay. 'This could be our only chance.'

'Your uncle is tired,' Rafi said.

'No one who is tired needs to stay,' Jay said, 'but some of us have plenty of appetite for more shikar. Don't we, Adela?'

She jolted at his sudden attention on her. Before she could answer, Jay went on persuasively, 'And you haven't had a chance to fire a shot yet. This shikar is especially for your birthday, is it not?'

'You are right, Sanjay,' said Kishan. 'Stourton was most ungallant for bagging Miss Robson's tiger.'

'I'm awfully sorry.' The Resident looked sheepish.

'No, really, I don't mind at all,' Adela assured him.

'But you must be allowed to stay longer if you wish it,' the Raja insisted.

'What do you say, Adela?' Jay challenged. 'Shall we go back and see if the tigress has returned for the bait?'

She didn't want Jay to think her weak, and she did want the chance to shoot at the man-eater.

'Yes, let's,' she agreed.

'Are you sure?' Wesley gave her a warning look.

Ignoring it, she smiled. 'Yes, I am. This might be my one chance of bagging a tiger before going back to England.'

'Then I will come with you both,' Wesley declared, casting a stormy look at the prince.

'There's no need,' said Jay. 'Your daughter is quite grown-up enough to look after herself.'

'No doubt of that,' said Wesley, 'but I'm not letting her out of my sight on this trip. I promised her mother that.' He gave a tight smile.

***

The Raja, Rafi and Stourton set off back to camp, the latter in a state of exhilaration and keen to oversee the gutting and beheading of his tiger. Adela, Wesley and Jay took a smaller number of shikaris and set off in the other direction.

'Be back by nightfall,' the Raja called out. 'We'll have a celebratory dinner!'

Back at the machans, Jay declared they should each have their own hideout. The heat was still intense and the large lunch had made Adela drowsy. She must have fallen asleep because she was roused by the machan being shaken. She sat up with a start. Was the tigress back? Then she realised someone was climbing the rope ladder up to her machan.

'Jay,' she gasped. 'What are you doing?'

'Coming to get you,' he whispered with a soft chuckle.

Her heart began to pound. Had her father seen him? He was so stealthy that she assumed not. She couldn't see her father's machan, each of them hidden in the thick foliage.

'You shouldn't be here,' she hissed.

'I've been trying to get you alone all day, but your father is far too possessive.' He dropped in beside her, jamming his gun in the corner. 'I've missed you, Adela.'

'Not enough to let me know what had happened to you,' she accused. 'Have you any idea the worry you put me through?'

He gave an apologetic smile. 'I'm glad you care that much about me.'

'But you don't care an ounce about me,' Adela said.

'I do,' he insisted, 'but the situation was very difficult for me. I had to get out of Nerikot without anyone knowing, or I might have been arrested.'

'Did you fire on any of those men, the protestors?' she demanded.

'Don't waste your pity on such scum,' he replied. 'They were armed and dangerous and out to harm my friend and his family.'

'So you did shoot at them?' She was appalled.

Jay flinched from her look and glanced away. 'I fired into the air to warn them off, nothing more. It was some of Nerikot's guards who lost their heads.'

She didn't know if she believed him. He took her hand and pressed it to his lips. She snatched it away, despite the pounding in her chest.

'You led me on,' she hissed, 'pretending we could be together when all along you've been betrothed to someone else.'

He gave her a bemused look. 'I never said I wasn't betrothed.'

'You never said you were,' she said, glaring.

'But you know what it's like for a man in my position: there are certain duties I have to perform, such as marriage and providing heirs for Gulgat. But what we have is different; we can still be together. You can travel with me when I go abroad; we can live in Delhi or the South of France – anywhere you want.'

'As your mistress,' she said with disdain. 'Never as your wife.'

'Is that so very bad? You will have anything you want in life, Adela.' His sensual mouth twisted in amusement. 'You gave the impression at Eagle's Nest that you were very happy to be my, er, companion.'

'I acted foolishly.' She blushed. 'I thought you loved me. You said you could defy your elders and do what you wanted. You promised me marriage.'

'We all say things in the heat of the moment,' Jay said. 'You came to me so willingly . . . eagerly—'

She slapped him hard on the cheek. He grabbed her by the wrist, thrusting his face at hers.

'Don't pretend to be the virtuous little memsahib now. It wasn't love we were after, it was pure pleasure.'

Adela swallowed back a denial; for a short while she had been mad with passion for him. She looked away, ashamed. He dropped his hold.

'I'm sorry,' said Jay. 'I should never have gone to Nerikot. If I hadn't, we might still be having fun in Simla.'

Adela felt leaden. That was all it had ever been for Jay: a bit of fun. Why had she ever thought it would be otherwise? She had ignored the warnings about his reputation, and then the romantic surroundings of Eagle's Nest had seduced her as much as his charm. Both had proved as transient as a summer's night. Deep down she knew there was another reason why she had given herself so impulsively to Jay: her anger at Sam for not loving her back. She had wanted Jay to fill the aching void and wipe out her feelings for Sam once and for all. As she sat in the cramped machan with her former lover, Adela realised that she had failed to extinguish her love for Sam – and she no longer wanted Jay.

'There is no reason I can see,' said Jay, taking her silence for agreement, 'that we can't pick up where we left off. I still find you very desirable.'

'Jay, I don't—'

'What on earth is going on over there?' Wesley shouted. 'Adela, are you all right?'

'Yes, Dad,' she called back. 'Prince Jay and I were just talking.'

'Well, you'll have frightened off the tigress. Sun's dipping. Let's call it a day.'

'No,' objected Jay, 'there's still time.'

'Sun down, gun down,' ordered Wesley. 'You know it's too dangerous to hunt after dark.'

'Dad's right,' said Adela, scrambling to her feet. Just as she was stepping on to the rope, there was a low growl right behind. She turned and froze. The tigress was poised on the steep bank behind the trees, tail twitching angrily. She was almost at eye level and a mere ten yards away.

'Jay,' she croaked. 'It's there.'

He swung round, saw the danger, reached for his rifle, cocked it and fired straight at its head. The tigress roared. For a moment Adela thought the beast would hurl itself right at them, and then abruptly it sprang away along the ridge and disappeared.

'I got it, I'm sure of it,' Jay cried.

By the time they'd swung down the rope ladders, Wesley was already waiting for them. Adela, weak-kneed with shock, fell into her father's arms. He rounded on Sanjay.

'What were you doing in my daughter's machan? Can't you see how you put her in danger with your arguing? You drew the tiger's attention.'

'I shot the tigress straight in the neck,' Jay retorted. 'She's mortally wounded. If we send in the shikaris, I bet we'll find her lying dead on the ridge.'

'She didn't look like she was dying to me.'

'Well, we'll see, won't we?' Jay challenged.

'We're not sending anyone after her now,' Wesley said. 'It's almost sunset.'

'I'm in charge of the shikar, not you,' Jay rebuffed him.

'Well, you shouldn't be putting any of your men in danger.'

'Please, Jay,' Adela intervened with a hand on his arm. 'Let's leave it till tomorrow. Then you can come back and claim her as yours.'

Jay flicked her a look, then turned to Wesley with a smile of satisfaction.

'You have a very persuasive daughter, Mr Robson. For her I will do anything.'

They returned to the elephants, Adela aware of her father fuming at Jay's taunting remarks.

'Ride back with me, Adela,' Jay commanded.

'She will come in my howdah,' said Wesley angrily.

'I will ride alone on Rose,' Adela said, tired of being fought over. How she longed to be back at camp and have a cool bath. Rafi and the Raja would bring peace and conviviality to the fractious hunting party.

Wesley fussed as she climbed into the howdah. 'I can manage myself,' she said irritably.

They set off back down the ravine and through the jungle, Rose leading the procession. Within a short while darkness fell as quickly as a curtain. The moon came up. They emerged into the clearing by the village; the temporary camp was gone, and small oil lamps glowed in the doorways of huts. The air was filled with the acrid smoke of cooking fires. Adela felt herself relax in the balmy evening.

The line of elephants plodded on through the trees and emerged on to the sandy riverbank. They were about half an hour's journey from camp. Something caught Adela's eye: a flicker of movement in the moonlight. She heard a strange spitting sound and then all of a sudden the tigress was there in front of Rose. Its face was bloodied; Jay must have hit it in the mouth. The beast opened its shattered jaws and roared. The next second the tigress was springing at the elephant. It clawed at Rose's trunk. The elephant bellowed in pain and tried to shake it off. Adela screamed. Behind, Wesley's elephant trumpeted in fright.

The mahout shouted a warning. He clung on to Rose's neck and ears as the elephant bucked and tried to escape its attacker.

'What's happening?' bellowed Wesley.

Adela was too terrified to answer. The howdah tilted dangerously, almost throwing Adela out. She screamed again and grabbed frantically to the sides of the basket. The air was filled with the snarling and roars of the demented tigress; it held on, sinking its remaining teeth into the elephant's hide.

'Help me, Dad!' Adela managed to shriek. 'Shoot it!'

Rose fought with the tigress, trying to stamp on its hind legs, thrashing from side to side. All at once Rose reared up, and the howdah tipped backwards, hurling Adela out. She landed on the ground with a dizzying thud; pain shot through her shoulder. She tried to get up; Rose's back feet could crush her at any moment. Screams, shouting, snarling and trumpeting rang out in the dark. Adela whimpered in terror.

Suddenly her father was there beside her.

'Stay down,' he barked. Then he took aim and fired. The deafening shot made her ears ring.

Wesley fired again. The tigress roared in fury and fell from the elephant. Rose bolted, with the mahout clinging on with all his might.

'Someone hold up a torch!' Wesley ordered as he frantically tried to reload. In that moment the wounded tigress leapt at him. Adela was so close she heard the claws rip into her father's bush shirt. He jammed his rifle sideways into her bloodied maw. She thrust him backwards, pawing at him like a kitten with a rag doll. Wesley howled.

'Jay, do something!' Adela screamed, scrambling towards her father.

In the flickering of flaming torchlight, Jay stood up high in his howdah. 'Roll out of the way!' he shouted at her.

Adela curled up small. Gunfire. The tigress gave a final furious snarl and fell back. There was shouting and confusion, the mahouts trying to control their agitated elephants while torch-bearing shikaris made sure the tigress was dead. Adela, panting and sobbing, crawled to her father.

'Dad? Daddy speak to me!'

He looked at her calmly. 'I'm all right, I'm all right.'

She wept with relief and put her arms about him. He moaned. She leant back, her arms sticky. She was covered in his blood. Jay was there beside her, pulling her away.

'He needs me.' She fought him off. 'He's bleeding.'

Jay began shouting orders. He pulled off his turban and attempted to wrap it around Wesley's gaping stomach, retching as he did so. Adela could think of nothing to do but hold her father's hand.

'You're going to be fine, Dad.'

As they waited for the men to bring a makeshift stretcher of poles and torn-up clothing, she felt his grip weaken. Her shoulder burned with pain.

'Send to the camp for help,' she cried.

'I've already done that,' Jay said, his eyes dark with horror in the moonlight.

The pole bearers ran with Wesley along the dried-up riverbed, Adela keeping up. She could hear his groans as they bumped and jolted him in their haste. *Please, God, let him live!* She repeated the words in her head like a mantra. A few minutes from camp, Rafi came out at the head of a rescue party. She ran to him.

'Help him! He's lost so much blood,' she sobbed.

Rafi put his arm about her and steered her back to camp. As soon as he saw the extent of Wesley's injuries, Rafi took control. 'The nearest doctor is at the mission hospital an hour away. I'll drive him there myself.'

'And I'll come with you,' Adela insisted.

The Raja hovered anxiously, his face haggard. 'How did it happen? Tigers don't attack elephants. The tigress must have been maddened. Your poor father. So brave to take it on.'

Jay steered Kishan out of the way. 'Let them go, Uncle. They mustn't waste a minute.'

Adela half hoped that Jay would offer to go with her, but he didn't; the Raja sent one of his guards to help.

'Please can someone fetch my mother,' Adela pleaded as they laid Wesley on the back seat of one of the Raja's cars and she climbed in beside him.

'Of course,' the Raja promised.

She glanced back, but couldn't read Jay's expression. Her last sight of the camp was of workers scraping flesh from the hide of the first tiger by torchlight. She ground her teeth to stop herself being sick.

As they rattled along the track, Adela crouched on the floor, gripping her father's hand and forcing back tears. The temporary dressings they had hastily bound on top of Jay's turban were already soaked in blood. The putrid sweet smell of her father's gored innards made Adela want to vomit.

'You're going to be okay, Dad, you're going to be okay. The doctor will fix your wounds. He'll make you better.'

He stared at her. She stroked back his hair; his forehead was clammy. Before they left the rutted tracks for the asphalt road, he was shaking uncontrollably.

'I think he's in shock,' Adela hissed at Rafi. 'He's cold and shivering.'

Rafi accelerated, bouncing them roughly. Wesley didn't groan. 'Talk to him,' Rafi urged. 'Keep him conscious.'

Adela gabbled at her father, talking about anything she could think of: his plans for the tea garden; whether they should get another dog; what she could bring back from England for Harry's fifth birthday.

Abruptly Wesley struggled to sit up. His eyes were clouded with pain. He sank back with an agonised groan.

'Don't try to move, Dad,' Adela said, a hand on his shoulder. 'We're taking you to the mission doctor. You're going to be fine.'

She picked up his limp hand and pressed it to her cheek. 'I love you,' she whispered. 'I love you very much. I'm so sorry. This is all my fault.'

Reaching the surfaced road, Rafi turned the car uphill towards the mission, revving the engine hard.

Wesley murmured something so faint that Adela thought it might just be a laboured breath.

'What was that?'

'Clarissa?' he asked in a stronger voice. 'Darling, is that you?'

Adela's heart turned over. She swallowed down tears.

'No, Daddy, it's me, Adela.'

He let out a long sigh.

'But Mother is coming. She'll be here with you very soon.'

They jolted along. He kept his eyes on her, but the lids began to close.

'Stay with us, Dad,' she pleaded, 'stay with us.'

A pained smile flickered across his face. 'Clarissa. My love.'

They were the last words Adela ever heard him say. By the time the car juddered into the mission compound, Wesley was already dead.

Chapter 14

Wesley's body was brought to the family plot at Belgooree for burial next to Clarrie's parents, Jock and Jane Belhaven. Adela's mother had resisted suggestions that he should be laid in consecrated ground in the British cemetery in Shillong, alongside other tea planters.

Clarrie's answer was simple: 'This is where Wesley belongs.'

On a sultry, overcast day, Adela stood at the newly dug grave with her mother, Harry between them holding a hand each. They were surrounded by their friends and throngs of tea workers. For three days Adela had felt completely numb, but now in the Belgooree garden her feelings were suddenly raw: every word, touch, birdsong and scent of roses caused her pain. The plain coffin was carried from the house by Rafi, James, Daleep and Banu, a grandson of Ama, the ancient village headwoman.

As they processed through the compound to the quiet burial grove, the drums of the villagers beat loudly and the women sang and cried out in grief. Adela was humbled by it. She knew how loved her mother was among the Khasis, but to see their outpouring of affection for her father squeezed her heart. Dr Black came to take the service and spoke eloquently about Wesley.

'We all loved and admired this man,' said the white-haired missionary, raising his voice for all to hear. 'Wesley Robson met with both respect and affection, whether it was in the Burra Bazaar in Shillong or the planters' clubs in Upper Assam. He was equally at home chatting about bows and arrows with Khasi hunters as he was taking tea with governors of the province or racing horses with his fellow planters.

'He had a commanding presence. In the early days of his time in India some – including his wife – might have called it a young man's arrogance.' He paused to give a wry smile, meeting Clarrie's tear-filled eyes. 'But everyone knew when Wesley Robson entered a room. It would be a livelier, more jovial gathering; there would be debate, as well as laughter. He was exceedingly knowledgeable about two things in particular: hunting and the tea trade. Wesley spent most of his days working hard to make Belgooree a success and to bring to the world the delicate mix of China and Assam tea that one more usually associates with Darjeeling. He has been a fine and fair employer – more than that, he has been like a father to the Khasi people who live and work here.

'Hunting too was a passion from his first days in India. It was on one such expedition here in the Khasi Hills that he first met his wife. So it is a terrible tragedy that he should die on shikar. But he did so defending his beloved daughter, Adela. That is the measure of the man.'

Adela felt a sob rise up from the pit of her stomach. Harry was crying, his eyes swollen and face puckered with misery. Her mother stood stoical, holding in her emotions.

'We all know the public man well – the planter, the horseman, the tea trader – but Wesley was above all a family man. He was happiest here at Belgooree with his wife and children. He doted on Adela and Harry; pride shone out of him when he talked of them. But it was Clarrie that he loved and depended on the most. He once asked me why I'd never married. When I said I was married to the church, he laughed and said, "There's no comparison with my Clarissa. If your love and passion for your church are as strong as mine for my wife, then Christianity is in good shape in these parts."'

Adela saw her mother's mouth twitch in a smile and a tear spill down her cheek.

'Wesley shared Clarrie's love of this place, its tea gardens and its people. Everything here at Belgooree he did for her. So let us now say our goodbyes to our good friend and commit his body to the ground and his soul to God. Let us draw near with faith . . .'

Adela hardly heard the words that followed as she broke down sobbing, her weeping and Harry's wailing echoed by the crying of dozens of the tea pickers behind. Tilly threw a comforting arm around her, and she buried her face in her auntie's plump shoulder.

Afterwards, they left the gravediggers to pile on the rich earth and returned to the bungalow. Mohammed Din had arranged a feast of pakoras, samosas, curry puffs, eggs, sandwiches, cakes and biscuits. Tilly and Sophie helped circulate among the funeral guests: planters and their wives, who had travelled from as far as

Tezpur, and officers from the barracks in Shillong with whom Wesley had ridden and hunted.

Adela, seeing how brave her mother was being, forced herself to stop crying and be hospitable. Harry was sent off to spend the afternoon with Ayah Mimi, while the Robson women mingled and entertained. Adela smiled when people recounted anecdotes about her father, even though it hurt, and she joined in the reminiscing. Never had she acted so convincingly, her outward appearance so at odds with the misery she felt inside.

Today everyone was their friend, and no one would think that her mother had ever been unwelcome at the planters' clubs or the drawing rooms of Shillong for being Anglo-Indian. They all knew how precarious life was on the plantations and how quickly life could be snatched away, even for vigorous men like Wesley, and they had come to give their support. Adela felt a surge of gratitude for the ruddy-faced men and their redoubtable wives, who filled the house with chuckles and kind words and left gifts of money for her and Harry and offers to visit them. As she watched her uncle James – Wesley's nearest adult male relative – shaking hands and thanking people for coming, Adela wondered how much he and Tilly had influenced people to attend at such short notice.

When all but the Khans and Robsons had gone, Clarrie was persuaded to lie down. She didn't appear again until late the next morning, her eyes dark-ringed, but with a smile for her friends. Adela had hardly slept a wink. Every time she closed her eyes, she was assaulted by the image of the leaping tigress and the sound of it tearing into her father. She could neither eat nor sleep.

Her mother would not speak about it. After the first horrific hours after Wesley's death, when Clarrie had been brought to the mission half hysterical with worry for them both, to find that her husband had already died, Clarrie had bombarded her with questions. Was she all right? Was her shoulder very painful? Why had they been out so late in the dark? Why was the rest of the party at the camp? What was Wesley doing out of his howdah? Who had wounded the man-eater in the first place? Why had Jay insisted on going back to find the tigress so late in the day? What on earth had Adela been thinking of, agreeing to go with him? Had Wesley suffered? Had he asked for her?

Adela had been too distraught to reply coherently; it was Rafi who'd tried to furnish Clarrie with answers and to shield Adela from the onslaught of questions. Perhaps it was Rafi's calmness and gentle concern that helped Clarrie summon all her courage, but she had insisted on helping to wash Wesley's body and wrap him in clove-scented winding sheets. Since then there had been no discussion of the terrible events.

For a further three days after the funeral the factory was closed and no picking was done in respect for Robson Sahib. But on the fourth day Clarrie ordered that the drying machines be switched on again and insisted on going to the factory to oversee production.

James protested that he could do this for her. Clarrie was firm. 'Thank you, but this is my garden and my responsibility. I know you are all trying to be kind and helpful – I couldn't be more grateful – but this is the only way I know how to cope. So please let me just go to work.'

By the end of the week Clarrie insisted on her friends going home and carrying on with their lives.

'James, I know how much you are needed at the Oxford Estates at this time of year. You really should go back. And Rafi, the Raja has been generous to spare you for this long, but Adela and I can manage.'

'But what are you going to do about Belgooree?' Tilly said. 'James can advise you. You can't make such decisions on your own.'

'I need time to think it through,' said Clarrie. 'When I'm ready to talk, I'll ask for help.'

'But you need help now,' James pointed out. 'Who is going to keep an eye on the coolies and do all the jobs my cousin did?'

'I will,' Clarrie said, 'and I have good undermanagers: Daleep in the factory, and Banu, Ama's grandson, as overseer in the gardens.'

'Dear Clarrie, I hate the thought of leaving you alone,' Tilly cried. 'Wouldn't you like one of us to stay with you?'

Clarrie squeezed her friend's hand. 'That's kind, but I have Adela and Harry for company.'

'Promise you will call on us whenever you need us,' said Sophie, 'and that goes for Adela too.' She turned with a smile of concern to Adela.

'Of course we will,' Clarrie agreed.

Adela felt panic tighten her chest at the thought of her aunties and uncles leaving. She felt safe with them around; hearing their voices around the house and their tread on the stairs was comforting, as if life could one day be normal again. At night, when she hardly slept, their presence kept the frightening shadows at bay.

But she bottled up her fears and told them she would be fine. She wanted to ask Sophie to write and tell her what was happening at Gulgat and with Jay, but she did not dare utter his name. Her feelings about him were so terribly mixed. His recklessness had led to the wounded man-eater mauling her father in a frenzied attack from which he could never have recovered. Only someone with her father's strength and bravery could have lasted the long hours of agony that he did. Yet Jay had been the one to finally shoot the tigress and had done all he could to try and keep her father alive. What was Jay thinking now? Did he regret his life becoming entangled with hers in the same way that she regretted ever becoming involved in his? But however much she railed against Jay's pleasure-seeking selfishness, she knew she would never blame him as much as she blamed herself for her father's death.

***

The days crept slowly by; the temperatures continued to rise. Adela's only release was to saddle up before dawn and ride out through the dewy tea bushes, watching the haze of smoke hanging over the village from early-morning fires and the pickers stream in a colourful wave, baskets strapped to their heads, up the plantation tracks. Her heart ached that her father would never again ride with her, or be by her side to wave to the women, as they had done together countless times before. She had lost the nerve to ride further into the forest.

Mainly Adela confined herself to the compound, trying to entertain a grieving Harry. Her brother wandered around like a lost puppy looking for its missing master.

'Delly, when is Daddy coming back?'

'He's not, Harry. I'm sorry.'

'Will he be here when I'm five?'

'No, he won't. You know he won't.'

'But he said he'd teach me how to fish when I'm five. He has to if he said he would.'

Each time he asked her, it opened up her raw grief anew. But worse was when he wanted to know about the tiger.

'Did you see it, Delly? Did it eat Daddy?'

'Of course it didn't!'

Harry's lip trembled at her cross tone.

'Mungo said it did.'

'Well, Mungo's a silly boy for saying so,' Adela snapped. 'He wasn't there.'

'Did the tiger just eat a bit of Daddy then?'

'Stop asking! It's a horrid thing to talk about.'

After that, Harry stopped pestering her with morbid questions. He stopped speaking to her at all. The unhappy boy became withdrawn and started wetting the bed at night. Adela felt consumed with guilt for being impatient towards him, but she couldn't smother her growing jealousy towards her brother for being able to comfort their mother when she could not.

Daily Clarrie seemed to grow more dependent on Harry. She allowed her son to clamber into her bed at night – he never seemed to wet hers – and yet when Adela asked one night if she could sleep with them, Clarrie had teased, 'I can't be coping with two babies. And darling, it's far too hot for us all to sleep together.'

It was the night the monsoon had started in earnest, rain battering the corrugated-iron roof like a thunder of kettledrums. Adela lay howling with the covers thrown off, glad of the noise that drowned out her noisy grief. Halfway through the night, wide awake, she went to the window in her nightdress and opened the shutters. Within seconds she was soaked through, her hair like wet ropes about her shoulders, the cotton nightdress stuck to her body like a watery shroud. She invoked the gods of the monsoon to come and take her, to strike her down with a lightning bolt.

'Why take my dad when you should have taken me?'

Three days later she was in bed with a fever, alternately shivering with cold and burning with heat. Her mother sent for Dr Hemmings.

'It's her own fault for standing out in the rain,' Clarrie said fractiously. 'As if I haven't got enough to worry about.'

Dr Hemmings prescribed tablets for Adela's headaches and an embrocation for her sore shoulder, which was still swollen from her fall from the elephant.

'Get MD to give her hot sweet tea and plenty of infusions to sweat out the fever.'

Ayah Mimi came in to nurse her. A week later Adela was up and about again, wobbly on her feet but calmer. The old ayah's tender care had been like a balm to her bruised heart, and she saw more clearly how hard her mother was struggling to keep the plantation and household going. It was no wonder she had no energy left to console her guilt-ridden daughter.

'What can I do to help, Mother?' Adela asked.

'Be kind to your brother,' Clarrie replied.

After that, Adela did her best to be more patient with Harry, taking him on the front of her pony for rides and down to the thundering waterfalls and swollen river pools to watch the villagers hauling in fish in their nets.

'What are we going to do, Mother?' Adela asked one evening after Harry had been put to bed. 'Are we still going to visit Aunt Olive in July?'

'You must go,' her mother said, 'but I can't – not now.'

'I'm not leaving you here on your own,' Adela protested.

'I won't be on my own. Harry will keep me company, and I have all our friends and helpers around me here.'

Adela swallowed. 'But it's you that Aunt Olive wants to see. I could stay here and look after things for you.'

Clarrie gave a soft snort. 'Running Belgooree is about more than riding around the gardens and drinking first flush.'

Adela winced. 'I know that but—'

'I appreciate you offering, darling, really I do. But I've decided I'm going to stay and make a go of things. My life is here, and it's all I want to do. I've written to Uncle James and Tilly. James has kindly agreed to help out when I need it – with negotiating prices and dealing with the Calcutta agents – and he'll come over once a month to make sure I haven't taken to the bottle.' Clarrie gave a wry smile.

'So it's all arranged?' Adela was astounded.

'Yes, as much as it can be.'

'But you've never asked me what I want to do.'

Clarrie avoided her look. 'No, I haven't. I suppose I assumed you would still want to go to England. I don't want you to feel tied to this place, and I know it can never be the same now without your father. You do want to visit Aunt Olive, don't you?'

'I suppose so. But not without you.'

'Well, I can't go just now. You must see that.' Clarrie finally met her look. 'I want you to go. I think meeting the rest of your family will be good for you.'

Adela swallowed. 'So you don't want me here?'

Her mother didn't answer directly. 'I've suggested to Sophie that she might like to take my passage instead. I know she would love to see Scotland again, and you would like her companionship, wouldn't you? I know how close the two of you are.'

Adela's spirits lifted a fraction. 'Yes, I would like that – but only if you really can't come.'

'That's settled then,' Clarrie said with a look of relief. 'I expect a reply back from her any day.'

***

By the second week in July it was all arranged. Clarrie's ticket had been transferred into Sophie's name, and in two days' time Rafi would come and collect Adela and drive them both to the railway station at Guwahati, where they would meet up with Tilly and Mungo at the start of the long journey to Britain.

On the final afternoon Adela had planned a ride to the waterfall and a picnic, but Clarrie was delayed at the factory, so Adela ended up knocking a tennis ball about with Harry until it was too late for the trip. They ate late. Adela wanted to sit up talking to her mother, but Clarrie resisted.

'I'm too tired and you have a very long day's travel ahead of you tomorrow. Best get to bed.'

Adela hardly slept. In the green light of dawn she slipped out of the bungalow and walked to the burial grove to stand at her father's grave. The monsoon had brought fresh green growth, so it was hard to tell the ground had been recently dug. It was marked by a simple cross, the grave still awaiting the elaborate headstone that her mother had commissioned.

She wanted to feel her father's presence there, but couldn't. He was somewhere else. The thought of his shattered remains lying below the earth made her stomach retch. She bent double and let out an animal cry.

'I'm so sorry, Daddy! I will never forgive myself for the way you died. Mother will never forgive me either. She hates me for it. I can tell. She can hardly bear to look at me. She's sending me away. I don't want to leave you, but I have to. It's the only way Mother can cope with what's happened. And I have no right to complain after what I've done to her – taken away the person she loved most in the whole world, will always love. It's like she can still see and hear you about the place. I know she talks to you. Harry says he hears her speaking to you during the night. It confuses him. He's so unhappy, and I feel guilty for that too.'

Adela rubbed her streaming eyes and nose on her sleeves. Through the trees the sky was filling with golden light, and the dew on the grass began to sparkle. The air was ringing with birdsong. Adela's weeping stopped. She felt as if balm were being rubbed on her sore heart; the sights and sounds of Belgooree would always be woven into the very fabric of her being wherever she went. She stood up.

'Thank you, Dad,' she whispered, bending to kiss the wooden cross. 'I promise I will try my best to make up for this terrible thing I've done.' She breathed in deeply, the earthy scented smell of Belgooree giving her courage. 'And I will come back – I promise you that. I *will* come back.'

Chapter 15

Adela leant on the ship's railing, staring back at the chaotic scenes on the Bombay quayside – the waving men, the scurrying porters, the fruit sellers and dockside officials – and watched India recede into the hot afternoon haze. The last three days of travel – the trains to Calcutta and on to Delhi and Bombay – had left her spent of emotion. Tilly had not stopped chattering and pointing things out to Mungo and talking of all the fun things they were going to do over the summer before he started school. Tilly was overjoyed that her closest friend in Assam, Ros Mitchell, was also spending the summer in Britain with her in-laws. She had already made arrangements to meet up with Ros, who would be staying at St Abb's in Scotland, close to where Tilly would be, in Dunbar, at her sister Mona's.

Adela stood drinking in the sights and sounds of India as if for the last time. Sophie was beside her, arm about her shoulder.

'I have mixed feelings too, Adela,' she murmured. 'This is the first time I've left India since we all came out on the boat in '22. The first time I've left Rafi since we got married.'

Adela saw that Sophie had tears in her eyes.

'I feel like I'm being banished,' Adela said unhappily. 'I don't really want to leave India at all.'

'Nobody's banishing you. And it's not for long,' Sophie encouraged. 'Maybe it will help ease the pain for a little while. I'm sure your aunt Olive and your cousins will be kind to you.'

'Yes, you're right. Cousin Jane is a very nice person if her letters are anything to go by. She sent such a sweet card of condolence by airmail. I should stop feeling so sorry for myself all the time. It's far worse for Mother being left to cope on her own. Do you think she'll be all right?'

Sophie nodded. 'I think if anyone can get through hard times it's Clarrie. She's the strongest person I know. But you shouldn't be so hard on yourself. You have lost your father – I know how close you both were – and you have every right to be feeling as grief-stricken as your mother.'

Adela whispered, 'It's not just grief, it's guilt. If I hadn't met Jay, if I hadn't agreed to go back and hunt the tigress, if we'd both just listened to Dad . . .' She broke off, too choked to speak.

Sophie squeezed her shoulders. 'You mustn't let regret consume you, darling lassie, else you will never find peace of mind. Whatever happened between you and Prince Sanjay is not the reason for your father's death. Wild animals are always unpredictable and every hunter knows that – Wesley most of all. He acted as he did because that was the kind of man he was. He would have done what he did for anyone, not just you. He saved the lives of the mahouts and the shikaris that night too.'

They stared out at the widening gap between the ship and land. The massive archway, the Gateway of India, stood out like a raised eyebrow as the face of the dockside grew indistinct. Adela felt numb as she thought of all those she loved and left behind: Mother, Harry, Mrs Hogg and her friends in Simla, the people of Belgooree, Rafi and James. Sam. Thinking about him made her heart sore. It was probable that she would never set eyes on him again. She couldn't explain how desolate that made her feel. It made no sense. They had only met a handful of times and yet he had had such a profound effect on her young heart.

She had fallen for his lean good looks, the sexy way his eyes crinkled when he smiled, his easy laugh and dishevelled hair. The touch of his strong work-roughened hands and the way his eyes lit with passion when he spoke about his work or his photography. The way he would speak to anybody, his humour and kindness. The intense way he looked at her that made the pulse jump in her throat. The firm mouth that she had longed to kiss and now never would. She kept the small photograph of the two of them tucked into an inner pocket of her handbag. It was all she had left of him.

'Come on, you two,' Tilly called from across the deck. 'Quickly!' She and Mungo had been looking west to the first blush of the sinking sun. 'Come and feast your eyes on this – Mungo's spotted a dolphin.'

Sophie pushed a handkerchief at Adela. 'Dry your eyes, sweetie. Auntie Tilly's on a mission to cheer you up.'

***

It was only much later, long after they'd left the boiling temperatures of the Indian Ocean and the dusty landscape around the Suez Canal, that Adela found the package. The ship was steaming through the Mediterranean, and cloudy skies and a stiff, cool breeze sent Adela to hunt out a warm jacket and discard her topee for a felt hat. In the jacket pocket was a small parcel wrapped in an old piece of the *Shillong Gazette*. Inside was a wad of tissue paper smelling of household spices with a folded note from her mother.

Darling Adela,

Try to enjoy your time in Newcastle. I think there is much you will love about it, not least the theatres and cinemas! I hope Olive will spoil you. She will certainly be better company than your sad old mother just now. I'm sorry I haven't had more time for you since your father's death. I will try to be better when you return. Perhaps it will do us both good to be apart from each other for a short while. The summer will rush by and you will be back in the autumn – unless you want to stay longer and Olive says you can. You mustn't think you have to hurry back – your father would never want me to stand in the way of your pursuing a career in acting if you get the chance in England.

I wanted you to have the enclosed necklace. It was given to me when I was your age and about to go to Britain for the first time, feeling very frightened and unsure of the future. The old swami at the ruined temple gave it to me as protection, and I have worn it almost every day since. Now I want you to wear it and always be under the swami's protection and my love.

Harry and I will miss you, darling one.

Take care,

Your ever-loving mother xxx

Adela wiped away the tears that spilled on to the letter and unfolded the tissue paper. Inside lay the pink stone on a simple chain that her mother always wore. Why hadn't she noticed that her mother wasn't wearing it the day she left home? She rubbed the smooth stone between her fingers – it was almost heart-shaped – and then fastened it around her neck. Kissing the stone, she pushed it under her blouse so that she would feel the weight of it against her skin, reminding her that her mother still loved her after all. She went up on deck with a lighter tread and a smile on her lips that felt strange after weeks of mourning.

She was going to make the most of this trip to Britain. From now on she would not look back and wallow in remorse. For the first time she felt curiosity about her Tyneside family and the big industrial port of Newcastle that was going to be her temporary home for the summer.

'Auntie Tilly,' Adela asked as she joined her on the bench, watching Mungo playing deck quoits with some of the other children. 'Tell me about the theatres in Newcastle. Is there a repertory company?'

'My brother Johnny used to act with an amateur dramatic society in Jesmond, but there's bound to be one. Your aunt Olive will be able to tell you. Oh, well done, Mungo!' She broke off to clap her adored youngest child. 'Are you thinking of joining a group while you're at home?'

'Perhaps,' said Adela. It sounded strange to have this unremembered city referred to as home. But then to Tilly, Newcastle had never stopped being home; even Adela was aware of that.

Tilly grinned and gave her a peck on the cheek. 'Glad to see you smiling again, dear girl. It's the fresher European air – lifts the spirits. Goodness,' she said, sighing happily, 'I can't wait to feel a good old North Sea mist on my face again.'

***

About the time Adela and her aunts were stepping ashore at Marseille in the South of France to board a train north – Tilly had decreed they take the train through France to save nearly a week of extra sailing around the Bay of Biscay – Clarrie was receiving an unexpected visitor.

Looking out from the tasting room, she saw a battered Ford passing the factory, heading towards the compound.

'What's wrong?' asked James. He had been staying for three days, helping with pricing the monsoon pickings, and had brought one of his mechanics to fix the ancient rolling machine that Wesley had always had the knack of repairing.

'Visitor, but I don't recognise the car,' answered Clarrie.

'I'll go and investigate,' he said at once.

'No, I will.'

'I'll come with you then.'

She gave him one of her looks, and James tempered his words. 'If you want me to, of course.'

Clarrie gave a soft sigh – half amusement, half impatience – and nodded. 'Thank you.'

Banu, on horseback, had stopped the car at the entrance to the compound. He was leaning down from the saddle, talking to the driver. Clarrie recognised the battered green porkpie hat.

'Sam Jackman? Is it you?'

Sam climbed out of the car and smiled. He came straight up to Clarrie, took her hands in his and gripped them.

'Mrs Robson, I'm so very sorry to hear about your husband's death. Dr Black told me. This must be a very trying time for you all. Please accept my deepest sympathy. I liked Mr Robson a lot. I just came here to see if there is anything I can do to help.'

Clarrie was suddenly overwhelmed by the young man's candid, kind words and the warm, strong hands around hers. She had heard so many platitudes of late – or worse were those who crossed the street in Shillong rather than deal with a grieving widow – that she thought she was immune to words of condolence. But something about Sam's directness and sincerity touched her to the core. Clarrie bowed her head and sobbed, feeling her legs buckling like a newborn foal. Sam pulled her into a hug and let her weep into his shoulder.

James squirmed with embarrassment and began to fuss. 'Look here, Jackman, there's no need to go upsetting her. Let's get her inside.'

They all got in Sam's car, and he drove them up to the bungalow. By the time they got out, Clarrie was once more composed and in charge.

'I'm sorry. What must you think of me crying like a schoolgirl? It's so kind of you to come and see us. You'll stay for some refreshment?' She disappeared to give orders for tea and tiffin to be brought on to the veranda. James turned to Sam while she was gone.

'I really don't think you should stay long, Jackman. Mrs Robson is in a very fragile state. She's just about coping, but she doesn't need reminding of Wesley every second minute, so keep the conversation light – and brief.'

Sam regarded James with interest. He had little respect for the tea planter who had ruled the Oxford Estates with an iron rod for years. Sam would never forget how, as a boy, he had seen desperate and dying coolies from the Robsons' plantations hurling themselves into the Brahmaputra to try and escape slavery and starvation. But he wouldn't be provoked.

'It's good to see that Mrs Robson has you to advise her. Are you staying long?'

James felt the blood rush into his thick neck. 'That's none of your concern. I'm here to help Clarrie as long as she needs me.'

'That's heartening to hear. Is your wife visiting too?'

'My wife has gone to England to take our son to school. It was her idea that I help out here when I can.'

James felt his anger quicken at the sardonic twitch of the young man's eyebrow. Damn him! He didn't need to explain himself to Jackman of all people. The young man was a dreamer who never stuck at hard work for long or faced up to responsibilities. He hadn't been fooled by Sam's overnight conversion to missionary zeal, and it didn't surprise him that he had fallen short of good conduct and gone off with some native woman. At best he was a well-meaning fool, at worst a dangerous subversive who had no loyalty to the British in India.

Clarrie returned before he could needle the missionary about the Sipi scandal.

'So what brings you back to these parts, Sam?' Clarrie asked as they drank tea out of thin china cups. In Sam's large hands the cup looked like it was from a doll's set.

'Dr Black's sister, Gertrude, died suddenly, so I came back for the funeral to support the doctor.'

'Oh, I am sorry. I hadn't heard.'

'You've had enough grief of your own to cope with,' James said, glaring at Sam as if it was his fault for bringing more to her door.

Clarrie ignored James's remark. 'What will happen to the school I wonder?'

'Dr Black is trying to sort things out and appoint a successor.'

'Are you still at the mission, Sam?' she asked.

He slurped and shook his head. 'Not exactly.'

'What does "not exactly" mean?' James frowned.

'I'm continuing much of the work I was doing – planting orchards, harvesting the fruit and helping the locals get it to market – but I no longer live at the mission house in Narkanda.'

'Where then?' asked Clarrie.

'Further east, towards the Tibetan border at Sarahan.'

'Is the mission still paying you a salary?' James asked.

'James,' Clarrie reproved, 'that's none of your business.'

Sam met his look, unperturbed. 'They buy the trees for planting, but I don't take any money for myself. Dr Black kindly pays a small allowance out of his own pocket for me and my, er, dependents.'

James was disbelieving. 'But you still manage to afford to drive a car?'

'Dr Black's car.' Sam smiled. 'He lent it to me so I could visit Mrs Robson and Adela.'

'Well, if it's Adela you want to see, you're too late there,' James said bluntly. 'She's gone back to England. Sailed with my wife and Mrs Khan.'

Clarrie saw the look of dismay on Sam's face and felt a pang of pity. She didn't know why James was being so prickly with the young man.

'She's gone to stay with her relatives in Newcastle,' she explained. 'I thought it would cheer her up to get away from here.'

'And get away from that wretched Gulgat prince who broke her heart,' James muttered.

This time it was Sam who felt himself redden around the jaw. 'Prince Sanjay you mean.'

'I'd rather not talk about it,' Clarrie said with a pained look. 'I can't help blaming the prince for his actions. If he hadn't insisted on pursuing the tigress, perhaps Wesley would be here today—'

'Don't think of it, my dear.' James reached out a hand and grasped hers. 'I shouldn't have mentioned him. Forgive me.'

Sam sat wrestling with his emotions. He had come here with high hopes of seeing Adela again and having a chance to explain everything, to get things straight between them. The last sight he had had of her was her aghast expression at the Sipi Fair when he made his split-second decision to intervene in the marriage barter and stop Ghulam being caught by the police. What else could he have done? At least he had saved Pema from certain slavery with a man who would have treated her as lesser than his hill dog, and she would never have to be at the beck and call of her abusive uncle again. But to the British community – liberal and conservative alike – he had acted beyond the pale. He, a missionary, had bought a heathen woman like chattel and taken her into his household.

'Tell me about the time Adela visited the mission in Narkanda,' Clarrie suddenly asked. 'Her letters were short, but I could tell it was a happy time.'

Sam felt his gut twist with the bittersweet memory. 'It was a happy time for me too.' He smiled. 'Your daughter is a natural with people; she made them feel better just by being around. And she'd make a good nurse – Dr Fatima was very impressed with her gentle but competent touch. No amount of blood or gore seemed to put her off.'

He stopped as Clarrie winced.

'Really, Jackman,' James protested, 'in the circumstances.'

'I'm sorry, I didn't mean to upset—'

'No, please go on,' Clarrie insisted. 'I want to hear more.'

Sam told her about the clinics and how hard Adela had worked, her manner always cheerful. He talked of her interest in the Gaddi nomads and how she had taken Fatima to meet them and give them medicines, how the women had taken her to their hearts. Clarrie listened with rapt attention.

It was a side of her daughter she had never really seen. She knew Adela could be fearless – reckless even – but usually it was in pursuit of enjoyment and self-interest. She had watched her daughter grow up into a beautiful pleasure seeker and worried that she and Wesley had indulged her too much. But Sam had let her glimpse another side of Adela, one that put others first and was brave in helping those at the margins of society. Clarrie had suspected that her daughter had only volunteered to help at the clinics in order to see Sam, yet Adela had proved herself courageous and compassionate.

Clarrie's throat tightened with emotion to think how she had judged her daughter too harshly over Wesley's death. Now she was thousands of miles away and far from her arms. She hadn't even been able to bring herself to give her daughter a parting hug, pushing her instead towards Rafi's car and telling her to hurry. It was kind Sophie who had put her arm about the unhappy girl and steered her into the front seat beside Rafi.

Just as she was struggling with her thoughts, Harry crept in from the garden. He didn't clatter around any more or jump around the furniture pretending to be a maharajah, so that often he startled her with his sudden appearance.

'Hello, you must be Harry.' Sam grinned and leapt from his chair, hunkering down in front of the boy by the veranda steps. 'Adela's told me all about you.'

Harry gazed at him with cautious dark eyes. 'Is Delly with you?'

'No, but she told me you like green sweets, so I've brought you this.' Sam pulled a slab of pistachio-flavoured fudge from his pocket. 'It's gone a bit soft in the heat, but it tastes just as good.'

Harry glanced at his mother to see if he was allowed to take this from the stranger. She nodded with a smile.

'This is Adela's friend Sam. You can have a bit now, then save the rest for after supper.'

Harry unwrapped it and rammed the end of the bar into his mouth. Joy spread across his solemn face. He sidled closer to Sam, leant on his arm and whispered, 'My Daddy died 'cause a tiger ate him. And Delly's gone away to a new castle. Now it's just me and Mummy and sometimes Uncle James. Would you like to stay and be my friend too, Sam?'

Sam ruffled the boy's hair – Clarrie's heart squeezed to see the fond gesture that Wesley had so often used – and said he would be happy to be his friend, but that he couldn't stay because he had work to do.

'I'll come back and see you another time,' Sam promised.

'And bring me sweets?' Harry asked.

'Of course.' Sam winked.

As Sam stood to go, Clarrie put her hand out and gripped his arm.

'Thank you, Sam. You're a good man. I can't tell you how much your visit means to me, and I'm sorry Adela wasn't here too. I know she would have wanted to see you.'

He gave a smile of regret. 'I don't deserve your praise, Mrs Robson. "Good" is not a word that usually goes together with "Jackman". But thanks.'

'Will you go back to Sarahan?' she asked.

Sam nodded.

'To your native wife?' James asked, his tone distasteful.

Sam answered with a defiant look. 'Yes, to Pema.'

He enjoyed the scandalised look on the tea planter's rugged face. Sam shook Clarrie's hand, nodded to James and jammed on his green hat. He put out a hand to Harry.

'Do you want a ride in my car down the drive?'

The boy brightened. 'Yes, please.'

'Come on then. You can toot the horn for me.'

Clarrie watched him swing the boy down the steps and into the Ford.

'I'll go with them,' James said, his look grim.

Clarrie watched them go. She knew James disapproved of the maverick young missionary – ex-missionary – but she found Sam endearing. It didn't shock her that Sam had taken the Gaddi girl as his wife, but she knew how much the news would upset Adela that Sam remained with Pema. Yet she felt grateful to Sam; he had given her a new way of seeing Adela and a way back to loving her daughter again. For a while she had so resented her, part blamed her for the tragedy. The sight of Adela's green eyes – so distressingly like Wesley's – staring at her full of misery and guilt had been more than she could bear. She had felt only relief when Rafi had driven away, taking Adela out of sight. But now she knew how unfair that had been. When Adela came back in the autumn, Clarrie would make it up to her. They would be a proper family again.

James was returning with a bawling Harry. Clarrie sighed. She knew Tilly's husband was doing his best to be of help, and she guessed all his fussing was masking his own unhappiness at his wife's departure with his youngest son, on whom he doted, but she was going to have to be firm and send him away. She would not become a crutch for him while Tilly was absent. Clarrie wanted above all to be left alone to grieve for Wesley in her own way.

Chapter 16

The train pulled into the cavernous Newcastle Central Station with a hiss and a billow of steam. Adela hugged her aunties and Mungo goodbye – they were all going on to Dunbar to stay with Tilly's sister Mona – and then they helped her out of the carriage with her two suitcases and hatbox.

'We'll meet soon,' Tilly promised. 'I'll come for a day out in Newcastle.'

'And don't forget you're invited on holiday to St Abb's in September,' Sophie reminded. 'See if Cousin Jane would like to come too.'

'I will,' Adela said, feeling suddenly teary that she was losing their company. 'Have a lovely reunion with Jamie and Libby. Tell them we'll play tennis together.'

'Will do, darling girl,' Tilly said, beaming and waving like an excited child.

Adela looked around for a porter. At any Indian station she would have been surrounded by red-jacketed coolies offering help and swinging her cases on to their heads before she could utter the words. As the train pulled away, she stood feeling foolish. She waved to a man with a trolley.

'Sorry, missus,' he said, 'I'm meetin' the posh uns in first class.' He called to a younger skinny man to deal with her.

The youth struggled with her two cases, while she carried the hatbox to the ticket barrier. Beyond was a crowd of expectant people come to meet passengers. Clarrie strained for a sight of any Brewises and worried that she wouldn't recognise any of them. A tall, thin young woman with a short pageboy haircut under an old-fashioned cloche hat raised her hand and gave an uncertain smile.

'Cousin Jane?' Adela called. The woman nodded. Adela muscled through the barriers, relieved that someone was there to meet her. She plonked down her hatbox and threw her arms around her cousin. Jane tensed, startled by the demonstrative greeting.

'It's wonderful to meet you at last.' Adela grinned. 'We could be sisters, couldn't we? Same dark hair and shape of the eyes.'

Jane blushed, pleased at the remark. 'You're much prettier.'

'No, I'm not.'

'George is waiting with the van outside. He's supposed to be at work, but he said he couldn't let you go on the tram.'

'That's very kind.' Adela smiled.

Under the blackened portico, Adela spotted a dark green van bearing the name of The Tyneside Tea Company, her uncle Jack's firm. The driver tooted, then jumped out and took the cases from the panting porter.

'Bloody lead weights,' the youth muttered, holding out his hand for a tip.

George paid him, then turned to Adela with a broad smile and an outstretched hand. 'So, you're my exotic cousin. You're even prettier than all your photos.'

Adela laughed and shook hands. 'And you're just as handsome as yours.'

She was amused to see his fair face blush. He was good looking, with well-groomed blond hair and regular features. Brother and sister were nothing like each other in looks, and by the way George chatted and Jane fell silent, Adela guessed they were opposites in temperament too.

They clambered into the front of the van, Adela squeezing in between her older cousins, and George was soon swinging the vehicle into the traffic.

'Sorry to hear about Uncle Wesley,' George said.

'Thank you,' said Adela.

'What a terrible business.'

'Yes, it was.' She dug her nails into her palms.

'He was really canny, your father,' said George.

'Canny?'

'Aye, likeable man – fun with us bairns. He taught me how to play cricket and took me riding the last time you were home. I must've been about nine.'

Adela's eyes prickled. 'I don't remember that.'

'You were just a nipper. Bet he was a great dad.'

Adela nodded, swallowing down tears. When would she stop wanting to cry at the very mention of her father's name?

Trying to think of something else, she gazed at the scene as they rattled over cobbles, noticing the fashions. The young women wore their hair shorter than in India, styled in waves, and many of the men wore large flat caps. There wasn't a brown face in sight, nor the dazzling colours of saris or gaudily painted rickshaws that would brighten up an Indian city. There were far more motor cars here and less horse traffic.

The sides of buildings bore huge advertisements for hot drinks or cleaning powders. They passed a theatre showing J. B. Priestley's play *Time and the Conways*.

'Oh, I'd love to go and see that,' cried Adela. 'Have you been yet?'

'Not into serious stuff,' said George. 'Prefer a good sing-song.'

'Well, you and I will have to go then,' Adela said, nudging Jane.

'My sister doesn't go to the theatre,' George answered. 'She gets nervy in crowded places.'

Adela looked quizzically at Jane, but her cousin glanced away and stared out of the window. Adela thought how different she seemed from the person who had written long newsy letters for the last ten years.

'Okay, Jane,' said Adela, 'we'll choose a very quiet matinée to go to.'

Jane's mouth twitched in a fleeting smile, but George snorted. 'Well, you can try.'

At the top of a steep hill he turned right and then left into a quiet terraced street and pulled up outside a house with a dark green front door.

'Number 10 Lime Terrace. Home sweet home,' George declared. 'You'll find the old girl indoors, but the old man won't be back till late. See you at teatime.'

He jumped out, retrieved the cases from among the packets of tea, opened the front door and dumped them in the hall.

'The maharani has arrived!' he bellowed, and then with a wink at Adela he sprinted back to the van and drove off, with it belching smoke and the horn blaring loudly.

Adela peered up a gloomy hallway, trying to adjust to the dimness after the sunshine outside. There was a smell of carbolic soap and disinfectant. A dark red narrow carpet runner disappeared up a black-painted staircase straight ahead, while three doors led off the hallway. It was colder inside than out.

'In here!' a voice called from behind the door to the right.

'Go ahead,' Jane said. 'Mam's in there.'

Adela quickly unpinned her hat and hung it on a high peg on the wall next to a man's coat, opened the door and stepped into a sitting room. It was crowded with solid dark furniture – two sofas, three armchairs, several nests of tables and a radiogram on a sideboard – with glimpses of a dark-blue-patterned carpet beneath. A strange-looking unlit fire was surrounded by brown tiles, and a large mirror hung on a chain above it. Adela wondered where her aunt was.

'Over here, lass. I've been watching from the window.'

Adela jumped. Turning towards the bay window, which was shrouded in net curtains and obscured by planters stuffed with ferns, she saw a thin woman stand up. She looked pale as a ghost in the filtered light, her oval face like delicately chiselled alabaster and reddish hair pulled away in a tight bun. She was dressed in a thick tweed suit despite it being the height of summer.

'Aunt Olive?'

'Of course it is. Come here, lass, and let me take a look at you.'

Adela rushed forward to kiss her aunt, but Olive stuck out her hands and held her at arm's length, surveying her. Her touch was cold and bony. Adela clutched her hands awkwardly, smiling.

'Eeh, just look at you, so like our Clarrie!' Olive cried. 'You're even bonnier mind. You've got your father's eyes; that's what it is. Your mam must be that proud of you. I wish I'd had a lass that took after me.'

Adela gave an awkward glance at Jane, but she remained impassive.

'And how pretty you look in that frock. Is that the fashion in India? Chintzy flowers and sweetheart neckline?'

'It's a couple of years old,' Adela admitted. 'Mrs Hogg's durzi copied it from a French magazine.'

'What's a durzi?' asked Olive.

'A tailor,' Jane answered.

'How on earth do you know that?' Olive exclaimed.

'Adela told me in a letter. Mr Roy, a durzi from Delhi, used to visit Simla during the cold season and go around all the British homes making clothes.'

'That's right.' Adela beamed. 'Aunt Olive, don't you remember the durzi from Shillong who used to make dresses for you and Mother? His son still makes clothes for us occasionally, though we mostly send to Calcutta or mail-order from Britain.'

Olive waved a dismissive hand. 'I've long forgotten all them foreign words. I hardly remember India at all. Now sit down, lass' – Olive patted the armchair by the window next to hers – 'and tell me all about yourself. Jane will pour the tea. It's Ceylon. My Jack thinks it's the best on the market.'

Adela settled into the leather seat, noticing how – although it was only early afternoon – the table in the window was already set with a silver tea service and a cake stand covered in a large linen napkin.

'It's very kind of you to have me to stay,' she said. 'Mother sends her love. She's sorry not to come, but she couldn't face leaving Belgooree at the moment. Not without . . . Well, you understand I'm sure.'

'Poor Clarrie. She'll be lost without Wesley,' Olive said with a shake of her head. 'He was her rock. Not that she appreciated him at first. Could have married him years earlier in India if she hadn't been so stubborn. But then that's Clarrie – just like our father: always thinking she knows best.'

Adela flinched at the blunt words.

'Well, as I say,' Adela repeated, 'she sends you her love.'

'It must have been awful for you being there when your da was killed. I can't imagine why Clarrie let you go off into the jungle full of tigers and wild animals.'

'It was my father's birthday present to me to go on shikar. Hunting is something we both loved doing.'

Olive shook her head. 'Well I would never let a daughter of mine go doing such dangerous things. Would I, Jane?'

Jane shook her head as she arranged dainty china cups on their saucers.

She served tea and milk from a silver teapot and jug, the milk and sugar basin covered in beaded nets to keep off nonexistent flies, and handed a rose-patterned cup and saucer to Adela.

'May I have mine without milk please?' Adela said, passing the cup on to her aunt.

'We don't drink black tea in this house,' said Olive, 'and that's too milky for me.'

'It's all right, Mam,' Jane said, hastily taking the cup from Adela. 'I'll have that one.'

She poured another cup without milk and gave it to Adela with a shaking hand. Jane then removed the napkin from the cake stand, revealing delicately cut sandwiches and slices of cake.

Adela took one of the sandwiches. 'These look tasty.' she said, smiling at her cousin. Biting into it, she found that the bread was dry; the sandwiches must have been made hours ago. The filling was fishy and bland. Adela swallowed it down, while Jane nibbled at hers and Olive didn't eat.

'Have another,' Olive encouraged. 'Looks like you need feeding up.'

Adela reached for a slice of Victoria sponge. It was dry too. She wondered how many times it had been brought out of a tin to sit uneaten on the plate.

'Does your cook live in?' she asked.

Olive gave a short laugh. 'We haven't had a cook for five years. Jane does the cooking. She's never going to win awards, but it's plain honest food you'll get here.'

'Lexy at the café taught me,' said Jane. 'She's good at pastries and cakes.'

'At Belgooree,' said Adela, 'Mohammed Din lets me stir the puddings sometimes too.'

'Well, you're welcome to help our Jane in the kitchen,' said Olive. 'In fact if you're going to stop around for long, I'll expect you to give a hand with the housework too.'

'I don't mind that,' Adela replied, wondering what it would entail. Did they have any servants at all? Jane used to mention a maid called Myra that she liked. Did they have sweepers to clean out the toilets or empty the baths?

Olive asked about Harry. 'Poor pet, he must be so sad. It's a terrible thing for a lad to lose his father. Lads need a man around the house. I went through hell during the Kaiser's war when my Jack was taken prisoner. The thought that he might die and George would grow up fatherless was more than I could bear.'

Her words pained Adela. 'At least Harry has Uncle James. He's coming over regularly to help at Belgooree.'

'James Robson, Tilly's husband?' Olive was taken aback.

'Yes.'

'While Tilly's away in England? That doesn't sound proper to me. But then Clarrie never cared what people said about us – not like I did. I'm the sensitive one. She just does what she wants.'

'She doesn't have much choice,' Adela defended. 'And it was Auntie Tilly who suggested it.'

'Strange man, James Robson,' said Olive. 'Never any good at polite conversation and never had any time for us Belhavens.'

'Well, he's making up for that now, helping Mother with the tea garden.'

Suddenly Olive put out a claw-like hand and patted Adela's knee. 'That's good. He didn't have a good word to say about Wesley when he was alive, but at least he's standing by family now.'

Adela changed the subject. She asked after Uncle Jack and his business.

'Works like a Trojan does my Jack,' said Olive, 'but business has been bad since the Slump. I don't know the ins and outs – he doesn't like me to worry – but we've had to tighten our belts. Still, he's been in charge of Tyneside Tea since Mr Milner retired five years ago, and I'm very proud of him.'

'And he has George to help too,' Adela said, smiling.

She saw the transformation on her aunt's face at the mention of George. Her taut features relaxed into a smile and her eyes glistened.

'Jack couldn't manage without our George; he's a born salesman. Got the gift of the gab, just like his father when he was first starting out. Jack used to bring tea to the house in Summerhill where we lived and to see me. That's when we started courting. Your mam was married to old Herbert Stock – she'd been his housekeeper. She never loved him, just married him for his money so she could start her own business. But me and Jack, we were a love match.'

'Mother married the love of her life,' Adela pointed out, 'when she married my father.'

'That's very true,' Olive conceded. She began to talk about George and his string of girlfriends. 'Not sure he'll ever settle down. He's always spoiling them rotten, then gets bored and finds someone new. Still, he's only twenty-five. I wouldn't want him rushing into marriage with the wrong lass. I don't think much of the current one mind. Barmaid at the cricket club.'

Jane spoke unexpectedly. 'Joan is canny. She's very sweet-natured.'

‘She sits there as quiet as a mouse – just like you,’ complained Olive. ‘George’ll get bored. He needs a lass who can string two sentences together, bonny, but not too bonny, and who can do more than pull pints. She only got the job at the club ’cause she’s the groundsman’s daughter. George needs to marry a lass from his own class with a bit of education.’

Adela steered the conversation to Jane. ‘How about you, Cousin Jane? Do you have a boyfriend?’

‘Our Jane!’ Olive exclaimed. ‘She’s much too shy. No one’s ever come courting her. What about you, Adela?’

Caught by surprise, Adela flushed. ‘No, I don’t have anyone special.’

‘But you’ve had a few lads court you, haven’t you? You’ve said so in your letters to Jane. What was the latest one I saw – wasn’t it some Hindoo prince?’

Adela looked aghast at Jane; it hadn’t occurred to her that her cousin would show her letters to anyone else. Jane was blushing and biting her bottom lip, her look apologetic.

‘I acted with a prince at the Gaiety,’ Adela admitted, ‘but I’m not courting anyone.’ She quickly changed the subject. ‘I’d love to visit Herbert’s Café. Would you be able to take me, Aunt Olive? Mother told me how beautifully you decorated it.’

‘I’m not well enough to go painting walls any more. I’m bad with my chest.’

‘I’m sorry to hear that,’ said Adela. ‘Mother said you’re a great artist.’

Olive smiled, pleased with the compliment. ‘I was once upon a time. But running a family and a house and looking after my Jack takes up all my time. Let alone the café. I haven’t had time for art in years.’

‘Well, while I’m here to help out, perhaps you could try dabbling again?’ suggested Adela.

Olive shrugged. Jane began to clear the tea plates and cups on to a tray.

‘I’ll take you to the café this afternoon if you like,’ her cousin offered.

‘I’d like that very much.’ Adela smiled, keen to get out of the depressing room and away from her aunt’s morbid preoccupations. She jumped up and began to help.

'No,' said Olive. 'We'll all go later, when George can run us down the hill. It's me who should show you the café – I'm the one who's been looking after it all these years. Leave Jane to do these. You go and unpack. You're sharing her room. Jane, pet, show Adela where your bedroom is and help her with those heavy cases; then you can finish off here. I'm going next door to see Mrs Harris for a cup of tea. I'll keep an eye out for George coming back.'

Jane's room was tidy and spartan. Half the wardrobe and a chest of drawers had been cleared for Adela's clothes, while a pull-out bed had been erected under the window and covered with a faded patchwork quilt of yellow, red and orange cotton prints. Jane's dark-framed bed was covered in a blue candlewick bedspread that matched the plain blue curtains. There was nothing to show what interested her cousin – no photographs, no keepsakes on the dressing table – except for a pile of books on the bedside table. They were library books: two history tomes, a travel book about Greece and two novels – *South Riding*, by Winifred Holtby, and *Gone with the Wind* by Margaret Mitchell. So there was a streak of the romantic in her apparently inhibited cousin.

Bored with unpacking, Adela went to the window. Below was a large backyard with a trough of geraniums and two outhouses, while opposite was an identical terraced row. Beyond that stretched other ranks of brick houses, dipping away towards a smoky horizon and the River Tyne. She unlatched the sash window and heaved it up. The breeze billowed into the antiseptic-smelling room. It was suddenly familiar: the mineral smell of coal fires. It brought back a memory of having a bath as a very young child in front of a crackling fire in a cosy, brightly painted house. Aunt Olive's? It certainly wasn't this dark, solidly respectable one.

While she was still unpacking and hanging up her dresses, Jane returned. At once she closed the window. 'Mam doesn't like the coal smuts flying in. Gets all over the house.'

'Sorry, didn't think. Where shall I put the empty suitcases?'

'Put them out on the landing. George can store them in the loft later. You can sleep in my bed, and I'll take the pull-out.'

'Certainly not,' insisted Adela. 'I'm not going to turf you out of your own bed. It's very kind of you to share your room with me.'

Jane gave a cautious smile. 'I hope you enjoy your stay here. I've been really looking forward to you coming – so has Mam. She wants to show you off.'

'Why would she want to do that?'

'She's always telling people how successful Aunt Clarrie is and boasting about being related to the Robson tea planters. You would think they owned half of India the way she talks.'

Adela laughed. 'Well, Robsons can be a bit full of themselves, that's true.'

'Oh, that's not a criticism of you,' Jane said hastily. 'It's just Mam trying to put herself above the folk round here.'

Adela eyed her cousin. She sounded resentful. Perhaps Jane wasn't as indifferent to Olive's carping as she appeared.

'Well, I'll try and put on a good show of being the memsahib.' Adela winked. 'Anyway, I brought this for you. It's not much, but you sounded so interested in India that I thought you'd like something to read.'

'You shouldn't have.' Jane eagerly took the proffered gift, carefully unknotted the string and unwrapped the brown paper. She smoothed a slim hand over the cover. '*Simla, Past and Present*, by Edward J. Buck,' she read aloud. 'Thank you. This looks really interesting.'

'It's got photos too.' Adela sat down on the bed beside Jane and turned the pages. 'That's just round the corner from Aunt Fluffy's cottage. The black and white doesn't do justice to the landscape or the sunrise.'

'I'm sorry about Mam and your letters,' Jane said quietly. 'I didn't show them to her; she came in here and went through my drawers. She used to make me read them out to her when you and I were younger, but I stopped doing that – you know, when you started writing about lads and feelings and that.'

Adela went hot at the thought of her aunt knowing so much about her. She tried to remember what she had written about Sam and Jay. It dismayed her that her twenty-three-year-old cousin couldn't stand up to Aunt Olive more.

'It doesn't matter,' Adela said. 'We'll just have to make up our own code in future. I did that with my school friends. Our code word for any action with boys was "Jubbulpore".'

'It won't get much use around here I'm afraid,' Jane said with a rueful smile.

'Well, I'm going to make sure it does while I'm here,' said Adela. 'I'm going to make it my mission to find you some Jubbulpore this summer.'

For the first time she heard Jane laugh, a deep, throaty gurgle quite at odds with her shy, humourless appearance.

Chapter 17

The household came alive when George burst back through the front door and shouted up the stairs.

'Come on, ladies, where are you hiding? Want a spin in the car, Adela? Thought I'd take you for a sightseeing trip. Mam says you want to visit Herbert's Café.'

Adela and Jane clattered out of the bedroom, where they'd been lounging on the bed absorbed in Jane's two copies of the new photographic magazine, *Picture Post*. Jane, it turned out, was a keen photographer, but couldn't afford to buy or develop much film. Adela was fascinated by the pictures of ordinary British life: miners walking to work in the mist; women wearing flowery aprons hanging out washing in cramped backstreets; a child riding to school on a bicycle.

'Yes to all of those,' Adela said and grinned as she jumped down the stairs.

Olive was already dressed for an outing in a green coat and matching hat.

It turned out that George had swapped the van for his father's car so he could ferry their visitor about. They all climbed into the small Austin, Olive up front with George, while the girls sat in the back.

'Don't drive too fast,' Olive said, tensing as George revved the accelerator and pulled on to the main road into town.

'This area is called Arthur's Hill, and we're joining Westgate Road,' George said, pointing out landmarks as they went. He drove them back past the railway station and the impressive Palladian buildings of central Newcastle, with their massive soot-blackened pillars and grand windows. They dipped steeply downhill towards the quayside.

'We don't want to see the mucky Tyne,' cried Olive. 'Adela will want to see the shops.'

'All in good time,' said George. He began to whistle 'The Lambeth Walk' and Adela immediately joined in singing.

'You know the show *Me and My Girl*?'

'We do get radio in India you know,' Adela said, smiling, 'and my theatre friend Tommy bought the sheet music.' She burst into a raucous rendition of 'The Sun Has Got His Hat On'.

'You've got a lovely singing voice,' said Olive. 'Maybe you can teach our Jane to sing. George takes after me – he's got a musical ear.'

'Mother said you used to play the violin beautifully,' said Adela.

'Haven't touched it in years.'

They drove under the solid metal Tyne Bridge, arching the brown river. The riverside was alive with activity: dockers unloading cargo and rolling barrels; wagons weaving through people and a flock of runaway sheep.

As they doubled back along the riverside, George and Adela sang 'The Teddy Bears' Picnic'.

'Sing something more romantic,' Olive demanded.

Adela sang 'I've Got You Under My Skin' in a rich, melodious voice.

'You'll break some poor lad's heart with that one,' said George, glancing at her in the rear-view mirror. She looked away, thinking with a pang how it reminded her of Sam. The newly popular tune had been played at her seventeenth birthday party.

Soon they were emerging into a working-class district of pubs and shops with striped awnings and merchandise stacked on the pavement to entice shoppers. There were a few people going in and out, but more were standing around in the hazy sunshine, hands in pockets, leaning against walls chatting or watching passers-by. Below were grimy sheds and engineering works that George said were gun factories.

'Work's picking up again since the Germans went into Austria,' he told her.

'Why? Are we selling guns to the Germans?' asked Adela.

'Don't be daft,' George said. 'They're making them as fast as they know how. We have to keep upsides, don't we? In case there's war.'

'Don't say that.' Olive shuddered.

'Surely that's not likely,' said Adela. She felt quite ignorant of what was going on in Europe. All the talk at home was of Indians agitating for home rule and the Japanese attacking China.

'It's becoming more likely, what with Hitler throwing his weight around and Musso cosying up to his fascist friend.'

‘Stop talking politics,’ Olive cried. ‘Look, here we are: Herbert’s Café. Goodness, the windows need a good clean.’

They came to a halt in Tyne Street. As they climbed out, a gaggle of young children surrounded them, shouting out, ‘Can I mind yer car, mister?’

George gave a coin to the oldest-looking boy and ushered the women inside the café. From the outside the tea room looked nondescript, but inside it had a scruffy charm. The yellow wallpaper was tinged brown from cigarette smoke, but there were large, brightly daubed paintings of local scenes and dusty palms in tarnished brass planters around an upright piano. The tables were covered in faded linen cloths, but someone had gone to the trouble of placing centrepieces of fresh carnations, now beginning to wilt. Most of the tables had one or two customers, some sitting reading newspapers, others chatting over empty plates. The room was stuffy and smelt of meat pies. Adela hid her disappointment; this was hardly the glamorous teahouse that her parents had often talked of so proudly.

A buxom middle-aged woman in a white blouse and black skirt with thick make-up and black hair that looked suspiciously dyed sashayed towards them.

‘Eeh, is this our little Adela?’ she cried, opening wide her arms. ‘Come and give Lexy a big hug, bonny lass!’

Adela was enveloped in hot arms, a slight sour smell of sweat masked by a cloying flowery perfume. She had a very vague memory of a loud laughing woman called Lexy who used to feed her cream cakes, but she remembered her as fair-haired.

‘Isn’t she the image of her mam?’ Lexy said to Olive. ‘How is Clarrie? Eeh, hinny, we were that sorry to hear about Mr Robson. He was a real gentleman. All the lasses here had a soft spot for him – not that we’ve seen him for years. But he helped us all. If it wasn’t for him, we wouldn’t be here. Saved this café from ruin and me from the workhouse, so he did. Lovely man.’

She swamped Adela in another hug. Adela was too overwhelmed to speak.

‘Can you bring us tea please, Lexy?’ Olive reasserted control.

‘And some of your cream buns,’ George said winking.

‘Just for you, bonny lad,’ Lexy said, tweaking his cheek. She issued instructions to a young girl called Nance, who wore an oversized apron and had large ears that stuck out under a frilly cap, and then showed them to a table near the piano. Judging by the film of dust on the lid, it hadn't been played in a while.

'Jane, I have a new recipe for you,' said Lexy. 'French custard tart. Had a Belgian sailor in last week whose family run a café in Antwerp. Rich and creamy; you'll love it.'

'Sounds expensive,' said Olive.

'I'll be back in tomorrow,' Jane said with more self-assurance than Adela had heard so far, 'and you can show me.'

Lexy sat with them until the tea and cakes arrived, plying Adela with questions about her family and Belgooree, then about Tilly and Sophie.

'They're spending most of the visit in Dunbar with Tilly's sister, but Tilly can't wait to have a trip to town.'

'You tell her to come here for her dinner and see me,' said Lexy. 'I'll make her steak and kidney pie and her favourite chocolate cake.'

'And you make sure she pays for it,' muttered Olive.

The order arrived, and the manageress watched with an eagle eye as Nance transferred the tea, cakes, china plates and cups to the table. 'Fetch an extra pot of hot water, lass. Adela will take hers black and it might be too strong.'

'How do you know that?' Adela laughed.

''Cause you're your mam's daughter.' Lexy smiled.

***

Afterwards, George drove them around the centre of town, pointing out the large department stores of Fenwick's and Binns and the Theatre Royal and various cinema houses.

'Can we all go to the pictures one evening?' Adela asked in excitement. She was thrilled with the bustling city centre and the wide choice of entertainment.

'George can take you,' said Olive. 'Jack and I are not ones for films and silly musical hall acts.'

Back at the house, Adela met her uncle Jack. He was a smallish man with receding fair hair and a wiry moustache that was already white. He looked frail, his suit a little big for him and his face deeply scored, but he had attractive eyes, and she could see how once he would have been handsome. George took after him. He gave her a friendly welcome before going off to wash and change. Olive fussed in his wake.

They all ate in the dining room at six thirty prompt. The room felt musty and cold, as if it was rarely used. George did most of the talking, regaling them with stories of his customers.

'Don't believe the half of it,' Jack grunted. 'Our lad likes to tell a tall tale.'

'Cousin George, you should go on the stage,' Adela said, laughing.

'Over my dead body,' said Olive. 'He'll be a respectable businessman like his father.'

'Well, that's what I want to do,' Adela announced, 'go into theatre.'

Olive shook her head and clucked in disapproval. 'Surely our Clarrie won't let you.'

'Mother doesn't mind. In fact she encourages it.'

'Good for you,' cried George. 'I'd come and watch you any day of the week.'

After that, Jack got up and retreated to the sitting room to doze over a newspaper in front of the unlit gas fire. George kissed his mother and went out, calling, 'Don't wait up. I've got my key.'

For the first time in her life, Adela helped with the washing-up. Jane had to show her what to do.

***

Adela soon settled into city life. She loved Newcastle, with its smoky bustling energy, its noisy riverside and grand buildings, its array of shops, from prestigious department stores to corner tobacconists, its clanking trams and the friendly people, who struck up conversations about football and the weather at tram stands or in shop queues. She didn't understand everything that was said – the accent was thick and the speech rapid – but she understood why Tilly hankered after her former home.

Olive paraded her around the neighbours in Lime Terrace, where they drank endless cups of strong sweet tea and ate jam biscuits that stuck to the teeth like glue. Morning visiting appeared to be socially unacceptable, and Olive only went out after three o'clock in the afternoon. Jane never came on these visits; she spent her time both shopping and cooking for the household and down at the tea room, helping Lexy. Adela asked her to show her how to cook, though her poor efforts were ridiculed by the family.

'Is that pastry or sludge from the sink?' George teased.

'I can't believe our Clarrie hasn't taught you any cooking,' said Olive.

'Mohammed Din sees to all that,' said Adela. 'He's very proprietorial over his kitchen.'

This caused great hilarity among the Brewises, and "Mohammed Din sees to all that" became a family catchphrase whenever Adela showed her ignorance about things domestic.

A Scotswoman called Myra came in twice a week to do laundry and cleaning. Adela found it strange to see a woman doing the jobs that low-caste men did at home. Myra was loud and cheerful and sang along to the radiogram as she polished, even though Olive repeatedly told her not to turn on the machine as it gave her a headache.

'Och, you need a good sing-song to encourage the elbow grease.' Myra laughed in defiance.

While Olive went to lie down, Adela couldn't resist joining in the singing. 'Whistle While You Work' became their shared theme tune as Adela pushed around the furniture for Myra, and the maid wielded the carpet sweeper.

'Mrs Brewis puts up wi' ma cheek,' Myra confided, ''cause naebody else round here will work for her. Always complaining. If I worked for free, she'd still say I was robbing her blind.' Myra laughed and continued in her forthright manner. 'That Mr Brewis is a saint putting up wi' her ways. And wee Jane should stand up for hersel' instead of cowering like a wee timorous beastie. I'd not let Mrs Brewis speak to me like Jane allows her to.'

But at the café Adela saw another side of Jane: her cousin was popular among the staff and customers. She was welcoming and efficient and seemed to know something about everyone who came in, chatting to the women about their families, the men about football and handing out sweets to children on their birthdays.

'Your mam started that tradition,' Jane told her. 'That's what Lexy says. It's one of my earliest memories being given a stick of liquorice in a bag of sherbet on my fourth birthday, even though it was just after the war and treats were hard to come by. I loved my aunt Clarrie.'

Adela enjoyed her visits to the tea room and the welcoming Lexy. She took little persuasion to lift the lid on the old piano and bash out popular tunes and sing along. She had learned to play at St Mary's, and Tommy had taught her a handful of more modern melodies. Lexy would join in, and the café would fill up more quickly as shoppers were drawn in by the music.

After two weeks of badgering, Jack gave Adela a tour of the Tyneside Tea Company factory. It was situated further upriver in an austere building with a once-grand frontage now flaky with peeling paint and grimy from smoke. Behind was a depot of delivery vans, a few motorised but mainly still horse-drawn. The air was full of the manure smell of stables and the occasional whinny of a workhorse. Adela was surprised that they weren't all out delivering.

She breathed in. 'Horse smell reminds me of Belgooree.'

'Wait till you smell the tea inside.' Jack smiled.

He showed her around the packing rooms, where loose tea was being poured into paper bags and sealed. The air was dusty with dry tea. The workers spoke to him with deference, but his manner with them was friendly and encouraging.

George joined them in the tasting room. Adela felt a pang of longing for the one at Belgooree; here as at home there was a simple bench lined up with white china tasting pots, spittoons and samples of different grades of tea.

'This is where we do our blending,' Jack explained. 'Gan on, Adela, and give us your opinion. Your mam was the best taster I ever knew. Let's see if she's taught you well.'

Adela worked her way along the line as George prepared the samples. She sucked through her teeth, let the liquid envelop her tongue and then spat it out.

'Full body, heavy soil, probably picked during the rains. Upper Assam. I'd mix it with something lighter.'

Jack nodded and she tasted the next. 'Umm, I like this. Bright, first flush, nice colour, soil more acidic. Darjeeling or Ghoom. A good breakfast tea.'

'Not on Tyneside,' said Jack. 'They like a bit more body to wake them up.'

She carried on tasting and spitting and giving her opinion. 'Fruity, apricot aroma, nice and balanced, mature, autumn flush, possibly Sylhet region.'

George was impressed and kept asking her about life on a tea plantation and how things were done at Belgooree. The more she reminisced, the more his enthusiasm grew.

'I'd give anything to travel out there and see where the tea gets grown. Must be a grand life. Do they play cricket?'

'They do, though there's not much time for it. Tennis is probably more popular.'

'Tennis is fine by me,' George said, grinning, 'especially mixed doubles.'

'You should come and visit,' Adela encouraged. 'Mother would love that.'

'Maybe I will.'

'You don't need to gan to India to know about tea,' said Jack. 'Everything you need to know about running this business you can learn from me, just like I learnt it all from Mr Milner. Besides, we can't afford for you to gan away. You're needed here, lad.'

Adela didn't push the idea further; she could see how it made her uncle agitated. 'Have things changed much since Mother was here, Uncle Jack?'

He sighed. 'It's been a tough few years, I'll not deny it. We used to sell tea all over the North East, selling it door to door. Customers are very loyal, 'specially out in the small villages and towns. But now these new chain shops have started up and they're undercutting us. They buy in bulk and sell cheap – no matter that the quality isn't as good. Folk go to them to save a few pennies, and who can blame them?'

'But you are still giving them convenience,' Adela encouraged, 'and personal service. Bet the likes of George brighten up a housewife's day.'

George laughed. 'I try my best.'

'We'll need more than George's patter to keep this business going,' Jack said morosely. 'I'd like to invest in new packing machinery and a couple of new motor vans, but we can't afford it. We've had to cut prices to compete. It's down to the bare bones.'

'I'm sorry, Uncle Jack. I wish we could do more to help, but Mother's first concern is keeping Belgooree going.'

'Of course it is,' George agreed. 'Da's not asking for financial help.'

Jack's look was haggard, and for a moment he said nothing. Then he rallied. 'If anyone can save a business, then it's Clarrie. I wish her luck.'

As they left the tasting room, Jack's frown returned. 'You'll not say any of this to our Olive, will you? Not about things being bad. She's such a worrier; it doesn't do to let her fret.'

'Course I won't,' Adela said, putting a reassuring hand on his arm. 'But wouldn't it be better if she knew what was going on? Then nothing would come as too much of a shock.'

Jack gave a hopeless shrug. 'I wouldn't know where to start.'

Adela worried about her uncle, but after that visit he refused to talk to her about the business and avoided being alone with her. Even a few words exchanged in the hallway seemed to annoy Olive. 'Don't you pester your uncle about his work,' she warned. 'When he comes home, he wants to leave all that behind.'

So Adela gave up trying to chat to her brooding uncle; he was so very different from the jovial, ambitious man that her parents had once described. She enjoyed George's company best of all. She went to watch him play cricket at the club and met his girlfriend, Joan. Adela thought she was a bit dull, despite her dreamy blonde looks, but she could see how George basked in her adoration. He took Adela out in the van around his delivery route to the pit villages south of the Tyne, and she stared in fascination at the clanking pit wheels, the coal-blackened miners trudging back from the morning shift and the women dashing into the street at the sound of George's horn. The miners' wives were cheerful and saucy and reminded Adela of the tea pickers, who would make ribald remarks about their menfolk when out of earshot.

She went with George to see Hitchcock's *The Lady Vanishes* at the nearby Pavilion Cinema, a former theatre which was still decorated with ornate pillars and busts of naked women. He took her to see *The Prisoner of Zenda* at the Gaumont, which Adela enjoyed so much that she went a second time, and she chivvied Jane into going too.

'Ronald Colman is to die for,' she said. 'We'll sit at the back by the aisle so you can make a run for it if you feel unwell. And there's a massive Wurlitzer organ gets played in the interval. George says they brought it over from the Bronx in New York. Isn't that exciting?'

Jane went reluctantly, but the trip was a big success. She didn't feel any panic sitting next to her chattering cousin, sharing a bag of lemon drops, and was so caught up in the film that she sat on to watch the credits. Sheepishly on the way home, Jane admitted that she hadn't been to see a film since she was twelve and had never been to a talkie before.

'I had this terrible memory of scary music being played while a monster came up on the screen. It seemed that real. I screamed and hid under the seat for the whole of the film. Mam was so cross with me for making a scene that she said she'd never go again.'

'And she never let you go either?'

'Said it wasn't worth the risk of me getting hysterical. I know it sounds silly,' Jane said and blushed, 'but I've always been frightened of the dark and being stuck somewhere where I couldn't get out.'

'It's not silly,' said Adela, 'but you don't have to be frightened any more. You've proved you can do it.'

'Yes, I have, haven't I?' Jane smiled.

'When that Essoldo opens at the end of August, me and you are going to be first in line,' Adela declared. 'We'll stuff ourselves with chocolates and swoon over the stars.'

The next time there was a social at the cricket club, Adela insisted Jane came too.

'I can't dance and I've got nothing to wear,' Jane protested in alarm.

Adela marched her upstairs and pulled out the summer dresses she had brought from India. 'Try them on.'

'But I'm taller than you.'

'We can let down the hem.'

'And you've got more, you know, bosom.'

'Only since you've started fattening me up with all your lovely cooking.'

They were reduced to giggles as Jane wriggled into Adela's clothes and paraded around the room wearing a topee and impersonating a memsahib.

Adela laughed. 'You're a good mimic.'

They decided on a full skirt in turquoise chiffon with one of Jane's white short-sleeved blouses, a wide pink belt and a matching diaphanous scarf, which Adela pinned around Jane's shoulders, and clipped a mother-of-pearl hairslide into her short dark hair. Adela allowed Jane to borrow her deep pink lipstick.

'You look gorgeous,' Adela gasped. Jane blushed at her image in the mirror, amazed at the poised dark-eyed woman who gazed steadily back at her.

Adela put on a bright yellow frock that accentuated her curves.

'I'll have to watch myself with your pies,' she joked, 'or this dress won't fit me much longer.'

She tied her hair in a golden snood, put bangles on her wrists and dark red lipstick on her full mouth.

Olive was sent into a panic when she saw them ready to go out.

'Lipstick!' she shrieked. 'Get that off now, do you hear?'

'There's no harm in it, Aunt Olive.' Adela stood her ground, catching Jane's hand so she couldn't run back upstairs.

'Jack,' Olive appealed to her husband, 'you don't want our Jane going out like that, do you?'

Jack looked up from his newspaper. He blinked in surprise at the young women.

'You look smashin', pet,' he said. 'You an' all, Adela. Pretty as your mam.'

Olive looked thunderous. She rounded on her daughter. 'You better behave yourselves mind. If I hear you've been making a fool of yourself, it'll be the last time you go. And no talking to lads.'

Jack spoke up. 'Haway, Olive, don't you remember being young once? You were happy enough to talk to me and go out on my arm.'

Olive's thin face tightened. 'That was done proper. I didn't gan out to parties wearing lipstick.'

'George will chaperone us,' Adela assured. As if on cue there was a hoot of the horn outside. 'Come on, Jane. Bye, Aunt Olive, Uncle Jack. We won't stay out late.'

In the car Jane laughed with relief as she recounted the confrontation to George. 'I don't know where you get the nerve,' she said in admiration.

'Aunt Olive isn't a dragon,' said Adela. 'She just worries about things that will never happen. That's no reason to stop you having a bit of fun.'

'You are my kind of girl,' George said and chuckled as he revved the car and they roared off up the street.

***

The cousins were in big demand on the dance floor that evening. Adela danced every dance, but got more enjoyment out of seeing Jane blossom under the attention of several of George's friends.

'Why have you been hiding your sister away for so long, Brewis?' demanded Wilf, a lanky joiner at Vickers-Armstrong's engineering works. He wanted to walk her home, but Jane resisted.

'Can I call on you?' Wilf asked eagerly.

'Mam doesn't like visitors.'

'Call into Herbert's Café,' Adela intervened. 'She's the manager there.'

'Not exactly—'

'The old tea rooms on Tyne Street?' Wilf's eyes widened. 'They serve canny pies there.'

'Jane's homemade recipe,' said Adela, linking arms with Jane and swinging her away before she could deny it. 'She'll be in tomorrow.'

As George drove them home, Adela said, 'Well, that definitely counts as some Jubbulpore.' The girls hooted with laughter in the back seat.

'What's all this talk about Jubbulpore?' he asked in bemusement.

But he got no sense out of his sister and cousin, who dissolved into fresh giggles. He started a sing-song, and they sang nonstop all the way back to Arthur's Hill.

Chapter 18

At the end of August, Tilly came for a visit to Newcastle with Jamie and Libby, leaving Mungo on the Dunbar farm with her sister and brother-in-law.

Lexy made a fuss of Tilly's red-headed children. Jamie looked older than his fifteen years. He had grown tall and had his father's square jaw, yet his interests were more in tune with his mother's; he was bookish and more bashful than Adela remembered. They had been firm friends as children. Libby was thirteen and had grown chubby and argumentative since Adela had last seen her in India as a seven-year-old. She sparked with her mother, who nagged her to sit up and keep her elbows off the table. Libby's answer was, 'Why? What harm are they doing?'

'Always got a cheeky answer.' Tilly gave an irritated sigh.

'It was a question actually,' said Libby. 'Miss MacGregor says we should question everything.'

'I'm tired of hearing about the opinionated Miss MacGregor,' said Tilly, rolling her eyes at Adela. 'Libby's history teacher is a bit of a firebrand.'

'Mother doesn't approve because Miss MacGregor is anti-imperialist,' Libby said, 'and so am I.'

Jamie patted his sister's back. 'We've been treated to daily lectures about the evils of colonial rule – in particular how awful we British are in India.'

Libby shook him off. 'We wouldn't like it if we were ruled by people thousands of miles away, would we?'

Adela was jolted by the words. She remembered Ghulam Khan being passionate about the same thing. How strange that she should hear it repeated by her youthful second cousin.

'Well, young lady,' Tilly said in exasperation, 'it's British people like your father who are working hard thousands of miles away who make it possible for you to go to your very good school. So you can tell that to your Miss MacGregor.'

'From what I remember,' Libby sparked back, 'it was hundreds of coolies who did most of the work. It's because they are paid so little that Daddy can afford to send me to school over here.'

'Don't be so rude!'

'Not that I got any say in the matter.'

Adela could see Tilly's eyes begin to fill. She knew how reluctant Tilly had been to send her children so far away for their schooling, so Libby's words were bound to wound.

'Don't start that again,' Tilly pleaded.

'I wish I'd been allowed to stay in India like Adela was,' Libby persisted. 'You chose your school, didn't you, Adela? And you ran away from the one you didn't like.'

'Well, it was my parents' decision to send me to St Mary's,' Adela replied, not wanting to fuel the argument, 'and it was your cousin Sophie who suggested it.'

'I wish she'd suggested that I go there too,' said Libby.

'And I'd wish you'd stop going on about it,' Tilly snapped. 'You're perfectly happy at St Bride's.'

Lexy saved the situation by bustling over with a fresh plate of cakes. Jamie and Libby tucked in, and for a while the conversation turned to what Adela had been doing in Newcastle. They were interrupted by the surprise appearance of George.

'Hello, Mrs Robson,' he said as he strode across and kissed Tilly robustly on the cheek.

'Goodness me, George,' she cried. 'What a handsome young man you are. Children, do you remember Adela's cousin George Brewis?'

Jamie stood and shook George formally by the hand. Libby sat up and smiled. George pecked her on the cheek, which brought the colour flooding to her face.

'Couldn't miss out on seeing the Robson family.' George winked. He sat down and helped himself to a sandwich. 'Come on you two; you have to finish these cakes,' he ordered, 'or Lexy will never speak to you again.'

He chatted easily, asking the youngsters about their holiday in Dunbar. Adela noticed how Libby's dark blue eyes shone as she looked at George and her cheeks remained flushed as she answered his questions. Adela recognised the yearning in the girl's face, her impatience to grow up and be treated as an adult. She had been Libby's age when she had fallen for Sam Jackman. Yet she had not rebelled against her mother as Libby was doing. But then the poor girl had been separated from Tilly for six long years, and her aunt Mona in Dunbar had become a mother substitute. Tilly wanted her to be the little girl she had left all those years ago, whereas Libby was on the cusp of womanhood and kicking against being treated as a child.

'Libby, would you like George and me to take you out in the van this afternoon?' Adela suggested. 'Let your mother and Jamie go to the library and art gallery.'

'Yes, I'd love that,' Libby said, beaming.

'What do you say, George?' Adela asked, conveying a certain look. 'We could help you sort out the orders.'

He read the signal. 'I'd be delighted to have the company of two charming ladies. I'm going upriver to Wylam. We'll have ice creams in Prudhoe on the way home.'

'That's very kind.' Tilly gave a smile of relief. 'You will behave yourself, won't you, Libby?'

'I promise not to put my elbows anywhere I shouldn't,' Libby answered with a grin.

***

At the beginning of September, before Tilly's children were due to start the new school year Adela was to join them in St Abb's on the Berwickshire coast. They were renting a solid stone house on the clifftop with Sophie for a week. Just before she went she received a parcel of Belgooree tea from her mother, which had been sent sea mail at the beginning of August. In it was a letter telling her about Sam's unexpected visit. Adela's heart quickened.

. . . He was sorry not to find you here. I could tell he was disappointed. James wasn't very kind to him – there seems to be some animosity there – so he didn't stay long. But I thought you'd want to know that he came to pay his respects to your father. Sam spoke a lot about your time at Narkanda helping at the clinic. I'm so proud that you did that, my darling. And here I was thinking you were spending most of your time in Simla just enjoying yourself! I'm sorry to have misjudged you.

Sam's no longer living at the mission, though he appears to be doing their work further into the mountains at Sarahan. Do you know it? He is such a nice man. I think it's very unfair of the British community in Simla to ostracise him for taking responsibility for Pema. I'm sorry to tell you though, my darling, that Sam is plainly living with her as man and wife – that's what he said . . .

As man and wife. The words were like a kick to the stomach. Adela felt desolate at the news. A part of her had still hoped that Sam was merely protecting Pema as one of his household. But no, he was living openly with her as her husband. She doubled up in pain at the thought of Sam and Pema living a life of intimacy. She thought she would be physically sick. Adela wished no ill on the Gaddi girl, and was thankful that she had escaped her cruel uncle, but would have given anything for it to have been any man in the world other than Sam who had stepped forward and saved her.

With a numb heart Adela prepared for her holiday in St Abb's. Olive rejected the gift of tea.

'Fancy Clarrie sending that. My Jack's a tea merchant; tea is the one thing we don't want for!'

'It's Belgooree tea,' Adela pointed out, 'to remind you of your old home.'

'I prefer Ceylon,' Olive said, 'and I don't want reminding of Belgooree. It hasn't been home for most of my life. My home is here with Jack and George.'

'And Jane,' Adela reminded. She was embarrassed that Jane was in the room, but not even mentioned.

'Aye, and the lass.'

Adela had been asking all week if Jane could go with her to St Abb's, but her aunt had stubbornly refused permission. She chose that moment to ask one last time.

'No,' said Olive. 'We Brewises don't take holidays; we can't afford it.'

'I'll pay for her train fare, and she won't need money for anything else,' Adela offered.

'And who will cook for George and Jack? No,' Olive said, quite adamant, 'she's needed here and at the café.'

Adela was tempted to retort that her aunt could do the cooking for once, but Jane's anxious look prevented her. Later Jane said, 'It's not worth the bother; Mam will only get upset.'

'You're twenty-three!' Adela protested. 'You're entitled to have a social life. Why don't you stick up for yourself? You won't even let Wilf take you out, though it's obvious how keen he is on you.'

'It's all right for you,' Jane retaliated. 'You're only here for a few weeks. You can swan in and do what you want, and then you'll be off back to India. This is my home, and I have to live by my parents' rules whether I like it or not.'

'Aunt Olive's rules.'

'Well, that's the way it is. Mam can't cope without me. She's frightened of being left on her own; that's why me and George take it in turns to be here. She can't help the way she is – she's always been delicate – and it doesn't help you stirring things up.'

Adela was taken aback by her cousin's sudden outburst. 'I'm sorry. I don't mean to upset Aunt Olive; I just want you to have a bit of fun.'

Jane looked away. 'I know you do and I appreciate it. But we're different you and me – we want different things. I'm happy with my life as it is.'

Adela left the next day. She wasn't totally convinced by Jane's protestations that she was content with the life she was leading, but perhaps she didn't know her very well after all. Soon she was too excited about seeing her Robson family and Sophie again to dwell on her unfathomable cousin. George dropped her off at the station with a cheery wave.

'Have a grand time,' he said, 'and send us a postcard.'

***

Adela took the Belgooree tea as a present for Tilly and Sophie, who accepted it with cries of pleasure. The sun shone most of the week, and the days were filled with picnics, clifftop walks, boat trips and swims from the sandy cove at Coldingham. They met up with Tilly's good friend Ros, who had them all to tea at the house of her parents-in-law, nearby.

Sophie was full of chat about her time in Edinburgh staying with her old employer, Miss Gorrie. They had gone on a tour of the Highlands with two of Miss Gorrie's friends and got as far as the island of Iona, where Saint Columba had first brought Christianity to Britain in the sixth century.

Both Sophie and Adela did their best to occupy Libby and keep her away from Tilly's fretful attention. Got on her own, the girl was good company, with a quick sense of humour and a lively interest in everything. She wanted to know what they thought of Hitler's aggressive stance towards the Sudetenland and the likelihood of going to war over Czechoslovakia.

'We mustn't go to war with Germany again,' Sophie replied. 'The last time was too terrible.'

'But we can't stand by and let Hitler and his bully boys walk into other people's countries, can we?' Libby challenged.

'Let's hope to heaven it won't come to that,' Adela said. 'They say Chamberlain is going out to Germany to talk some sense into Hitler.'

As the week came to a close, tension from the outside world seemed to seep into the carefree holiday. Tilly became fiercely demonstrative towards Mungo, which made him uncharacteristically clingy. Libby squabbled with Jamie when he baited her about having a crush on George. But when Mungo unburdened his fear of starting at Dunelm School, it was Libby who reassured the anxious boy.

'You'll be in the same house as Jamie, so he'll look out for you and we'll meet up at half-term at Aunt Mona's – that's only five weeks to wait. Then we'll be together for Christmas. And I'll write to you every week. St Bride's is only an hour away from you by train, so perhaps I could come through to see you one weekend.'

On the final evening Sophie took Adela aside and asked, 'Have you decided if you're going to stay in Britain longer or come home with us in October?'

'I'm still not sure,' said Adela. 'I don't know how much longer I can carry on living at Aunt Olive's – she's growing tired of having me around, and I don't want to outstay my welcome. But from Mother's letters, she seems to be coping fine without me.'

She had told her aunties about Sam's visit to her mother, but didn't say how much the news of his settled life with Pema had upset her. She was plagued by thoughts of them being together, working side by side, laughing over meals, sharing the same bed . . . Jealousy clawed at her insides. But she was powerless to change the situation. Now that Sam was quite out of her reach, there was even less reason to go back to India.

'So?'

'So, I've been thinking. When I go back to Newcastle, I might try and see if I can join the local repertory theatre, even if it's just to give a helping hand behind the scenes to start with.'

'That sounds like a good plan.' Sophie smiled. 'I think Newcastle suits you – you're looking really well. Don't tell Tilly how much fun you're having though, or she might insist on staying with you and refuse to get back on the boat at the end of next month.'

The three women agreed to meet up in October before they were due to sail. By then Adela would have made her final decision. Libby slipped Adela a folded piece of paper as they were packing up.

'Will you give that to George for me please?' The girl held her look, but there was uncertainty in her deep blue eyes. 'It's a cartoon.'

'Of course I will.' Adela took it. 'Am I allowed to look?'

'You can, but don't show it to anyone else.'

Adela opened it up. There was the unmistakable image of George – the wave in his blond hair exaggerated, and half his face taken up with a huge grinning mouth – and he was whacking a cricket ball high in the air. Below the giant hurtling ball, and running for their lives, were tiny figures in Nazi uniforms, with Hitler leading the retreat.

Adela chuckled at the likeness and the pithy message. 'He'll like that – hero George to the rescue.' She smiled at the girl. 'You've very talented, Libby.'

'I wish Mummy thought I was,' said Libby, then hurried off before Adela could protest that Tilly did.

***

Back on Tyneside, Adela put her plan into action about finding a job in the theatre. She had a fruitless week tramping around the theatres for a paid job and ended up getting a part-time position as an usherette at the Stoll Picture Theatre. By the end of the month the talk was all of Chamberlain, the prime minister, returning triumphantly from his negotiations with Hitler waving a peace agreement with Germany, Italy and France. Adela wondered what Libby and Miss MacGregor would make of it all.

In early October Adela's job became full-time, and when she wasn't at the cinema she was helping out at Herbert's Café. Sometimes before a shift she would end up drinking tea in Lexy's small flat above the café, encouraging her to reminisce about the old times, when her mother was in charge. Adela rarely spent time at Aunt Olive's any more, just returning to sleep and share in the occasional meal. She insisted on giving her aunt some money for her bed and board.

'It's very good of you to let me stay so long,' Adela said. 'When I've saved a bit more, I'll look for digs.'

'Why ever would you do that?' Olive exclaimed. 'No, you can keep on sharing with our Jane. What would Clarrie think of me if I allowed you to go living in lodgings like some working-class lass? I'll not have the neighbours saying I can't look after my own.'

Adela was enjoying her job – it meant she got to see all the latest films, even if it was in snippets, and she still had the occasional evening off to meet up with George and his friends. Now that the cricket season was over, they went dancing or to the musical hall. Jane did not go out with them and had rebuffed Wilf enough times for the amiable joiner to look elsewhere. He was courting Nance from the café. Adela was perplexed as to why her friendship with Jane had cooled since her going away to St Abb's. Her cousin was polite, but distant. Perhaps she feared Aunt Olive's censure, or maybe they were just too different to be close friends.

Two days before Adela was due to see Tilly and Sophie, Myra the cleaner waylaid her on her way out. She kept her voice low so Olive, sitting at the front-room window, keeping a watch on her neighbours, didn't hear. 'Away in the kitchen a minute, hen.'

'I don't really have time, Myra; I'm due at work in twenty minutes. Can it wait?'

'Better now while Jane's out and Mrs Brewis is on the sherry.'

Adela gaped. 'What do you mean, on the sherry?'

Myra gave her a look of disbelief. 'You must hae noticed?' she whispered.

'No—'

'I have to buy it in – as well as the cough sweets to mask the smell. She thinks Mr Brewis and Jane don't know, but they do.

We all pretend it's medicinal. Her morning medicine, she calls it. Helps her get through the day.'

Adela was stunned. 'I had no idea.'

'Anyway, that's not what I wanted tae say.' Myra nodded towards the kitchen and Adela followed her in.

'Take a seat, hen.' When Adela had sat down at the kitchen table, Myra continued. 'I do all the laundry here, including all of yours, am I right?'

'Yes, it's very good of you.' Adela was distracted, still trying to take in the news that her aunt was a secret drinker. Was that why she was so contrary in her moods and never left the house until well into the afternoon?

Myra waved a dismissive hand. 'I don't mind; that's ma job. But you don't dae any of yer own washing – nothing personal?'

'The odd pair of stockings if I need them for the following day.'

'I don't mean stockings, lassie. But I have nae washed any of your sanitary towels. You've been here over three months and you've never had a bleed.'

Adela stared at the woman, nonplussed. 'Well, I'm never very regular,' she said and flushed, acutely embarrassed.

'That's what I thought,' Myra said, eyeing her, 'at first.'

'What do you mean?' Adela's heart began to thud.

'I know the signs, hen. Your breasts are bigger and you've put on weight. And lately you've stopped drinking tea. I went off tea when I was expecting.'

'Expecting?' Adela gasped. 'I'm not . . . I can't be—'

'Aye, lassie, I think you are. And I tak' it from the shock on yer face that yer family dinnae ken.'

Adela swallowed down hard. Pregnant? She couldn't possibly be! She didn't feel any different, and she could go months without a period. Her pulse began to race. How many months this time? She racked her brains, counting back. She'd had a bleed two weeks before the *Arabian Nights* opened at the Gaiety, so end of April, beginning of May. Before her affair with Jay. Over five months ago.

Adela put her head in her hands. 'Oh my God!' she wailed.

'Wheesht, lassie.' Myra bustled round and put her arms around her shoulders. 'Worse things have happened at sea. Is it one o' George's friends? He'll just have tae dee the honest thing and put a ring on yer finger before it really shows. And you'll have tae pick the right time tae tell the sherry queen in there. It's a shame yer that far frae hame.'

Adela felt a sob rise up. 'I can't.' She gulped. 'It's not one of George's friends. It didn't happen in Newcastle, it was in India.'

Myra sighed. 'Oh, lassie,' Myra sighed, 'then I don't know what yer gangin' tae dee.'

Chapter 19

Adela pleaded with Myra to tell no one. She went off to work, her head reeling. It couldn't be true. It mustn't be true! She did her job distractedly. Lying on the pull-out bed that night, listening to Jane's even breathing, she wondered if her cousin had had her suspicions. Was that why Jane was avoiding her? Did she think it was contagious, or did she worry at what Aunt Olive would do if she found out? *When* she found out! Adela felt waves of panic pin her to the bed. The shock to her aunt might tip her over the edge into hysteria.

In a week's time she could be sailing back to India. That's what she'd do: return home to Belgooree. Her mother would know what to do. But Mother would be furious too – or worse, she'd be ashamed and feel let down by her only daughter. She couldn't bear her mother's disappointment after the pain she'd already caused her. God, she was a hateful person! A stupid, selfish girl! And what if Sam were ever to find out about it? She went hot and then cold at the thought. His censure would be the worst of all. She would not be able to endure it.

In the early hours of the morning, still sleepless, Adela thought about Jay for the first time in an age – properly thought about him. She was sure that he had taken precautions; he'd talked of coitus interruptus and said there was no chance of conception. She'd believed him just like she'd believed everything else he'd told her. How selfish of him! But what a fool she had been. How could she not have guessed that she was pregnant? The signs had been there if she'd thought about them: the weight she was gaining and the strange queasy metallic taste in her mouth. Had she deliberately ignored the changes in herself because she couldn't bear it to be true? The thought that she was now carrying his seed inside her filled her with fear and revulsion. The last thing on earth she wanted was a baby – especially not that man's baby! He had already brought so much heartache to her and her family.

She couldn't go home; it was her last thought before falling into a troubled sleep. She woke exhausted two hours later and dragged herself down for breakfast, forcing down porridge and tea. She mustn't do anything to cause suspicion.

Two days later she met Sophie and Tilly on the Town Moor for a walk and then lunch at Fenwick's. Adela put on make-up and wore a new woollen skirt and jumper she'd bought in the market that didn't accentuate her shape. She put on a cheerful face.

'You're absolutely sure you don't want to come back with us?' Tilly said in dismay.

'I'm having too much fun here,' Adela replied. 'And I'm still hopeful of getting into a theatre company soon.'

'Yes, you'd be silly to give up the chance,' Sophie agreed.

'We'll miss you, dear girl.' Tilly sighed.

'She'll be able to keep an eye on the children for you,' Sophie pointed out.

Tilly brightened. 'Oh yes, will you?'

'Of course,' Adela promised.

'Perhaps you could go to Mona's for Christmas. If your aunt Olive can spare you. I'd so love it if I thought you'd be there with my darlings.' Tilly turned tearful and fumbled for a handkerchief. Adela thought it best not to linger.

'I have to work at two,' she said, getting up. In the buzz of the restaurant, she briefly hugged her aunties and forced a cheerful goodbye. She felt sick inside having to leave them, but she couldn't let them guess her state of turmoil or let them cling on for close hugs.

She turned at the door and gave them a broad smile and a final wave, then hurried down the stairs. By the time she was out in the sharp autumn air, tears were coursing down her cheeks. She didn't really have to go to work for another hour, but she couldn't have kept up the pretence any longer. How many times was it on the tip of her tongue to blurt out her troubles to her closest friends and confidantes? Over the following days Adela wondered again and again what Sophie and Tilly would have said and done if she had let them into her shameful secret.

But the day of their sailing came and went and Adela would never know. She had got herself into this mess and was going to have to deal with it herself. Was it still possible to get rid of the thing inside her? Perhaps Myra would know. Could she confide in Lexy and ask her advice?

As she returned home to Lime Terrace late that night after work, she felt a strange sensation in her stomach. At first she thought it was from walking too quickly uphill in the cold damp air; it was like a hard pulse. But it wasn't regular. It stopped, then five minutes later began again, this time more like the flutter of a tiny bird. She'd felt it before, but hadn't thought anything of it. Now she instinctively knew what it was. Her baby – Jay's baby – was stirring inside her.

***

'What did you say?' Olive clutched at the chair and then sank into it.

'I'm having a baby,' Adela repeated, rushing forward in alarm. Her aunt had gone chalky white.

She had brooded on her problem for a month, but by November she knew it was only a matter of time before rumours would start. She had a pot belly under the layers of jumpers and cardigans that she wore, pretending that she was always cold in England.

'Don't touch me!' Olive screeched.

'I'm sorry, Aunt Olive. I've been trying to pluck up the courage to tell you.'

'Whose is it?' Olive asked. She looked terrified. 'Some docker you've met at the cinema or the tea room?'

Adela shook her head.

'Someone from the cricket club then? That's it, isn't it? I knew I should never have let you gan to that dance. And to think you took our Jane with you!'

'It's no one from the cricket club. It doesn't matter who it is.'

'Doesn't matter?' she hissed. 'Of course it matters. You'll have to marry him double quick.'

'I can't.' Adela tried to stay calm. 'And I wouldn't want to.'

'Not *want* to? I've never heard a lass so brazen! Who is the father? It's not my George?' she gasped, clamping a hand to her mouth.

'Of course not!' Adela was appalled her aunt could even think such a thing. 'It's nothing to do with your family or any of their friends. No one here is to blame except me and the man who did this, and he can't possibly help me now.'

'How could you do this to your mother? Clarrie will be that ashamed of you. What will she think of me an' all? Not able to keep you from going with men like a common tart. Is it that Wilfred who was after Jane? Did you oblige him instead?'

'No,' Adela insisted, 'it's no one you know. It happened in India.'

'India?' Olive echoed. 'How far gone are you?'

'Six months.'

'Oh my God!' Olive swore, close to tears.

'I know it's a terrible shock,' said Adela, 'but I'm not going to keep it. I just wanted you to know that I'll have it adopted as soon as it's born. Then I'll move out and find somewhere else to live.'

Olive stared at her. 'You can't stay here. Not in your condition. What would the neighbours say? And my Jack; he'd have a fit! No,' Olive said, standing up in agitation, 'you'll have to find somewhere else till the bairn's born. No one must know.'

Adela's spirits plunged; this was the reaction she had feared most but had suspected would be the most likely. She watched her trembling aunt cross over to the sideboard, reach inside for a bottle of sherry and pour herself a full glass. She glugged it down in one go.

'Myra knows,' said Adela, 'and I think Jane might suspect.'

Olive looked at her, horrified. 'If you've corrupted my lass—'

'I've done no such thing. Jane's a grown woman.'

'Myra will have to go,' Olive fretted, 'or she'll be telling all the other housewives in the street she works for.'

'Please don't sack her! Myra won't tell a soul – she's promised. She's the one who noticed first, not me, and she's not breathed a word for over a month.'

Olive poured and drank a second glass. Then she rounded on Adela.

'Tell me who the father is.'

'You don't need to know.'

'It might not be too late to get him over here sharp and marry you. Does he have money? If it's one of your posh friends, he could fly. They say it only takes four days.'

'He's got money but he's engaged to someone else – has been for years.'

Olive's expression changed. The fear returned. 'It's not that Indian you acted with?'

When Adela didn't deny it, Olive advanced, face contorting in horror. 'You went with a native? How could you? Have you got a half-caste in your belly?' Adela winced at the disgust in her voice. 'A bastard Eurasian!'

'Stop it, Aunt Olive!' She faced her squarely. 'It's not as if that hasn't happened in our family before.'

'What do you mean?'

'I know all about our family. Mother told me. Your Indian grandmother went with a British clerk, and Jane Cooper, your mother, was the result. So we're all half-castes.'

'How dare you!' Olive struck, half slapping, half clawing at Adela's cheek. Adela recoiled, clutching at her face.

'Don't you ever dare say such a thing again,' Olive cried. 'George and Jane know nothing of all that, so don't you say a word. You're a disgrace to the family. You can't stay here. So get out of my sight!'

'So you'd put me out on the street at six months gone?' Adela cried. 'Mother would never do that to one of yours.'

'No daughter of mine would have been so shameless.' Olive glared.

Adela swallowed and took a deep breath. 'You're right to be angry with me. I'll regret what I've done for the rest of my life. But please, Aunt Olive, help me. We're family.'

Olive collapsed into her chair again. 'What am I to do with you?'

'Perhaps I could go and stay in the flat with Lexy.'

'No. Not the café. We'd be the talk of the town. You'll have to stop going round there.'

'Then where? Let me at least go and speak to Lexy and see if she can help.'

'Very well,' Olive agreed. 'But Lexy is the only one you're to tell. And I'll not have you sharing with my Jane any longer, so you better get summat sorted quick.'

***

Lexy was shocked by Adela's news but soon recovered. 'Of course I'll help you, lass.'

'Aunt Olive says I'm to move out of Lime Terrace and I'm not to come near the café either.'

‘She’s a coward,’ Lexy said crossly. ‘Always has been. To think of the times Clarrie helped her sister and looked after her bairns; the least she could do now would be to help you out. Is that how you got them marks on your cheek?’

Adela ignored the question. ‘There must be places I could go till the ba—, till my time comes.’ Adela thought of the grim stories she had heard of homes for fallen women, part of the workhouse system. She shuddered at the thought.

‘I’ll not have you put away in one of them places.’ Lexy was adamant. ‘We’ll sort summat. I’ve got half an idea already.’

Two days later Lexy sought out Adela at the cinema as she was coming off shift and told her the plan.

***

Olive made the announcement around the tea table later that week.

‘Going to Edinburgh?’ Jane asked in dismay. ‘That’s very sudden.’

‘Well, I’ve got the chance of some theatre work,’ Adela lied, ‘and a lift up the Great North Road from someone at the cinema. So it has to be tomorrow.’

‘That’s grand, lass,’ Jack said.

‘Congratulations!’ George cried. ‘Which theatre?’

‘The Playhouse,’ said Adela. She hoped there was such a place, or if not that her cousin’s knowledge of Edinburgh was as vague as hers.

‘Maybe I’ll come up and see you perform.’ He grinned. ‘You’ll be a star, I know it.’

‘I’m glad for you,’ Jane said without enthusiasm, ‘though I’m sorry to see you go.’

‘Thank you.’ Adela was surprised and touched by her cousin’s obvious disappointment.

Olive sat smiling tensely throughout the meal, hardly touching her food. Adela was relieved when it was over and she could retreat to the bedroom. Jane followed. She watched as Adela packed a few clothes into the smaller of the two suitcases.

‘How long will you be gone? Will you come back for Christmas?’

'I'm not sure. I'll just see how it goes.' She closed the suitcase. 'If there's anything of mine in the wardrobe you'd like, then please help yourself.'

'But you'll need them when you come back.'

Adela hesitated. 'In the meantime you can wear them.'

'You are coming back?' Jane looked at her in alarm.

'I'm sure I will be.' Adela smiled. Her aunt's anger she could shoulder, but her cousin's unhappiness at her going made her suddenly teary. She turned quickly away and heaved the case from the bed.

'Did you really get those marks on your face from falling on the ice?' Jane asked. 'They look like nail scratches to me.'

'You're right,' Adela said. 'It was a drunk at the cinema. But they don't hurt anymore.'

That night she hardly slept. She was sick at having to lie to her cousin and was impatient for the dawn. In the early morning she rose and dressed in the cold bedroom while Jane cooked a breakfast of fried eggs and bread. Adela was nauseated by the smell. Jack left swiftly, wishing her well. Olive stayed in bed and didn't appear when Adela was ready to leave.

'Say goodbye to your mam for me, won't you?' she asked Jane. 'And tell her thank you for having me to stay all this time.' The cousins hugged.

George put her case in the van, and she climbed into the seat beside him. The last sight of Number 10 Lime Terrace was of Jane standing on the doorstep in the chilly purple dawn, waving.

George dropped her outside Central Station. 'Shall I wait till your lift turns up?' he asked.

'No need,' Adela said hastily. 'They'll be here any minute. You get off to work.'

His look was considering. She leant across and pecked him on the cheek before he started asking any awkward questions. 'Thanks for making my stay here so much fun.'

He grinned at her. 'No, the pleasure was mine. I can't remember the last time we had so many laughs in our family. Jane will miss you. She's really come out of her shell since you came.'

'Really?' Adela had felt a failure with Jane. Sticking up for her cousin had just seemed to make things worse for her.

'Really,' George assured. 'The old Jane would have sat at the table and not said two words.'

'Make sure you fight her corner,' said Adela. 'She thinks the world of you.'

George promised he would, kissed the top of her head and said, 'Out you get then, or you'll make me late for work.'

He hooted as he drove off. Adela watched till he was out of sight before turning away and walking into town.

***

Lexy was waiting at the bus station with their tickets bought. On the way towards the coast, she told Adela what to expect.

The icy sea air hit them sideways as they climbed down from the bus. The North Sea was grey and churning, capped with white waves. They walked south from Whitley Bay, passing closed-up hotels and respectable villas, Lexy insisting on carrying her case. Adela shook with cold and nerves, her hands frozen in her pockets. Eventually they stopped at a row of squat cottages overlooking a steep cliff. On the beach below a fishing boat was being pulled ashore. Two women sat on stools in nearby doorways mending a net, seemingly impervious to the cold. The air smelt fishy and salty.

At the end of the row stood a small house on its own, its windows opaque with sea spray. From what Lexy had told her, Adela knew this had belonged to a coastguard, now dead. His ancient widowed mother still lived here, looked after by one of Lexy's friends. These old women were to be Adela's guardians and companions for the next three months.

The woman who came to the back door in a purple housecoat had a lined leathery face and untidy grey hair. She smelt strongly of stale cigarette smoke.

Her face broke into a piratical grin – half her teeth were missing – and she held out her hands.

'Eeh, you're just like your mam! Welcome to Cullercoats. Come away, hinny. Don't let the cold in a minute longer.'

Lexy pushed Adela forward into the house. The door led straight into a low-ceilinged kitchen with an old-fashioned black range. Mingling with the aroma of potato soup was a smell of incontinence. A tiny woman in a 1920s black dress sat by the range. She looked very old, her hair sparse and her pale skin stretched over the bones of her nose and cheeks.

'I'm Maggie,' said the first woman, 'and this is Ina. We're old friends of your mam's; Ina used to work at the tea rooms with Lexy. We'd do owt for Clarrie.' She raised her voice and bellowed at the old woman by the fireside. 'Wouldn't we, Ina? We'd do anything for our Clarrie. This is her lass, Adela.'

Ina peered myopically across the room. She beckoned Adela over with an arthritic hand.

'Gan on,' Lexy encouraged. 'Don't be frightened. Ina doesn't bite. She can't see you till you're right up close.'

Adela went forward and put her hand into Ina's. The woman's confused expression changed into that of wonder. 'Clarrie,' she croaked, 'you've come back to see me.'

Adela felt tears welling in her eyes. These complete strangers were showing her such kindness – and all because of their love and respect for her mother. Ina thought she *was* her mother. She gently squeezed the old woman's hand and smiled. 'Yes, I've come back to see you, Ina.'

Chapter 20

Adela stuck to the house during daylight hours, helping with Ina, keeping the fire stoked up and making endless pans of vegetable soup. Around the house, Adela wore a pair of bright orange pantaloons that she had brought from India to wear as pyjamas, letting out the drawstring for comfort. Maggie did the shopping. After tea, when they'd put Ina to bed, Adela would dress warmly and go out in the dark around Cullercoats, walking along the promontory north towards Whitley Bay or south in the direction of Tynemouth, wondering if Sam's mother still lived nearby. Strange that she should end up at the small fishing village from where Mrs Jackman came. At first Maggie would protest at these nocturnal rambles.

'What you want to do that for? You'll catch your death or slip on the icy pavements and hurt yourself or the baby.'

But Adela would not be kept indoors. 'I'm not an invalid, Maggie. I need fresh air and exercise. I promise not to go far.'

Lexy had given her a cheap ring to wear on her wedding finger, and the story to neighbours was that Adela was a young widow helping with the housework for bed and board. If anyone suspected she was with child, no one said so, but Adela was increasingly self-conscious and preferred to go outdoors when most folk were in their homes. Besides, she didn't want to run into anyone who might know her from Newcastle. She existed in a strange state of limbo, anxious at the ordeal to come but impatient for it to be over. She missed her mother more every day, yet the women were kind and never once made her feel ashamed for her predicament.

Wanting to show her gratitude to her mother's friends, Adela risked going out to the shops in broad daylight just before Christmas. With the last of her wages she bought some treats: tangerines, bars of chocolate, and chestnuts for roasting; lavender water for Ina; and cigarettes and a soft woollen scarf for Maggie in her favourite purple. For Lexy she wrapped up the colourful bangles she had worn in the summer and that Lexy had admired. It was on this day that Adela spotted a small shop selling sewing supplies: needles, threads, buttons and bolts of cloth.

Glancing up at the name above the door, she felt her stomach somersault. Jackman. She stood rooted to the spot, heart hammering. How could just the sight of Sam's surname upset her so? But why was it such a shock? She knew that Sam's mother came from this fishing village and had probably returned here. Ever since Adela had come to live in Cullercoats, the thought of bumping into Sam's mother – maybe even seeking her out – had nagged at the back of her mind, disturbing her thoughts. Or maybe this shop had nothing to do with Sam's mother at all.

Adela forced herself to peer in the door and saw a small plump woman behind the counter, who beckoned her in.

'Can I help you?'

Adela felt her mouth dry and throat tighten. She couldn't speak. Forcing a smile, she shook her head and hurried away. Maggie was concerned by her agitated state when she returned home out of breath and clutching her shopping. Later, after Adela questioned her about Jackman's shop, Maggie told her that the woman had once lived abroad in a hot country, which hadn't suited her. Adela was sure it must be Sam's mother. She longed to go in and ask her, but what on earth would she say if the shopkeeper said yes? The woman might get upset or angry. Adela would be doing it for selfish reasons, to be able to talk about Sam and somehow feel closer to him by being with his mother. But it might also lead to awkward questions about her pregnancy and what she was doing there. So Adela stifled her curiosity and kept increasingly at home.

***

Adela grew fond of her mother's old friends. Maggie had had a very hard life with a low-paid job in a laundry and a husband who regularly beat her. When the laundry had closed five years ago, a year after her husband's death, she had been almost destitute. She'd gone to Lexy for help. Lexy had fixed her up with a job looking after their old friend Ina. Ina was struggling to manage the family house after the death of her bachelor son and was becoming increasingly confused. Three of Ina's five children were now dead, and of the remaining two, daughter Sally had emigrated to Canada with her husband, while Grace was married to a lighthouse keeper and lived in a remote part of the Scottish Hebrides. Ina's son had left enough modest savings for Maggie to keep house for them both.

Ina was sweet-natured and never complained of being housebound with a bad hip that had got worse over the years. She talked of her dead offspring as if they were still alive and frequently called Adela Clarrie.

'She was widowed very young,' Maggie told Adela, 'but raised five bairns on her own. Wor Ina sold second-hand clothes all over Tyneside to feed 'em, and they all got on in life.'

Of them all, Adela grew closest to Lexy. No matter how many hours the extrovert manager worked in the café, she always found time to come two or three times a week to visit and make sure Adela was all right. With Lexy's irrepressible optimism and bawdy humour, she lifted all their spirits.

The café was closed on Christmas Day and, despite Lexy having numerous sisters, nephews and nieces who had invited her to spend the day with them, Lexy chose to go to Cullercoats and share a meal with her friends. She brought a pudding and crackers to go with Maggie's goose and roast vegetables. For Adela, there were letters from her mother and from Sophie and Tilly, along with small gifts of clothing, a brooch and more Belgooree tea, all of which Olive had handed over to Lexy. They had agreed with Olive to keep up the pretence to Clarrie that Adela was still living with the Brewises in Newcastle. Any letters Adela wrote home were posted by Lexy in the city. To pre-empt the likelihood of any Robsons trying to track her down, Adela had taken the precaution of writing to Tilly to say that she wouldn't be able to see her children over the Christmas holidays, but hoped to see them at Easter.

Adela shared out the presents but said, 'I'll read the letters later, thanks,' knowing how emotional they would make her. How would her mother and Harry be spending the first Christmas without her and her father? She had thought it would be easier to be so far away from home without the constant reminder that her father wasn't there, but it was worse not to have the comfort of her mother and brother. Inside she carried a leaden weight of grief for her beloved father, and she felt on the verge of tears all day. She made a huge effort not to let it show.

They ate well and, encouraged by Lexy, Adela led them in a sing-song. For Ina she sang an old song popular in the Great War that her mother had taught her, 'Red Sails in the Sunset', which made the old lady cry. This sparked off a series of more cheerful hit songs: 'Life Is Just a Bowl of Cherries', 'Sally' and 'On the Sunny Side of the Street'. But when Maggie started a rendition of 'Tea for Two', it was Adela who burst into tears.

'Reminds her of her da,' Lexy explained, giving Adela a hug. 'They used to sing it together.'

'Eeh, sorry, hinny,' Maggie gasped.

'D-don't be,' Adela said weepily. 'It's comforting to be with people who knew him.'

'Aye, he was a real gentleman, your father,' Maggie said, squeezing Adela's arm. 'Wish I'd had a man half as good as him.'

Afterwards, they sat around the fire in the lamplight, peeling hot roast chestnuts, smoking cigarettes and reminiscing about the days when Lexy, Ina and Maggie had lived in the west end of Newcastle and patronised the Cherry Tree pub. It was there that they had befriended Clarrie, who was working all hours for her father's cousin, Jared Belhaven, and his wife, Lily.

'An old witch was Lily,' Lexy said, 'but Jared was canny enough.'

'That's 'cause he paid you lots of attention,' Maggie cackled, 'and swept you off your feet after old Lily died.'

'He didn't do much sweepin'.' Lexy chuckled. 'He was lazy that way. But I had a few happy years with your Belhaven cousin, Adela, before he died.'

'And you made his last days happy an' all,' Maggie said.

Adela encouraged them to talk about the old days; she liked to hear how her mother had coped with coming to a strange land from India. From what the women told her, her mother had had a much tougher time than she had. It made her ashamed that she was so caught up in her own worries over the pregnancy when she had friends to help her. Whereas her mother and aunt had come to Newcastle not knowing a soul apart from a Belhaven cousin, whom they had never met and had been treated little better than slaves.

It was these women – poor, rowdy and big-hearted – who had helped her mother through the first frightening months, when she had still been mourning the death of her own father, Adela's grandfather, Jock. It was these same friends who still had little material wealth, but were prepared to share with her what little they had, when her own aunt had turned her out.

'What was Aunt Olive like in those days?'

'Always frightened of her own shadow,' Maggie said. 'She would never have survived at the Cherry Tree if it hadn't been for Clarrie protecting her from Lily and doing the brunt of the chores. It was Clarrie getting that job with the Stocks that saved them both and helped them up in the world.'

'Not that Olive gave her any thanks for it,' Lexy said. 'For a while after your aunt married Jack, she didn't even give Clarrie the time of day – cut her out of her life. Your mam was very hurt – not that she said so, but you could tell.'

'Well, Olive was jealous of Clarrie, wasn't she?' said Maggie.

'Jealous?' puzzled Adela. 'Why? Because she married the rich lawyer Herbert and got the café?'

'No, 'cause Clarrie had been courted by Jack Brewis before your aunt was.'

'Really?' Adela gasped. 'I never knew that.'

'Aye,' said Maggie. 'Jack's first choice was your mam.'

'I think Olive has spent all her married life worried that Jack still liked your mam best.'

Adela was shocked by the thought – both that Uncle Jack had desired her mother and that Olive should have punished Clarrie for it. Was that why Olive had been so protective of Uncle Jack while she had stayed at Lime Terrace? Was it possible that her aunt resented her being there because of long-ago jealousy towards Clarrie over Jack? How sad to allow bad feelings to fester over the years; she was quite sure her mother was unaware of them. It made Adela think of her mother in a new light; she had once been a beautiful young woman whom other men had fallen in love with – Jack, the elderly Herbert Stock, and Wesley. But Adela was in no doubt that it was her father who had been the love of her mother's life.

They carried on talking about Olive.

'She's still terrified of the world,' Lexy said with a sigh. 'I can't help feeling sorry for her. I just wish she wouldn't be so hard on Jane. She used to be such a loving lass and bright as a button, but over the years Olive has heaped all her cares on the lass's shoulders. Course your aunt always favoured George, right from when they were bairns.'

'Aunt Olive drinks sherry on her own every day,' said Adela. 'I suppose it's to give her Dutch courage to go out and face the world.'

'Aye, I know,' said Lexy, 'and she uses the profits from the café to buy it.'

'It's the tea rooms what prop up your uncle Jack's business an' all,' said Maggie. 'Isn't that right, Lexy?'

'Hush, Maggie man! I don't want Adela to worry about that in her condition.'

'Is the café in danger of closing?' Adela asked in concern.

'Not if I can help it,' said Lexy. 'I was hoping Clarrie would have come over with you and sorted things out with Olive and Jack. But with your da dying – well, I don't like to bother her with any of it.'

'But legally the café belongs to the Brewises, doesn't it?' Adela frowned. 'Mother said she signed it over to Aunt Olive when she was last in Newcastle when I was little.'

'Aye, but your mam and da were still investing in the café,' said Lexy. 'What they didn't know was that since the Slump their money was going into the Tyneside Tea Company more often than not.'

'Clarrie has a right to know.' Maggie was indignant. She eyed Adela through a cloud of cigarette smoke. 'Maybes you should be the one to tell her, hinny.'

Lexy said, 'Adela's got enough on her plate without worrying about the café. If I thought we were in real trouble, I'd write to Clarrie me'sel'.' She smiled at Adela sitting cross-legged by the hearth, leaning against Ina's chair. 'Knowing your mam, she'd carry on paying to keep Jack's business afloat – anything to help Olive and her children. It's a crying shame Olive isn't half as big-hearted.'

***

The year 1939 came in with a clatter of hailstones and anxious talk of military build-up on the Continent. The newspapers speculated whether Hitler would extend his occupation of the Sudetenland into the rest of Czechoslovakia. The government were compiling a register for war service, and an Auxiliary Territorial Service for women had been set up. On Ina's crackling radio they talked about the manufacture of Anderson shelters for civilians.

'What's one of them when it's at home?' Maggie asked.

'Some sort of shelter to stick in the garden,' said Adela, 'and protect you from bombs.'

To Adela it all seemed too far-fetched to be true. She was more interested in finding music on the radio. 'Blue Skies Are Round the Corner' became her favourite, and she clung on to it like a mantra as her belly swelled and the creature inside her squirmed restlessly and left her out of breath as she climbed the stairs to her tiny bedroom.

Lexy came at the beginning of February with news about the adoption. Through the minister at the seamen's mission, Lexy had made contact with a church that arranged adoptions for unwanted babies.

'Most of the bairns are sent abroad to the colonies – Canada and the like. They get a good, healthy outdoor life working on farms. That's grand, isn't it?'

Adela's heart beat erratically and her palms sweated. 'I suppose so.' She didn't really want to dwell on such things. To her, this baby was a deep source of shame. She didn't want to think of it as a person who would have a future life somewhere else. Once it was born, it would no longer be her concern. She wanted rid of it as soon as she possibly could.

'I don't want to know anything about it after the birth,' she said, 'not even if it's a girl or a boy.'

But as the time of birth drew nearer and the baby turned in the womb, Adela couldn't help dwelling on what would become of it. Her mind was filled with images of street children in India abandoned to poverty with no parents to fend for them, at the mercy of disease and hunger, begging for food.

When Lexy next came, Adela said, 'I want it to go to a good home. How will I know it will be cared for? Can't a childless couple in Britain take it in? So it can get a good schooling and be more than just a farm labourer or housemaid.'

Lexy fixed her with a look. 'I'm not a miracle worker, lass.'

'Sorry.' Adela looked away. 'You've done more for me than I ever deserved. I know I've no right to ask.'

Lexy said, 'I'll put in a word. They're good church people. It's not all the bairns that gan abroad.'

A week later, as Adela was helping feed Ina some broth, she felt a gush between her legs. Mortified that she'd wet herself, Adela was reassured by Maggie.

'It's your waters breaking, hinny. Your time's nearly come.'

She put Adela to bed, lining it with towels and brown paper. Nothing happened. Adela watched the first fat flakes of snow glide past the window as she waited. The sky darkened. Dread paralysed her. She had seen tea pickers go into labour among the tea bushes and be rushed to the compound, but she had always been bustled out of sight while her mother went to help with the births. She was ignorant of what she would experience next. How she longed at that moment for her mother! Even the lowliest tea worker had had Clarrie's fussing attention, yet here she lay thousands of miles from home, without a mother's love and reassurance at the birth of her firstborn. It was a moment that they would now never share, and she had only herself to blame. Feeling horribly alone, she got up again to help with the dishes, but Maggie chased her back upstairs.

'I'm not in labour,' Adela protested. 'Let me help with Ina.'

Half an hour later she was twisting in agony and shouting for her mother. Lexy appeared as if by magic.

'It's snowing hard,' she said, stamping her feet and bringing in a blast of icy air.

She coaxed Adela on to the bed and through the pain. 'Breathe easy. That's it, lass.'

But the pain grew unbearable; it was red-hot and came in ever-increasing waves. Is this what the Khasi hill women had had to endure? And the women on Fatima's purdah ward? She had never appreciated the agony they must have gone through.

Adela shrieked, 'I'm going to die!'

'Stop being so dramatic.' Lexy laughed. 'I've helped ten nephews and nieces into this world, as well as me youngest sister. I've never lost any of 'em. So be me guest and scream the house down.'

It felt like for ever, but there was still a streak of light left in the sky when Adela's baby came pushing out on to the lumpy bed. The labour was swift – no more than two hours – and the birth uncomplicated. Within minutes it was giving a lusty wail.

Lexy saw to the umbilical cord and wrapped the baby in a clean sheet.

'Do you want a hold?' she asked.

Adela lay back, panting. 'No.'

'Want to know the sex?'

Adela shook her head. Her eyes felt hot and watery. She squeezed them shut.

'Let me know if you change your mind. If we get snowed in, you'll have to feed the bairn anyway.'

Adela dozed. She woke to hear the women below laughing and cooing over the baby. She turned on her side, tears stinging her eyes. Tears of relief. But once they started, she couldn't stop them. She had a vivid memory of her mother holding newborn Harry in her arms, her tired face suffused with love, completely absorbed in the joy of cradling her son. It left her winded. Burying her face in the pillow, she muffled her sobbing and cried herself into exhausted sleep.

In the night she awoke and climbed out of bed on wobbly legs, needing to relieve herself. She used the chamber pot. There was an odd noise coming from below. Adela descended. In the firelight she could see Lexy asleep on the sofa. Within touching distance, the baby was lying in a scrubbed-out fish box, swaddled in blankets, making snuffling, whimpering noises that were growing louder.

Adela steeled herself to bend down and look. It had a crown of black hair and a dark pink face. She brushed it with a finger. It opened its eyes – dark pools in the dim light – and for an instant focused on her. She felt a jolt of alarm and withdrew her hand. A minute later the baby was crying loudly enough to wake Lexy.

'You'll have to feed him.' She yawned.

'Him?'

'Aye, it's a lad. Best you know, lass. You might spend the rest of your days wondering. Tak' him back upstairs, and I'll help get him latched on.'

'I'd rather stay down here by the fire.' Adela went back and fetched covers from her bed. She piled them by the hearth and lay down. With Lexy helping, Adela propped herself on her side and guided the infant to her breast. She winced at the first sharp tugs.

'How does he know what to do?'

'Just nature, isn't it?' Lexy smiled.

Adela watched the baby's earnest face as his tiny rosebud mouth sucked rhythmically, his soft hair shiny in the firelight. He fascinated her. Soon he tired and loosened his hold, his eyes closing as he fell asleep. Adela closed hers. In that half-conscious state between being awake and oblivion, she was struck by the thought that her father, had he lived, would now have been a grandfather. This tiny creature, lying in a Cullercoats cottage, was the grandson of Wesley Robson. Part of her was thankful that her father would never know of the shameful birth, and yet she was filled with sorrow that the two would never know each other. Despite her regret that she had fallen pregnant with Jay's child, she was sure that her father would not have rejected this baby, might even in different circumstances have grown to love him. Adela was overwhelmed with bittersweet regret. She bent to kiss the infant's soft, downy head and was taken aback by a brief surge of longing – whether for her father or the baby she was too tired to fathom.

***

Adela refused to give the baby a name. 'It's not mine. Let the family he goes to give him a name.'

'You have to register him, hinny,' said Maggie. 'Anything will do.'

In the end Lexy went to register the birth, saying that the mother was too ill with milk fever to do it herself. 'I called him John Wesley, after your Belhaven grandda and your da.'

Adela's heart squeezed at the mention of her father's name. 'What did you put for the father?' she asked in panic.

Lexy was blunt. 'Unknown.'

Adela felt tears brim as she nodded. If she'd been truthful and declared that the father was an Indian prince, they would have accused her of being a fantasist or a liar.

She fed the baby for four more days, until the snow cleared, but never again experienced the intimacy and wonder of that first suckling by the fire of the old black range. It was as if she had wrapped her heart in bandages to staunch any feelings towards the boy. She was unable to care for him, so why make it harder by allowing herself to feel any affection? It would just make it worse for them both. She was impatient for him to be gone, her thoughts already turning to when she would leave the confinement of the cottage.

She would look for a job in Whitley Bay or back in the city. She might head for London and try her luck in the theatres there. She would cut her hair shorter and buy a new lipstick. In a few months she would forget she'd ever had a baby or made such a foolish mistake. She would put it all behind her. Adela determined she would make enough money to pay for an inside toilet to be plumbed in for Ina so she didn't have to do her business on a smelly commode. She'd buy Maggie new clothes and Lexy a holiday, for she owed them so much. Nothing could repay their kindness, but she would try.

The day the church people came to take away the baby, Adela said she would go out for a walk. She didn't want to see them or be seen. At the last moment she felt an overwhelming desire to do something for her son – to compensate in some small way for turning her back on him. With trembling fingers, she took off the pink stone necklace that her mother had gifted her and gave it to Maggie.

'See that the church folk take this and keep it for the baby. It's all I've got to give him, and it comes from India, like he does. It's from a holy man and will give him protection.'

Adela left swiftly. She was almost physically sick as she stepped into the raw grey day, suppressing the urge to turn around and look at the boy one last time. Gulping at the salty sea air, she hurried out of sight.

Roaming around aimlessly, trying to think of anything except what was going on back at the cottage, she found herself once more in front of Jackman's haberdashery. She almost went in, had her hand on the brass handle of the sewing shop door, but lost her nerve again. What would she say? Would Sam be angry with her for interfering? Would Mrs Jackman be upset to be reminded of her failed marriage and motherhood? Adela walked away. It was none of her business. But it left her feeling more upset than before. She wanted Sam's mother to be able to stop the aching misery that gripped her, to give her reassurance that it was possible to survive such heartache and disappointment.

As she dragged herself back in the direction of the coastguard's house, it struck Adela why she had been drawn to

Mrs Jackman's door. It wasn't Sam's mother that she longed to meet, it was Sam. She yearned for Sam's strong comforting arms around her, to look into his handsome face and see the compassion in his hazel eyes and his kind, lopsided grin. But that was never going to happen. Even if by some miracle they were to meet again, things could never be the same between them as when she had first fallen in love with him. The day at the Sipi Fair and its aftermath had changed their fate for ever. How he would despise her now for her selfish affair with Jay and abandoning her child! She couldn't bear the thought of him finding out. Better that she never saw Sam again than to witness his contempt at what she had done.

Back at the cottage it was strangely quiet and empty. Maggie had been crying. It suddenly struck her that the women had enjoyed having the baby to fuss over. While she had been irritated by his crying, they had rushed to pacify him. They had more motherly feeling in them for her baby than she ever had. It made her wretched.

'I'll make tea tonight,' Adela announced.

She cooked sausages with creamed turnip and mashed potato sprinkled with nutmeg, like Mohammed Din used to do. Lexy returned, bringing a bottle of barley wine.

'Don't give me that look, Maggie man,' said Lexy. 'I'm not ganin' to touch the stuff, but I thought Adela might need a drink.'

The alcohol went straight to Adela's head. She welcomed the instant numbing of her senses. She sang all the songs she could remember. They put her to bed, and she went into an exhausted dreamless sleep. When she awoke at dawn, she had several blissful moments of her mind being quite empty. And then she remembered where she was, and the painful memories of the past few days and giving birth to a son assaulted her anew.

Chapter 21

Despite all Adela's intentions of leaving Cullercoats as soon as she could, Lexy insisted she stayed on at the house until her body recovered. Maggie bound up Adela's sore breasts to hasten the drying up of her breast milk, and it was a month before her bleeding stopped. That spring she tried to avoid listening to the increasingly worrying news on the wireless. Yet she couldn't help knowing that Nazi troops had marched into Czechoslovakia and Italy had invaded Albania.

'They're calling up men of twenty and twenty-one,' Lexy told Adela and Maggie. Ina started talking about the Kaiser and fretting about Will.

'Who's Will?' Adela asked.

'Your mam's stepson, Will Stock,' said Lexy. 'He was the canniest lad you could ever meet. Clarrie thought the world of Will – we all did. Died in France after the war ended. Your da served with him. By, Wesley had us all in tears at the memorial service with the canny things he said about Will! Reckon that's when your mam realised Wesley was a good 'un.'

Growing impatient to be doing something useful, Adela said it was time she started earning a living again.

'Please can I come and live with you at the café flat?' she asked Lexy. 'I don't think I can face going back to Aunt Olive's, even if she'd let me.'

'Course you can, hinny,' Lexy said, beaming. 'I'd be happy to have your cheery face around the place. It'll be just like when me and your mam used to share it.'

Adela's return to Newcastle was greeted with enthusiasm by Nance and the other waitresses at the café, as well as her cousin Jane.

'Did it not work out for you in Edinburgh?' Jane asked with a look of curiosity.

Adela shook her head. 'I don't really want to talk about it,' she said, not wanting to make up any more lies about the past few months.

'I would have sent on your mail,' said Jane, 'but Mam told me to give it to Lexy to do.'

'Thanks, that was kind of you.' Adela deflected any further questions with talk about the new films at the Stoll and Essoldo. But Jane persisted.

'So you won't be coming back to Lime Terrace and sharing a room with me.'

'Your parents were very kind to have me for as long as they did,' said Adela. 'I can't expect them to keep me indefinitely. Anyway, Lexy offered, and I'll help out at the café as much as I can.'

She wasn't at all sure that Jane believed that she had been in Edinburgh all this time, but George didn't question her story.

'Good to see you back, lass,' he said as he grinned. He picked her up and swung her around. 'Newcastle's been a dull dog without you.'

'Don't believe you.' Adela laughed. 'Are you still courting the gorgeous Joan?'

George winked, which Adela took to be a yes.

Within a week Adela had talked her way into a job at the new Essoldo cinema, working as an usherette and helping out in the circle lounge café. At Lexy's encouragement, she decided to pay a visit to The People's Theatre in Rye Hill. The keen amateur group ran a thriving theatre in an old converted chapel uphill from Herbert's.

'Don't spend all your spare time helping out here,' said Lexy. 'Go and have a bit o' fun with the players. See if you can do a bit o' singin' and dancin'.'

'The People's don't do variety.' Adela smiled. 'They're much more serious.'

'Well, you can liven them up then.'

Calling round one early-summer's evening, Adela found the stage door open and discovered Wilf, George's cricketing friend, who had briefly been out with Nance, helping with carpentry behind the scenes.

'Fancy finding you here!' Adela exclaimed.

Wilf blushed. 'Just filling in for a lad I work with.' He quickly led her into the main hall where the players were rehearsing a satire about war, George Bernard Shaw's *Arms and the Man*. When they took a break, Wilf introduced her to a gaunt middle-aged man called Derek, who was producing the play. He eyed her suspiciously when he heard she'd done all her acting in Simla.

'Not one of those prima donna memsahibs, are you?'

'Chance would be a fine thing,' Adela sparked back. 'I was usually the third spear carrier or a monk.'

Nearby, a round-faced woman blew out cigarette smoke and chuckled.

Derek frowned. ''Cause we don't hold with imperialists here,' he continued. 'We have a proud socialist tradition of radical plays. If it's singing and dancing you want, try the operatic society.'

'I've done Shaw as well,' Adela persisted. '*Saint Joan*. Was understudy for the main part at my boarding school.'

'Boarding school.' Derek gave a snort of derision.

'Stop teasing her,' the plump woman said, grinding out her cigarette in a saucer and stepping forward. 'I'm Josey Lyons. We welcome anyone here who wants to help out; you don't have to be a working-class warrior like Derek.' She shook Adela by the hand and smiled. 'In fact,' she said in a loud whisper, 'even Derek's roots are suspect. His father was a station master, which makes him lower middle class.'

'Signalman,' Derek protested. 'He was a signalman, and my grandfather was a miner.'

'Helps if you have a miner in your family tree,' Josey said with a wink.

Adela decided to keep quiet about her family of tea planters. 'Farm workers a couple of generations back,' Adela said. 'Does that qualify me to help out behind the scenes? I'll do anything.'

'Of course it does,' said Josey, offering her a cigarette. Adela hesitated, then took one; this was more nerve-racking than she'd anticipated.

Josey said to Derek, 'Let's try her out. If she auditions well, she can be my understudy for Louka.'

'The saucy chambermaid?' Adela exclaimed. 'I'd love that.'

'You know the play then?' Derek said with a sceptical look.

'Went to see the film three times,' she replied. 'Tried to style my hair like Anne Grey. She was wonderful as Raina. And I know it's an anti-war play and that's why you're probably putting it on now, even though it's a comedy.'

Derek raised his bushy grey eyebrows. 'All right. You can sit here and prompt,' he agreed. 'Just no more mention of boarding school.'

***

Adela went to the theatre in Rye Hill whenever she had a free moment. She found keeping busy was the best remedy for her shattered emotions. By filling every waking minute, she didn't have to dwell on the traumas of the past year, the grief for her father and the way she had messed up her life. Relief came from helping others and not brooding on her mistakes. Activity alleviated the gnawing emptiness inside.

Adela helped with costumes and painting the scenery, prompted at rehearsals and learnt the part of Louka by heart. Determined to impress the lugubrious Derek, she helped sell tickets around the town, advertising the play at Herbert's Café and mentioning it to regular cinemagoers at the Essoldo. The rest of the cast were friendly and helpful – thirty-year-old Josey in particular was easy to like. She was well-spoken – her voice gravelly from constant smoking – yet dressed like a tramp, in old corduroy trousers and misfit jackets. She lived in cheap digs off Westgate Road run by a retired Co-operative bookkeeper, with an assortment of bohemian spinsters.

'I've lived with them for a dozen years now. They're my family,' explained Josey to a curious Adela after one rehearsal. 'Much better than the real thing.'

'Why do you say that?' Adela asked as they walked back into town together.

'Mine were ghastly. My father went to prison for fraud; no idea where he is now. Mother couldn't cope without servants and money so threw herself at the mercy of my rich uncle Clive. Ten years ago they sold up and emigrated to Argentina. My brother went with them, but I refused point-blank. I'd already joined the People's, and it was just as we were expanding the theatre and moving into the old chapel. So I stayed. That's why Derek likes me; even though I grew up posh, I turned my back on all that. Even changed my surname.' She gave a chuckle of amusement. 'Picked Lyons after my favourite restaurant.'

'You were very brave to do it all on your own,' said Adela. 'I couldn't have left home and come all this way without having family here to stay with.'

'You're very mysterious about your background.' Josey smiled. 'Don't be cowed by Derek. Was it Burma you said you came from? Are you the daughter of some famous governor general or commander-in-chief?'

'India,' said Adela. 'Assam – tea-growing country – though I went to school in the hills at Simla. And no, I'm not the daughter of anyone high up. My father's a tea planter . . .' Adela faltered, winded by her own words. 'Was a tea planter. He died last year very suddenly.' Her eyes filled up with tears as the familiar pain of grief gripped her.

'I'm so sorry,' Josey said, quickly steering her towards a low brick wall in front of someone's house and sitting her down. Adela found herself weeping into Josey's comfy shoulder and telling her some of the details of Wesley's gruesome death and her overwhelming feeling of guilt.

When she drew away and blew her nose, Josey was giving her a strange look.

'You must think I'm awful,' Adela sniffed.

'Robson did you say your name was?' Josey's tone was sharp. 'Your mother isn't called Clarrie, is she?'

'Yes,' Adela said. 'How did you know?'

Josey let out a low whistle and reached for her cigarettes. She lit up before answering. 'So Clarrie and Wesley Robson are your parents. Who would have thought it?' She turned and eyed Adela. 'Yes, I can see the resemblance now.'

'How do you know my mother?' She felt a fresh pang of longing.

Josey gave a wistful smile. 'Clarrie was my step-grandmother.'

'Grandmother?' Adela was astonished. 'How can that possibly be?'

'She was married to my grandfather, Herbert Stock. I adored Clarrie as a child. Once a week my twin brother and I were taken to spend the day with Clarrie and Grandfather Herbert. I spent all week longing for those visits. After we started school, we saw her less often. Then Grandfather died. There was some sort of falling-out with my parents – they blamed your mother for their financial difficulties – but no doubt it was my father's fault. He was hopeless with money.'

Adela gazed in amazement at Josey. To think this woman had known her mother since she was a small child! 'Tell me more about my mother,' she urged, 'please.'

Josey blew out smoke, her look reflective. 'Clarrie was more of a mother to me than my own mother ever was. Verity's a cold fish – can't abide children. She hated me always asking to go and see Clarrie. When your mother married Wesley – he was some sort of relation of my mother's – my brother and I got a wedding invitation. My parents were furious and threw it on the fire.' Josey gave a mirthless laugh. 'I sneaked out of school and went anyway. Trouble was I'd remembered the time wrongly, and the whole thing was over by the time I got to Herbert's Tea Rooms, and everyone had left.'

'Did my mother ever know that?' Adela asked, feeling a wave of pity for the young Josey.

'No, I just went away and never said anything. Didn't like to approach Clarrie's family again, 'cause I was aware how bad relations were with my parents. But over the years I've popped into Herbert's for a bite to eat and earwigged on the gossip. Knew from that nice Lexy that Clarrie had gone abroad years ago.'

Adela put a hand on Josey's arm. She felt a flood of affection. 'I'll write and tell Mother. I bet she'll be over the moon to hear about you.'

'Do you think so?' Josey looked unsure. She ground out her cigarette.

'Yes, I am.' Adela gave a reassuring squeeze. She felt suddenly close, delighted that they now shared a bond with her mother.

'I did wonder,' Josey said.

'Wonder what?'

'About a small gift of money I was given when I turned twenty-one.'

'Go on.'

'It was just at the time I was defying my mother and uncle about going abroad,' said Josey. 'The money was a godsend and helped me stay on at my digs while starting to act. Mother said it must be from my father, but I never believed that. I think it might have been from Clarrie and Wesley. My brother blew his amount on a brand-new Austin Windsor, which he drove into a lamp post and wrecked.'

'I'm glad you stayed and made a go of things here.' Adela gave a trembling smile. 'Do you realise something?'

'What?' asked Josey.

'If my father was a distant relation of your mother's, then we must be related.'

Josey's eyes widened. 'So we are!' She laughed and swung an arm about Adela's slim shoulders. 'My cousin Adela.'

'My cousin Josey!' Adela grinned, leaning into her hold and feeling her spirits lift.

***

Adela had been dreading June, the month of her nineteenth birthday and the first anniversary of the nightmarish tiger hunt and her father's appalling death. She wasn't sleeping well and often on the point of sleep was disturbed by vivid flashes of memory that left her shaking and upset. Worse were the dreams that she could tell no one, for they were about her baby. They were filled with panic – Adela trying to hide him away – and then she'd wake with a start to find him not there. She'd get out of bed, restless with a feeling of loss, and gaze out of the window, wondering what had happened to him. Sometimes the impulse to find out was so strong that she had to grip the windowsill to stop herself running out into the night to search for him.

'You're grinding yer teeth at night,' Lexy told her in concern. 'Perhaps you should get yoursel' to the doctors for a bit o' sedative.'

But Adela refused, not wanting to have to explain her shameful secrets to anyone else. It was Josey who saved her sanity. In Herbert's granddaughter she had found a kindred spirit: someone who enjoyed life, the theatre and having fun, as well as being a link to her parents. It was Josey who got her through midsummer with her humour and kindness, keeping her busy at the theatre and protecting her like an older sister. She introduced Adela to her eccentric friends at the rambling house on Westgate Road and their welcoming landlady, Florence. It turned out that she too had known Adela's mother in the early days of Herbert's Tea Rooms.

'Clarrie was wonderful to us suffragists,' Florence enthused. 'She let us use Herbert's for our protest on Census Night before the war. And we often met in her café to discuss tactics, and she'd send over extra cake to keep us going. You will send my fondest regards, won't you, dear?'

Adela thirsted for these stories of her mother; they made her feel closer to her faraway parent. She wrote letters home telling Clarrie about Josey and Florence. Her mother wrote back, thrilled at the news and sending her love and greetings, especially to Josey. She admitted that the modest amount of trust money had been her idea, and Wesley had arranged it. But nowhere in her letters did Clarrie encourage Adela to come home. Quite the opposite. Yet she kept to herself how upsetting it was that her mother was still pushing her away.

I'm glad things are working out for you in Newcastle and that you are having some fun along the way. It was the right thing for you to go. Stick in at the theatre; you never know what might come of it. I get quite nostalgic at the thought of you sharing the flat with Lexy. What a great friend she has been to us both.

You don't say much about Olive and the family any more. I hope everything is all right with the Brewises. You would tell me if there was anything to worry about, wouldn't you? Give them my love as always . . .

This galvanised Adela into calling on her aunt. She had only made one brief, awkward visit to Lime Terrace since she had returned to Newcastle, to tell Olive in confidence that the problem of the unwanted baby had been taken care of. She had invited her aunt to a birthday tea at Herbert's on 13 June that Lexy and Jane had organised, but Olive had not come.

One late June evening she took Josey round to meet Olive and Jack.

Adela's uncle was bashful but welcoming. 'Josephine Stock! I remember you from family gatherings at Summerhill. Full of chat. And good at sharing the toys with our George – not like your twin brother.'

Olive seemed agitated by the appearance of someone from her past.

'Your mam and dad never made a secret of how they looked down their noses at the likes of us,' she said.

'Sounds like them,' Josey said, not taking offence. 'I remember you doing lovely drawings. Do you still draw, Mrs Brewis?'

'No, not for years.'

'And those paintings in the café – you did those, didn't you?'

'Yes, but I'm not well enough now.'

'Pity,' said Josey. 'You've got such talent. If you ever decide you want to paint again, we'd love some paintings to hang in the theatre. We encourage local artists, as well as actors.'

'That would be canny,' said Jack, 'if you picked up a paintbrush again.'

'It's not that easy,' Olive said, her hands squirming in her lap. 'You all talk as if it was easy.'

Adela wished she'd made sure George was at home before calling. He would have lightened the atmosphere. She quickly diverted the conversation. 'We wondered if you'd both like to come to see the play Josey is in next week. I've got you complimentary tickets.'

Neither her aunt nor uncle looked enthusiastic. Jack put on a show of being pleased.

'That's very kind.'

'You know I can't go to crowded places,' Olive said with an expression of panic.

'Perhaps George would like to take Joan,' Jack suggested.

Adela left the tickets on the table. 'Whatever you decide is fine,' she said and smiled, not wanting to make her uncle feel uncomfortable. She made excuses to leave quickly. Outside, as they walked away, she apologised to Josey.

'Sorry for dragging you along. I thought it might help my aunt to meet someone from the past – something to spark her interest. She's almost a recluse these days.'

'I don't remember Olive well – except that she had beautiful red-gold hair – but she was nothing like that frightened skinny woman in there.'

'That's it,' agreed Adela. 'Everything seems to frighten her.'

'How sad,' said Josey, linking an arm through Adela's. 'But whatever your aunt's problems are, you are not to blame for them. Come on, we've a show to put on.'

***

The People's Theatre group played all week to packed audiences. Adela helped as much in the preparation as she could, though her job at the Essoldo meant that she missed most of the performances. The Wednesday matinee was her afternoon off, and so she determined to watch the play herself that day. A hurried note from Florence came to Herbert's that morning, where she was helping Lexy serve breakfasts.

'Josey has been sick all night. She's asking if you could possibly stand in for her this afternoon.'

'Poor Josey,' said Adela in concern.

'Aye,' said Lexy, 'but this is your big chance to shine on stage. Take that pinny off and get yoursel' up to the theatre.'

Derek's grumbling at the last-minute change was half-hearted; he had watched Adela rehearsing the part with Josey and already knew she was capable of doing a cheeky, flirtatious Louka. In his opinion, Josey was a talented character actress carrying off her role with the force of her personality rather than her looks. Adela – if she didn't get stage fright – would be funny, as well as engaging to look at.

As soon as Adela stepped on the stage and felt the heat and glare of the spotlights, she was exhilarated. Everything else in her life vanished: all anxious thoughts, past traumas, pain and regret were pushed from her mind as she became Louka. She revelled in the part, playing the coquettish servant for all it was worth. The laughter from the audience made her as heady as if she'd been drinking champagne.

Afterwards, as she sat in the cramped dressing room taking off her make-up and chattering with her fellow players, Josey walked in with Derek behind.

'Are you all right?' Adela sprang up.

'She seems to have made a remarkable recovery,' Derek said dryly. 'In fact she was feeling well enough to sit and watch the matinée.'

Adela gaped.

'You were wonderful, Miss Robson.' Josey grinned and gave her a peck on the cheek. 'I'm beginning to think I made a huge mistake picking you as my understudy.'

‘Did you pretend to be ill just to let me perform?’ Adela asked. ‘You did, didn’t you?’

‘Put it this way,’ Derek grunted, ‘she’ll be in the pink and back on stage tonight.’

Adela was overwhelmed with gratitude. ‘Thank you,’ Adela said, hugging her friend.

‘And that’s not all,’ said Derek. ‘Cecil McGivern was in the audience and was asking who you were.’

Adela gasped. ‘The BBC producer?’

Derek nodded. ‘He acted with The People’s years ago, long before he started making dramas and documentaries.’

‘What did you say about me?’ Adela was wide-eyed.

‘That you were a posh flapper from Simla, but you were useful to the wardrobe department.’

Josey spluttered. ‘Flapper? Nobody uses that expression now. You’re showing your age, Derek.’ She turned to Adela. ‘And he’s only teasing. I heard him positively gushing about you to Cecil.’

Derek gave the flicker of a smile. ‘Well, he’s making a radio programme about The People’s – past patrons, like George Bernard Shaw and Dame Sybil Thorndike, are going to be interviewed – and I wanted to give us all a bit of credit.’

Adela was touched by his gesture. ‘Thanks, Derek. I’ve hardly been here two minutes, so it was very kind of you.’

‘Don’t thank me. I would have disowned you if you hadn’t given a good performance up there,’ he said. ‘You’re not bad for a member of the ruling class.’

***

That summer Adela continued to fill every moment of every day with activity: working at the Essoldo, helping at the theatre, learning to bake cakes and pies at Herbert’s under Lexy’s and Jane’s instruction, and visiting Maggie and Ina in Cullercoats. Lexy tried to encourage her to take the occasional evening off.

‘Why don’t you go to the cricket dance on Saturday?’ she suggested. ‘George will stop asking you to go if you keep turning down his invitations.’

'George doesn't mind,' said Adela. 'He's only asking out of politeness. And I don't think Joan likes me. It would just be awkward.'

Lexy gave her a pitying look. 'Listen, lass. You made a mistake and got in trouble. Plenty do. But you don't need to punish yourself for ever. Find a lad who'll treat you well.'

Adela's heart squeezed as Sam came vividly to mind. For the umpteenth time she was flooded with regret at the rupture of their friendship. How different things might have been if she had never met Sanjay, or if Sam had not been at the Sipi Fair that fateful day the previous May. If only she had let Sam know her true feelings for him before all that happened. She was sure that he had felt something for her too. And on hearing about the death of her father, Sam had travelled to Belgooree to see her. Was that just because he had been in the area and was making a polite call to offer his condolences, or had he been genuinely disappointed to find that she had gone to England? She might never know. He had made no attempt to write to her.

If he had held feelings for her once, circumstances had prevented them from growing. He had Pema to take care of now. Besides, as a missionary he would be horrified if he ever learnt of her getting pregnant and having Sanjay's baby out of wedlock. She was filled with shame at the thought of his finding out. She would never be worthy of his love now, and the thought made her desolate. Yet would the day ever come when she didn't feel pain in her heart at the thought of Sam Jackman? Just the sound of a tugboat hooting on the river or a pile of ripe red apples was enough to bring him to mind. She would have to harden her feelings if she was ever to get over him.

'I'm not looking for a lad,' Adela replied, masking her unhappiness. 'They're nothing but trouble.'

'What a cynic for one so young,' said Lexy.

'Well, you took your time before settling down with Cousin Jared,' Adela reminded her.

'Aye, I wouldn't have looked at him twice when he ran the Cherry Tree,' Lexy admitted, 'but he mellowed in later life. I had fifteen happy years with Jared, so I've no complaints.'

Adela was adamant. 'Well, I'm not going to rush into any more romances either.'

'Suit yourself,' said Lexy, 'but from what Josey tells me, half the lads at the theatre are in love with you. You'll have a hard job ignorin' 'em.'

***

There was one area in Adela's life in Newcastle that continued to bring upset: she could do nothing to please her aunt Olive. She had suggested they redecorate Herbert's, but Olive had rebuffed any attempts to get her to come to the café and give her opinion. Adela worried about her aunt's increasing isolation at Lime Terrace, knowing that she took solace in drinking sherry alone and ruminating. According to Jane, Olive hardly left the house any more, not even to visit her neighbour, Mrs Harris.

'She's worrying about war breaking out on the Continent,' said Jane, 'and George joining up.'

'It won't come to war – and he wouldn't volunteer, would he? Uncle Jack needs him in the business.'

'That's what Father keeps telling her, but she won't listen,' Jane confided. 'Keeps going on about the Great War and how Father nearly didn't come back.'

One July afternoon Adela called to see her aunt, but no one came when she rang the bell. She knocked on the bay window.

'Aunt Olive, it's me, Adela. I know you're there. Please let me in. I've brought you a piece of lemon cake.'

She could almost feel her aunt holding her breath behind the net curtains and potted plants, waiting for her to go away. What would her mother have done? Adela wondered. Probably gone round the back and climbed in at the kitchen window, forcing Olive to speak to her and confront her fears. But Clarrie was probably the only person to whom Olive might listen. She certainly wouldn't have her anxieties dispelled by anything Adela could say to her.

Adela gave up and turned away. Olive's rejection hurt her deeply. She wanted to befriend her aunt if only for her mother's sake; she recalled Clarrie's words urging her to be helpful. *Do all you can for our Olive; she's one of life's worriers.* Yet even when her aunt had welcomed her into her home the previous summer, Adela had never felt close to her. There was a reserve about Olive and an ever-present tenseness, as if she was constantly bracing herself for some catastrophe. Was it possible that she was still jealous of Clarrie after all these years and resented Clarrie's daughter swanning in from India and monopolising her family? Lexy had said as much when she'd told her about Olive's fear that Jack still loved Clarrie.

Adela retreated down the hill back to Tyne Street. She had failed her mother again. Her eyes stung with tears of frustration as she was overwhelmed with a sudden pang of homesickness for Belgooree, her mother and her dead father. What was she doing here in Newcastle? It wasn't her home. Despite her one heady appearance on stage, she'd been given no acting parts. Her days were filled with doing menial jobs; after long shifts at the Essoldo or the café, she had to do her own chores. Many were the nights when she was still washing out underwear and stockings at midnight in preparation for the next day. She did jobs here that she wouldn't have dreamt of doing at home.

And yet. If her mother wrote to her tomorrow asking her to come back and be with her and Harry, would she go? Adela gazed about in the hazy sunshine at the rows of scruffy terraces banking down to the grey oily river – the jumble of rooftops, church spires and bridges that marked the teeming heart of the city. She knew it would be bustling with shoppers and traders down there. Within ten minutes of where she stood she could enter a dozen cinemas, scores of shops and cafés, listen to dance music on a hundred different radio sets.

For the first time in her life she was living independently, with no one to tell her how to organise her day. She was content living with Lexy in her tiny flat, fuggy with cigarette smoke, where they swapped stories over cups of tea at the day's end. No, Adela realised, she didn't want to go home – not yet – despite the tugs of homesickness. She would have felt differently if there had been the slightest chance of Sam coming back into her life. But that was a pipe dream. He had put himself beyond her reach by taking Pema as his wife, and she had ruined her chances of being with him when she'd chosen to have the affair with Jay – a choice she would regret for the rest of her life.

Besides, her mother wasn't calling her home, so she just had to make the best of her life in England.

Walking in at the back door of the café, Adela saw Jane's face light up. Adela could hardly bear her cousin's look of expectation.

'Sorry, Jane, she wouldn't even answer the door—'

'Didn't think she would.' Jane grabbed her hand and pulled her across the kitchen. 'We've been waiting for you. You're going to get such a surprise. Come in the café now!'

Adela let herself be dragged through the swing door. The room was busy with customers taking tea and children digging long spoons into tall glasses of ice cream. Lexy was chatting to someone at a table that was obscured by a huge potted palm. Lexy caught sight of Jane leading Adela by the hand and waved them over, her heavily made-up face smiling.

As Adela reached the table, there was a chorus of 'Surprise!' She gaped at the array of grinning faces – Tilly and her children.

'Auntie Tilly!'

Tilly, clad in a garish flowery cotton frock, stood up and flung out her arms. 'Darling girl!' she cried. 'We've had to eat far more cake than is good for us waiting for you.'

Adela felt her knees weaken at the excited looks around the table and Tilly's loving expression. It was as if they had been conjured up by magic to stop her feeling sorry for herself. How strange that her mind had been full of thoughts of home and India. She fell into her friend's embrace. 'What are you doing here? I can't believe it.'

Abruptly a sob rose up and engulfed her. 'How I've missed you!' She clung on to Tilly as if she were her own mother and wept loudly, unable to stop.

Tilly just held her and stroked her hair as if she were a child, while Jamie, Libby and Mungo looked on in embarrassment. Adela didn't care. What mattered at that moment was the feel of Tilly's plump, warm arms around her, telling her more than words could possibly say that she was dearly loved.

Chapter 22

'It was my friend Ros Mitchell who put the idea in my head,' Tilly explained once Adela had brought her crying under control and was sitting beside her at the table. 'Her husband, Duncan, has been posted back to Newcastle. You know he works for Strachan's agency? Well, their headquarters are here. Ros is simply my very best friend in Assam, and I really can't bear the thought of her being here and me out there. But that's as may be. She suggested I keep her company on the ship home – come back for the summer.'

'Why didn't you say you were coming?' Adela smiled tearfully. 'Mother never mentioned it.'

'It was all very last minute. I was lucky to get a berth on board. But there have been cancellations – some people aren't sure if coming home is a good idea.' Tilly paused and glanced at her children. 'Their father wasn't happy. He's got it into his head that Europe's on the verge of war.'

'He's right: it is,' Libby interrupted. 'Hitler's got his sights on half the Continent. Poland will be next and—'

'All right, we don't need a political lecture, thank you, dear.' Tilly waved an impatient hand.

'I hope there is a war,' eleven-year-old Mungo said in excitement. 'I'm going to join the army as soon as I'm allowed and fight the Germans.'

'Don't be stupid,' said Jamie. 'War's a horrible thing, and you're just a kid.'

'Don't be unkind; he's only being patriotic,' Tilly said, defending her youngest and putting a protective hand on his head of unruly red curls.

'Idiotic,' muttered Jamie, lolling back in his chair. At sixteen, Adela noticed, he was gangly and slightly clumsy, as if not sure what to do with his long limbs. His voice had deepened in the past year. Libby was still plump-faced and wearing her hair in girlish plaits, but her figure was developing. She kept crossing her arms self-consciously over her breasts, as if by doing so she could hide them. Adela felt a pang of pity for the awkward fourteen-year-old.

'Anyway, I'm just here for the summer holidays,' Tilly continued. 'Ros has kindly invited us to stay at their house in Jesmond. It's just two streets away from my old home – can you believe it? We're going to spend a week in St Abb's with Ros's in-laws, and of course we'll visit Mona at Dunbar, but most of the time we'll be here in Newcastle.'

'That's wonderful,' cried Adela. 'We'll be able to see lots of each other.'

'Exactly,' Tilly said, covering her hand and squeezing it.

'You never came to see me at school,' Libby said, giving Adela a steady look with her dark blue eyes.

Adela flushed. 'No, I didn't and I'm sorry. It's been a hectic year.'

'I was really looking forward to it,' said Libby.

'Don't be rude, darling,' Tilly intervened. 'Adela is a busy young woman.'

'We'll spend some time together this holiday,' Adela said hastily. 'I could take you to The People's Theatre and introduce you to the cast.'

'Is that the socialist theatre?' Libby asked, her interest sparking.

'I think so,' said Adela. 'It grew out of the Clarion Theatre.'

'It is then.' Libby smiled. 'I'd love you to take me there. When can we go?'

'Goodness me!' Tilly exclaimed. 'Stop badgering poor Adela. And do sit up straight; you'll end up with round shoulders like me.'

Libby flushed and sat back with a mutinous look.

'We'll go at the weekend, Libby,' Adela promised, 'just you and me.' She turned to Tilly. 'How is Mother coping? And what news of Sophie and Rafi? I want to hear everything.'

'As expected, your mother is being a tower of strength,' said Tilly. 'She is coping amazingly well with the tea garden and the business side of things. And Harry keeps her busy too. I don't know when she has time to sleep. Of course she has a very good undermanager in Daleep, and James gets across about once a month to make sure things are running smoothly. I usually go with him. The climate is so much better at Belgooree. I'm getting the most awful night sweats at Cheviot View, and on top of the prickly heat, I'm getting no sleep at all. I'm just not made for the climate in Assam. I can't tell you what a relief it is to be back in Britain, where the wind doesn't feel like a blast from a furnace.'

'And Sophie?' Adela prompted.

'Oh, you know Sophie – enjoying the jungli life. We managed to meet up at Belgooree in the cold season so that James could join a fishing trip with Rafi and the Raja. Sophie went too, of course, while I reread Clarrie's set of Dickens on your lovely veranda. But no doubt they both wrote and told you all about it.'

'Yes, but not in any detail,' said Adela. 'Was . . . was Prince Sanjay on the trip?'

'Oh no, he wasn't invited. Rafi thought it might be difficult for Clarrie to have to entertain him – bring back memories of the ghastly tiger hunt.'

Adela winced. 'Yes, of course.'

'Sorry, dear girl!' Tilly grabbed her hand and squeezed it. 'Let's not talk about the wretched prince. As far as I know, he's not even living at Gulgat. Gone off to continue his playboy existence in Simla or Bombay.'

Adela's insides churned at the thought of Jay charming some other naive girl into his bed. She went hot with shame to think of how she had succumbed to him so easily. She turned to the others. 'Enough talk about India.' Adela forced a smile. 'I want to hear all about you chaps and what you've been doing at school.'

***

The summer passed quickly with Tilly and her family around for company. They were a comforting link with home, and Tilly was in high spirits to be back in Newcastle. Twice Adela went round to the Mitchells' house in Jesmond for Sunday lunch – Ros was a quiet antidote to Tilly, and Duncan a genial host – and once they went on the train to the coast and played beach cricket. Libby was surprisingly quick and had a better eye for the ball than Jamie, and she was just as keenly competitive as her brothers.

But the biggest revelation was taking Libby to The People's Theatre. Away from her family, she lost her sullen expression and combative manner and became animated and good fun.

When she laughed, her dark eyes lit up, and her chubby face was transformed. 'Bonny' was how Sophie would have described her. Even Derek was captivated by her enthusiasm for their theatre and her knowledge of the class struggle.

'A little charmer, that cousin of yours,' he said approvingly. 'You can bring her again.'

So Adela did. As the summer advanced, sometimes Libby would go to the theatre alone and help out. She was very organised and had a good head for numbers, so Derek put her to work in the office, sorting out their haphazard filing. Libby took to Josey at once, just as Adela had, and the actress mothered Libby in a way that Tilly didn't. Rather than nag or criticise, Josey encouraged her. One time, when Adela and Libby went to Rye Hill together, the girl confided in Adela and Josey.

'I wish I could live with you in Florence's house, Josey. You treat me like a grown-up. Mummy still treats me like a baby.'

'From what I hear, your mother is an angel compared to mine, believe me,' Josey said, laughing.

'It's just that Tilly doesn't want you to grow up too quickly,' said Adela, 'not while she's thousands of miles away from you. She finds that very hard.'

'It was her choice to have us go to school halfway round the world,' Libby pointed out.

'Probably your father's,' said Josey.

'Well, she didn't try to stop it, did she? And anyway, I think she's glad I'm so far away. It's only my brothers that she misses. She's always telling me off, but never the boys,' Libby complained. 'I can't do anything right in her eyes.'

'It's a difficult age,' said Adela.

'You sound just like Mummy,' snorted Libby.

Adela laughed. 'Sorry. It's just I remember so clearly being your age and desperate to be taken seriously by adults. I was in such a hurry to grow up. But if I've learnt anything in the past five years, it's that it's best not to rush.'

'Still,' Libby said, sighing, 'I can't wait to leave school and go and live in a house full of interesting people like you, Josey.'

***

Libby and Adela were at the theatre on a day in late August when alarming news broke of a non-aggression pact between Germany and the Soviet Union.

'Stalin's done a deal with Hitler,' Libby said in disgust.

Derek was incredulous. 'I don't believe it. Must be anti-socialist propaganda.'

'It's true, Derek,' said Josey. 'The Soviets have got into bed with the Nazis.'

'It doesn't make sense,' Derek railed. 'The communists hate the fascists more than we do.'

'It's obvious,' said Libby. 'Miss MacGregor warned it would happen. Both powers want to export their revolutions and dominate their neighbours.'

'But not if it means supping with the devil,' Derek protested. 'The Left have always stood up to the fascists. Look at Spain. Even in Germany itself.'

'And they've lost every time,' said Libby. 'This way both Stalin and Hitler get to grab land without the other interfering. Poland will be first. They'll be carving it up between them just like in the last century.'

Adela was astounded at the girl's knowledge of current affairs. 'But that was history. This is 1939,' Adela exclaimed. 'We won't let that happen.'

Libby's dark eyes looked troubled. 'No, we probably won't,' she answered, 'and that means war.'

***

Perhaps Adela had been too eager to ignore what was happening in Europe, so bound up was she in her new life in England. After the distress of her pregnancy and the shameful birth of her baby, all her energies had been channelled into forging a fresh existence with new friends and interests. If news came on the wireless in the flat, she would turn it off or retune it to popular songs or band music. She was always singing. 'My little nightingale', Lexy called her. When Adela sang, it made all other thoughts go away.

But after the discussion at the theatre that day, everything seemed to move with dizzying speed. Within a week Hitler was threatening to march on Danzig in Poland, and Britain and

France had restated their pledge to protect Poland's independence. Emergency powers were introduced to put the country on a war footing. Schools practised evacuating children to the countryside, kerbs were painted white in anticipation of night-time blackouts, gas masks handed out and restrictions put on carrying cameras in certain areas. Each day the newspapers and newsreels carried instructions to civilians, while soldiers and sailors had leave cancelled and hurried to report to barracks and ports.

Tilly came round to the café in a panic. 'They're saying the Admiralty is stopping British shipping from entering the Mediterranean. It's out of bounds. What does that mean for boats to India?'

'I don't know,' Adela said, trying not to show alarm, 'but we could go down to the shipping offices on the quayside and find out.'

On the way they noticed the frantic activity. People were sandbagging buildings, and throngs of men in uniform were milling about the lofty entrance to Central Station. The offices of the shipping lines were besieged by people wanting to know about sailings across the Atlantic to America and Canada, as well as to the East. Adela steered Tilly away after a harassed clerk suggested that they'd do better going to India by aeroplane.

'You can fly to Karachi in four days via Cairo and Damascus,' he said. 'That's what I'd do if I wanted to get back out to my family.'

Adela's stomach clenched in fear. It all seemed like a bad dream. But the man's anxiety was infectious. War was coming. Neither woman spoke as they toiled back up steep Dean Street into the town. Adela steered Tilly into a café and ordered them coffee. The older woman was perspiring, her brow creased in worry.

'What do you want to do?' asked Adela. Her mind was in turmoil. She couldn't think.

Tilly stared at her coffee, stirring it with a spoon though she'd forgotten to put in sugar. Finally she glanced up and met Adela's look. 'My family is here,' she said quietly. 'I won't go back to India without them.'

'And what about Uncle James? He'll be expecting you back.'

Tilly gave a small shrug. 'He will cope, like he always does. Besides, this whole thing might still blow over. I wasn't due to go back till after the children start school again in mid-September.'

Tilly put a hand out and covered Adela's. 'What about you?'

Adela had refused to think about her situation up till now. She had been sure that war would be averted – somehow, by someone – but she could no longer ignore what was happening. If war was coming, her mother would want her to come home, wouldn't she? India held those most dear to her – her mother, her brother, Sophie and Rafi, Aunt Fluffy, and somewhere in the mountains Sam lived his life. She felt the familiar hollowness inside at the thought of him. He seemed further away now than ever.

Yet if Tilly was to stay . . . ? Here in Newcastle, Adela had her new life and friends, and she felt she owed them her loyalty too. She had a feeling that to turn her back and run away to safety in India would be a betrayal of these people, who had opened their hearts and homes to her: Lexy and the waitresses, Josey and the players, Maggie and Ina, her Brewis cousins and Uncle Jack. Even if Aunt Olive had found it difficult to love her, the others had shown her friendship and support. She held on to Tilly's hand.

'I feel so torn,' Adela admitted. 'I'm not sure what to do.'

Tilly squeezed her hand. 'I understand. You need time to think about it. It's different for me. The children are my first priority.'

They left the café, their coffees cold and half-drunk. On the walk back to Tyne Street, Adela wrestled with her thoughts. Tilly's fierce protectiveness towards her children plagued her. Deep down Adela had another reason to stay in England that she could hardly even admit to herself. Her baby. John Wesley was a quiet, insistent pull on her heart. She knew it was irrational, for he could never be hers. How could she even acknowledge that she'd ever had a son? She had no idea if he was still in the country – most likely not – yet she couldn't bring herself to leave this place where he was born. Those strange intense weeks with the women at Cullercoats and the few days with the baby were dreamlike now, but they tied her to the area. Adela drew comfort from living with Lexy, who knew what she'd been through and what she had given up, and that she had once been a mother. None of this she could ever say to Tilly, but by the time they reached Herbert's Café, Adela had made up her mind.

'Auntie Tilly, if you're staying,' she said tentatively, 'then I think I will too. At least for the moment, while things are still uncertain. Like you say, it might all blow over.'

Tilly brightened. 'Are you sure?'

Adela nodded.

Tilly's face broke into a smile of relief. 'Oh, darling girl! That's what I hoped you'd say.'

The following day the prime minister, Neville Chamberlain, announced over the airwaves that Britain was at war with Germany.

Chapter 23

Belgooree, India, August 1940

The hills beyond the veranda were wreathed in mist, the air heavy with moisture after a torrential downpour. Clarrie, newly returned from supervising the monsoon pickings, stood dripping on the worn wooden floor, reading Adela's latest letter and ignoring Mohammed Din's entreaties to change out of her wet clothes.

'In a minute I promise.'

The thin blue airmail paper was turning soggy in her hands, but she eagerly read it from start to finish and then read it all over again, as if she could somehow conjure Adela to her by memorising the words.

Dearest Mother,

I don't know what news you are getting at home, but you mustn't worry. It really hasn't been bad here at all. Of course we get air-raid warnings, but that's just part of life now. We all know what to do and where to go and life goes on.

Now for the really exciting news – we had auditions last week for Pygmalion *and guess what? Derek has picked me for Eliza Doolittle!! I'm so thrilled to finally get a big part. I'm sure if Josey had been here she would have got the part in a flash. We were all very worried about her for a while. I probably told you in my last letter, but no sooner had she joined the Entertainments National Service Association than she was sent to France. What with all the confusing news about Dunkirk and not knowing who'd got safely back across the Channel, we just kept praying she hadn't been captured.*

But two weeks ago I got a letter to say she was back in London – she'd got out on a cargo ship from Saint-Malo and sounded as chirpy as ever. She couldn't say where she and her troupe are going to be sent next, but I know if she comes anywhere near Newcastle she'll pop in to see us. Derek pretends he doesn't care – he's still annoyed that she volunteered for ENSA instead of helping to keep The People's going. He said munitions and factory workers and miners deserve entertainment as much as the forces. But I know he really misses her.

Libby is helping out again at the theatre over the summer holidays, despite Tilly wanting her to stay at Mona and Walter's farm with her and the boys. Lexy said she could sleep at the flat if I'd be responsible for her. She's such a plucky girl and helps me at the station canteen. It's been busier than ever since the troops came back from France. We get everyone passing through, from Polish sailors to Free French airmen, as well as our own boys. Libby is cheery to them all, though she can get on her high horse at times and give them a history lesson.

I hope this finds you well. Give Harry a kiss from me – and a big one for yourself. Tell Uncle James that Tilly and the family are safe and in good spirits (perhaps you shouldn't mention about Libby being in Newcastle without her mother – just say they are all well, which they are).

All my love,

Adela xxx

Clarrie's eyes smarted at the tender farewell. Her daughter was safe and sounded happy. She noted the date. It had been written a month ago. Her stomach clenched in fresh anxiety. Anything could have happened since then. She knew from crackling bulletins on the wireless that since the fall of France in June the Luftwaffe had begun dropping bombs over British cities. Tyneside had been mentioned.

It amazed Clarrie that any letters got through these days. Now that Italy had declared war on Britain, no ships coming through the Mediterranean were safe from attack, and flights were now almost impossible. Mail came by sea around the Cape, but how much mail had been lost along with devastating numbers of merchant shipping? Adela had referred to some earlier letter about Josey joining ENSA that she'd never received.

For an instant she felt again the hurt that her daughter had chosen to stay in England instead of returning to India and safety. At first, she had been disbelieving and then angry at the decision, wondering unfairly if Tilly had put pressure on her to stay. But her anger had turned swiftly to guilt. She had pushed Adela away. Was it any wonder that she hadn't come rushing back to her? For a time she had worried that her daughter was unhappy in Newcastle – for a couple of months the previous year Adela had not written to her at all – but since the outbreak of war her spirits appeared to have revived. Perhaps she had a new sense of purpose.

Clarrie went to change out of her sodden clothes. There was no sign of Harry, who would still be with Banu, the garden overseer. If Clarrie allowed it, the boy would spend every daylight hour out riding with the patient Khasi manager or playing with Banu's children. Perhaps she was wrong to let the boy run free, but he was not yet seven, and she wanted him to enjoy his childhood at Belgooree and be accepted by the local hill people in the way that she had been.

Ayah Mimi, frailer now, still kept an eye on him at the house when Clarrie was busy at the factory, and between them they were teaching him the basics of reading and counting. He loved Ayah's stories of Hindu gods and goddesses. Formal education could wait. She wanted to keep Harry with her as long as possible. He was her final link with Wesley and each year grew more like his father: the unruly waves of dark hair, the lively green eyes that creased when he laughed and his passion for the outdoors.

Adela was so far away and might never want to live at Belgooree again. Was she being selfish wanting to hang on to Harry and not send him to school, Clarrie wondered? Adela! What was life really like for her vivacious daughter? She knew that Adela was playing down the danger she was in; after all, the tea rooms were close to the munitions factories and shipyards of the Tyne, which would surely be a target for enemy planes.

Her anxious thoughts were interrupted by the sound of a car engine grinding up the drive. She quickly stepped into a loose cotton frock and pulled a brush through her wavy damp hair. Minutes later James was striding up the steps, looking dishevelled, as if he hadn't slept for days, his expression grim.

'Whatever's happened?' Clarrie asked, her stomach knotting. 'Is it news from Tilly?'

'Lack of news,' James growled, thrusting his hat at Mohammed Din. He accepted a glass of nimbu pani, which he downed thirstily.

'Please, James,' Clarrie urged. 'Sit down and tell me why you're so upset.'

'Tilly's not answering my telegrams.' James plonked himself down in a battered cane chair. It creaked under his solid frame.

'When did you last hear from her?'

'Two weeks ago. She's refusing to bring the children out here; says the risk of travelling is worse than staying put.'

'Perhaps she has a point.'

'Do you have any idea of what's happening at home?' James demanded. 'Tyneside is in the firing line with its shipyards and ammo factories. Last week the Germans were bombing Newcastle in broad daylight. The BBC reported that squadrons operating in the North East had brought down seventy-five bombers. But they never said how much destruction they managed before our boys destroyed them.'

Clarrie felt sick with anxiety, but she tried to calm him. 'I just received a letter today from Adela.'

His haggard face brightened for an instant. 'You have?'

'Yes, and she says they are all safe and well – told me to tell you especially that Tilly and the . . . the children were staying with Mona on their Berwickshire farm. So well out of harm's way.'

'When was it written?'

'July,' Clarrie admitted.

James let out an oath. 'She should have got out in June, when I told her to,' he fretted. 'Jean Bradley managed to get back safely to Assam with her two children – the Oxford Estates moved heaven and earth to get our employees' wives and families on to planes. But not Tilly.' He stood up and paced to the balcony. 'I never knew she could be so stubborn – or so irresponsible.'

'Isn't it of some comfort that she's there with the children?' Clarrie asked. 'At least they're all together.'

He turned and glared. 'I want them here with me, damn it! How can I protect them when they are thousands of miles away? Britain's on the verge of being invaded. I don't even want to think what that might mean! They're completely isolated – Denmark, Norway, Holland all under the Nazis' jackboots, and now France. It's just a matter of time. Good God, woman! Don't you worry about Adela?'

'Of course I do!' Clarrie jumped up, stung by his accusation. 'But there's nothing we can do out here.'

'There must be something.' James gave her a desperate look.

'Hope and pray, that's all,' Clarrie answered, digging her nails into her palms to stop herself breaking into tears.

James turned away, gripped the balcony rail, and bowed his head. His broad back and thick shoulders, straining in his crumpled linen jacket, began to shudder. In alarm Clarrie went to him.

'James?' She put a hand on his shoulder. He let out a low howl. He tried to shake her off and hide his face, but she pulled him around. His craggy features were flushed and streaked with tears.

She rubbed his arm. 'Don't give up. We'll be strong for each other.'

He gazed at her with intense blue eyes. His voice when he spoke was a hoarse whisper. 'How will I manage without my Tilly? She's the reason I get up in the morning and do my job. Cheviot View is so lonely without her, so bloody lonely!'

'I know,' Clarrie said gently. 'All you can do is be brave and carry on doing your job. Some day soon, God willing, Tilly and the children will return, just as Adela will come back to Belgooree.'

'Do you really believe that?' asked James.

'I have to – and so do you.'

Just then Clarrie heard a child's shout and a clatter of feet. Harry was back.

'Hello, Uncle James.' He grinned. 'I saw the car coming and ran home. Are you staying?'

'Yes, he's staying,' Clarrie said at once.

'Have you been running?' Harry asked in curiosity. 'You look all pink in the face.'

James straightened up and rubbed his eyes on his sleeve. 'No, just a bit of grit in the eyes.' He ruffled the boy's hair. 'But your mother got rid of it.' Over Harry's head, he gave Clarrie a grateful smile.

***

James stayed on for three days, doing a tour of the gardens and factory with Clarrie, their talk businesslike. No further mention was made of Tilly, and the tea planter resumed his usual brisk manner. Yet Clarrie could not forget her glimpse of a more vulnerable James, one who had let down his emotional guard and shed tears for his wife and family. Under all his bluster and forthright opinions, James had a soft heart – at least when it came to Tilly. Clarrie felt a fresh pang of loss for Wesley. Perhaps the Robson cousins had been more alike than she'd ever imagined: loyal and loving under their tough manliness.

Before he left to return to Upper Assam, James made a suggestion. The day before, they had been discussing Harry's education. James had been critical of Clarrie's reluctance to send her son away to school, even to St Mungo's in Shillong, where he could return to her at weekends. James had pointed out that Harry would be seven in a couple of months' time and that he was bright enough and ready for school. But Clarrie had been firm and told him that the decision was hers alone.

'I know you think it's none of my business,' he said, 'but I have a very talented young assistant, Manzur Ahmad, who wants to be a teacher. He's my bearer Aslam's boy. His mother, Meera, was the children's ayah. Perhaps you remember her.'

'Of course. Meera has been here on several occasions – a sweet woman. Didn't you and Tilly pay for Manzur to go to school?'

'Yes, we did. Tilly took a shine to the boy and said we owed it to Meera for all that she'd done for our children. Well, you know Tilly – daft about kiddies.'

'It was a kind gesture,' Clarrie said, waiting for him to explain why he was talking about Manzur.

'The thing is, his father wants Manzur to train as a clerk in the plantation office – that's where he's been for the past year since finishing school – and he's very efficient at what he does. I don't want to lose him, but he's a bright young man with a mind of his own, and I'm worried he might just up and off.'

'So, what are you thinking?' Clarrie probed.

'That if I offered him some tutoring over here, say once a month, with young Harry, then Manzur might be content to stay.' James added dryly, 'Then both Aslam and I would be happy.'

Clarrie considered. It might do Harry good to have a young tutor with the energy and patience to teach him. She was touched that James had been giving the problem some thought.

'If Manzur would be willing to do that,' Clarrie said and smiled, 'then yes, I'd be very grateful for your offer. Perhaps we could try it out for a couple of months and see how Manzur gets on with Harry.'

'Good idea,' James said, nodding.

He left whistling 'The British Grenadiers', which Clarrie knew was a sign that James's spirits were reviving.

Chapter 24

Newcastle, autumn 1940

Adela never mentioned anything about the bombing raids in letters to her mother. The first one in July had been terrifying. The sirens had wailed their warning on a late Tuesday afternoon just as she'd been in the middle of replenishing the tea from the urn in the voluntary canteen at the railway station. She had put down the large metal teapot and hurried out with her fellow workers and customers to the underground passage between the platforms, which doubled as a temporary air-raid shelter.

A sailor had played his harmonica to keep their minds off what might be happening above. Adela's chest had tightened till she could barely breathe as they waited. The first bombs had sounded like the thunder of a distant train. In the dark somebody reached out for her hand. She held on to it tightly, until her fingers were numb.

The bombing had grown louder and more intense, shaking the walls, while the sailor carried on playing. Adela's teeth had jarred as she clenched them shut to stop herself screaming. She thought her end had come and prayed that Lexy and the others would survive, that the café was still standing and that her Brewis family and Tilly were safe.

When they had emerged, shaking and laughing with euphoria at having survived, fire engines and ambulances were hurtling along the street heading for the quayside. Later she had discovered that the bombers had struck as close as the Spillers factory by the river, a split second away from the High Level Bridge. The air had reeked with burning rubber and metal, and palls of black smoke had blocked out the sun. Jarrow, the shipyard town on the south bank of the Tyne, had also been ablaze. The death toll that day had been thirteen, and the injured well over a hundred.

The raids carried on over the summer and into September, but Adela learnt to mask her fear and make jokes like others did.

'Hitler must have heard you'd put yourself forward as Henry Higgins in our play,' she teased Derek.

'And Josey must be performing in London then,' Derek replied with dark humour.

They knew that however bad it was in Newcastle, it was worse in London, which was being hit night after night. Adela hoped fervently that her friend was on tour and out of the capital. She would be forever grateful to Josey for her caring attention of the previous summer, when life had never seemed so tough. Adela's body and emotions had still been in shock after childbirth and giving away her baby, and grief for her father had swamped her anew on the anniversary of his death. Josey had not pried into her unhappiness or fussed over her, but her warmth and humour had helped her through the worst of it.

More children were evacuated to the countryside, and Libby's school was relocated to a rambling stately home north of Alnwick. She wrote impatient letters to Adela about how she wished she was in Newcastle being useful and vowed that once she turned sixteen, she was determined to leave school. Tilly was renting a terraced house in South Gosforth to provide a home for the children and, at Libby's insistence, had taken in two Polish refugees through the Red Cross. Tilly had thrown herself enthusiastically into war work, volunteering with the Women's Voluntary Service, helping at rest centres doling out clothes and food for those made homeless by the bombing.

Although the cinemas had reopened again after being closed at the beginning of the war, Adela had gone part-time at the Essoldo so that she could help out more at the services' canteen and at Herbert's. The latter was staying open till late to provide a fuggy haven for the flood of new workers at the armaments factories. Any spare time she had was spent at the theatre on Rye Hill.

Just before Christmas, as they were rehearsing *Cinderella* – Adela was playing Prince Charming – in walked Josey. Adela flew at her and they hugged tightly.

'No, you can't have my part,' Adela said, laughing, 'so don't even ask.'

'Love the long boots, Miss Robson.' Josey grinned. 'Derek never let me wear anything that fetching.'

'You'd never fit those thighs in them, that's why,' Derek grunted, but couldn't resist giving her a peck on the cheek.

They celebrated in the green room with a bottle of whisky Josey had been given by a grateful quartermaster at the barracks in Ripon, and she regaled them with stories of her touring.

'It's not all whisky and after-show parties in the sergeants' mess you know,' said Josey. 'It's damn hard work, and some of the places we've stayed in I don't think they'd changed the sheets since the Napoleonic War.'

'Remember it, do you?' said Derek.

'No, but I remember you talking about it,' she said, sticking out her tongue.

Josey had two weeks off before her next contract.

'Florence has let my room to two munitions workers,' she said with a grimace. 'I don't blame her, and she's been good about storing a trunk for me, but it means I'm homeless.'

'Stay and have Christmas with us,' Adela urged. 'You can have the camp bed in my room.'

Lexy was as accommodating as ever, agreeing at once to Adela's request that they take in a friend in need of a home. The three of them got on well, Josey and Lexy sharing a sometimes bawdy sense of humour. For Christmas, Lexy suggested cooking a meal at the café for the Brewises, as well as Tilly and her family.

'Won't you be expected at one of your sisters' or nieces' homes?' asked Adela.

'I can see them any day of the week,' Lexy said, 'and I'd only end up doing all the washing up. If I stay here, you and Josey can do that.'

Tilly accepted with alacrity. 'Ros is going to Duncan's parents in St Abb's for Christmas. Strachan's seem to be able to get hold of petrol without too much trouble. She invited us along, but the children would rather be in Newcastle.'

'So you're intent on staying and seeing the war out here?' Adela asked her.

Tilly's expression was pained. 'I know James is hurt that I haven't gone beetling back to him and India. But I couldn't do it. Not while all three children are here. And I won't risk a sea voyage.' She put on a brave smile. 'Besides, we've survived so far, haven't we? And the Nazis haven't invaded. So this Christmas, at least, we have something to celebrate.'

'Yes, we do,' Adela agreed. She wondered if Tilly woke each morning with the same queasy anxiety that she did. Would today bring further bombing raids or news of another ship sunk? For one day at least they could try and forget the ever-present dangers and join together to lift each other's spirits.

Aunt Olive, however, took a strong dislike to Adela and Lexy's plans and refused to leave Lime Terrace. Jane was apologetic but loyal.

'Mam's better where she feels safe, and that's at home. It's not really her fault. She can't stop fretting that our George is going to volunteer – he's been talking about wanting to join the Fleet Air Arm.'

'No wonder she's worried,' Adela sympathised, dismayed to think of George going away. 'But won't he get called up soon anyway?'

'That's what George keeps saying,' Jane replied. 'And he wants to be able to choose where he goes.'

'What does your dad think he should do?'

Jane sighed. 'Father just says whatever he thinks will stop Mam worrying. He says George is needed to run the business, and he'll say so in front of any tribunal. It's causing a bit of friction at home I can tell you.'

'What about Joan? She won't want George joining up either, will she?'

Jane pulled a face. 'Joan's putting pressure on him to get wed – says all her friends are doing it – but I think that's another reason he wants to up and off.'

On Christmas Eve a card came from Adela's dear old guardian, Fluffy Hogg, with seasonal good wishes. Scrawled on the back was a message. Adela caught her breath at the familiar name.

'*I thought you'd want to know that your missionary friend, Sam Jackman, has left the Sarahan district. I heard it from Fatima. He came to see her, but unfortunately she has been away in Lahore seeing to her sick mother so missed him, and he left no onward address. We think that the mission might have given him a second chance and sent him somewhere else to start afresh at short notice.*'

Adela reread the tantalising short message several times with a thumping heart. It told her so little. Why had Sam left? Where had he gone? Had he taken Pema with him? To hear of him in this way was upsetting. He had disappeared from the Himalayas, and the chances of her ever seeing him again were even more remote than before. *Oh Sam! Where are you now?* she wondered bleakly.

Adela couldn't bear to have the card on display so slipped it into her bedside drawer under her nightie, alongside the photograph she had kept of her and Sam on the Narkanda veranda. Briefly she gazed at the photo. How happy they looked together! Her heart twisted to think of what might have been. But it was a glimpse into a past life that would never be hers again.

***

On Christmas day, with the café decorated with homemade paper streamers and old Chinese lanterns (that Tilly remembered Clarrie using for her long-ago twenty-first birthday party), the Robsons, Lexy, Josey and Derek all came together to share a meal. Tilly and Josey took to each other at once – Tilly remembered Josey as a lively child at a Christmas party of Clarrie's during the Great War – and the café rang with their raucous laughter as they swapped anecdotes about their growing up in Newcastle among eccentric and bossy relations.

Later, as the short day waned and they pulled the blackout curtains, George and Jane turned up with a bottle of homemade ginger wine and a crate of beer that George had somehow got hold of in return for tea.

Adela and Josey played duets on the piano and they began a sing-song. Libby gazed at George with adoration and joined him in renditions of 'Blaydon Races' and 'Teddy Bears' Picnic', even though Tilly shrieked that it was like a cat's chorus.

'A very pretty cat,' George said with a wink, throwing an arm around the girl and making Libby blush puce with pleasure.

They ended up with Josey getting George to carry her gramophone downstairs from the flat – they took so long that Lexy made lewd comments about what they might be doing – and the party went on long into the evening as they danced to Glenn Miller and Henry Hall and the BBC Dance Orchestra.

Mungo curled up and went to sleep under a table, and Adela, tipsy on unaccustomed beer, sang 'Cheek to Cheek', 'Smoke Gets in Your Eyes' and 'The Nearness of You', which reduced an emotional Tilly to tears.

'How Clarrie would love to hear you, dear girl,' she said and sniffed.

This made Adela tearful. How she wished they could all be together!

'If only Daddy could be here too.' Libby sighed. Adela reached over and pulled her into a hug.

Swiftly, George stood up and refilled their glasses. 'Before we all go home and leave these lovely ladies in peace,' he said, raising his glass, 'let's all drink to absent family and friends.'

'To family and friends!' they chorused.

Adela had a sudden image of Sam with his battered green hat pushed back on his untidy hair and his lean face grinning down at her, his look playful. She felt anew the upset of the previous day, when she'd learned that Sam had disappeared once more. *My darling Sam, may you stay safe and happy,* she wished silently as her eyes smarted.

George, mistaking her emotion for homesickness, gave her shoulder a squeeze. 'Maybes next Christmas you'll be with your mam.'

Adela forced a smile and nodded.

After that, in more sombre mood they all hugged each other as Jane and George went into the pitch-black night. How Adela would miss George if he enlisted; he was a tonic for them all. Adela persuaded Tilly to stay, not wanting her to risk a long walk home and getting into trouble with ARP wardens. Together the women took Tilly and her children upstairs to sleep in Lexy's small sitting room.

It had been a special day, a brief respite from the daily hardships and tensions of war, where they had joked and comforted each other. Proof, thought Adela as she bedded down, that what mattered most in these uneasy times was friendship and love.

Chapter 25

September 1941

Tilly picked her way through the smouldering wreckage, trying not to gag at the stench of charred buildings and bodies. A pall of thick smoke hung over everything, making her eyes stream and throat sore. In the distance flames from the goods station on New Bridge Street lit the early morning. Ambulance and fire-engine bells clanged. Never in her worst nightmares did she ever think she would have to witness such scenes.

'Over here!' an ARP warden hollered. 'I hear something.'

Tilly, armed with blankets, hurried over and peered into the half-collapsed entrance of an Anderson shelter. The house had taken a direct hit; it was a pile of scorched bricks. There was nothing much left of the whole street. The night had been one of terror, as the city had been showered with scores of high-explosive bombs, incendiaries and parachute mines. They had worked through the night to bring people to safety in the Shieldfield school that was a temporary rest centre and give them food and reassurance, not knowing if they would be the next target.

'Wait,' ordered the warden, kicking debris out of the way and venturing into the shelter.

Tilly felt completely exhausted. The air attacks had started again in April. Would they ever be free of the fear of screaming bombs? Had she been wrong not to try to get back to India with the children when she'd had the chance? Too late for doubts. At least Mungo and Libby were safely back at their schools – Libby mutinous, but persuaded by Miss MacGregor to stay on into sixth form at least for a year. Jamie had also had his arm twisted to begin his degree in medicine rather than enlist. He was somewhere in the city helping out at a first aid station.

The warden reappeared, carrying a whimpering bundle. Tilly went immediately to help.

'Little laddie,' said the warden.

'Give him to me,' she said, holding out her arms, swapping the infant for the blankets, keeping one to wrap around him. He stared at her with huge eyes out of a face covered in soil. 'There,

there, little man,' she crooned, gently rocking him, 'you're safe now.' She glanced at the warden. 'Anyone else?'

He shook his head, his look harrowed. 'Couple killed on the steps. Must've been on their way in. Maybe his parents.' He held out a small metal cash box. 'Mother was clutching this.'

Tilly swallowed down tears. Another child orphaned. What a hellishly cruel world they were living in. 'Give me the box. I'll take him up to the school and get him cleaned up. Poor wee scrap.' She kissed the child's head of matted hair. He was trembling in her arms, though his crying had stopped.

Back at the rest centre, the scene was less chaotic than a few hours ago. The newly homeless were helping the volunteers rig up temporary dormitories, while others queued up for porridge and tea. Through the steamy atmosphere, an acrid smell pervaded. Perhaps it was on her own clothes, Tilly wondered.

'You look done in,' a fellow WVS worker said. 'Go home and get your head down. I'll look after this one.'

'I think he's just lost his parents,' said Tilly, hanging on to the boy. Her eyes stung with tears. 'I feel like taking him home. Who will look after him now?'

'We will,' said the matronly woman with a kindly smile. 'And maybe someone in his family has survived and will claim him.'

Tilly left details of where they had found the boy and went home to sleep. A couple of days later she heard from a neighbour in the same bombed-out street that the boy was called Jacques, the only child of a Belgian couple called Segal.

'Father was an electrician. Canny couple. Bonny mother.' The neighbour shook his head in incomprehension. 'Must have thought they'd be safer here than in Belgium.'

'So there might be family abroad,' Tilly said in hope.

The man gave her a glum look. 'Didn't know them well enough to know.'

Tilly found her greatest release after such upsetting days was to go to Herbert's and share a pot of tea – however watered down – with Adela and Lexy. Under Jane's guidance the café had become a distribution point for free meals to the homeless – part of Newcastle's Communal Feeding Scheme – and Tilly often called in on behalf of the WVS to liaise. Her friends recognised that what she really wanted was a moment of snatched camaraderie and Adela's gossipy banter about the theatre.

Adela had no idea how much Tilly relied on her to cope with the horrors and fears of their daily existence. Tilly told herself constantly that if Adela at her young age and far from home could remain brave and cheerful, then she, silly Tilly, had nothing to complain about. Sometimes Tilly felt a guilty stab that she hadn't tried to persuade Adela to return home to her mother, and might even have encouraged Adela to stay by choosing to remain in Newcastle herself. She hoped that Clarrie didn't resent that she saw so much of her spirited daughter, yet Tilly was just thankful to have the girl nearby.

But today Tilly knew that after such a savage air raid, Adela and Lexy would be frantically busy coping with a new influx of dazed and destitute civilians.

So it was a few days later that she called round to the café. She found Adela in a state of excitement.

'I've got an interview with ENSA,' she told Tilly. 'I'm to go to London next week. Josey's been badgering me for months to apply, but it's really thanks to Derek.'

'Derek?' Tilly said, trying to mask her dismay. 'Didn't think he'd want to lose you.'

'He's sick of me going on about wanting to help the war effort more – especially now they're training up so many more troops to go out to North Africa. Remember that BBC producer, Cecil McGivern? Well, he's down in London now, and Derek asked him to put in a good word for me with the ENSA lot,' Adela explained. 'I didn't think I'd be good enough, but they're taking on more amateurs now. Anyway, I got a letter inviting me to audition at the Theatre Royal in Drury Lane and see what I can offer. Isn't that exciting?'

'Of course it is.' Tilly smiled. 'I'll keep my fingers and toes crossed for you.'

How pretty and animated the girl looked. Ever since Gracie Fields had visited Tyneside in July to boost morale after a series of attacks on the shipyards and city, Adela had been restless to do more than help out at the local canteen.

'I want to sing for my country too,' she had declared, high with emotion after attending one of the concerts for factory workers that Wilf had smuggled her into.

Tilly thought what a duller place it would be without Clarrie's daughter. At twenty-one, Adela had matured beyond her age. Always vivacious and a little headstrong, the precocious adolescent of Belgooree days had turned into someone much more stoical and selfless. Lexy, Jane, Derek and herself were just some of the people who relied on Adela's tireless energy and good humour to get them through the day.

As she left, Adela walked out into the street with her. 'There's one thing worrying me about going,' she said. 'I wanted a word out of earshot of Jane.'

'Go on,' said Tilly.

'It's likely that Jane will get called up before the year is over. All women under thirty will be eventually, so it's just a matter of time.'

'You're worried about Lexy coping without her,' Tilly guessed. 'I'd be happy to help out more.'

Adela smiled and put a hand on her arm. 'That's kind, Auntie Tilly. Lexy would be glad of the offer I'm sure. But that's not my main concern: it's Aunt Olive I worry about. Now that George is away training with the Fleet Air Arm, I can't see her managing without Jane. She'll go to pieces.'

'I don't know Olive well,' said Tilly, 'but from what I do know she's a bag of nerves. In my opinion she should pull herself together and get out more.'

Adela's look was reflective. 'She hasn't always had an easy time of it, but Aunt Olive finds the littlest things daunting. I'd hate to be that scared of life.'

'Yes, me too.' Tilly sighed. 'So what are you suggesting?'

'I wrote to Mother about her and she came up with an idea. It'll either work or have Aunt Olive screaming the house down.'

***

A few days later, armed with half tins of unused paint from The People's Theatre, Adela, Tilly, Jamie and Derek descended on Number 10, Lime Terrace. Jack, primed by his daughter, had persuaded Olive to go out for the day with him on a rare trip to the Tyneside Tea Company to taste a new blend.

By the time she returned, the sitting room at Number 10, where Olive spent most of her waking hours, had been transformed.

Gone were the drab wallpaper and sombre colours of mud brown and dark red. It glowed yellow and peach, and across one wall was a huge mural of a whitewashed bungalow surrounded by lush green foliage and bright blossoms of pink and crimson. Vivid green parrots flew through the air, and three figures stood at the veranda rail: two young women and a turbaned servant.

Adela could hardly keep still. She was jumpy with nervousness. Perhaps it was all too gaudy for her aunt's taste. She knew she would take the brunt of Olive's tongue-lashing if it displeased her.

Olive shrieked in horror at seeing it and sank into a chair. 'What have you done? Jack, did you know what they were doing? I'll never forgive you!'

Adela's stomach churned. She bit the inside of her mouth to stop her tears. 'You can blame me and Mother. It was our idea,' she defended her uncle. 'Mother said how you used to paint everything in bright colours. This dark room wasn't your taste at all.'

'How dare you!' Olive spluttered. 'What would you know about my tastes?'

'Mam, don't—' Jane tried to intervene.

'Did I ask for your opinion?' Olive cried.

'Aunt Olive,' Adela appealed to her, 'Mother thought if you were going to spend a lot of time sitting here, it might cheer you to be reminded of Belgooree.'

Olive looked at her in stupefaction. 'Belgooree?'

Adela ploughed on. 'Look, that's you and Mother leaning on the balcony. And that's your old khansama, Kamal. I hope it looks something like him.'

Olive gave her a suspicious look and then turned back to the wall. She clutched her chair arms while peering at the mural. She gave a small gasp.

'Kamal?'

Then abruptly the indignation went out of her. She crumpled forward, head in hands, and began to sob.

Jane rushed at once to comfort her. 'Don't be upset, Mam. We can paint over it. I should have known you wouldn't like it.'

'No.' Olive jerked up.

They watched as she got unsteadily to her feet and walked across to the painting. She put out a tentative hand to the figures on the veranda. Adela held her breath.

'Clarrie and me,' she murmured, tracing a finger over the dark-haired woman and the red-haired girl. 'And dear Kamal.' She stroked the figure of the Indian servant.

'Yes,' Adela said. 'Mother insisted on him being there.'

'Don't change it,' she whispered. She turned and eyed Adela tearfully. 'Tell Clarrie thank you.'

Instinctively Adela rushed forward and hugged her aunt. For an instant Olive tensed, and then she responded with a gentle pat on Adela's back. It was an awkward gesture, but Adela knew that for Olive it was a brief sign of affection. For the past two years she had felt guilty for adding to Olive's worries with the shock of her pregnancy. Now perhaps they could put that distressing time behind them. The redecorating was a success. Her mother would be proud, and that filled Adela with joy.

***

Tilly went to see Adela off at Central Station. The young woman was still euphoric at their transformation of Olive's lair.

'How did Mother know Aunt Olive would be so pleased with the painting of Belgooree? I've hardly ever heard her mention it all the time I've been here.'

'I suppose it brought back memories of a happier time in her life,' Tilly mused, 'when she wasn't so afraid of everything. It seemed to be the figure of Kamal that had most effect.'

'Yes,' Adela agreed. 'Mother said Olive was particularly fond of their khansama. Took her a long time to get over having to leave him behind when they came to England.'

'Well, it was a kind and brave gesture.' Tilly smiled. She took Adela's hands in hers. 'Will you stay down in London if you're accepted?'

'I don't know. It depends what they want. *If* I get accepted.'

'They'd be mad not to have you. You'll cheer up the grumpiest of soldiers.'

Adela's eyes swam with tears. 'Thanks, Auntie Tilly. I'll give it my best shot.'

‘I know you will. And I’ll pop in to see Olive now and again for you, so you don’t need to worry about her. Libby’s another matter. I don’t know how I’m going to break it to that girl that you’ve disappeared off to London. She’ll make my life hell.’

Adela hesitated. ‘Be kind to Libby – just like you are to me.’

Tilly flushed at the gentle rebuke. How she wished she could love her daughter as easily as she did Clarrie’s. It wasn’t just that Adela was pretty and engaging and got on so easily with people; Libby might blossom in time and learn to listen rather than lecture. But of all her children, Libby was the one with whom she sparked and became too quickly irritated. Jamie was sensitive and amiable, like her own brother, Johnny. Even though she hadn’t seen Johnny for several years – a regimental doctor, he was somewhere in Mesopotamia – she had always loved him best of her siblings. Her youngest son, Mungo, was a boisterous, uncomplicated boy who followed orders and gave her little trouble. But Libby was single-minded and responded neither to cajoling nor threats. She was her father’s daughter; Libby was so like James. Tilly wondered if that was why she was harder on Libby than the others. Was she jealous of Libby’s adoration of James, even though it was her husband’s insistence and not hers that the children should be sent back to Britain for their schooling?

Oh, James! She didn’t want to think about her husband. It made her feel wretchedly guilty for failing to return to him. Yet a part of her felt relief at not having to live the isolated life of a tea planter’s wife. Here in Newcastle she was her own person again, able to choose where to live and what to do. She did miss him. Not so much physically – her appetite for sex had dwindled ever since Mungo’s difficult birth – but she missed his companionship and solid, reassuring presence. She forced her mind back to Adela’s request.

‘I’ll try my best,’ Tilly promised. They kissed cheeks like grown-ups, then Tilly said, ‘Oh, give me a hug, won’t you!’

They clung on for a moment, and then Tilly let her go. As she watched Adela thread her way along the crowded platform, she fought back tears and the fear that she might not see the girl again for a long time.

‘Goodbye, my darling girl,’ Tilly murmured, and blew a kiss as Adela turned one last time to wave before boarding the train.

Four days later a telegram came. Adela was a new recruit in the Entertainments National Service Association.

Chapter 26

Upper Assam, May 1942

James looked through his field glasses with disbelief. The road dipping down from the hills was filled with bedraggled soldiers. They came like an army of locusts, covering the slopes, trudging forward in the saturating heat or on open trucks that did for ambulances. A couple of aeroplanes buzzed overhead and then veered out of view in the direction of the Burmese border.

All spring the talk at the club had been of the shock invasion by the Japanese army, rushing like tigers through Malaya and then on into Burma after the capture of Singapore in February.

'We'll hold the line at Sittang River,' James had said bullishly, knocking back a double whisky. He had started drinking more heavily in Tilly's absence.

But in Burma, the 17th Infantry Division of the Indian Army under General Smyth had been quickly outflanked and pushed back north and west. By early March the capital, Rangoon, had fallen. Mandalay in the centre had followed. The Indian army made a desperate fighting retreat across the Chindwin River and through the almost impenetrable jungles and mountains to India. James had hunted in those teak forests as a young man when Burma had still been a part of India. He knew planters who had gone to work there and some of their Indian staff.

The news had grown ever grimmer. By April the Japanese had occupied the Andaman Islands and were bombing naval bases in Ceylon and Southern India; Madras was being evacuated. The tea planters, coal mine managers and oil workers of Assam were in near panic at the speed of events. A year ago they had thought India was 'safe as houses', as his fellow manager and neighbour, Reggie Percy-Barratt, had claimed. Now they were being forced to contemplate sending their families to safety in Calcutta or Delhi – always supposing anywhere in India was now safe.

The enemy was pressing towards their border. Burma had gone up in flames; cities and oil fields were ablaze, whether set alight by the invaders or the retreating British, James didn't know. Rumour had it that thousands of stranded Indians were fleeing too: plantation workers, shopkeepers and clerks with their families.

'Well, the Europeans had to be given priority on the ships, didn't they?' said Percy-Barratt defensively. 'Rangoon couldn't handle such numbers of evacuees.'

James had been uncomfortable at the thought. These Indians were in Burma working for the British and were subjects of King George. Knowing the terrain and the stifling heat of West Burma, it would be a near-impossible trek for women and children. He doubted many could survive even if they evaded the pursuing Japanese. He looked again through his binoculars. It amazed him that so many troops had made it back across the border. It was rumoured that thousands hadn't; whole units had been either killed or taken prisoner.

He agonised about what to do: hurry back to the Oxford Estates and make preparations to evacuate the remaining wives and families of his staff, or continue up towards the border to see what he could do to help.

'Damn it!' he cursed under his breath. Turning to his assistant, Manzur, he said, 'Come on. You can drive me up to Kohima.'

They found the border village in chaos. Army tents and temporary shelters were erected on the lawns of British bungalows. Tennis courts and paddocks had been given over to emergency field hospitals, vehicles, mess awnings and equipment. Exhausted men in grubby, sweat-stained uniforms milled around. But what lay beyond, corralled on the hillside, struck horror into James's chest. A seething mass of people – emaciated, collapsing, beseeching, half naked, filthy, diseased – were camped out in the open as far as the eye could see. He was appalled at the almost Biblical scene of suffering.

The border officials were completely overwhelmed by the situation. James tried to get some sense out of one young man.

'It's not my fault,' he said defensively. 'We've been told to only let Europeans into Assam.'

'They'll die if you don't,' James said.

'What can I do?' the man said, removing his spectacles and rubbing his eyes in exhaustion.

'Show a bit of compassion, man!'

But the clerk remained obstinate. 'Take it up with my superiors. I'm just trying to do my job.'

James stormed off. He could see the situation was hopeless. He ordered Manzur to drive him back to the plantation.

James sighed in frustration. 'We'll offer some provisions to the army – maybe some labour to help them build defences or supply roads. See what they need. If the Japanese are coming, we're going to be on the front line.'

On the way back his young assistant suggested, 'Sahib, we could extend the lines, build some temporary shelters. Take some of those people in. They'll have to let them across the border sooner or later.'

James just grunted. He should upbraid Manzur for being impertinent; it was none of his business what the authorities chose to do. But he didn't. He had a growing respect for the young man and was secretly admiring that he had the confidence to voice his opinion to his boss. Clarrie liked Manzur too. He had proved a patient and encouraging tutor for Harry – who was turning out to be rather a serious child – and Clarrie had been pleased with his efforts. Clarrie would be outraged at the treatment of the fleeing civilians from Burma.

That night James couldn't rid himself of the image of the destitute refugees on the hillside. They reminded him of bad memories from twenty years ago, the camps of absconding plantation workers that had lined the ghats of the Brahmaputra River. He sat on the veranda in the dark, drinking and thinking back to the time when he'd brought Tilly to Assam as his wife. He'd been embarrassed that her first sight of his domain was scores of cholera-raddled troublemakers. They had been desperate and destitute, but he had seen them only as a burden and the makers of their own misfortune. He had been further irritated by Clarrie's high-handed comments about how all the tea planters should rally to help them. My God! She'd even talked about defying the tea association and putting up wages unilaterally, a sure way of causing further disturbance and dissension in the tea gardens. How contemptuous he had been of her suggestions and of Wesley for letting her take such a hand in business at Belgooree.

James slugged back his whisky. Strange how he was seeing things through her eyes now. Something must be done about the refugees from Burma. He stood and went to lean on the balcony railing. The trees below pulsed with night sounds in the warm, sticky air. The monsoon would come soon. Perhaps that was the only thing that would keep the Japanese invasion at bay: flooded and impassable jungle ravines. But it would also bring fever and further misery to those fleeing and struggling to reach the border.

'*It was your fault, Robson!*' an angry young man had once shouted at him at the club in Tezpur, years ago. '*Those poor runaway bastards. Saw them as a boy. Never forget. No one deserved to die like that.*'

Sam Jackman. He'd been thrown out of the club for disorderly behaviour. At the time James had not understood. But Jackman – amiable and amusing when sober – had gained a reputation for maligning tea planters when in drink. Especially over the coolies' agitation twenty years ago. Some men made excuses for him; he had taken the death of his father, the old steamship captain, badly. James had been less tolerant, indignant at being blamed for any of it.

He sighed deeply, wondering what had become of the ardent young man with a passion for justice, as well as a weakness for cards. He hadn't seen him since the disgraced missionary had visited Belgooree four years ago in the wake of Wesley's death. James winced to recall how spikily unpleasant he had been to the lad at the time. Sam hadn't deserved his needling remarks. James wondered if Jackman had enlisted or whether he still remained in India. Poor Sam; he had been dashed to hear that Adela had gone to England. James now knew what it was like to pine for a woman.

He stood up straight, glancing dolefully at his empty tumbler. Whisky seemed to be one of the luxuries still plentiful in Assam, no matter how perilous their situation. He really ought to cut down. Tilly would be telling him to if she were here. But she wasn't. James felt a fresh wave of anger at his errant wife. He might be dead in a few weeks, bayonetted by the Japanese. Then she'd be full of remorse for abandoning him!

'*Stop feeling sorry for yourself.*' That was what an exasperated Clarrie had said to him when he'd whined to her recently about Tilly. '*Just be glad you have a spouse, even if she's halfway across the world. She's looking after your family after all.*'

James grunted out loud. 'You're right, Clarrie Robson. I've got nothing to complain about. Tilly will come back to me – if there's still somewhere to come back to – when this bloody war is over.'

He turned from the starlit view with a new determination. He would go back to Kohima and force the authorities to begin letting in the refugees. The Oxford would accommodate some – or help them on their way. He wasn't going to be accused a second time of turning a blind eye to suffering.

'If we're all going to die,' James said to the night, 'let us at least fight and die together on Indian soil.'

Chapter 27

October 1943

The Toodle Pips dance trio received a raucous reception from the audience of Land Girls, who were packed into the barn of a stately home in Cumberland.

'They'll eat you alive, Tommy,' Adela teased as she came off the rickety stage with Prue and Helen. They were clad only in black leotards and purple tutus, breathless from singing their signature song, 'Don't Sit Under the Apple Tree'.

Tommy Villiers adjusted his bow tie and winked. 'Thanks for nicely warming up my audience, girls. Now watch the master perform.' He extinguished his half-smoked cigarette, slipped it into his dinner jacket pocket, took a deep breath and sauntered on to the stage.

Prue and Adela watched from the wings. 'Listen to them laughing at his jokes,' said Adela. 'Half of them want to mother him, and the other half want to take him to bed.'

Prue snorted. 'They'd be sorely disappointed. He's only got eyes for Henry Bracknall Junior.'

'Don't be such a gossip,' said Adela, shoving her friend in the arm.

'Well, you know it's true.'

'Henry just gives him a billet when Tommy's in London.'

'Precisely' said Prue, tapping her nose conspiratorially.

'Well,' Adela said with a rueful smile, 'they'd make a lovely couple. Henry is such a sweet, kind man – nothing like his overbearing father.'

'You're not still holding out hope Tommy'll fall in love with you?'

'Course not.' Adela laughed at the idea. 'Even in Simla he was more like a brother than a boyfriend.'

They hurried off to change into their ENSA uniforms. If they got an encore, they'd be ready to sing 'My Hero' from *The Chocolate Soldier*.

What a happy day it had been, Adela recalled, when Tommy had come back in to her life. She'd just done her audition at the Theatre Royal and was waiting tensely in one of the dressing rooms that had been converted into an office. There was an air of excitement and semi-organised anarchy about the place. Beyond the door she'd heard a familiar laugh and ribald comment and had dashed out.

'Tommy Villiers?'

'Adela Robson? Adela, my gorgeous girl! What on earth are you doing here?'

'Come to clean the floors. What do you think I'm doing here?' She had stuck out her tongue and then hugged him.

He had made her a cup of disgusting ersatz coffee while they had caught up on the past three years.

'Came back to help the Mother Country,' Tommy had said, 'in the only way I know how.'

'You never answered my letters about Sophie Khan and whether you might be her brother,' Adela had chided.

'All that weird and wonderful stuff about carved heads on bracelets? Seemed too Agatha Christie for words.'

'Sophie was so hoping to meet you. You could at least have sent a reply.'

Tommy had given her a strange look and dropped his air of insouciance for a moment. 'I'm not sure I want to be reinvented as someone's brother. It would change everything – and I don't want to be changed. I know who Tommy Villiers is. I don't know what sort of person Sophie Khan's brother might be. Does that make any sense to you?'

'Yes, I suppose it does.' She had kissed him on the cheek and never mentioned Sophie again. They had only spoken once about the painful ending to Adela's last summer in Simla and her being ostracised by her theatre friends over her behaviour with Jay. Tommy told her that Nina Davidge's mother had swiftly married a widowed district officer and gone to live in Sialkot, dragging Nina with her.

'Nina wanted to stay in Simla, but her mother wouldn't hear of it. Never thought I'd feel sorry for the girl, but her mother was a gorgon.'

'So Nina never did go to RADA then?' Adela had asked.

Tommy had snorted. 'You have to be able to act to do that.'

Adela had expected to feel a flicker of triumph that the privileged, popular Nina had not had it easy after all. But she felt nothing except a small twinge of pity. The gut-wrenching emotion that the name Nina Davidge had provoked for so many years had vanished.

Deborah Halliday, Tommy told her, had returned to Burma. They had worried about what might have become of the Hallidays, but Tommy had lost touch with Adela's one-time school friend and didn't know. The news from Burma grew ever grimmer, and Adela was always trying to glean information. Her beloved Assam was now on the front line.

The last she'd heard from her mother was that Uncle James had been working himself into the ground directing labour to help build defences. While other companies had pulled out their personnel, the tea planters had rallied round to defend Assam's upper valleys. But there was precious little about it in the newspapers. The censors appeared to be throwing a blanket of secrecy over that theatre of war that just increased her anxiety. Adela had pangs of guilt that she hadn't returned to Belgooree at the start of the war. But how could she possibly have guessed that India would be threatened with invasion by Japan? She knew now the dread that her mother must have experienced at the thought of her only daughter being encircled by the enemy. Yet it was useless to dwell on past decisions, as she could do nothing to change them. So Adela learned how to mask her constant fear for her family and homeland by keeping busy and acting cheerful.

It was when they were putting together a review troupe to tour Scotland in early 1942 that Prudence Knight had walked in, whistling and offering to paint stage scenery. Adela had been overjoyed to meet her old Simla school friend, and when one of the three Toodle Pips went ill with measles, brunette Prue stepped in and took her place. Her dance steps were a bit wooden and not always in time, but Prue had a rich alto voice and enough bravado to make up for it.

Josey sometimes joined them too – when she wasn't in a touring play – and performed in a series of sketches that Tommy had written. The rest of the show was made up of two acrobats who could unicycle, a crooner with a husky smoker's voice, a mediocre ventriloquist and a jaunty band consisting of an accordionist, violinist and drummer who always got feet tapping. If there was a piano at the venue which was moderately in tune and had most of its keys, Adela would also sing solo, with Tommy bashing away on the piano.

For the last eighteen months they had criss-crossed Britain in overcrowded trains and battered trucks with their show – from Newquay in the south to the Orkneys in the far north; from Blackpool in the west to Lincolnshire in the east. They performed in vast army camps, RAF aerodromes, garrison theatres and village halls, sometimes to hundreds of men and at other times to a handful in some remote anti-aircraft battery. They toured hospitals, factories, mines and prisoner-of-war camps. On one occasion, when Tommy's comedy routine was met with silence and stony looks, The Toodle Pips were sent back on to save the show. Afterwards it was discovered that the baffled audience were a group of Polish airmen, who hadn't understood Tommy's quick delivery or humour. Josey had teased him for weeks afterwards. 'Give us your best Polish jokes, Villiers.'

Their schedules were relentless, the travel gruelling and the accommodation often primitive, but they knew they were doing it not just to entertain, but to lift morale among jaded troops and nervous trainees. They were never off-duty on these tours, but expected to socialise and dance afterwards.

'Always make a beeline for the sergeants' mess,' Josey had advised. 'They give you hot meals and lashings of tea – as long as you don't mind it brewed up in the urn with tinned milk and sugar.'

'Sugar?' Tommy had cried. 'What heaven!'

But often the women were monopolised by the officers and ended up in late-night drinking parties and slow dancing. They had been warned at the outset by an ENSA official, 'Be friendly and chat to the boys – they'll need cheering up most likely – but don't be flighty or lead them on.' She had fixed the new girls with a look and said words that made Adela flinch. 'No loose behaviour or babies on tour, do you hear?'

Prue was often quoting this in mock-severe tones, unaware of just how painfully it reminded Adela of her shameful mistake with Jay. Her friend was always one of the last to leave the fun and revelled in the attention.

'You're such a prude,' Prue would tease Adela. 'You won't even let them give you a goodnight kiss.'

'Can't be flighty,' Adela would quip, and change the subject.

When she thought back to her time in Simla and her infatuation with Prince Sanjay, she wondered if that could really have been her. She could think of him with dispassion now – he'd been handsome and charming – but she felt no flicker of desire or emotion towards him. But Sam was another matter. She looked at the young officers and soldiers who were eager for friendship, and none of them stirred her heart in the way Sam still did. Sometimes she would glimpse a ruffled head of fair hair or a pair of muscled shoulders that made her insides somersault, and for a split second she thought she had found him again, was desperate for it to be Sam. Always her hopes were dashed, and she would turn away and hide her desolation. Adela knew she would never be able to fall for another man the way she had for Sam. It made it easier to resist the advances of other men yet left her feeling alone and yearning for what she couldn't have.

After the show in Cumberland to the Land Girls, Adela and her companions travelled south. With one week left of their six-week tour, conversation turned to what they might do next. Tommy raised the subject of going abroad.

'You know they're wanting more of us to volunteer for North Africa now that the Germans have surrendered there. Desert is positively groaning with army boys with not enough to keep them from going mad with heat and boredom.'

'I'd heard ENSA is wanting to send touring parties further east to India,' said Josey.

'India?' Adela felt a quickening of interest. 'Really?'

'I heard Basil Dean discussing it when I was last in London. Thinks Mountbatten's South East Asia Command troops are being neglected as far as entertainment goes – they're the forgotten army.'

'You'll not get me going out there,' said Helen, a fellow Toodle Pip. 'It's all disease and creepy-crawlies and horrible heat, isn't it?'

'Not all the time,' Tommy said, winking at Adela.

'Do you think there's a real chance ENSA will get sent there?' Adela asked.

'Not if we're all as squeamish as Helen,' Josey said in derision.

'Would you sign up for it if you could?' Tommy asked her.

Adela didn't hesitate. 'Yes. What about you?'

Tommy looked unsure.

Prue said, 'I'll go if Adela does. Come on, Tommy, we're The Simla Songsters. We have to stick together.'

Tommy gave a wry smile. 'I'd much rather stay in Blighty and see out the war here. But if you insist on making me sail dangerous seas to perform in a country on the point of being invaded, then I suppose I must.'

'You're such a drama queen, Villiers,' snorted Josey. 'I might just have to come too.'

***

By November Adela, Prue, Tommy and Josey had signed up for a nine-month contract to the Middle East and India. Blonde Helen resolutely refused to go, so they replaced her with an older dancer called Mavis, who claimed she'd once been a Bluebell Girl in Paris.

'The Bluebell Inn at Pontefract more likely,' Tommy muttered to Adela.

'Her dancing is okay and she's got a blonde wig,' Adela replied, 'so let's take her.'

The only other one from their review who was prepared to go all the way to India was the accordionist, a middle-aged Scot simply known as Mack. Tommy complained at the paucity of talent going with them.

'An impressionist who can't do anyone famous, a juggler who drops everything and an alcoholic magician. Oh, and not one but *three* ukulele players. I can't stand the ukulele.'

'Well, the boys will love them,' said Josey.

'We'll be laughed off stage.'

'Laughter is better than booing.' Adela smiled. 'And you'll look after them all like a mother hen, just like you do us.'

With passports and nine inoculations in order, costumes made and scripts and routines practised, Adela and Josey managed to get away to Tyneside for a final week of leave before embarkation. Taking a night train, Josey found no difficulty in falling asleep on a prickly seat, but Adela's nervous excitement kept her awake. She hadn't been back to Newcastle for over a year. Since then George had come back from flight training long enough to marry Joan, which had lifted Olive's spirits, according to a letter from Jane; her cousin was working in Yorkshire, helping operate searchlights and an anti-aircraft gun. Her letter sounded happy, and she got home every few weeks, but had missed her brother's snap wedding in July.

'*A small do – registry office and tea at Number 10. Lexy made a cake. Joan's moved in with Mam and Father.*'

That had really surprised Adela. She wondered how Joan would cope with being at Olive's beck and call. But perhaps Joan's placid nature would be good for Olive, and Adela was glad Jack had someone who could share the burden of keeping Olive's melancholia at bay.

Tilly was as busy as ever with her WVS duties and still had one of the Polish refugees lodging with her. Libby had left school at seventeen and for a while had returned to Newcastle to volunteer at the services' canteen again. The last letter from Tilly had said that Libby, now eighteen, had enlisted and been drafted into the Land Army. She was working on a farm near Morpeth in Northumberland, and Tilly complained she hardly saw her now. Lexy never wrote; she just waited for Adela to turn up and resume their friendship. The thought of seeing her soon brought a wide smile to Adela's lips.

Rattling over the High Level Bridge as the dawn broke over a smoke-hazed Newcastle, Adela leant out and breathed in the acrid smell of coal fires and felt a pang of affection for her adopted home. The women went straight to Herbert's Café for breakfast and received an ecstatic welcome from Lexy.

'Why didn't you say you were coming, lass? I'd have got something special baked.'

'Didn't know till the last minute. We've brought you jam, coffee and American chocolate bars,' Adela said and grinned. 'Been saving them from our trip to a US airbase.'

Adela was astonished to find Maggie working in the café kitchen and living with Lexy.

'Old Ina died in October,' Maggie explained. 'She didn't suffer, but she'd had enough. Hated all them sirens and that. Thought I was her daughter at the end.'

'Dear Ina,' Adela said, her eyes prickling with emotion to think of her weeks of refuge in the old lady's house nearly five years ago. Ina had given her sanctuary when her own aunt had not. It all seemed a lifetime ago.

Over a meal of scrambled powdered egg, thin rashers of bacon and fried bread, Adela caught up on all the news. The most startling was that George's new bride, Joan, had given birth to a baby the previous month.

'A baby?' Adela exclaimed. 'But—'

'Aye,' said Lexy, 'three months after the weddin'. We can all do the sums. It's a lass. Joan's called her Bonnie after that bairn in *Gone with the Wind.*'

Adela felt her insides clench. She tried to hide how flustered the sudden news made her. 'Well, she always did like going to the pictures,' Adela joked.

'She certainly does,' Josey agreed, 'and not always with George.'

They all stared at her.

'What do you mean?' Adela asked.

'Oh, nothing,' Josey said. 'Don't listen to me.'

Adela tried to shake off her upset feeling. 'Bet George is pleased to be a dad.' She forced a smile.

'He hasn't seen the baby yet,' Lexy replied. 'His ship sailed for Ceylon the week before the birth.'

'Oh, that's terrible,' Adela cried. 'Poor George.'

'Aye,' Lexy said and sighed, 'and poor bairn. Not likely to set eyes on her dadda till this war's over.'

A silence fell over them. How uncertain life was for all of them, Adela thought. There might be signs of the war turning in their favour in North Africa and southern Italy – and the Russians had held off the Nazis in Eastern Europe – but most of the Continent was still in enemy hands.

'Come on.' Josey roused her from jittery thoughts. 'Let's go and see Tilly. We can leave baby worship and the Brewises till later.'

'Yes, let's.' Adela smiled gratefully. She was far closer to Tilly than she would ever be to her own flesh-and-blood aunt, and Josey knew that.

***

Both Adela and Josey stayed at Tilly's house for the week; Josey found Tilly's easy-going household refreshing, and Tilly mothered her as much as she did Adela. They had a carefree few days, dropping into the café daily and visiting Derek and their friends at the theatre, who were gearing up for a production of Oscar Wilde's satire *The Importance of Being Earnest*.

'It's the nearest I'll ever get to putting on a panto,' Derek said with a lugubrious smile.

Libby, on hearing that her cousin and friend were briefly in Newcastle, hitched a ride in a milk delivery lorry to come and see them.

As she bounded in and greeted them with robust hugs, Adela was amazed how Libby had suddenly grown into a woman. She had lost her childhood plumpness, and her body was toned and fit from outdoor work. Even her face seemed to have changed shape from round to oval, accentuating her plump mouth and her deep blue eyes, which still flashed with a familiar bold look. There was a sprinkling of freckles across her small nose that added to her prettiness and air of good health. Her unruly waves of dark red hair shone like fire in the wintry sun.

'Libby, you look wonderful!' Adela cried. 'Your mother never told me how pretty you've grown.'

'No, she wouldn't,' said Libby, giving a deep-throated laugh.

'She's always been pretty,' Tilly said without really sounding like she meant it.

They spent a happy winter's afternoon by Tilly's kitchen fire, toasting stale bread and drinking tea from a special hoard that James had managed to send from the Oxford. Libby stayed the night and left before dawn.

'I'll catch a lift going up the Great North Road,' she told her fretting mother. 'Be back for breakfast. They won't have missed me.' She turned to a sleepy Adela, who was wrapped in a blanket, yawning.

'I'm so jealous that you're going to India,' she said. 'You'll see Daddy before I will.'

'I hope to get to Assam,' said Adela, 'but who knows where we'll be sent?' She smiled sympathetically. 'Any messages for him if I do?'

Alarmingly she saw tears well up in the girl's eyes; Libby hardly ever cried.

'Tell him I send my love,' she said, her voice cracking, 'and that we'll all come back as soon as we can. Tell him that.'

Libby planted a swift kiss on Adela's warm cheek and then bolted into the dark.

***

With two days left of leave, Adela realised she couldn't put off going to visit Aunt Olive any longer. She was baffled by her own reluctance to do so. Perhaps it was just the effort of being cheerful in the face of her aunt's habitual complaining.

'Will you come with me?' she asked Josey.

'Reinforcements at the ready,' Josey agreed.

To Adela's delight she found her aunt in better spirits than she'd ever seen her. Olive greeted them at the door in a bright blue dress instead of her usual drab black or grey, and her hair was neatly permed.

'Come in, come in! I heard you were back. Thought you would have been round before now.'

'Sorry, Aunt Olive—'

'Well, you're here now. Come away in, the pair of you.'

The sitting room was still painted in its bright colours and the sombre furniture had been covered over with gaudy blankets and pushed back to allow baby paraphernalia. Joan, her blonde hair swept up in a loose bun and her figure voluptuous in a loose shift and long cardigan, looked up from kneeling on a baby blanket, and smiled.

'Hello, Joan,' said Adela, stepping nearer. 'I hear double congratulations are in order.'

As Joan shifted to one side, Adela saw the baby wriggling on the blanket. She was dressed in a yellow woollen suit, and her starlike hands were waving. She gave out tiny popping noises from her pink bud lips. Adela stopped in her tracks.

'Hello, Adela. This is Bonnie.' Joan swept the baby from the blanket and into her arms and stood up. She kissed her daughter's fluff of fair hair and lapsed into a babyish voice. 'You're Mammy's good little lass, aren't you, bonny Bonnie? Yes you *are*! Come and say hello to your cousin Adela. She's a famous actress. Yes she *is*.'

Beaming with pride, Joan advanced towards Adela and held out her baby. Adela froze. She couldn't look at it. Her eyes met Joan's. The young woman's look was bashful, expectant. Adela knew she was longing for her approval. As Adela made no move to take the infant, Joan's blissful look faltered.

'Go on, she won't bite.'

'Yes, go on,' encouraged Olive. 'She's a little jewel – my first grandchild. I've beaten Clarrie there, haven't I?' Her aunt gave a small triumphant laugh. It was as if Olive had wiped from her memory that Adela had ever been pregnant or given birth.

Adela felt sick; her pulse began to race. She couldn't bear to touch the baby. Her heart would shatter into tiny pieces. She took a step backwards.

'Sorry, I'm hopeless with babies.' She forced a laugh. 'Don't want to drop it . . . her.'

Josey intervened. 'Here, let me. I never get the chance.' She almost snatched Bonnie from Joan's arms. The baby wailed at the sudden movement, but Josey walked to the window, joggling her in her arms and singing, 'I'm Just Wild About Harry', adapted to Bonnie's name.

It gave Adela long enough to recover her poise. They stayed half an hour – to Adela each minute was purgatory, as Olive and Joan talked endlessly of the baby – until Bonnie needed feeding. Joan took her baby to the kitchen so Bonnie could suckle in the warmth of the back room. As Josey said goodbye to Olive at the door, Adela braced herself to nip into the kitchen to apologise to Joan. She felt awful for disappointing George's wife and didn't want her to think she didn't like her baby. Joan was sitting in a low chair, the baby snuffling but hidden under a shawl.

'We're off now. She's gorgeous, your Bonnie. Suits the name. Sorry about before.'

Joan eyed her. 'I know what you're thinking. That I'm not good enough for George.'

Adela was taken aback. 'I never thought—'

'You think I'm too common for your cousin. But now we're married and everything's canny.'

'I'm glad for you.'

'And it doesn't matter if the bairn came three months after we were wed. At least Bonnie was born in wedlock and I've got a ring on me finger. That's what matters, isn't it?'

Adela felt her heart begin to pound. 'Yes, that's good.'

Joan gave a pitying look. 'Not like you.'

For a moment Adela couldn't breathe. She gripped on to the door frame.

'I don't know what you mean.'

'Aye, you do,' said Joan. 'I saw you in Cullercoats walking along the cliff when you were supposed to be in Edinburgh. I was on a bus. It was dark, but I could still tell it was you. You were big enough to burst. I never said anything to your family. I felt sorry for you.'

Adela swallowed hard. 'Thank you.'

'And I won't ever,' said Joan. 'Just as long as your friend doesn't go telling tales about me.'

'Josey?'

'Aye, her.' Joan blushed. 'I was being friendly, that's all. It's what us lasses do to help the war effort, isn't it? We have to bring comfort to the lads.'

Adela was baffled. 'She won't say anything against you, I promise.'

'Did you give your bairn away?' Joan asked.

Adela's chest constricted as she nodded.

Joan put a protective hand on Bonnie's head. 'I can't imagine doing that. I'm sorry for you, I really am. Would the lad not stand by you?'

'No,' Adela whispered.

'George would never have left me in the lurch.'

'No, George is a good man.' Adela's eyes stung with tears. 'Take care of yourself and Bonnie.' Adela managed a smile and, before Joan could ask anything more, fled from the stifling kitchen with its smell of milk and baby.

***

Josey took her for a walk. They sat on a park bench in the chilly dank November air while Adela poured out her heart. She told her friend everything about her affair, the pregnancy and giving away her baby – the pain that had not diminished over the years, but had grown into a hard knot of regret deep inside.

'I've never told as much to anyone before,' Adela said tearfully, drained after the telling. 'The only people I thought knew were Lexy, Maggie, Aunt Olive and her cleaner, Myra. Jane might have guessed, but never asked. Yet all this time Joan knew as well. Why didn't she say anything?'

'Maybe she really did feel sorry for you,' Josey said. 'Joan is not the brightest penny in the till, but she's not so stupid that she can't imagine it happening to her. If it hadn't been for George hastily marrying her, she would have been in the same boat.'

'What is it that you know about her?' Adela asked.

'I saw her with another man at an after-show party last year. Sub lieutenant in the navy. Dancing cheek to cheek they were. One of his shipmates said his friend was head over heels, so I got the impression it wasn't the first time she'd met him.'

'And she recognised you too? Was she embarrassed?'

Josey gave a short laugh. 'Not in the least. Came right up to me and said how much she'd enjoyed the show, and did I have news of you? There really isn't much mental activity going on between her ears.'

'Poor George,' said Adela.

'Maybe it's what he wants,' Josey said with a shrug, 'an uncomplicated pretty wife at home to think about while he's overseas.'

'I hope so.'

***

On her last day in Newcastle, Adela chose to be alone. She took the train down to the coast and the row of cottages at Cullercoats, and stood in front of the old coastguard's cottage where she had lived with Maggie and Ina – and given birth to her son. For the first time in nearly five years Adela allowed herself to remember – *really* remember – what it had been like to give birth. She had been so young and her feelings so confused; she'd been frightened, ashamed, resolute, shocked at the pain yet exhilarated to survive and to hold a new life in her arms. A baby boy: a warm, blood-pumping, heart-beating, squalling, bright-eyed boy with dark hair as soft as duck down and a trusting look. Her breasts tingled as she thought of his suckling. John Wesley. Her sweet son.

Only the sight of baby Bonnie, her cousin's beautiful daughter, had finally brought home to her what she had given up. Bonnie had torn open the emotional wound that she had managed to cauterise the day she had abandoned her boy.

Adela stood on the cobbles in the raw sea air and allowed a gigantic wave of remorse and sorrow to engulf her. She had been so determined to put the pregnancy behind her and to dismiss her affair with Jay as a terrible, juvenile mistake. At the time she had considered the baby as a nuisance, a shameful secret to be hidden away.

Yet the boy had been *hers* too and not just a manifestation of a past lover for whom her feelings had long since vanished. Somewhere out in the world she had a son. Did he look like her or like Jay? Did he have his grandmother Clarrie's nose or his grandfather Wesley's eyes? Did he run like Harry or have long dextrous fingers like the Rajah's? Adela would never know. As she turned from the cottage with tears stinging her cold cheeks, she prayed that he was safe and healthy and being loved. She hoped that, after all, he had been taken safely to Canada or America to a life of opportunity and the clean outdoors.

The beaches along the coast were fenced off and the promenades still restricted, despite the threat of imminent invasion having long past. Adela took a back lane towards the station and found herself at the end of the street where Jackman's Sewing Shop stood. She stopped outside. Was Sam's mother equally remorseful for having turned her back on her only son? Was it ever too late to try and heal the wounds of betrayal that Sam felt so keenly? Perhaps it was within Adela's power to attempt to mend the rift between him and his estranged mother.

There was a handwritten notice in the window advertising an alteration and mending service. There was no light on in the shop on this dull grey day, but she tried the door anyway. It opened with a tinkle of a bell. The same woman she had seen behind the counter several years ago was sitting in the pool of light from the shop window, round spectacles poised on the end of her nose, sewing the hem of a utility skirt. Less plump and a lot greyer than before but recognisably the same woman.

'Can I help you, dear?' She looked up and smiled. She didn't look like the type of woman who would walk out on a husband and a small son. But then who was she to judge?

'I'm Adela Robson. I was brought up in Assam on a tea estate. Belgooree. Did you used to live in Assam, Mrs Jackman?'

The woman looked at her in astonishment, her mouth falling open. After a moment she nodded. 'A very long time ago.'

'It's just that I'm a friend of Sam Jackman's,' Adela ploughed on before her courage failed. 'And I wondered if he was . . . if he is your son.'

The woman half rose. Her sewing dropped to the floor. 'Sam?' she gasped. 'You know my Sam?'

Adela nodded. Mrs Jackman burst into tears.

***

Later Adela talked it over with Tilly and Josey: the spur-of-the-moment encounter and Marjory Jackman's emotional outpouring.

'She insisted that she'd never meant to abandon Sam, wanted to take him with her, but old man Jackman wouldn't hear of it. Marjory said she couldn't stand another minute of India – the climate, the isolation, her husband taking her for granted.'

'I can sympathise with that,' Tilly murmured.

'She said they had terrible rows. She told him he should just as well have hired a housekeeper rather than married her. And why had he dragged her all the way out there just to ignore her and live on his blessed boat all the time? Marjory said she'd have gone back to England sooner if it hadn't been for Sam.'

'But she did desert Sam, didn't she?' Josey pointed out.

'She claimed her husband threatened her with the police. She made arrangements to take Sam anyway, but Jackman took him on the boat and wouldn't let her see him, so she knew her husband would never let Sam go.'

'What a terrible dilemma,' said Josey.

'I'd still have stayed,' said Tilly. 'At least I think I would have – for Sam's sake. He was only very young, wasn't he?'

'About seven I think,' said Adela, feeling a stab of pain. Not a lot older than her lost son was now.

'So why didn't she fight harder for poor Sam?' asked Josey.

Adela sighed. 'Marjory was pretty hard on herself. Said that her husband, for all his faults towards her, was a good father to their boy. A better parent than she was.' Adela swallowed, feeling tearful. 'She gave up Sam because she thought he'd be better off with his father.'

'What sort of mother does that?' Tilly exclaimed.

Josey gave Adela a sympathetic glance. 'A brave one.'

They lapsed into silence. Tilly broke it. 'So did she give you a message for Sam?'

'She wanted his address so she could write to him, but I've no idea where Sam is.' Adela felt her heart squeeze. 'So I gave her Mother's address at Belgooree. Said we'd try and find out through Dr Black; send on any letters if and when we know Sam's whereabouts.'

'That was kind of you,' said Tilly. 'Though from what you've said of Sam, he might not thank you.'

'No,' Adela admitted, 'he'll probably be mad at me for interfering. But isn't it better that he knows that his mother cared for him and didn't want to leave him?' Her throat tightened with emotion.

'Yes, of course it is,' agreed Josey.

'I hope you manage to track Sam down.' Tilly gave an encouraging smile. 'Just think: in a few weeks' time you'll be back in India.'

Excitement fizzed inside Adela at the sudden thought. After the emotional turmoil of the last few days, she clung to the thought with hope. How she longed at that moment for her mother and home! For the first time in over five years, she knew she was ready to return to the land of her birth.

Chapter 28

India, 1944

It was February before Adela finally reached India again. They had spent a month in North Africa on the way, entertaining at military hospitals and desert camps, before taking the train to the end of the Suez Canal and embarking at Port Tewfik on SS *Port Ellen*. It was a small ship carrying parts for Spitfires and Hurricanes, with only a couple of hundred passengers, mainly American airmen and Royal Navy personnel. Their passage on a large troop carrier through the Mediterranean in December had been anxious – a ship carrying ENSA members had been torpedoed two months earlier – but Adela felt no such fear as they steamed across the Red Sea to meet a naval escort at Aden.

The sight of porpoises and flying fish leaping from the azure sea had quickened her excitement for the East and quelled any nerves at their daily emergency boat drill and submarine watch. How she wished Josey had been with her to share her excitement, but her friend had come down with pneumonia on the eve of departure and was still convalescing in Newcastle at Tilly's. With huge disappointment, Adela had gone without her.

Prue, however, had been enjoying the attention of an American airman called Stuey, with whom she played regular deck tennis and cards. She and Adela had slept out on deck under the stars so that Prue could chat late into the night with Stuey. Adela had lain restless, wondering if she would be able to get to Belgooree during the tour. And now she had this new quest on behalf of Marjorie Jackman to put her in touch with Sam, which gave Adela an excuse to discover what had become of him.

Her greatest fear was that Sam had settled down somewhere with Pema and begun a family. But she had to know; not knowing was ten times worse. Lying on the warm deck, she would be beset by old doubts; Sam's feelings had never been as strong as hers, and once he knew her shameful secret, even those feelings might be blighted.

Adela clung to the thought of getting back home; Belgooree would be a balm on her sore heart. And there was the joyous possibility of seeing her beloved Auntie Sophie.

Rafi had been seconded to timber production for the forces and was based at the Gun Carriage Factory in Jubbulpore. Even though he travelled all over India sourcing timber and inspecting factory production, Sophie had set up temporary home in the garrison town. Prue's parents were also still living there, and the two friends had talked excitedly about the likelihood of them getting to see their loved ones. But by the time the tugboats and small islands around Bombay hove into view, Prue's talk was only of her romance with Stuey. She declared she was head over heels in love with the airman from North Carolina and that they were unofficially engaged until Stuey could seek her father's approval.

'I predict that will be the first of many plightings of troth for our dear Prue,' Tommy said dryly, tapping out his pipe. He had taken to smoking one since leaving London; even though he didn't like the taste, he thought it made him look distinguished.

'God this place pongs!' cried Mavis. 'Worse that the fish quay in Grimsby.'

The city was teeming with servicemen in uniform, alongside the brilliant colours of sari-wearing women and the dazzling white suits of high-caste Hindus. Mavis was full of complaints about the state of the dingy and overcrowded hostel where they were billeted. Adela took her out sightseeing before Tommy choked on his pipe with exasperation. But the things that were endearingly familiar to Adela – the oily smells of cooking, and the red spit from paan chewing that spattered the ground – caused Mavis to squeal with horror and retreat indoors.

Mavis had the knack of irritating others without realising it. Tommy couldn't forgive her for ruining their first show in Egypt; it was only then that they had discovered she sang out of tune. After that, Tommy had ordered her to mime the words to all The Toodle Pips' songs, while Betsie, one of the ukulele players, sang off stage on her behalf.

They hardly saw Prue for three days while she spent snatched hours with Stuey, eating ice cream at the Taj Mahal Hotel and going to dances. Then the troupe was boarding a train for Lahore, and Prue was saying a tearful goodbye to her American fiancé. From Lahore they travelled by truck along dusty roads to Rawalpindi and stayed in Flashman's Hotel while they gave two performances every day for a week to the many servicemen billeted in the army town. Every night they were entertained at mess parties and plied with whisky while the officers gossiped and asked for news of home.

The next month was spent in the north of India. They toured the tribal territory of the North-West Frontier under an armed escort of Sikh soldiers in a convoy of lorries that kept breaking down. Adela and Prue wore bandanas to keep the dust off their hair, and Mavis moaned about her feet swelling in the heat.

'Call this heat?' Tommy derided. 'This is a spring picnic. Wait till we get to Calcutta and Bengal – fires of hell. That's when you'll really start to melt.'

The days were hot in the rocky, barren hills around Peshawar, but the nights were still cool. They performed to pilots training with the Indian Air Force, to Gurkha soldiers and British conscripts. The paratroopers at one remote camp made so much noise with rude comments and ribald laughter that they could hardly hear themselves sing.

'ENSA – Every Night Something Awful!' one shouted out when the juggler dropped his batons for the third time.

They mocked the impressionist and booed the ukuleles. At his wits' end, Tommy sent The Toodle Pips back on again, which received rousing cheers.

'Think I prefer the officers' wives knitting in the front row at Rawalpindi to this lot,' Mavis panted, her face beetroot red and her blonde wig awry after a final encore.

They travelled on to Risalpore, where they played to RAF audiences. Then March came and they moved up into the hills around Murree. Leaving the plain, with its walled villages, temples and bullocks, they climbed steep, winding roads surrounded by thick emerald-green bushes. As they gained altitude quickly, Adela felt a jolt of familiarity. She leant out of the truck window and breathed in the sweet scent of pine and was transported back to Simla.

Arriving in the hill station of Murree, Adela was struck by how similar it was to her former home in the British-Indian capital. Wooden bungalows, hotels and shops were strung out along a ridge, which was milling with rickshaws, the road being closed to motor traffic. It too had a Cecil Hotel, with dizzying views over a sheer drop away to the distant hazy blue plain, and a bazaar spilling down the hillside that throbbed with activity and noise in the rarefied air.

The chalet where they were staying, with its flight of wooden steps up from the hotel lawn and the glimpse of Himalayan mountains beyond the fir trees, reminded Adela nostalgically of her home with Fluffy Hogg. Her eyes smarted to think of her carefree life with her kind guardian. Fluffy had kept in touch by occasional letter. From her she knew that Sundar Singh had distinguished himself in North Africa fighting the Italians and that Boz had re-joined the army and was training mortar gunners. Fatima was still at the hospital in Simla, working all hours. But there had never been any more news of Sam or where he had gone.

Adela stood on the veranda, gazing at the peaks of Kashmir, and felt anew the sharp tug of longing for Sam Jackman. She was older and wiser than the impulsive seventeen-year-old who had fallen so deeply for the handsome former steam captain that heady spring of '38, but her feelings for him had not abated. Despite the intervening years and the separation of continents, she knew she still loved him – and now back in India, that love flared ever stronger. It had taken just the sweet smell of pines and the sight of snowy peaks to conjure up Sam's lean smiling face and vital eyes, his deep laughter and passionate talk.

From the breast pocket of her uniform, Adela drew the photograph of her with Sam at Narkanda. It was creased and dog-eared from use, but the image of Sam still set her heart hammering.

'Where are you, Sam?' she whispered.

Adela vowed to herself that she would not leave India a second time without knowing what had happened to him.

***

'Dancing up here is worse than the heat,' Mavis gasped. 'You can't catch your breath.'

Her litany of complaints had gone on all month as they ventured to outlying camps. They travelled up hairpin bends, where the narrow road was sometimes washed away, and had to clamber out of vehicles while their drivers negotiated the ruts and avoided toppling into ravines. At other times they had to squeeze past oncoming local buses, with only inches to spare above dizzying drops. One evening, as the temperature plummeted their truck skidded and slewed towards the cliff edge. The driver ordered them all out as he fought for traction and managed to regain the bend.

'Got nerves of steel, these Indian laddies,' accordionist Mack said in admiration.

'They're hopeless mechanics,' Mavis retorted. 'The motor vehicles are always breaking down.'

'Well, go by bloody mule then!' Prue snapped. 'There's a war on and we're not priority. They do their best.'

Tempers were frayed after the nonstop series of shows and the nerve-racking travel. They shared tin-roofed huts with giant red cockroaches and changed for shows all together in the same small tent, without chairs or mirrors. Monkeys invaded and ran off with costume jewellery and hats, the juggler got dysentery and the magician fell off a rickety stage and broke a leg. They had to leave him behind in a hospital in Abbottabad, to follow on when he could travel. And Mavis had a point about the thin air: singing required double breaths that left the singers feeling faint.

For Adela, all the tension and exhaustion was worth it for the moments of comradeship with the men – seeing their faces relax as they enjoyed the show and forgot about the war for a few precious moments. They danced in mess tents with the sound of jackals in the forests beyond and sat cross-legged with troops around campfires singing all the songs they could think of until they grew hoarse. The women were in high demand as penfriends for homesick conscripts, who were on the verge of being sent into action in Burma.

'Be my girl and write to me' was a constant refrain. Prue took on the task with enthusiasm.

'What about Stuey?' Mavis pointed out. 'You've already got a man.'

'Most of these boys have also got girlfriends,' said Prue. 'That's not the point. They just want letters. It's what they live for.'

Nobody would tell the entertainers what their impending orders were, but it was obvious that the fightback against the Japanese army on the fringes of India's eastern borders had begun. The mood in the camps was jittery.

Adela and Tommy had renewed an old habit of slipping off to the cinema together whenever there was a free afternoon at their base in Murree to watch out-of-date newsreels. There was footage of General Orde Wingate and his guerrilla force, the Chindits, being airlifted into Burma, and reports of their successes, but the film was six months old. From what Adela could glean, there had been fierce fighting on the Arakan peninsula near Chittagong since December. What she wanted to know was the present situation further north, on the Assam border.

When they returned to Murree from Abbottabad, there was a letter awaiting her from her mother. Adela sat on the chalet steps and read it eagerly. Clarrie and Harry were well and managing things at Belgooree. Her mother was worried about James pushing himself to the point of exhaustion, taking on numerous civil defence duties, as well as the work of the plantations.

'I've forbidden him to come to Belgooree while the present crisis is on,' wrote Clarrie, 'as I can manage perfectly well with Daleep's and Banu's help.'

What present crisis was she referring to, Adela worried? Was it the war in general or Assam in particular? Familiar tension curdled in her stomach.

I had a visit from Sophie last week. She has volunteered with the Red Cross as a driver and was on her way up to Dimapur in Upper Assam. She is so plucky and brave. It doesn't seem to bother her that she is heading into a war zone – she was as cheerful as ever. She said that Rafi fully supported what she was doing – besides, he's away such a lot that she hardly sees him. She is very excited to think she might come across your show and see you if you are sent up to Dimapur. Selfishly, I hope you won't go anywhere near. There's never any mention in the press about the Japanese being on Indian soil, but from what James tells me, Imphal is under threat and Kohima too – do you remember playing tennis up there with your father one Christmas holiday? One of his fishing friends had a bungalow with a tennis court. How long ago that all seems now.

Adela could hear the longing in her mother's words. It was nearly six years since her father's death. For Adela, the pain of loss had eased to the point where she could think about him and smile rather than be choked with tears. But she sensed that, for her mother, the grief was as raw as ever.

Adela was folding up the letter when she saw a postscript on the back. Her heart skipped a beat to see Sam's name.

PS As you asked me to, I wrote to Dr Black to see if he knew the whereabouts of Sam Jackman. I just heard back last week. It seems that Sam enlisted with the Royal Air Force. Dr Black says he was on operations in Iraq, but since returning to India he's been assigned to the film unit. The doctor is not sure where he is, though he suspects it might be Chittagong or somewhere on the battlefront, but a letter care of the Public Relations Directorate in Delhi would probably catch up with him eventually.

Adela's heart thudded at the unexpected news. So Sam was an airman and working in films. She felt light-headed. For so long she had known nothing, had invented a dozen stories of what might have become of him, but never guessed that he'd joined the RAF. The relief of finally knowing made her euphoric. He would be in his element behind a camera, even if it was just propaganda newsreels and photographs. But her joy turned quickly to dread to think he might be on the embattled Burmese border. Was he still flying for the RAF too? Or was he part of the ground crew? All the rest of the day she see-sawed between exhilaration at knowing what had become of Sam and anxiety to think of him in constant danger.

***

A week later, in early April, they were packing up and heading back to the plain.

'Typical disorganised ENSA,' Mavis grumbled. 'Just as everyone else is heading for the hills in the hot weather, we're being sent back to fry in the sun.'

To Adela and Prue's disappointment, the planned tour to Jubbulpore was cancelled and instead they were sent to Bihar to perform to camps of field companies: engineers, gunners, transport and supplies men and medics. The heat became fierce and the dust blew into everything.

'Now you know what it means to sing through gritted teeth,' Tommy joked.

Adela found herself endlessly trying to soothe tempers among her fellow dancers and keep Mavis and Prue apart, except on stage. Prue fretted that she wouldn't get to see Stuey before he was deployed to Burma. His training in southern India was over. They picked up an anxious rumour from loose talk in the officers' mess that Imphal was besieged and that there was fierce fighting around Kohima. The supply basis at Dimapur was under threat. If the Japanese broke through at Kohima, then Dimapur and the rest of Assam would be theirs for the taking. Adela wore herself out worrying about Sophie in the front line and James and his fellow tea planters at imminent risk. Belgooree was a few days' march from there. But there was no official news of any conflict; the authorities had brought down a safety curtain of ominous silence. She tried to keep her fears to herself and put on a brave face, but Tommy understood.

'Singing and dancing are your weapons,' he said, giving her a hug, 'so go out and use them. With a voice like yours, we're not going to lose India.'

***

By May they were on their way to Calcutta, a journey that should have taken three days. Five days of slow trains, stopping at endless chaotic stations and Mavis complaining about everything from kerosene-tasting tea to the stench of dung fires pushed Prue to breaking point.

'If you don't shut up, I'm going to ram this tiffin tin into your miserable mouth and push you off the train!'

'There's no need talk like that,' Mavis said, quite taken aback.

'There's every need. You're driving us all mad.'

'I'm just saying what everyone else is thinking,' panted Mavis, fanning herself with an old newspaper. 'India is stinky and sweaty and we all want to go home.'

'No,' Prue cried, 'the only stinky and sweaty person here is you! I knew you should never have come. You can't sing and you're only a half-decent dancer. Call yourself a Bluebell? The nearest you ever got to a bluebell was in a wood.'

'Well, I've never been so offended!' Mavis spluttered. 'And if we're talking about dancing, you dance like you've got two left feet.'

Adela tried to intervene. 'That's enough, both of you. Let's all just calm down and try to get some sleep. It's just the heat talking.'

'I'm not going to dance with her again,' declared Mavis, 'not till she apologises.'

'Apologise?' Prue exclaimed. 'You're the one who should be apologising to the whole show for being the worst performer. We'd be better off with two Toodle Pips rather than two plus a panting elephant.'

'That's it!' shouted Mavis, puce-faced. 'I'm not dancing with you ever again.' She turned to Adela, her eyes welling with tears. 'You'll have to decide.'

'Decide what?'

'Which of us you want as your other Pip. My Pip suits your Pip better than her Pip.'

At that moment Adela caught Tommy's look. He always kept out of the arguments, but she could see him trying to suppress a snort of laughter at Mavis's plea about pips. Adela felt a laugh bubble up inside. She clapped a hand over her mouth, but couldn't stop it. In seconds both she and Tommy were doubled up and clutching their stomachs from spasms of laughter, filling the fetid carriage with their hoots of amusement. Mavis burst into tears. Prue looked at them as if they had lost their senses. But it was infectious, and soon the whole carriage was in giggles, even Mavis, relieving the frayed nerves from months on the road and the ever-present fear of being invaded.

***

Calcutta was a shock. Adela had not seen it for six years, but she was appalled at the scenes of destitution along the railway tracks. She had heard from her mother about a terrible famine in Bengal the previous year – there had been almost no news of it back in Britain – but nothing had prepared her for the grim sights that still lingered. Skeletal naked people with shrivelled limbs and huge staring eyes in skull-like heads lay by the rails or under bushes. It was impossible to tell if they were men or women; they were just husks of their former selves. Adela was nauseated. How could it possibly have got this bad? Surely the authorities could have done something for them.

Outside the station was also crowded with the moribund. The ENSA group looked about them in disbelief. Adela saw some of them recoil as sticklike arms gestured towards them for food. Their army escort instructed them firmly not to give away their rations.

'Sorry, but those are the rules. You'll get used to it I'm afraid.'

Adela knew about Indian poverty and beggars who lived by alms, but this was wretchedness on a sickening scale. She wondered what the effect must be on Indian troops to see their fellow citizens reduced to skin and bone, dying in front of their eyes. What would Rafi think, and had he seen the effects of the famine on his travels? For a moment she thought of Rafi's brother Ghulam, so passionate and angry about the treatment of Indians under the British. Adela had no idea what had become of him.

They hurried from the sound of empty tin bowls being tapped on the hard ground and the sour smell of rotting humanity, guilty at their healthy flesh and the knowledge that they would be fed that night.

Central Calcutta, around Chowringhee Street, where the city teemed with troops and airmen on R&R from the China-Burma theatre of war, was a different world. Here, the bars, hotels, cinemas, clubs and ice-cream parlours were busy with trade and awash with money as British and Americans spent their pay.

Adela and her fellow players were taken to the Grand Hotel. It advertised seven-course meals and the downstairs dining room was packed with young officers entertaining servicewomen and Anglo-Indian secretaries. Jazz played in the crowded bar while the drinkers knocked back gins and lime and talked about sport and home. But the bedrooms were airless and cramped. That night Adela lay sweating and sleepless as a single fan turned the hot soupy air and she listened to someone throwing up in the room next door.

Two days later they were sent off to Panegar, SEAC's vast camp for the Burma front, situated on the baking plain. Huts and tents sprawled across the wasteland, broiling in the pre-monsoon heat and infested with insects. They performed four times a day in a shed on a makeshift stage. Despite the unbearable temperature, they kept their coats on in the dressing room to keep the mosquitoes at bay. The walls were crawling with them.

Tommy, usually so mild-natured, started throwing props at the walls to kill them and shouting incoherently, till Adela pushed him back on stage to accompany her on the piano.

It was almost a relief to return to the vast, overcrowded Grand Hotel, even if it meant sharing a room with an unhappy Mavis, who was suffering from mosquito bites and thought one of the staff was stealing her make-up.

'Aye, it's that laddie sweeper going around with purple eyeshadow and red lipstick – that's the giveaway,' Mack teased.

Prue, though, was deliriously happy to find a note from Stuey saying he was due three days' leave in Calcutta before operations. While Adela and Tommy went to play and sing at a hospital, Prue slipped off to join Stuey at the Tollygunge Club. She returned two days later with an engagement ring on her finger – her father had written giving reluctant consent – yet heartbroken that Stuey was off on some dangerous mission into Burma.

***

News was filtering out of Assam that the Indian Army had broken the siege at Imphal and gone to the relief of Kohima. This was the first time that the authorities had even admitted that Kohima had been at risk of being overrun. There had been a breakthrough further south in the Arakan too. Adela and Tommy rushed off to the cinema for the latest news, but it was full of the courageous landings by the Allies in Northern France in early June and the opening of the second front in Europe, so long awaited. To the south, in Italy, Rome had been liberated by troops that numbered among them the Indian Army's 4th Infantry Division.

Heartened by the news, the ENSA group joined in celebrations with other servicemen and women, yet they all wanted news of Burma. A week later Adela, Tommy and Prue were back at the cinema, and this time there was footage of Assam.

The battle that had been raging for six months in the Arakan had finally been won by British and Indian troops. Reinforcements had then rushed north to relieve Imphal and Kohima, where heroic fighting had saved India from invasion.

News footage of the Battle of Church Knoll, Kohima, came next: a mortar trench in the foreground, thick vegetation and a dark ridge beyond. Adela watched in astonishment as she recognised an artillery officer looking through binoculars and pointing out a target on the hillside.

She grabbed Tommy's arm. 'That's Boz! I'm sure it is. Uncle Rafi's old forestry friend. He was in Simla. Don't you recognise him?'

'Keep your voice down,' Tommy said in amusement.

The jaunty clipped voice of the commentary was already on to the next scene, describing the soldiers crouching behind a wall – men of the 15th Punjab Regiment – waiting for the order to rush forward and take the hill. The film cut to a wounded major lying on a stretcher and smoking while having his abdomen dressed by a nurse.

'I wonder if Sophie is anywhere near there,' Adela whispered, hardly daring to blink in case she missed any details.

The camera panned to Hawker Hurricane fighter-bombers flying low overhead and dropping bombs on the far side of the ridge. Soundless plumes of smoke rose up, obscuring the view. The final footage was of a mule train returning to base and the muleteers struggling to offload heavy panniers of equipment before rubbing down their animals. In the foreground a group of officers was drinking tea, as if they had just come back from a fishing expedition.

There was a cheer in the cinema at this. Adela's eyes smarted.

'I hope they're drinking Assam tea.' She smiled.

'Of course they will be,' Tommy assured her with a pat on the arm. 'Belgooree's best.'

As they left the cinema, Adela wondered if Sam had been the one to film the action at Church Knoll. Or had he been flying overhead in a Hurricane? Seeing Boz on the screen in the hills of Assam made her all the more determined to get to the front. She knew it must be a sanitised view of what was really going on up there, but she felt reassured by the stoical troops on screen.

Over the next few days she could think of nothing else. She knew that a few members of ENSA had gone to Chittagong in June; Vera Lynn had flown in for a short hectic tour of Chittagong and the Arakan. There was talk of sending some to Imphal when it became less hazardous. But most troupes were too large and unwieldy to travel to these forward positions on the front line. Adela kept pressing their entertainments officer in Calcutta for a smaller group of them to go.

Finally, in July, ENSA agreed to send a group up the Brahmaputra River to Assam. By this time the monsoon had come, bringing relief from the intense heat, but also swampy pools rife with mosquitoes and roads turned to churning mud. Insects crawled out of the walls, and Mavis's wig was eaten by white ants. Half the show had come down with malaria or jaundice and was being packed off to Darjeeling in the mountains to recuperate. To Prue's relief, Mavis, dispirited at losing her wig, went with them.

But nothing would keep Adela from volunteering for Assam. Together with Tommy, Prue, Mack, Betsie and a couple of dancers from another troupe, they took the train out of Calcutta. Two days later they were transferring to a boat on the swollen Brahmaputra. She thought of Sam and his steamship and knew he would rail at the conditions on board, with workers in steerage crammed in and enduring the suffocating heat while the ENSA members and a handful of British officers enjoyed the relative comfort of crowded cabins on the prom deck. It would have been far easier to go by aeroplane, but all available space on planes was taken up by priority troops and their supplies.

It was sweet agony to Adela to sail past Guwahati and know how close she was to her mother and brother at Belgooree, and yet not be able to see them.

'Write her a letter,' said Tommy, 'and maybe you can meet her on the way back.'

'She'll only worry if she knows I'm anywhere near the war front,' Adela replied. 'If I get the chance on the way back, I'll surprise her.'

***

The views of the towns they passed were depressing: ghats and streets filthy and crowded with the poor – perhaps refugees from Burma who had struggled back to India two years previously and got no further. Then, after days on the overcrowded boat, they transferred to a train again to get up to Dimapur. Adela's heart raced at the sight of emerald-green hillsides of tea bushes rippling away in to the sparkling heat. They weren't the Oxford's, but it made her feel pangs of homesickness for the tea gardens she knew so well.

Dimapur, a mass of grey dripping roofs, was squalid from its swollen population: injured and battle-fatigued sepoys; coolies and porters who were helping with the back-breaking building of roads; suppliers, cooks, camp followers, medics, railway workers, undertakers and refugee families. Asking around at the army divisional hospital for Sophie Khan and the Red Cross, Adela was told she was most likely helping up at Kohima.

They performed at the hospital and nearby barracks. At one show a group of Gurkha children crept in and giggled at the front. Afterwards, Adela and Tommy went to chat to them. It hadn't occurred to Adela that the men might have their wives and families with them. Suddenly the little dark-eyed boy she had been talking to caught sight of his mother and ran off, throwing himself at her legs and laughing. Adela was winded by the sight of his simple adoration of his young mother. For a moment she was paralysed by a fresh wave of grief for having given up her own son. She had hoped that the vast distance she had put between herself and Newcastle would have helped dull the ache for her baby. Instead, the sight of the Indian children just made her long for him more keenly.

Within days they were being jostled in a truck up to Kohima Ridge among the Naga Hills. The former village of the Naga tribe and the bungalows of the British officials had been obliterated. It was now one large military camp, surrounded by glittering rain-filled craters, burnt-down buildings and a landscape shattered by intense bombardment. The Toodle Pips – with Betsie drafted in to take Mavis's place – did their first performance on an open patch of ground, their audience a straggle of tired soldiers standing around, grinning in amazement to see the women and whistling loudly through their fingers.

Over the next days they went about the camps, performing up to six times a day, their reward being the gratitude of battle-weary men, some of whom had been away from home for years. Everything was soaked daily by the monsoon: tents and trees dripped, their costumes stank of sweat and mould, and they all turned a yellowish hue from the amount of Flit sprayed on them to keep mosquitoes at bay. Adela took up smoking cigarettes to burn off the purple leeches that sucked at her ankles, thighs and arms.

Yet all the discomfort was forgotten when, to Adela's joy, she encountered Sophie at a field hospital. She recognised her bob of fair hair and her trim figure in jodhpurs and uniform shirt as soon as she climbed down from the cab of a Red Cross truck.

'Sophie!' Adela screeched and ran at her mother's friend. They hugged in delight.

'Adela, my darling.' Sophie grinned, her eyes glinting with tears. 'I can't believe it! You're so grown up. Are you well? You look wonderful.' She hugged her again.

'I'm fine. So glad to see you. I've missed you and Rafi so much. And mother. You saw her recently?'

'Yes, and she's as amazing as ever. Running everything without a fuss. Missing you, of course.'

Adela gave a rueful smile. 'Maybe.'

'Not maybe. Yes!' Sophie insisted, swinging her arm around Adela's damp shoulders.

They hardly had time to gabble out their news before Sophie was due to make the arduous drive back to Dimapur with two wounded sappers.

'Poor boys. Got burnt in a mess-tent accident. One will need an amputation unless we can save his arm at the main hospital. Besides, the field hospital is packing up and moving down beyond Imphal.'

'Haven't things stopped for the monsoon?' Adela asked.

'Apparently not. Looks like the orders are to push on into Burma after the Japanese, despite the monsoon.'

'Sam Jackman's flying planes,' Adela blurted out. 'And making films for the forces. Have you come across him?'

'No,' said Sophie with a sympathetic smile, 'but that doesn't mean he's not here. There are thousands of us.'

'Of course,' said Adela, feeling foolish and adding hastily, 'I saw Boz in a newsreel about Kohima. He looked very calm and in charge.'

Sophie gave a broad smile. 'Good for Major Boz. I'm so glad to hear it. I knew his artillery company was here, but I haven't come across him either. He could be on leave or moved further to the front.'

They kissed goodbye. 'You'll find me at the divisional hospital in Dimapur,' Sophie said. 'Please call on your way through, won't you?'

'Promise,' Adela said and smiled, hating to be parted so soon after being reunited.

'And take good care of yourself!'

***

Over the next few days Adela badgered for them to be sent on to Imphal. 'From what I hear, the place is chock-a-block with front-line troops, as well as a major field hospital.'

Tommy tried but failed to get them taken by plane, but a week later, in mid-August, they took the more hazardous road route among a convoy of engineers. After two days' travel through shattered jungle, along roads on which sappers worked like Trojans in the incessant rain to lay tracks in the liquid mud, they reached the amphitheatre of Imphal, nestled in the hills.

That afternoon The Toodle Pips performed in a makeshift overflow ward of the field hospital for bed-bound officers, a mixture of newly arrived wounded and sick from the front. There appeared to be more men dying from illness – dengue fever, malaria and an outbreak of typhus caused by ticks – than from battle wounds.

After they finished and were leaving, a man from a corner bed called out hoarsely, 'Miss Robson! Brava, Adela!'

She turned in surprise. He was gaunt and sallow-faced – probably jaundiced – and his hair shorn. Something about the brown eyes was familiar.

'You don't remember me, do you?' he said, attempting a smile, his eyes betraying disappointment. 'Jimmy Maitland. Simla, '37. I was on leave at Craig Dhu, the officers' hostel.'

'Jimmy!' Adela gasped. 'Of course I remember.' She hid her shock at the change in him. The young Scots artillery captain who had dated her that Simla summer had been robust and athletic, with thick dark hair and a cheeky dimpled smile. She had corresponded with him for a few months and then lost interest. 'How wonderful to see you. Not in here, of course, but good all the same. How are you?'

He smiled. 'All the better for seeing you. You're as bonny as ever – and sing just as sweetly as I remember.'

'And you're as charming as I remember.' Adela grinned. 'So you're one of the heroes of Imphal?'

He shook his head. 'I didn't do anything more than the other boys.' His expression tightened. She sensed the subject was too raw to talk about. Instead she asked him about his family. He'd been back home on leave in Scotland when the war broke out.

'And you, Adela?' He reached for her hand with his bony one. 'No ring on your finger yet. Does that mean there's still hope for a love-struck major?'

'Major now, are you? Well, you never know.' Adela laughed.

'I'm sorry we lost touch,' said Jimmy. He was too gallant to blame her for stopping writing.

'I left Simla in '38 and went to England,' Adela explained. 'I should have let you know.'

'Not at all,' Jimmy said. 'I should have been more persistent.'

'I better go now,' she said, smiling, 'but I'll come back and see you.'

'Will you?'

'Of course.'

'I'd like that. Just to talk to you would be a better tonic than the stuff they're making me swallow.'

'Jimmy.' She squeezed his hand. 'I promise I'll not leave Imphal without seeing you again.'

She went quickly, before he saw the tears of pity in her eyes. The number of shattered lives that they had seen on their tour was sometimes overwhelming. But to suddenly come across a man that she had known before the war – had been a little in love with – and see him reduced to a husk of his former self was heart-wrenching.

Each morning before their hectic schedule of performances, Adela made the effort to go early and visit Jimmy. Most of the nurses on duty encouraged it, as it raised the morale of the whole ward when she sang them songs over breakfast.

At the end of their second week in Imphal, rumours spread of the imminent arrival of a VIP.

'Could be Mountbatten come to dole out medals,' Tommy speculated.

'Oh, I hope so.' Prue grinned. 'He's a real dish. Do you think we'll get to perform for him?'

But before it could happen, Adela, Tommy, Prue and Betsie agreed to go to a casualty clearing station at Tamu sixty miles away to perform to medics and patients. The monsoon rains had eased and the roads were drying out. They crammed into a jeep without room for props or costumes and were driven south by a cheerful Gurkha. The friends were nervous at going nearer to the front – Jimmy had pleaded with Adela not to go – but the joyful surprise of the hard-pressed staff at their surprise arrival was worth it.

The clearing station was a huddle of canvas buildings in a forest clearing by a river, with patients lying on stretchers that were kept off the ground by forked sticks. The nurses had dispensed with the starched-white uniforms of hospital and were living in tents with holes in the ground for latrines and sustained by food dropped from the air. To Adela's amazement she came across an old school friend from Shillong, the only girl who had ever been a true friend, however briefly.

'Flowers Dunlop! I don't believe it!'

The young woman in slacks and shirt, and her dark hair still worn in a thick plait, gaped at her. At once they were hugging and giggling as if they were thirteen again.

'I've been sent up from an army hospital in East Bengal to help,' Flowers explained. 'We've got so many cases of fever coming in, and it's hopeless sending them to hospital in the plains in the hot season, as it just makes them worse, so we're treating as many as we can here and keeping them in the hills to recuperate.'

'Yes, I've seen some of them at Imphal – including an old boyfriend,' said Adela. 'I sing to them over their egg and toast.'

'I bet that cheers them up,' Flowers said, winking.

Later, after Adela had sung with her friends to patients babbling with delirium and groaning in pain, she sat on Flowers' camp bed under a mosquito net as they drank tea by the light of a hurricane lamp. Flowers told her about training as a nurse and how she had been working in Rangoon when the Japanese invaded Burma. She had escaped on one of the last overcrowded ships to leave the port. After that she enlisted as an army nurse and was sent to the Middle East.

'Since coming back, I've worked in Calcutta and then with a specialist neurosurgical unit in Comilla before coming here.'

'Gosh, you're adventurous,' Adela said in admiration, 'and brave.'

Flowers flashed her an amused look. 'Not what you would have expected from the timid girl you knew at St Ninian's?'

'No, not really,' Adela admitted. 'But we were very young then.'

'But you were always brave,' said Flowers. 'I wish I'd had the courage to run away like you did. I hated school. And you caused such a fuss, you wouldn't believe it. Especially when you didn't come back.'

'I hope they didn't pick on you more because I wasn't there,' Adela said with a guilty pang.

'They did,' Flowers answered bluntly. 'But it made me stronger. I kept telling myself that I was better than them and that I'd make something of myself – not just learn the social graces and make myself pretty for a husband. You did that for me, Adela. So thanks for getting yourself expelled.' Flowers gave a wide grin.

They laughed and drank more tea. Adela gave a brief outline of what she'd done in the intervening years, leaving out the painful details of her affair and illegitimate child.

'I'm sorry to hear about the death of your father,' said Flowers. 'My father's health is not good. My mother wants him to go to the convalescent home in Simla, but he won't desert his duties as station master, even though their house got requisitioned by the army and they are living in a leaking bungalow in Sreemangal.'

'Jaflong would be closer than Simla for a spell of R&R. Doesn't your mother come from there?'

Flowers smiled. 'Fancy you remembering that. Yes, it would be closer, but the railways would pay for him to go to Simla if he made a good case. But he will never ask.' They fell into silence, each thinking about their parents. Flowers murmured, 'It's funny being up here, close to the tea plantations. I hope I have the chance to see Assam while I'm here.'

'Why? Does it remind you of the Sylhet gardens of home?' Adela asked.

'Not because of that. It's something Daddy said. He was born on a tea estate. I never knew that until he told me on my last visit home. All the talk of Kohima and Assam lately got him reminiscing; said his father was a Scots tea planter. Daddy grew up in Shillong, so I don't know how that fits in, but he seemed quite proud of the connection.'

'You'll have to ask him more about it when you next see him,' said Adela, feeling a sudden pang of homesickness for Belgooree.

Soon after, Adela crawled into the tent she was sharing with Prue and fell into exhausted sleep. In the morning she was woken by screams. Scrambling from the tent with Prue, they saw Betsie cowering in a canvas bath behind the tent flap.

'Stop them!' she squealed.

'Stop who?' Adela looked around wildly for attackers.

'Up there!' She waved a hand.

Adela looked up at the tree above. A crowd of monkeys were chattering loudly. Suddenly one hurled a twig at the naked Betsie. Prue picked it up and flung it back.

'Don't!' Adela cried. 'You won't win.'

A shower of sticks rained down on them. Adela grabbed Betsie's towel and held it over her. 'Finish off quickly,' she ordered and ducked at the same time. Prue took refuge in the tent. A minute later Adela was following, with Betsie bundled in the towel. They collapsed, laughing, in a hysterical heap. It was minutes before they could draw breath.

'Are you boozing in there?' Tommy shouted through the canvas. 'What's going on, girls?'

'Monkey business,' Adela snorted, which set them all off again.

They stayed three more days before the driver returned to collect them. On the last night one of the orderlies chucked a grenade in the river, which brought fish to the surface and a smile to the nurses' faces when they dined on fish that evening.

Early the next morning Flowers and Adela hugged and wished each other good luck, promising to stay in touch. The ENSA troupe bumped their way back in the Jeep, their bodies jarred and bruised by the rutted road. The driver kept the hood down to allow the breeze to cool them, so that by the time they arrived back in Imphal they were all covered in a thick brown dust.

Chapter 29

Wavell, India's new Viceroy and former Commander-in-Chief, was flown into Imphal on a Douglas Dakota transport plane, along with other dignitaries: Lieutenant-General Stopford, of the Indian Army's 33rd Corps; Air Commodore Vincent; and Bodhchandra Singh, the Maharajah of Manipur, in whose state they had landed.

For once Sam was not piloting the plane. He had been detailed to make a film of the prestigious event for the SEAC film unit. It was to be a much-needed morale booster for the Indian army. There had been plenty of bitter talk, among officers as well as lower ranks, about their forgotten war on the Burma front. Sam, who had spent the past dangerous months flying supplies to beleaguered troops behind the Japanese lines and had witnessed the Herculean efforts of infantry, gunners and engineers to keep Kohima and Imphal from falling into enemy hands, knew more than most how deserving of their medals were the surviving soldiers.

His own fellow airmen had been no less heroic – the men of 194 Squadron whom he had joined near Rawalpindi in '42. They had become his family – navigator 'Chubs' MacRae, his wireless operators and the ground crew of experienced older men who did twenty-hour shifts to keep the planes maintained. The camaraderie of the squadron had earned it the nickname 'The Friendly Firm'. For weeks on end they had flown in supplies, transported troops, evacuated the wounded under cover of darkness and navigated the treacherous mountainous terrain without proper maps or radar systems. Using the stars and rivers on clear nights and memorising the lie of hills and valleys, Sam had got to know North Burma like the back of his hand.

He had landed on precarious strips of cleared jungle for Wingate's Chindits, avoided Japanese night fighters to drop ammunition and water by parachute, and coaxed skittish mules on to his aircraft for use in the Burma mountains. The operations had been endless and punishing, but the worst risk to their transport drops so far was not enemy attack or the terrain, but the order to continue flying through the monsoon – and in daytime.

There was nothing as terrifying as flying into giant cauldrons of cumulonimbus clouds and being hurled around while deafening hail clattered like bullets on the metal aircraft. Sam's jaw continually ached from being clenched. His heart would race, until he found the all-important hole in the cloud into which he could dive, hoping to find their drop zone and not a mountain wall. Chubs, clutching his homemade pinpoint map, stayed as calm as if they were scouting a picnic spot.

'Anytime now would do nicely, Padre,' he would encourage. Chubs had nicknamed Sam 'The Padre' after they discovered he'd once been a missionary.

Back at their Assam base at Agartala, in the humid officers' mess they would toast their survival in gin and throw treats to their mascot in the compound, a pet Himalayan black bear. After a few snatched hours of exhausted sleep, their bearer would shake them awake, and the relentless round of flights would begin all over again.

But today Sam had a welcome diversion and respite as documentary maker. He relished being behind the camera observing once more.

He took close-up footage of the Viceroy inspecting troops of the 15th Punjab Regiment, Durham Light Infantry, Royal Berkshires, Royal Welsh Fusiliers and 1st Gurkha Rifles. Wavell presented medals. Sam filmed the men showing captured military hardware: mountain guns with wooden spoked wheels. Three prisoners of war were spoken to through a Japanese-American interpreter. Sam knew the significance of this: to show the world that the Allies treated their captured POWs with humanity – at least with food, shelter and medicines.

Next Wavell visited the hospital. Sam took some shots. The censors at the War Office could decide if the pictures of men shrunken by fever or bandaged beyond recognition were to be shown more widely. To him, these men should not be hidden away from a squeamish public; they deserved to receive just as much recognition as the medal wearers. But he doubted that they would.

As the VIPs took refreshment with the doctors, Sam stepped outside, enjoying the warm sunshine on his back. He never minded the heat in the hills; it was the humid, claustrophobic cities, like Calcutta, that sapped his energy and spirit.

As he finished a cigarette and waited for the Viceroy, a dusty Jeep drove into the compound and was stopped by guards. Sam was surprised to see three women clamber out of the back, their topees tipped back jauntily, laughing and shoving their male colleague playfully at some remark he must have made. They were blatantly flirting with the guards, trying to wheedle their way into getting a closer view of the VIP visit. Sam snorted in amusement. On a whim he raised his camera, which was strung around his neck, and focused it on the group. Through the lens he could just pick out the ENSA badges on their shirts. Nice, shapely figures. The dark-haired one pulled off her filthy hat and shook out her hair. A double for Vivien Leigh.

Sam's heart thudded in his chest. It couldn't possibly be. Without hesitating, he started to stride towards the noisy party. As he got close, the young woman looked over. Her eyes widened. Then she smiled and his stomach flipped over. Her face was streaked with dust and sweat, but she was even more beautiful than he'd remembered.

'Adela.'

'Sam.'

She came up to him and held out her hand. He shook it, feeling ridiculously formal. What he really wanted to do was crush her to his chest and not let go. They stood grinning at each other. She didn't seem so shocked to see him. Sam was almost speechless.

'I'd heard you were in the RAF,' she said, 'and making films for them. Are you travelling with Wavell?'

'Yes.' His voice sounded embarrassingly husky in his ears. 'When did you join ENSA? Have you been back in India long?' He was still gripping her hand. 'I want to hear everything.'

She laughed. It made his chest constrict. How had he forgotten how much he loved the way she tilted her head to one side and half closed her eyes in amusement?

'Since February,' Adela said. 'We all have. Do you remember Prue and Tommy from The Simla Songsters?' She dropped his hand as she turned to the others. 'And this is Betsie, who hasn't quite recovered from being attacked by monkeys in the bath.'

Sam exchanged greetings with them all.

'Can we meet the Viceroy?' Prue asked with a wink.

'We don't want to get on film looking like this,' Betsie said in horror.

'Perhaps on our return,' Sam suggested, 'you could perform something for the camera. I could suggest it to the ADC.'

'Return from where?' Adela asked.

'We're off to Bishenpur this afternoon and then on to Kohima.'

Her face fell. 'So soon? But you're coming back?'

'Tomorrow night, before returning Wavell to Calcutta.'

'Good.' She smiled. 'Then we'll put on our glad rags for the Viceroy.'

There was no time for further conversation, as one of Wavell's aides summoned Sam back. He gave a regretful shrug and a lingering look, before striding away.

***

The rest of Sam's day passed in a blur. They descended through clouds to the camp at Bishenpur, the mountains hidden from view. Sam's nerves jangled, as they always did when he was a passenger rather than pilot. As the ceremony of medal giving began again – he focused in on a gunner from the Gordon Highlanders who was being honoured – his mind was only half on the task. He had thought of Adela often over the intervening years, yet imagined her in Britain. She would be doing something for the war effort or working as an actress or married to some lucky man in the tea business and raising his children.

In times of fear, exhaustion or the adrenaline-pumping moments of this hellish war, Sam had tortured himself with thoughts of Adela. In some perverse way it made it all seem more bearable to think of her living, breathing and laughing somewhere in the world rather than to imagine a world without her. Even if he never saw her again, just to think that she lived a life under the same moon and stars was a comfort; it made the world worth fighting for.

Yet there she was in Imphal just a few hours ago, stepping out of a filthy Jeep and into his life again. Sam mocked himself for his runaway thoughts. Just because she looked pleased to see him didn't mean she shared the same strong feelings. How could she? They hadn't met for over six years. Adela had been hardly out of girlhood. He had known back then that she had cared for him – until his impetuous actions at the Sipi Fair. At least he would have the chance to explain all that to her. If they ever got back to Imphal on schedule. Impatience curdled in his gut.

Sam set to the task of filming as they travelled on to Kohima. He had seen it all from the air, the carnage and devastation. It was amazing how just one monsoon was already covering the pounded earth and the mass graves with lush new growth. He took footage of Wavell looking through binoculars at recent battle areas. As the cloud cleared over the Naga Hills, the courageous tribesmen who had helped the Allies, lined up to salute the Viceroy and the Maharajah in the traditional way by putting their hands to their noses.

Sam was suddenly overwhelmed. Their villages and animals had been destroyed by someone else's war, yet the Nagas greeted the British with gifts of machetes and homespun cloth. Sam felt a lump in his throat at their generosity and lack of reproach. Yet again he felt humbled by the lion-hearted spirit of India's hill people.

***

Adela had no idea how she had kept so outwardly calm at seeing Sam again. Sam! He had stridden towards her, camera swinging from his chest as if he had been waiting for her to arrive. He looked older, his tanned face scored with deeper lines around his hazel eyes and firm mouth. His hair was cropped short, his cap stuffed into his belt out of the way for filming. But his easy smile was just as broad, and his eyes shone with the same mixture of warmth and mischief that made her pulse race.

Then he had taken her hand and almost crushed it in his. Her heart had felt as if it would explode out of her chest at his touch. Surely he had been aware of her shaking or seen the flush rise up her neck.

'So you're just as keen on Sam Jackman as ever?' Prue teased her.

Adela gave a rueful laugh. 'Was it that obvious?'

'It was to me,' said Prue, 'but then you have talked a lot about him since we've got back to India.'

'Have I?' Adela put her hands to hot cheeks.

'Yes. And he couldn't take his eyes off you either.' Prue smiled. 'I predict a possibility of some Jubbulpore when he returns tonight.'

'Not if he's still married to Pema.'

'That wasn't a proper marriage,' Prue said dismissively, 'just a Sipi tradition.'

'But Mother said ages ago that he lived with Pema as her husband,' Adela fretted.

'Well, you'll just have to come right out and ask him. In true forthright Adela style.'

The following day a message came through that Wavell's party would like to attend an ENSA performance that evening, which threw the small troupe into a panic.

'I can't play ukulele to the Viceroy!' Betsie shrieked. One of the dancers started throwing up.

Tommy came up with a compromise and made arrangements for an army concert band to play with them.

Prue had an uncharacteristic fit of nerves as darkness fell and word came through that Wavell's party had arrived back in Imphal. 'I don't think we can wear our leotards in front of all those VIPs, can we? Won't they be shocked?'

'Who cares about them?' said Tommy. 'You'll send the lads off in high spirits, and that's what counts.'

Just before they were due to start, they learned that the Viceroy had left for Calcutta, pressure of work not allowing him to stay another night. Adela tried to hide how upset she was. Prue gave her shoulder a sympathetic squeeze as they took to the stage. Adela paused to take three deep breaths and then smiled into the lights, determined to give a good show no matter how disappointed she was.

The Toodle Pips received a rapturous reception from the audience of NCOs and privates; the stuffy tent was crammed with men, their sweating faces shining in the lamplight.

When they came off and the army band came on, Tommy took her by the arm and said, 'Take a peek. You've just been filmed.'

Adela peered from backstage. Halfway down the room, there was Sam crouching behind his camera. Her heart leapt. He had stayed behind to film. Would he have to go straight off afterwards, or would she get to see him for more than a snatched moment? As the band played popular tunes, she felt a confusion of excitement and anxiety. She changed quickly into her evening dress of green silk that she'd had made in Bombay on their arrival back in India.

Then it was her turn to go on and sing, with Tommy on piano. The instrument sounded tinny from heat damage, but her friend attacked the keys with gusto. Adela sang 'A Lovely Way to Spend an Evening' and 'A Nightingale Sang in Berkeley Square'. Her third song was supposed to be a light-hearted one from the musical *Oklahoma!* On the spur of the moment she touched Tommy on the shoulder and murmured, 'Play "You'll Never Know".'

He gave her a pitying look. 'No guesses who this is for.' But he played the opening bars.

Adela announced, 'I'm going to sing a special song that Alice Faye made popular in last year's film *Hello, Frisco, Hello*. This song is for all your sweethearts at home who are missing you – may you soon be reunited.'

She began to sing the tender song of yearning, of a woman declaring her love for a man who doesn't seem to notice how much she loves him. He will never know how much she misses him; he has taken her heart with him, and if he doesn't realise how deeply she loves him now, then he will never know. Adela sang straight to the camera, her heart swelling with the bittersweet words. If she never got another chance to speak properly to Sam, then she hoped fervently that these words would say all there was to say.

As she finished, there was a moment of complete silence, and then the room erupted in applause and cheers. Adela smiled, took Tommy's hand and they bowed together. Betsie came on with her ukulele and gave them two jaunty numbers, and then The Toodle Pips returned for their final signature song, 'Don't Sit Under the Apple Tree'.

Afterwards they were swept into the sergeant's mess for drinks and almost mobbed by the high-spirited men. There seemed to be a feverishness in the air, as if everyone knew that their respite in Imphal was coming to end and they would soon be back in action.

Adela began to worry that her chance of seeing Sam was slipping away. Suddenly she spotted him in the crush of people – a head taller than most – and moving towards her. With just a smile and no words, he reached for her hand and hung on to her as he pulled her back through the crowds. Some ribald comments were shouted after them and grumbles about officers always getting the ENSA girls. But Sam ignored them as he steered Adela out of the hall, leaving Tommy playing away on the mess piano.

He led her to a row of officers' bungalows that had remained intact through the siege, round the side of one to a small garden with a bench and a view of the eastern hills, bathed in moonlight. The noise of crickets pulsed in the undergrowth, and the trees were restless with night birds.

'I hope you've taken your Mepacrine,' Sam joked. 'I'd hate to be responsible for you catching malaria on my account.'

'I have,' said Adela, 'but we could share a cigarette and keep the moskies at bay.' Silently she hoped it might steady her nerves at being suddenly so close to Sam in the dark. After six long years apart, would they still have anything to say to each other? Would he still be the same man with a zest for life who had made her feel so alive and special when they had worked together in Narkanda?

He lit two cigarettes and gave her one. 'You start first,' he ordered, 'and tell me about the last six years.'

Perhaps he was wondering the same about her. Adela gave the same sanitised story that she had trotted out for Flowers Dunlop, making him laugh with stories about her Brewis relations and the characters at the theatre in Newcastle. They finished their cigarettes. He took her hand gently, firmly between his two.

'I'm so very sorry about your father's death, Adela. I came to see you at Belgooree, but you'd already gone to England.'

'Yes, I know. Mother wrote and told me. It was kind of you.'

'Not kind – I wanted to see you and to explain about the Sipi Fair.'

Adela's heart banged with excitement at his touch, but also fear at what he might be about to say. Abruptly she said, 'Don't say anything yet.'

'But it's important that you know. I think we cared for each other then—'

'Kiss me, Sam,' Adela interrupted. 'Kiss me first before you say anything else.'

They looked deep into each other's eyes, and then Sam was pulling her towards him and lowering his mouth to hers. He kissed her long and hard, as if he had hungered for this moment for years; she knew that she had. His hands held her body; her heart drummed under his touch. His kisses consumed her, stirring her longing for him. She ran her hands over his face and hair, wanting to feel his skin under her fingers. She had felt passion before, but this was more than physical lust: she wanted every part of his being.

They paused for breath. Sam murmured, 'I've loved you for so long.'

'Truly?' Adela marvelled at the thought.

'I've longed for you,' he insisted.

She said, 'I've dreamed of this happening so many times.'

Sam went on, 'That's why I want to set things straight about Sipi.'

Adela braced herself. 'I don't really want to know. I don't want to hear about your wife, even if it wasn't a proper marriage. You made a choice over Pema – a brave and honourable choice – but it changed everything.'

Sam gripped her. 'It doesn't have to. She isn't my wife. I gave her a home, but we never lived as man and wife.'

'But Mother said you did.'

Sam gave an exasperated cry. 'Your uncle James was needling me – I let him believe what he wanted to believe.'

'So it isn't true? You never lived together?'

'Not in the way you mean. I stood by her while she needed me. Pema gave birth to a child,' Sam admitted. Adela gasped. Sam's look bore into her. 'But not my child.'

'What do you mean?'

'The poor girl was already carrying a baby when I rescued her at the fair. Her uncle had forced himself on her, and that was why he was getting rid of her at Sipi.'

Adela moaned, 'How terrible.'

'She has a son.'

Adela looked at him with dismay. 'You can't just abandon them, Sam.'

'I haven't.' Sam's hold slackened and his tone hardened. 'I would never abandon a child – not like my mother did me. What sort of woman would give up her son?'

Adela felt her insides go cold. Sam didn't notice her tense.

'Well, I made sure that Pema wasn't put in that position. My servant Nitin is her protector now. He fell in love with Pema, and I encouraged him to take on her child. They married five years ago – a proper Hindu marriage – and they have a daughter now too. You couldn't get a prouder father than Nitin.'

Adela swallowed. Her heart was racing. 'You're a good man, Sam,' she whispered.

'No, I'm not. I've done some idiotic things in my life. The worst of them being allowing you to leave Simla thinking I didn't care for you. I know I hurt your feelings – I saw you that day at Sipi with Prince Sanjay. I was mad with envy, especially after Fatima told me she had warned you about him. You were such an innocent. But you didn't love him, did you?'

Adela squirmed at his words. 'No, I didn't.'

Now was the moment to confess everything, tell Sam about her affair and the baby and how she had been one of those terrible women who gave their sons away. Let him know what sort of person she really was – not the innocent girl of his dreams, but a foolish and heartless one.

Yet she couldn't bring herself to tell him. She couldn't bear to see the loving expression and passion in his eyes turn to disillusion and disappointment. He pulled her into his arms once more and kissed her tenderly. Adela felt slow, hot tears trickle down her cheeks. Sam pulled away.

'Adela, my darling, what's wrong?' He looked at her with such loving compassion that she thought her heart would break in two.

'Nothing,' she said. What a coward she was! 'I better get back.'

'Adela.' He stopped her getting up. 'Speak to me. Have I gone too fast? I don't want to put you off, but I thought we felt the same about each other. I'll wait if that's what you want.'

She looked away. 'I do love you Sam, so very much. But—'

'But what? Is there someone else, Adela? Have you promised yourself to another man? I wouldn't blame you after all this time.' When she didn't answer, he dropped his hold and sighed. 'I thought it was too good to be true that you weren't already spoken for.'

'It's not like that,' Adela struggled to explain.

'Then what is it, my darling?'

Adela stood up. She mustn't lead him on. She had ruined their chance of being happy together when she had chosen to have the affair with Jay. She knew Sam would despise her for what she had done – perhaps not the affair, but her abandoning of her child. That, in the eyes of Sam Jackman, with his fierce sense of loyalty and justice, would be unforgiveable. Suddenly it became clear in her mind as it had never been before: she would never be at peace unless she returned to Newcastle and tried to find her son. If he had remained in an orphanage and not been adopted, then she would claim him back. Her heart yearned for that – perhaps more than the love of any man.

'There is someone – someone whom I must go back to England for after this war is over.' She forced herself not to weaken in her resolve. 'My loyalty lies with him. I'm so sorry, Sam.'

He looked at her, stunned. The confusion on his handsome features made her wince in shame. Sam stood too, trying to put on a brave face.

'Lucky chap,' he said.

Adela knew in that moment that she would probably never see Sam again. She could do one last thing for him, even though he might not thank her for it. She told him about visiting his mother in Cullercoats.

'She was a nice woman – kind. She made me feel at home.'

His expression turned from regret to disbelief. 'Why would you do that? Why go and see that woman?'

'I thought it might help reconcile the two of you. She was full of remorse at leaving you behind. She said she'd tried to take you with her, but your father wouldn't let her. Threatened her with the police.'

'That's a bloody lie!' Sam's anger ignited. 'She was just saying that so you wouldn't think badly of her. I can't believe you were taken in. You better not have raised her hopes that I wanted anything to do with her. Did you, Adela?'

'Yes, I did.' She faced him. 'I said she could write to Belgooree, and I would send on any post when I found out where you were. Then when I heard you were filming for SEAC, I wrote and gave her the Delhi address. Has she written to you?'

'No, thank God!' He glared at her. 'Please tell me you didn't just play along tonight so that you could get me to write to my mother.'

'Of course not!' Adela reached out a hand. Sam kept his fists balled by his side. 'Why are you so hard on her? She made a mistake in giving you up, but she longs to be reconciled. Can't you ever forgive her?'

'No!' Sam said, his jaw clenching. 'When she walked out on me and my father, she tore my family apart. I've never known family life – not until I joined the squadron. They're my family now. I can rely on them to always be there – we protect and look out for each other. That's what people do when they care.'

That was the last Sam spoke until he had walked her safely back to her quarters. He nodded a curt goodnight. 'Look after yourself, Adela. I hope you have a happy life and that the man you love deserves you.'

Adela rasped, 'Take care too, Sam.'

She stood in the dark, watching him go. For a long time she remained there, listening to the harsh sound of jackals calling in the jungle, echoing the desolation in her heart.

Chapter 30

The only way Adela knew how to ease her broken heart was to work ever harder. She drove herself relentlessly, pushing the troupe to do extra performances and staying up late being a confidante to homesick and war-weary men. They spent another month on the Burmese border, but she never came across Sam. She heard that 194 Squadron were on operations further into Burma. She prayed that he would stay alive and might one day forgive her for hurting him.

At times, lying awake in uncomfortable billets, she wondered if she had made a terrible error in not giving Sam the full facts about what she had done, to let him choose whether he still wanted to be with her. But she always concluded that his love would have been poisoned by the knowledge; she would have reminded him too much of his inadequate mother. She couldn't have suffered his contempt.

Prue and Tommy could not fathom what had gone wrong.

'He was asking for you at the hospital the morning he left,' Prue told her. 'One of the nurses said. He'd heard you came to sing to the patients early. What on earth did you say to put him off?'

Adela never replied to her friend's exasperated questioning.

'Well, I wouldn't have let him slip through my sticky paws,' Prue declared, and gave up asking.

They returned to Calcutta. In October their nine-month tour was at an end. Adela's spirits revived to discover that Sophie and Rafi were in the city too. Rafi was sourcing goran wood from the Sundarbans for making tent poles as an alternative to traditional hardwoods, which were in short supply since the occupation of Burma. Sophie had secured a transfer so that she could be with her husband and work at the Calcutta Red Cross depot. Adela spent a happy couple of days with them in their cramped temporary quarters. Rafi had aged; the hair at his temples and moustache was grey and his handsome face more hollowed. He looked tired out, but greeted her with his habitual warmth and cheerfulness.

'You can see my husband is working too hard,' said Sophie, 'and worry over Ghulam has produced more grey hairs.'

'What's happened to Ghulam?' asked Adela in concern.

'Worn himself out trying to help victims of the famine,' Rafi said, sighing, 'and not looking after himself.'

'But he won't let us help him,' explained Sophie. 'Prefers to stay angry and live like an outcast.'

'We've sent for Fatima,' said Rafi dispiritedly, 'she's the only person he might listen to.'

Adela could see how the subject pained Rafi so asked instead about the Raja. Krishan, Rita and their daughters were well. The Raja had encouraged many of his Gulgat subjects to enlist in the Indian Army to defend the country, though the family spent much of their time in Bombay, where Rita was happiest. Sanjay was married and living in Delhi, but still leading the playboy life. Sophie showed her a recent newspaper photo of him attending a polo match.

'Losing his good looks already,' Sophie pointed out. 'Too much good living.'

Adela stared at the grainy picture; Jay's figure was stouter and his face had filled out. She knew Sophie was trying to make her feel better that Jay was out of her life. But there was no need. Adela could hear his name mentioned now and see his image without the slightest tug of emotion.

'You look weary, lassie,' Sophie said with a concerned smile. 'Why don't you go home for a visit and let your mother spoil you?'

***

While the ENSA troupe decided whether to sign on for another stint in India, they were given two weeks' leave to spend in the hills.

'Typical.' Tommy laughed. 'Just as the cold season starts, they send us to freeze in Darjeeling.'

He and Prue decided to go to Jubbulpore instead and stay with Prue's parents, Prue ever hopeful that Stuey might get a few days' leave to join her. Adela, encouraged by Sophie's suggestion, sent a message to her mother and headed to Belgooree. She faced the truth that, despite her yearning to go home, deep down she had been putting off going back because of the pain it would stir up over her father's death and the rift it had caused with her mother. However many fond and caring letters Clarrie had written to her in the intervening years, Adela knew that her mother had blamed her for the tragedy in Gulgat. But Adela couldn't avoid the issue for ever; better to clear the air now so that they could try and recapture the loving relationship they once had. With her heart torn in shreds over Sam, she needed her mother more than ever.

Adela felt her spirits rise the closer she got to home. From the ferry she took a crowded local bus to Shillong, where Daleep was waiting with her father's rusting car. Harry, was standing up in the passenger seat, waving. For a heart-stopping moment she saw the likeness to their father.

'You're so tall,' Adela cried as she pulled him down for a hug. The eleven-year-old was suddenly bashful and brushed off the kiss she planted on his cheek. She laughed.

Daleep chatted about the gardens all the way back up to Belgooree. Adela half listened as the familiar landscape rolled by, and she was flooded with memories of doing this drive with her father – and with Sam. She smothered such thoughts as Daleep honked the horn to signal their arrival. Minutes later she was rushing up the veranda steps and into her mother's arms.

***

For the first few days Adela did little more than sleep. She got up for meals – Mohammed Din spoiling her with all her favourite dishes – but even when she sat on the veranda to read the letters she had picked up from the ENSA office before leaving, she fell asleep for hours at a time.

Clarrie was busy every day at the factory. Harry was having his fortnightly lessons with the handsome young Manzur. Clarrie was trying to be firm that Harry would go to St Mungo's School in Shillong after Christmas; she had already put off his going twice. Now that the threat of invasion was receding, she felt better about allowing Harry out of her sight.

Adela went to visit Ayah Mimi, who continued to live contentedly in a hut in the garden, and she put flowers on her father's grave. She wept fresh tears, but felt his presence strongly, and it eased her sore heart. Once her energy began to return, Adela would go riding in the morning while Harry had his lessons and then take her brother fishing.

It was only at the end of the week, when Manzur had left, that she finally had time alone with her mother to talk. After Harry had gone to bed, the women sat on the veranda sofa together with the windows closed against the cool night air of October, and Adela read out the letters she had brought from Calcutta.

There were two from Jane, who was still relishing her job at the air defence battery; Olive continued to dote on Bonnie and looked after her while Joan worked in the café. George had been away for over a year with the Fleet Air Arm, but his infrequent letters sounded cheery.

The other letters were from Tilly and Libby. Tilly's was full of home news: Jamie was working hard at the hospital, Mungo was loving school sports, Josey was staying with them while having a break from touring, and Libby was just being Libby. Libby's letter, on the other hand, hardly mentioned her family at all, but was exultant about Paris being liberated by the Allies. She was funny about her Land Girl job and some prank she and her friends had played on Italian POWs who had come to help with the harvest.

'James misses his family terribly,' Clarrie said. 'He seems to miss them more as time goes on, not less, poor man. I've written to tell him you're here, so you can give him first-hand news if he can manage to get away for a day or so. You don't mind, do you?'

'Of course not,' Adela said, 'I'd love to see him. It was frustrating being close to the Oxford Estate and not getting there when up at Dimapur. And I can tell him how much his family misses him too. Libby especially. I think the only time I've seen her cry was when she knew I was likely to be seeing her dad before she would.'

'Dear Libby,' said Clarrie with affection. 'She was always the most demonstrative of the three.'

'She certainly speaks her mind,' Adela said with a rueful smile.

Adela talked about her tour. She told her mother about meeting Flowers Dunlop again after all these years, and Jimmy Maitland.

‘He was recovering, thank goodness,’ she said, ‘and has been sent to the army hospital in Comilla now that the hot weather is over.’

‘Will you stay in touch?’ Clarrie asked.

‘Just as a friend,’ said Adela. ‘Jimmy knows I don’t have feelings for him other than affection.’

Her mother let her talk on. When she paused, Clarrie asked, ‘Adela, is there something troubling you? Something you haven’t told me about?’

Adela’s stomach knotted. She hesitated. Suddenly the burden of carrying her secret for so long was too much to bear. If she was ever to regain closeness to her mother, then she could no longer bury the deep hurt inside her. Tears stung her eyes as she looked at her mother’s concerned face.

‘I met Sam Jackman again in Imphal. It was wonderful – he loves me. He never did live with Pema as husband and wife; she’s married properly to his old bearer, Nitin. But I sent Sam away letting him think there was someone else – even though I love him too with all my heart.’

‘Why would you do that?’ Clarrie asked gently.

‘Because there is someone else.’ Adela swallowed hard. ‘A five-and-a-half-year-old boy.’

Clarrie’s expression was puzzled. Then something changed in her dark eyes, a dawning understanding. She reached out and put a hand on her daughter’s knee.

‘Tell me,’ she encouraged.

It all came pouring out: the whole confession about her infatuation and affair with Prince Jay at the same time as loving Sam; wanting to seal off her hurt at Sam’s impulsive local marriage to Pema. She spoke about her discovery of being pregnant – of maid Myra’s discovery – her utter shock at her situation and Olive’s horror.

‘I don’t blame Aunt Olive in the least,’ said Adela, ‘and you mustn’t either. She was so scared of what people would say. But Lexy stood by me. She was incredible. All your old friends were – Maggie and dear old Ina too.’

Clarrie squeezed her hand. She seemed too overcome to speak, just nodding for Adela to continue. So Adela talked about the birth of her son – tenderly and with the profound joy of a mother – in more detail than she had ever done before. Then she steeled herself to tell her mother about giving the baby away and how at first she had felt nothing but relief.

'It was only much later that I came to regret what I'd done,' she admitted. 'Bitterly regret. The moment Joan tried to get me to hold Bonnie, I thought I would faint from the pain inside. Even then I believed I'd done the best thing for him. But now I have this yearning to try and find him. Perhaps he never got adopted because of his Indian blood. And even if he did, I just want to know what happened to him. Can you understand that?'

Her mother's face was wet with tears, yet she had said nothing while Adela unburdened herself.

Finally Clarrie swallowed and said in a trembling voice, 'Of course I do, my darling.' She pulled Adela into her arms and held her, rocking her as if she were a child. 'I'm so very sorry you had to endure all that on your own. I should have been there when you needed me, but I was selfish in my grief for your father and sent you away. I hope you can forgive me.'

Adela hugged her mother tighter. 'None of it was your fault,' she whispered. 'It's me that's sorry for what happened to Dad. Not a day goes by when I don't regret that terrible trip. I wish I could undo everything. But I can't. The only decent thing to come out of it all is that sweet baby boy.'

Clarrie smoothed back Adela's hair and kissed her forehead. 'Did you give him a name?'

Adela shook her head. 'But Lexy did – insisted on it. She called him John Wesley – after Granddad Jock and Dad.'

Clarrie let out a whimper. 'Dear Lexy.'

'I did do one thing for my baby,' Adela said. 'I gave him the swami's pink stone to protect him. I hope he still has it. Do you think it will keep him safe?'

Clarrie nodded and kissed her brow. For a while they just sat holding each other, their emotions too strong to put into words. Adela felt more at peace than she had since the death of her father. It was such a blessed relief that her mother knew – and did not hate her for it. She shared her mother's handkerchief to wipe her tears.

'Is that why you pushed Sam away?' Clarrie asked.

'Yes,' Adela admitted, feeling a new wave of regret. 'He was so angry at his own mother for giving him up that I knew he would hate me too.'

'You don't know that,' Clarrie pointed out. 'Isn't it a little unfair to Sam, letting him go through life thinking you love someone else? It would take courage to tell him, but if he rejected you because of it, then he wouldn't be half the man I think he is, and you'd be better off without him.'

Adela was startled by her mother's blunt words. It was distressing to think she might have made the wrong decision. Clarrie stood up.

'It went quite out of my head,' she said, 'but you mentioning Sam and his mother has just reminded me.'

'Reminded you of what?' Adela asked.

'A package came weeks ago addressed to you. I put it in the trunk to stop ants eating it. No idea what it is, but the address was Cullercoats and the name was Jackman.'

Adela followed her mother into her bedroom. In the soft lamplight three framed photographs glinted on the dressing table, the large one of her parents in their wedding finery and two smaller ones of Adela on a pony, grinning, and Harry sitting on a tricycle, frowning with impatience. Her mother unlocked the zinc-lined trunk in the corner and rummaged under a layer of clothing. She pulled out a small brown paper parcel tied with string and handed it over.

They returned to the veranda while Adela pulled it open.

She gasped. 'It's a shawl from Sam's mother. Isn't that kind of her?'

She part unfolded it. It was soft to the touch, made of thin creamy wool with elaborate green and turquoise embroidery around the edge.

Clarrie fingered it. 'It's beautiful. Cashmere I'd say.'

'Why would she send it to me?'

'She doesn't have a daughter to pass it on to. What does the letter say?'

Adela reached for the letter and leant towards the lamp to read it. Her heart began to thud. She read on, her astonishment mounting. She reread it over again, her heart now pounding. She could hardly believe what Mrs Jackman had written. Was it possible? She looked up at her mother, gaping.

'What is it?' Clarrie frowned.

Adela passed her the letter. 'Read it. This changes everything.'

As her mother reached for her glasses to read, Adela fully opened out the shawl and found the other gift that Sam's mother had sent her.

Chapter 31

Sam picked up the letter that was awaiting him at the officers' mess in Jessore; it had been forwarded from Agartala. For the past month he had been training with a new Special Duties squadron in East Bengal, including pilots newly out from Europe with experience of special ops. With regret he had left 194 Squadron, The Friendly Firm, but he relished the new challenge. What was there to lose? He cared not for danger; he had no ties and no obligations except to his fellow crewmen. By December he would be flying into Eastern Burma and dropping men and supplies in the Toungoo Hills to carry out guerrilla warfare and intelligence gathering. They just awaited the first full moon.

He had managed to function after Adela's rejection, day by day, flying sortie by sortie. An emotional numbness cocooned him. His last morning in Imphal he had gone to the hospital to try and see Adela, apologise for taking out his anger at his mother, on her. She hadn't been there, and the nurse on the officers' ward had been trying to calm an agitated young major, a Scot called Maitland.

'She can't come every morning,' the nurse had said. 'There'll be a good reason.'

Sam tried to cheer the man. Then Maitland had told him how in love with Adela he was – had known her since their days in Simla – and how he planned to propose once he was on his feet again. Sam had walked out, determined to bury all feelings for Adela once and for all.

But now a letter had come from her. He stuffed it in his pocket, unsure whether he should read it. He had found equilibrium in his life; reading what she had to say might destroy that. Half an hour later he could ignore it no longer. He went outside, lit up a cigarette and opened it, annoyed at his fumbling fingers.

Dear Sam

I know you won't be expecting to hear from me – will probably be cross that I am writing to you after the way I let you down. But I hope this message gets to you. I have something really important to tell you, and I'd rather not write it in a letter. Is there any possibility that you could meet me in Calcutta so that I can explain in person? I know you sometimes go there in between operations. I'm not asking this for myself but for someone close to me. I've been having R&R at Belgooree – it's been a little piece of heaven. But I return to Calcutta next week and will be staying with Sophie and Rafi (at the address at the bottom of this letter). You can get a message to me there.

Please come, Sam.

Yours most affectionately,

Adela

Sam didn't know what to make of it. What could be so important? Was there a change in her circumstances and she now wanted to be with him? His initial leap of hope was quickly dashed as he reread it. She wasn't asking on her own behalf. He felt a flash of irritation. Was she doing it on behalf of his mother? When would she stop interfering! But then that was Adela all over – stubbornly sticking up for others. Sam let out a long sigh.

That night he sent a letter back, agreeing to meet her the following week – if he could get away.

***

Adela answered the door to the Khans' flat, her heart drumming painfully. Sam was looking lean and handsome in his pilot's uniform.

'Thank you for coming.' She smiled nervously. 'Please come in.' Her words sounded ridiculously formal, but she wasn't going to let her own emotions get in the way of what had to be said. He looked as ill at ease as she felt.

'Sophie's here. She's making tea in the kitchen. Rafi will be back later. I hope you'll stay to meet him.'

Sam didn't answer. He followed her into a small sitting room, its ugly army furniture softened by colourful blankets and cushions. A gramophone and a pile of records took up space on the dining table. Adela indicated they should sit down next to a low carved table.

'Adela, what is this about?'

'Let's have tea first. I promise to explain.'

Sam put his cap on the table and ran a hand over his cropped hair.

'What are you doing at Jessore?' she asked.

'Special Duties.' He didn't elaborate.

'But not with The Friendly Firm anymore?'

'No. Except for Chubs MacRae. He's come with me.'

'I'm glad.'

'Adela!' He gave her a helpless look. 'I'm finding this very hard.'

At that moment Sophie came in, carrying a tray of teacups and a teapot.

'Sam, hello. It's been years since we've met. I know it must look strange me acting as bearer, but I thought it would be easier if it was just us.'

Sam got up and took the tray from her, placing it down on the table. Then he shook her hand.

'I bet you don't remember me,' Sophie said and smiled. 'You were just a boy when I travelled on your father's steamboat in '23.'

Sam smiled. 'I do remember, because you bothered to speak to me – not like most of the memsahibs. And I've heard about you from Adela since.'

'Of course.'

Adela poured out the tea, while Sam asked politely after Rafi. She felt a pang of affection for him, attempting to be sociable when she knew how confused and on edge he must be. Adela got up and fetched the package from the dining table.

'I'm going to tell you something, Sam, and I don't want you to interrupt until I've finished. It's quite hard to take in. At the end you can ask any questions you like.'

He looked at her, baffled.

'Last week Mother gave me this parcel. Your mother sent it a couple of months ago.' Adela held up her hand to stop the protest that was rising to his lips. 'I thought the gifts were for me, but they weren't. They're for you.'

She took out the shawl from its brown paper and handed it to him.

'Mrs Jackman explained in her letter how she came to have it. She's not your real mother, Sam. The woman who gave birth to you was Jessie Logan, a tea planter's wife. When you were a week old, she saved your life by bundling you up in this shawl and giving you to her ayah to take to safety. She also gave the ayah an ivory bracelet to buy food or anything you might need, until she could rescue you. That never happened, because her husband, Bill Logan – your real father – shot Jessie and then turned his gun on himself.'

Adela paused. Sam was staring at her intently, his face in shock.

'The deaths were covered up because things were volatile at the time – it was fifty years after the sepoys' Mutiny, and the authorities feared unrest on the anniversary. The police officer who suppressed the truth of the murder also made sure that the ayah handed over the baby to him. He gave you to the Jackmans because Mr Jackman was a fellow Mason in the Shillong Lodge. They couldn't have children of their own and were more than happy to take you on.'

She stopped to allow Sam to take in her momentous revelation. He shook his head in disbelief.

'It's impossible,' he said. 'It's just another story concocted by that woman to make you feel sorry for her, to get to me.'

'No, Sam, it's all true,' Sophie spoke up. 'Open the shawl and you'll find the bracelet. Look at it now.'

Sam did as she told him. He held up the small circle of carved elephants' heads, yellowed by age. Sophie pulled back the sleeve of her cardigan. She was wearing an identical one.

'See. It's the same. I was given one just like it. My mother was Jessie Logan too. I was in the bungalow at Belgooree that day—'

'Belgooree?' Sam gaped.

Sophie nodded. 'Our parents were renting it – trying to save their marriage perhaps, away from the gossip of the Oxford Estates. It was my sixth birthday, and I saw Ayah Mimi running off with you. Mother made me go and hide. I never saw her again . . .'

Abruptly she stopped, her eyes welling with tears.

Sam whispered, 'Are you telling me that you're my sister?'

'Yes,' Sophie said through her tears, 'and you're the brother I've been searching for. To think we were living in the same part of India and have known of one another for years!' She held out her arms to him. 'Can I have a hug from my wee brother please?'

They stood up and went to each other. Sam put his arms gently around Sophie and rubbed her back. Adela gulped back tears of her own. She rose, feeling suddenly an intruder on their emotional reunion. Sophie broke away from Sam.

'It's thanks to Adela that we've found each other.' She smiled. 'If she hadn't got in touch with Mrs Jackman and befriended her, this would never have happened.'

Sam looked at Adela. She saw him struggle with conflicting emotions. It would take time for him to come to terms with the truth.

'I'll leave you both for a bit,' she said, smiling, 'so Sophie can tell you more about your family. I'll be at the Grand Hotel with Prue.'

She picked up her jacket and went to the door.

'Adela,' Sam said, his voice husky. 'Thank you.'

***

Adela didn't return to the flat that night, and Sam didn't come looking for her. She bedded down with Prue, who talked of her exploits in Jubbulpore and her frustration at not seeing Stuey.

'Sounds like you found other distractions at the Gun Carriage Club,' Adela teased.

'Well, being a grass widow – or a grass fiancée – doesn't mean you can't have fun,' said Prue breezily.

'Is there such a thing as a grass fiancée?' asked Adela.

'If there isn't, there should be.' Prue sighed. 'My parents aren't at all keen on my engagement to an American; they think it's all too quick. But I'd marry him tomorrow. What's the point of looking into the future when there's a war on? Take happiness where you can say I.'

They discussed staying on to do another tour. 'I'm keen if you are,' said Prue. 'We might get sent further east if they ever retake Rangoon – then I'm more likely to see Stuey.'

'Yes, I'll stay,' agreed Adela, 'till the war ends.'

The next day she went back to the Khans' flat, but Sam had gone. Sophie was still very emotional. 'We sat up half the night just talking and talking. He wanted to know everything about our parents – not that I could tell him that much, but I told him about Auntie Amy in Edinburgh and how wonderful she had been to me as my guardian, and Great Uncle Daniel in Perth, who taught me to fish. And of course it means that he's now second cousins with Tilly. He was overwhelmed by it all. I think that's why he left. He said he had to get back to base, but I think he needs a bit of time to think it all over.'

'Did he say when he might come back again?' asked Adela.

'No.' Sophie gave a look of regret. 'His squadron's gearing up for something big I think. He wouldn't say what.' She sighed. 'It's so hard. I've just found my brother, and now he's flying off and I'm going to worry about him all the time until I see him again.'

Adela felt her eyes prickle. Sophie's look was sympathetic. 'You're feeling the same too, aren't you, dear lassie?'

***

Adela couldn't settle to anything. They were rehearsing new songs and dance routines for their next tour, this time to southern India and Ceylon. Tommy and Prue were growing exasperated with her lack of concentration.

'For pity's sake,' cried Prue, 'go and see that man before he flies off. If Stuey was based just a couple of hours away, I'd go like a shot.'

'And say what?'

'That you love him of course!'

That night Adela sat down and wrote Sam a long letter, pouring out her feelings for him and telling him about her illegitimate baby.

I won't blame you if you never want to see me again, but I've come to realise that the worst thing is to have secrets from those you love. When this war ends – and please, God, it will one day soon – I will go back to England to find out what happened to my boy. There is no other man in my life – no one has ever come close to you in my heart – so I wanted you to know that it was my son that I meant when I spoke of loyalty to another.

Take good care of yourself please, Sam. You are dearer to me than the stars.

Love you forever,

Adela.

She didn't post it. Instead she put on her ENSA uniform, persuaded Tommy to go with her, took a train to Jessore and hitched a lift in a Jeep going out to the airbase. They talked their way in, Tommy saying he'd come to arrange a performance on the base. They were shown into the officers' mess.

'Flight Lieutenant Jackman is on training ops,' they were told.

'We'll wait,' said Adela.

'He won't be back till after dark.'

'Come on, girl,' said Tommy, 'we can't stay. Leave your letter for him.'

As they were escorted back to the gates, planes flew in overhead.

'They're not Dakotas,' Tommy said with a pitying look.

***

Back in Calcutta, Adela threw herself into rehearsals; hard work was her best remedy for a bruised heart. When she was on stage singing or dancing with The Toodle Pips, she blanked out everything else. In a week's time they would be taking the train to Bangalore. While she had heard nothing from Sam, Sophie had received a long, affectionate letter telling her how pleased he was to have discovered a special sister and a whole new family of cousins through Tilly. One day he hoped to meet them all. Adela had read the letter with a mix of joy for Sophie and pain for herself. She was forced to accept that Sam no longer wanted her.

Late one evening she was drinking in the hotel bar with Tommy, Prue, Betsie and Mack after a long day of rehearsals. It was Tommy, sitting opposite, who made a soft whistle and said, 'Brace yourself, Robson, for incoming fire.'

Adela glanced round to see a tall figure elbowing his way through the throng towards them. Her heart jolted. It was Sam. He was still in sweat-stained and creased pilot's fatigues, as if he had rushed straight from the cockpit. He greeted the group with a distracted smile, but his eyes focused only on Adela.

'I just got your letter. The sergeant mislaid it. I commandeered a car to get here.'

'Can I get you a drink?' asked Tommy. 'Looks like you could do with one.'

'Thanks. Maybe in a minute. First I want a moment alone with Adela.'

Adela got up quickly, ignoring Prue's arching eyebrows. 'Let's go outside, Sam.'

On the roadside, beyond the covered portico, soft lights from stalls illuminated the line of waiting tongas, their drivers hunched in blankets against the chill of early December. Ignoring the passers-by, Sam took her hands and pulled her round to face him.

'Adela,' Sam said, looking down at her. She had never seen his eyes look so intense, almost feverish. 'Your letter – did you mean what you said?'

'About my baby?' Adela whispered, her heart knocking with fear at what he might say.

'No.' His expression softened. 'Not about that. How could you think I would reject you because of what Jay did to you? I hate to think of what you've been through on your own. And I'm not one of those puritans who blame women for having babies out of wedlock. If society wasn't so quick to blame, then women wouldn't be under the pressure they are to give up their children.'

Adela's eyes stung at his kind words. 'I thought you would hate me for giving away my boy; you were so angry with your own mother.'

Sam's grip on her hands tightened. 'Not my mother. My real mother sacrificed her own life to save me and Sophie. That other woman – the one who deserted me – was so unhappy that she couldn't have stayed, not even for the adopted son whom she tried so hard to love. I see that now, and I don't feel the same anger towards her any more. I've written to say so – and to thank her for having the courage to tell me the truth. Adela,' he said, his look tender, 'I can't thank you enough either.'

'Is that why you came, Sam?' She was trembling under his touch.

'No, I came to tell you that I love you, Adela, as much as you say you love me. No other woman has ever come close to making me feel the way you do. As soon as I saw you again in Imphal, I knew I was still hopelessly in love with you.'

Adela gave a tearful laugh. 'I was filthy and a terrible sight.'

'A beautiful sight.' Sam smiled. 'But I need to be sure that you are not promised to any other – to that Major Maitland in the hospital.'

'Jimmy?' Adela said in surprise. 'No, we were never more than friends.'

He pulled her closer. 'Then marry me, Adela. Marry me now before we're parted again.'

Adela's heart soared. With a gasp she asked, 'Here in Calcutta?'

'Yes, before I have to leave for Burma and you for the south. I have five days.'

Adela thrilled at his words. 'Yes.' She grinned. 'Yes, of course I'll marry you!'

She threw her arms around his neck as he pulled her into his arms, and they kissed on the dusty pavement as people stepped around them. A group of sailors, meandering by, whistled and cheered.

They broke apart, laughing. 'Sam Jackman, how I love you!' Adela cried.

***

Three days later Adela and Sam were married by a magistrate and by special licence. Tommy and Prue were witnesses, and Sophie and Rafi held a celebratory lunch in their flat. Clarrie, too far away to get there in time, sent a telegram of congratulations and love.

'Can't believe you've beaten me to the altar,' Prue teased. 'Now Stuey will have to buck up his ideas.'

Rafi arranged for him and Sophie to stay with a colleague so that Adela and Sam could honeymoon in their quarters for the two precious days that they had left together.

'It's our wedding present to my special brother and my favourite lassie,' Sophie said, beaming.

'Thank you,' said Adela as they kissed goodbye.

Afterwards Sam took Adela by the hand. 'Finally I get you alone,' he said and smiled.

They went straight to bed and made love as the dying winter sun lit the room with a blaze of orange. They carried on until well after dark and then lay entwined, hearts thumping after their passionate coupling.

During the two euphoric days together, they talked of many things: how they might return to the Himalayan foothills and plant new orchards or live at Belgooree for a while and help in the tea garden, or travel around India making films.

'Whatever we end up doing,' Sam said, 'I promise you we will also go to England and look for your baby.'

'Thank you, my darling,' Adela whispered, and kissed his lips tenderly.

The day of parting came. At the seething railway station they clung to each other in a fierce embrace. Adela had never felt such strength of emotion, desperately sad at Sam's going and yet flooded with the deepest love for the man who was now her husband.

'When the war ends, we will never be apart again,' Sam said, kissing away her tears. 'Until then, my darling Adela, you'll be in my heart every hour of every day.'

'And you in mine, Sam,' Adela said and smiled, her green eyes brimming with love. 'Always.'

~~~
~~~

Some Anglo-Indian Terms

Begar	System of forced labour
bidi	Indian cigarette
Box-wallah	Person in trade
Burra bungalow	Main bungalow
Burra memsahib	Head lady
chai	Indian tea
Chai-wallah	Tea worker/seller
chaprassy	Messenger
Chee-chee	Indian accent (derogatory)
Chota hazri	Breakfast
Dak	Post or postal service
Durzi	tailor
Godown	Storage shed
Gur	Type of raw sugar
Jalebi	Chewy, syrupy sweets
Jungli	Lives in jungle/'gone native'
Khansama	Head servant
Lathi	Long stick/truncheon
Machan	Tree hideout for hunters
Mali	Gardener
Memsahib	Madam
Mohurer	Bookkeeper
Nimbu pani	Lemon drink
Paan	Chewable areca, spice, betel leaf
Puri	Deep-fried puff bread
Sahib	Sir
Sepoy	Private in Indian Army
Shalwar kameez	Loose-fitting trousers and tunic
Shikar	Hunting
Shikari	Hunter/tracker
Swaraj	Freedom
Syce	Groom/stable boy
Topee	Sunhat

Acronymns

WVS	Women's Voluntary Service
SEAC	South East Asia Command
ENSA	Entertainments National Services Association
RAF	Royal Air Force
NCO	Non-Commissioned Officer

SECRETS OF THE TEA GARDEN

A powerful and heartrending novel set in the turbulent times of post-Second World War India and Independence: India Tea Series - Book 4

She's gone in search of happy memories. But was her idyllic childhood in India an illusion?

After the Second World War, Libby Robson leaves chilly England for India, and the childhood home where she left her heart—and her beloved father, James—fourteen years ago.

At first Libby is intoxicated by India's vibrant beauty: the bustle of Calcutta, the lush tea gardens of Assam. But beneath the surface a rebellion is simmering: India is on the brink of Independence, and the days of British rule are numbered. As the owner of a tea plantation, James embodies the hated colonial regime, and Libby finds herself questioning her idealised memories—particularly when she meets the dashing freedom fighter Ghulam Khan.

As Independence looms, life in India becomes precarious for Libby, James and even Ghulam. And when James reveals a shameful family secret, Libby is forced to question her past—and her future.

Acknowledgements

I'd like to thank my husband, Graeme, for encouraging the trip to India and helping me trace the footsteps of my intrepid grandparents Bob and Sydney Gorrie through the foothills of the Himalayas. In the course of our research we had the thrill of discovering the house in Shimla where they had lodged with my two-year-old mother, Sheila, in the winter of 1928. Many people made our stay in India special, but particular thanks go to Sanjay Verma, our guide around Shimla and the area, for his knowledge of local history and his interest in my family's links to his town. We also experienced a little bit of heaven on the Glenburn Tea Estate, near Darjeeling, and would like to thank the management and staff for their kindness. Appreciation also goes to Lis van Lynden, of Haslemere Travel, for putting together the specialised itinerary for the research trip.

About the Author

Janet MacLeod Trotter is the author of numerous bestselling and acclaimed novels, including *The Hungry Hills*, which was nominated for the *Sunday Times* Young Writer of the Year Award, *The Tea Planter's Daughter*, which was nominated for the Romantic Novelists' Association Novel of the Year Award and *In the Far Pashmina Mountains*, which was shortlisted for the RNA Historical Romance of the Year Award. Her novels have been translated into nine different languages. Much informed by her own experiences, MacLeod Trotter was raised in the north-east of England by Scottish parents and travelled in India as a young woman. Fascinated by family links between Scotland and India, she discovered diaries and letters belonging to her grandparents, who married in Lahore and lived and worked in northern India for nearly thirty years, which served as her inspiration for the India Tea Series. Find out more about the author and her novels at www.janetmacleodtrotter.com.

Printed in Great Britain
by Amazon

22323687R00229